Zendegi

Other books by Greg Egan:

An Unusual Angle
Quarantine
Permutation City
Distress
Diaspora
Teranesia
Schild's Ladder
Incandescence

Greg Egan

NIGHT SHADE BOOKS
San Francisco

First Edition

ISBN: 978-1-59780-174-4

Night Shade Books
Please visit us on the web at
http://www.nightshadebooks.com

PART ONE
2012
۱۳۹۱–۱۳۹۰

1

Martin stared anxiously at the four crates full of vinyl LPs in the corner of the living room. A turntable, amplifier and speakers sat on the floor beside them, their cables draped in dust; it had been three weeks since he'd sold the shelving unit that had housed the components. The records would be far too heavy to take with him on the plane to Iran, and he didn't think much of their chances if he sent them separately as surface freight. He'd contemplated putting them in storage, as he'd done when he'd gone to Pakistan, but having already spent a month selling furniture and throwing out junk he was determined to complete the process: to reach the point where he could fly out of Sydney with no keys in his pocket, leaving nothing behind.

He squatted beside the crates and did a quick count. There were two hundred and forty albums; it would cost more than two thousand dollars to replace them all with downloads. That seemed like an extravagant price to pay in order to end up exactly where he'd started, give or take a few minor scratches and crackles. He could always just replace his favorites, but he'd been lugging these crates around for decades without discarding anything. They were part of his personal history, a diary written in track lists and sleeve notes; there were plenty of bizarre and embarrassing choices, but he didn't want to forget them, or disown them. Whittling the collection down would feel like a kind of revisionism; he knew that he'd never part with money again for Devo, The Residents or The Virgin Prunes, but he didn't want to tear those pages from his diary and pretend that he'd spent his youth entirely in the exalted company of Elvis Costello and The Smiths. The more obscure, the more dubious, the more downright cringe-inducing the album, the more he'd have to lose by excising it from his past.

Martin knew what he had to do, and he cursed himself for not facing up to it sooner. Normally he would have scoured the web for the pros and cons of different methods, then spent another week mulling over the choices, but he had no time to waste. The crates held almost seven days' worth of continuous music, and he was flying out in a fortnight. It was not impossible, but he'd be cutting it fine.

He left his apartment and walked two doors down the hall.

At the sound of his knocking, Alice called out grumpily, "I'm coming!" Half a minute later she appeared at the door, wearing a wide-brimmed hat, as if she was about to brave the afternoon sun.

"Hi," Martin said, "are you busy?"

"No, no. Come in."

She ushered him into the living room and motioned for him to sit. "Would you like some coffee?"

Martin shook his head. "I won't take your time; I just wanted some advice. I'm going to bite the bullet and put my vinyl on computer—"

"Audacity," Alice replied.

"Sorry?"

"Download *Audacity*; that's the best software to use. Plug your turntable preamp into your sound card, record everything you want and save it as WAV files. If you want to split each album side into individual tracks, you'll have to do that manually, but it's pretty easy." She took a small notepad from the coffee table and scribbled something, then handed him the page. "If you use these settings it will make life simpler if you decide to burn CDs at some point."

"Thanks."

"Oh, and make sure you get the recording level right."

"Okay." Martin didn't want to appear rude, picking her brains and then rushing away, but since she hadn't taken her hat off he assumed she was itching to get moving herself. "Thanks for your help." He rose to his feet. "It looks like you were going somewhere—"

Alice frowned, then understood. "You mean this?" She took hold of the hat by the brim and pulled it off, revealing a mesh of brightly colored wires tangled in her short dark hair. "I didn't know who was at the door, and it takes me ten minutes to stick all the electrodes back on." Though it didn't look as if any hair had been shaved off, irregular partings revealed patches of white skin to which small metal disks adhered. Martin had a disconcerting flashback to his childhood: grooming the family cat in search of ticks.

He said, "Can I ask what they're for?"

"There's a Swiss company called Eikonometrics who want to see if they can classify images by flashing them on a monitor subliminally and looking at the viewer's brain activity. I signed up for one of their trials. You just sit and work normally; you don't even notice the pictures."

Martin laughed. "Are they paying you?"

"One cent per thousand images."

"That'll catch on."

Alice said, "I expect they'll replace the micro-payments with some kind of privileges scheme. Maybe give people free access to games or movies if they're willing to wear the electrodes while they watch. In the long run they're hoping to get it working with a standard gamer's biofeedback helmet instead of all this DIY-neurologist crap, but off-the-shelf models don't have the resolution yet."

Martin was intrigued. "So what's your angle?" Alice earned her living as a website designer, but she seemed to spend most of her spare time on mildly nefarious projects, like the "Groundhog Cage" she'd constructed that made thirty-day free-trial software think it was always on the first day of the trial. Apparently this was harder than simply lying to the software about the true date; there were exchanges with distant servers to be faked as well.

"I'm still analyzing the system," she said, "trying to figure out how to game it."

"Right." Martin hesitated. "But if the experts can't write software that classifies images as well as a human brain can, how are you going to write a program to simulate your own responses?"

"I don't have to," Alice replied. "I just have to make something that *passes for* human."

"I don't follow you."

"People aren't all going to react identically," she said. "There might or might not be a clear majority response to each class of image, but you certainly won't get the same signal from everyone. Some participants— through no fault of their own—won't be pulling their weight; that's a statistical certainty. But the company wouldn't dare discriminate against people whose brains don't happen to go *aaah* every time they see a fluffy kitten; they'll still get the same rewards. I want to see if I can ride the coattails of the distribution."

"So you'd be satisfied with passing as a low-affect psychopath, just so long as you don't actually come across as brain-dead?"

"That's about it."

Martin rubbed his eyes. Though he admired her ingenuity, there was something about her obsessive need to prove that she could milk the system that felt every bit as crass as the brain-farming scheme itself.

"I'd better go," he said. "Thanks for the tips."

"No problem." Alice smiled, suddenly self-conscious. "So when are you flying out?"

"Two weeks."

"Right." Her smile stayed awkwardly frozen, and Martin realized that it wasn't her eccentric head-ware that was making her embarrassed. "I'm really sorry about you and Liz," she said.

"Yeah."

"How long were you together?"

"Fifteen years," he said.

Alice looked stunned; she'd been their neighbor for almost a year, but the subject had probably never come up before. Alice was in her mid-twenties; fifteen years would sound like a lifetime.

Martin said, "I think Liz decided that Islamabad was the last hardship post she was willing to put up with." He couldn't blame her; Pakistan and Iran were not the most appealing locations for Western women with no reason of their own to be there. Liz worked in finance, for a company that didn't mind where she lived so long as she had an internet connection, but Martin suspected that somewhere in the back of her mind she'd imagined that the years in Purgatory were going to be rewarded with Paris or Prague. Martin's employers reasoned instead that his time in Pakistan was the ideal preparation for their new Tehran correspondent, and after twelve months slacking off as an online news editor in Sydney, a return to the field was long overdue.

"I'm sorry," Alice repeated.

Martin waved her crib-notes in thanks and replied with a parody of a honey-toned late-night DJ from the eighties, "I'd better go spin some disks."

Martin started with the Eurythmics' *Touch*. He fussed over the cables and the software settings, checking and rechecking every option, and when he'd finished the recording he played back the entire album to be sure that everything had worked properly.

Annie Lennox's voice still gave him goose-bumps. He'd only seen her performing live once, in a muddy field in the countryside north of Sydney in January 1984. Talking Heads, The Cure and The Pretenders had all played at the same festival. Unseasonal downpours had drenched the campgrounds and he could still remember queuing in the rain to use the unspeakable toilets, but it had all been worth it.

Martin had been eighteen years old then; he would not meet Liz for more than a decade. In fact, all of his vinyl predated her; by the time they moved in together he'd bought a CD player and now the soundtrack to their entire relationship was already on his hard drive, safely out of sight. These crate-loads of old music would carry him back to the era before her—and with the possible exception of Ana Ng, you couldn't miss someone you hadn't even met yet.

It was an appealing idea, and for a few hours he lost himself in Talking Heads, drinking in their strange, naïve optimism. But by late evening he'd started on Elvis Costello and the mood was turning darker. He could have hunted through the crates for something cheerier—there was a Madness compilation in there somewhere—but he was tired of steering his emotions. Even when the music simply made the years melt away, the time-tripping itself was beginning to leave him maudlin. If he kept this up for two weeks he'd be a wreck.

He continued with the recording marathon, flipping and changing the albums like pancakes, but he turned down the playback volume so he wouldn't have to listen anymore. Better to start thinking of the imminent future; Martin opened his browser and began catching up on the news from Iran.

The opposition group that had garnered the most attention in the run-up to the impending parliamentary election was Hezb-e-Haalaa, literally the "Party of Now." Tongue-tied foreigners occasionally pronounced this almost indistinguishably from Hezbollah, "Party of God" (not to mention confusing the Iranian Hezbollah with the Lebanese group of the same name), but the two could not have been more different. Among other things, Hezb-e-Haalaa had announced a policy of recognizing Israel; as Dariush Ansari, the party's founder, put it: "Iraq killed a million of our people in the war, but we now have normal diplomatic relations with them. In proposing the same with Israel, I am not giving my blessing to anything that nation has done, any more than our esteemed leaders who sent their ambassador to Baghdad were giving theirs to the invasion of our territory and the slaughter of our people."

Ansari traveled with a bodyguard to discourage freelance zealots from physically rebuking him for this line of reasoning—and there was still a chance that his big mouth would get him sent to Evin Prison—but his positions on economic, legal and social reform were far less controversial and received substantial support in opinion polls. Even in a perfectly fair and open ballot, Hezb-e-Haalaa probably would not have won a majority in the Majlis—a body that had only limited power, in any case—but in combination with other reformists it could still have embarrassed the conservative president.

However, the final say on eligibility fell to the twelve-member Guardian Council, who had just declared every candidate who happened to belong to Hezb-e-Haalaa unfit to stand in the election. There would be no need to engineer the results to keep them out of the Majlis—risking fresh cries of "Where's my vote?"—now that they had been pre-emptively wiped right off the ballot.

The flight to Singapore left Sydney at the very civilized hour of nine a.m., but Martin had been up for forty-eight hours dealing with a plethora of last-minute tasks and his biological clock no longer recognized the distinction between good and bad times to travel. He spent the journey drifting fitfully in and out of sleep. Eight hours later as he strode through Changi Airport he still felt like a pared-down version of himself, an automaton with tunnel vision ignoring everything but signs that promised to take him closer to the right gate for Dubai. He actually had a ninety-minute layover, but he could never relax until he knew exactly where he had to be at departure time.

On the flight to Dubai the mental fog began to lift. He knew he'd have a headache for the next few days, but at least he was sure that he'd ticked everything off his list and wouldn't have to send a stream of emails back to Sydney begging people to tie up loose ends for him. If the plane went down over the Indian Ocean he could drown in peace, with no fear of real estate agents blacklisting him in the afterlife for failing to dry-clean his curtains.

The passenger in the seat beside him was a telecommunications engineer named Haroun who was headed for Abu Dhabi. When Martin explained that he was going to be covering the Iranian election, Haroun replied good-naturedly that he doubted it would be as newsworthy as the previous, presidential vote. Martin couldn't argue with that prognosis; after the turmoil of 2009 this was likely to be the most tightly managed poll in decades. Still, no one believed that the fire beneath the ashes had been extinguished.

In his present state it was pointless re-reading his background notes on the election; he slipped on his headphones and started up iTunes. The music library software had provisions for storing cover art and he'd started out taking photos of each album himself, but it had been hard to get the lighting and the angles right, so he'd ended up grabbing images off the net instead. Many of the sleeves had also included lyrics, notes or extra artwork, but he hadn't had time to digitize any of that. The day before he'd flown out he'd taken the crates to a charity shop in Glebe, but they'd told him that unless he had collectors' items, vinyl wasn't worth their shelf space. By now, it would all be landfill.

Martin flipped through the cover art. It was certainly a richer cue for memory than a mere list of names, but though the images had been endowed with perspective and reflections in some imagined glossy shelf-top, the faux-3D effects made it look like a museum exhibit trying too hard.

No matter; he had the music itself, and that was the main thing. He'd even diligently backed up everything to an external drive; his laptop could fry itself and these memories would still survive intact.

He wanted to hear something by Paul Kelly, but he couldn't make up his mind where to start so he let the software choose. "From St Kilda to Kings Cross" filled the headphones; Martin closed his eyes and leaned back in the seat, beaming nostalgically. Next came "To Her Door," a song about a break-up and reconciliation. Martin kept smiling, focusing on the power and simplicity of the lyrics, refusing to countenance any connection to his own life.

Something made a loud crackling noise. He tugged off the headphones, wondering if he was missing an emergency announcement by the pilot. But the plane was silent, save for the engines' monotonous drone, and he could see a flight attendant chatting calmly with a passenger. Perhaps it had been some kind of electrical interference.

Halfway through the next song, "You Can't Take It with You," he heard the crackling sound again. He paused the song, skipped back a few seconds and replayed the same section. The noise was there again, as if it was part of the recording itself. But it didn't sound like dust on the stylus, a scratch on the vinyl, or some random electronic pollution that had snuck into the circuitry from a mobile phone or fluorescent light. As Kelly's voice surged it *became* the noise, as if something mechanical inside the headphones might be scraping against its housing when the sound became too loud. But when Martin replayed the track with the volume turned down two notches, the noise was still there.

He started playing other tracks at random. His heart sank; about a third of them had the same problem, as if someone had gone through his record collection with a piece of sandpaper. He pictured Liz flipping through the crates in the dark, urged on by the ghost of Peter Cook from *Bedazzled*. But petty vindictiveness wasn't her style.

Haroun said, "You seem very angry with that machine. You're welcome to borrow my laptop if it's any help."

Martin wondered nervously if the obscenities that had been running through his head had remained entirely unvocalized; it didn't take much erratic behavior for an overzealous flight marshal to pump you full of horse tranquilizer and lock you in the toilet. "That's very kind of you," he replied, "but it's nothing urgent. And I don't think the problem's with this laptop."

He explained what he'd done with his music collection. "I checked the first seven or eight albums and everything sounded perfect."

"May I listen?"

"Sure." Martin cued up an example of the strange blemish and passed Haroun the headphones.

After a moment Haroun gave a smile of grim satisfaction. "That's wave shaping. I'm afraid you're right: there's nothing wrong with your playback, it's part of the recording."

"Wave shaping?"

"You set the recording level too high."

"But I checked that! I adjusted the level when I did the first album, and it was fine for at least six more!"

Haroun said, "The signal strength would vary from album to album. Getting the right level for the first few would be no guarantee for all the others."

No doubt that was true, but Martin still didn't understand why the effect was so ruinous. "If the level from the turntable was too high for the computer, why doesn't the recording just... fail to be as loud as the original? Just lose some dynamic range?"

"Because when the level is too high," Haroun explained patiently, "you're not shrinking the waveform, you're decapitating it. Once the voltage exceeds the highest value the sound card can represent as data, it can't take it upon itself to re-scale everything on the fly. It just hits the maximum and draws a plateau there, in place of the true signal's complicated peaks. And when you truncate a wave like that, not only do you lose detail from the original, you generate noise right across the spectrum."

"I see." Martin accepted the headphones back from him and tried to laugh off the setback. "It seems I'll be paying these starving musicians a few more cents after all. I just can't believe I wasted so much time and made such a bad job of it."

Haroun was silent for a moment, then he said, "Let me show you something." He booted up his own laptop and summoned a website from his browser's offline cache. "This book is a translation into English of a story in Arabic; it was published in the nineteenth century, so it's now in the public domain. An American company obtained a copy and scanned it, making it available to the world. Very generous of them, no?"

"I suppose so." Martin couldn't see the screen clearly from where he was sitting, but the title bar read *The Slave Girl and the Caliph*.

"Optical character recognition isn't perfect," Haroun said. "The software can sometimes recognize that there's been a problem and call on human help to patch things up, but that process isn't perfect, either. This story is obscure, but my grandfather gave me a copy when I was ten, so I know that the heroine is named Mariam. This digital version, scanned from the English translation, has turned the 'r' and 'i' in her name into an 'n' throughout. Mariam has become *Manam*—which, other than being an island off the coast of Papua New Guinea, so far as I know means nothing in any language."

Martin said, "That doesn't sound like a mistake the translator would have made. Not unless he was in the middle of an opium-smoking competition with Richard Burton."

Haroun closed his laptop. "I'm sure no human was involved, beyond feeding the book down a chute, along with ten thousand others." He was smiling, but Martin could see the frustration in his eyes. He'd probably tried emailing these custodians of culture to put them straight, to no avail, while the grating error had seeped into mirror sites, multiplying irreversibly.

He gestured at Martin's own damaged library. "With time and care everything could be preserved, but no one really has the patience."

"I was about to leave the country," Martin explained defensively. "I had a lot of things to do."

Haroun inclined his head understandingly. "And why wouldn't any traveler want to turn their fragile music into something robust and portable? But so many processes are effortless and automatic now that it's easy to forget that most things in the world still play by the old rules."

"Yeah." Martin had to concede that; having treated the first few albums with care, he'd let himself imagine that the rest would follow as easily as if he'd merely been copying files from one hard drive to another.

"We're at the doorway to a new kind of world," Haroun said. "And we have the chance to make it extraordinary. But if we spend all our time gazing at the wonders ahead without remembering where we're standing right now, we're going to trip and fall flat on our faces, over and over again."

2

"Bidar sho! Agha Martin? Lotfan, bidar sho!"

Martin stirred, his head throbbing. He squeezed the button for the light on his watch; it was just after two in the morning. He recognized the voice: Omar, his neighbor from downstairs, was banging on the door, pleading with him to wake.

What was Farsi for fire? Martin had picked up a smattering of Dari—the Afghani dialect of Farsi—when he'd been stationed in Pakistan, but even after two months in Iran, most of it spent working with a professional translator by his side, his Farsi remained rudimentary.

"Aatish?" he called back. That was fire in Urdu, but he was fairly sure it was the same in both languages.

"Na!" Omar's tone was impatient, but not baffled, so at least the question had made sense. *"Lotfan, ajaleh kon!"* Omar usually spoke English with Martin, but whatever the emergency was it had apparently driven the language from his brain.

Martin switched on the bedside lamp, got into his trousers and stepped out into the entrance hall of the cramped apartment. When he opened the door, Omar was tinkering with his phone. Martin suppressed a groan of irritation; it had been bad enough in Sydney, but in Tehran nobody could go five minutes without whipping the things out and doing something pointless with them.

Omar handed the phone to Martin. Sometimes the tinkering wasn't so pointless: the screen displayed an email message that had just been translated into English by a web service. It took Martin a while to make sense of the mangled syntax, but he suspected that in their present state he and Omar would have needed an hour playing charades to get the same

12

information across.

There had been an accident on Valiasr Street, one of Tehran's main thoroughfares. The two drivers, along with two passengers from one of the cars, had been taken to hospital with minor injuries. One of the passengers was Hassan Jabari, a high-ranking jurist and politician. The other passenger's identity was unknown, but a bystander had filmed the aftermath of the accident on their phone and a still from that movie was embedded in the message.

Martin squinted at the ill-lit image of a paramedic helping a woman from the wreck. "Could that be his wife?"

Omar roared with laughter; his English hadn't deserted him completely. The woman was flashily attired, with glittering pendant earrings and a tight-fitting evening gown. Tehran certainly had its Gucci set, and behind closed doors—or the tinted windows and dividing partition of a limousine—even the most respectable woman was no longer bound by the rules of *hejab*. But looking again at the still, he thought perhaps that was stretching the bounds of probability.

"Okay, so it's his mistress. Or a prostitute." Even so, Martin was a little surprised that Omar and his friends would treat such a revelation with anything more than cynicism. Dozens of young Iranians had told Martin that their rulers were two-faced hypocrites, moralizing endlessly in public while they embezzled oil money and lived like kings. One student had shown him a famous cartoon: in the first panel, the despised former Shah cupped his hands beneath a torrent of gold falling from the sky, with just a few stray coins spilling out from between his fingers to reach his subjects below. In the second, a glowering, bearded mullah stood in the Shah's place—and this time every last coin was caught, with nothing slipping through.

Omar wiped tears from his eyes. "*Bebin!*"

Martin looked at the picture again, wondering what he was missing. The woman was statuesque, with striking bone structure—was she a famous actress, or a singer? Perhaps it was just the poor quality of the image, but there was something theatrical, almost mask-like, in the excess of make-up she was wearing—

"*Mibinam,*" he said. "*Mifahmam.*" He understood, now, why Omar had woken him.

Hassan Jabari, former government prosecutor and current member of the Guardian Council—the body that had declared more than two thousand aspiring candidates for last month's election to be insufficiently loyal to the principles of Islam—had just been caught in his chauffeured Mercedes Benz in the middle of the night in the company of a glamorous, begowned transsexual.

"*Berim be—*" Martin struggled.

"Hospital?" Omar suggested.

"*Dorost,*" Martin agreed.

Behrouz, Martin's translator, had taken a fortnight's leave to visit his parents. With the non-event of the election over and half the country shut down for Noruz, the Persian New Year, Martin was officially on leave himself, but he'd decided to stay in Tehran and catch up on paperwork.

As they drove into the city, Martin contemplated the task ahead of him with unease. He recoiled from the prospect of treating anyone's sex life as news—least of all when there was a potential death penalty hanging over the participants—but the email was already circulating, the revelation a *fait accompli.* The real story now was not Jabari's behavior, but the way the regime and the public would respond to the exposure of his hypocrisy.

"We should call him 'Hugh Grant' Jabari," Omar suggested—rather proudly, as if the time was long overdue for an Iranian celebrity to grab the attention of the international tabloid media.

"I'm pretty sure Hugh Grant was caught with a woman," Martin said.

Omar racked his brain. "'Forty-Eight Seconds' Jabari."

"Keep this up and you'll be hosting the Oscars."

Omar owned a shop that sold consumer electronics—and the odd bootleg DVD under the counter. His English had come back to him completely now, but Martin wished he wasn't so reliant here on Omar's help. Omar was a partisan player in all this, an unashamed pro-reformist; Martin was grateful for his tip-off, but it would be both naïve and unfair to expect him to act as an impartial colleague, like Behrouz.

They drove down Taleghani Avenue, past the "Den of Espionage" formerly known as the US Embassy. The walls of the compound were emblazoned with bombastic slogans—helpfully translated into English for the edification of tourists—and a series of murals that included a skull-faced Statue of Liberty that would not have looked out of place on a Metallica album. Even at this hour Tehran's traffic made Martin nervous, with the ubiquitous Samands and old fume-belching Paykans weaving between lanes without warning, and motorbikes zigzagging into every tiny space that opened up before them.

As he turned his company Peugeot Pars into the cramped hospital car park he hoped they hadn't arrived too late. In a perfect Orwellian police state, Jabari's companion—and every witness to the crash—would already have vanished without a trace, but Tehran was a very long way from Cold War East Berlin. He doubted that Jabari's double life had been an open secret among the rigidly pious regime's upper echelon, and while elements of VEVAK, the intelligence service, might have known about it—keeping it on file for a time when a political favor was needed—it would not surprise him in the least if they had not yet even heard about the accident; the email had been distributed in encrypted form to a relatively small number of people. In the first instance Jabari's driver would be charged with keeping everything under wraps, but if he were out of action, who would call in the fixers?

Martin turned to Omar. "So what does a paramedic do when he comes across a man dressed as a woman?" He was assuming Jabari's companion was pre-operative, though that wasn't necessarily the case; Ayatollah Khomeini, no less, had issued a startlingly enlightened fatwa in the eighties, declaring that gender reassignment surgery was a perfectly acceptable practice.

Omar said, "For a heroin addict lying in an alley, who knows? But for this, I think he acts like he doesn't notice. Why make te-rouble?"

Martin pressed the heels of his palms against his eyes. A male paramedic had an excuse to play dumb, but what happened when a female doctor examined the patient more closely? Notwithstanding Khomeini's ruling, there was no guarantee that a man who took estrogen and put on an evening gown was going to sail through the segregated medical system without igniting some form of commotion.

"Are you sure you want to do this?" he asked Omar. "If I screw things up myself, the worst anyone's going to do to me is deport me."

Omar looked irritated. "I want you here as a witness, but no way you could do it alone. *Berim.*"

It was a busy night; Omar spent ten minutes in a queue at the reception desk before a polite but harried woman could speak with him. Martin stood at his shoulder and tried to follow the conversation without letting the effort show. Omar said his wife had been in an accident. What was her name? *Khanom Jabari*: Ms. Jabari. Martin's skin crawled at the audacity of it, but this scenario offered them their only chance. Iranian women kept their family names when they married; Hassan Jabari's sister would remain *Khanom Jabari*. If Jabari's companion was still passing as a woman, it would surely be too risky to register as his wife, so claiming to be his sister was the only respectable option left.

The receptionist typed something into her computer, then glanced up at Omar. "Shokouh Jabari?" She gave a date of birth.

"*Dorost, dorost,*" Omar replied impatiently, as if these details were trivially familiar to him. Martin waited to see if the receptionist would ask Omar to confirm his own name against a recorded next of kin, but she had better things to do. "*Bekhosh shishom,*" she said. Ward six? Omar was already walking.

Martin caught up with him. "Your first wife will be thrilled by this addition to the family," he joked.

"Fuck you!" Omar snapped back angrily. Martin was startled by the intensity of his reaction, but on reflection he realized that he had no right to be surprised. Omar loathed political and religious extremism, but the DVDs under his counter tended more to *Rambo* than *Transamerica*; on this issue he was probably to the right of the ayatollahs. He was here for the sake of political expediency; this was not some humanitarian rescue mission.

At the entrance to the ward, Omar spoke with the nurse on duty; she glanced inquiringly at Martin, and Omar said something that sounded like *dayeam*: my uncle. The nurse summoned someone else to organize the visit; fifteen minutes later the two of them were led into a small, curtained-off space, where a figure dressed in a baggy gray manteau and a black shawl and head-scarf sat in a wheelchair, one foot bandaged and elevated. For a moment Martin thought there'd been a mistake, but the hospital must have supplied the modest clothing. The angular face beneath the scarf was the face from the emailed image of the crash site.

The three of them were left alone.

"*Salaam khanom*," Omar greeted Shokouh nervously. "*Chetorin?*"

"*Bad nistam*," Shokouh replied. "*Shoma chetorin?*" Martin found it hard to judge how her voice would sound to a native speaker; she spoke quietly in a slightly reedy falsetto, but it was not forced or uneven.

"Tell her we're her friends," Martin said, "or she'll think Jabari sent us." Shokouh looked up at him, startled, and he realized he'd just managed to put that idea right out of her head. "*Ruznaame negaaram*," he explained. I'm a journalist.

Omar spoke in a low voice; Martin could follow only a small part of what he was saying. Shokouh replied, heatedly, at length.

"She wants to go to Europe," Omar announced, dismayed. "She'll only come with us if we es-wear to get her to la France." On their drive into the city Omar had mentioned safe houses, but his plans clearly hadn't stretched as far as Paris.

Martin said nothing. He still had the phone numbers of some people-smugglers in Quetta he'd interviewed for a story a few years before, but he decided against offering Omar an introduction; the smugglers had sometimes dealt with Iranian clients, but he doubted that Shokouh would be safe traveling through Baluchistan, even fully veiled in a burqa. In any case, he was meant to be covering this story, not orchestrating it.

"Maybe there's a way," Omar mused. He sounded doubtful, but then he added decisively, "If we do it, we should do it quickly. Before everyone wakes up and knows what they're missing." He spoke with Shokouh again, and they seemed to reach an agreement. He told Martin, "I get the—" He mimed crutches, and disappeared in search of a nurse.

"*Ingilisi baladin?*" Martin asked Shokouh.

"Very less," she replied. "Parlez-vous français?"

"Une petite peu." He'd studied it in high school, but by now his French was probably worse than his Farsi.

Shokouh lowered her gaze to the floor. Martin set his frustration aside; if Omar could pull off this miracle, Sandra Knight in the Paris bureau could interview her face-to-face in a language they both spoke fluently. Even if he'd had Behrouz beside him it would have made little difference; whatever promises of discretion he'd offered, Shokouh would have to be crazy to disclose a long list of potentially suicidal details while she was still in the country.

Omar returned with a pair of crutches and together they helped Shokouh to her feet. There was some paperwork to complete, but Shokouh had already been medically cleared to be discharged.

As they were leaving the ward, the nurse stopped them. There was a brief exchange before they moved off down the corridor. Once the nurse was out of sight, Omar's forced smile evaporated, and he urged them forward.

"What was that about?" Martin asked.

"She said Khanom Jabari's cousin has arrived at reception, wanting to make a visit. I said tell him we'll meet him there. But maybe he doesn't want to wait."

"Okay." Martin digested the news. "At least it wasn't another husband; that would have been awkward."

They reached an intersection with a side corridor; Omar tilted his head and Martin took Shokouh's arm and helped her to make a sharp right turn.

They should have borrowed the wheelchair, Martin realized belatedly. This was hopeless; the "cousin" would reach the ward and double back to find them before they could get even halfway to the car park, and if he had colleagues covering the exits—

"We're screwed," he said.

"Not yet," Omar declared.

Martin glanced at Shokouh. She was hobbling as quickly as she could, but her face was tensed against the pain. They'd moved away from the wards into some kind of service area, and only every third of the ceiling bulbs were lit.

Omar tried a series of doors in succession until he found one that opened into a tiny utilities room. There was a mop, bucket, cleaning products, and a small sink. Omar and Shokouh had a terse exchange.

Martin said, "What's the plan? We can't hide in here all night."

"You hide. I'll send someone to get you."

"Me? It's not me they're looking for."

"We need your ca-lothes," Omar explained. "For disguise."

Martin's stomach clenched painfully. "No, no, no!" He gestured at Shokouh. "It won't work! Look at her eyebrows!"

Omar addressed her in Farsi. Shokouh took off her scarf and shawl; the earrings from the crash were long gone. She went to the sink and, with the aid of a few drops of floor-cleaner, washed off every trace of make-up. Then she ran wet fingers through her thick black hair, quickly reshaping it. The end result was a slightly dated male Persian pop-star look, the fringe flopping down to all but conceal her forehead. With no pencil darkening her plucked eyebrows, close up she looked more like a burn victim than anything else.

Martin said, "Whoever's looking for her, they'll know she can pass as a man."

"But if we're quick," Omar countered, "they won't expect it. The nurse will tell them one woman, two men."

There was no denying that a rapid switch could improve the odds. Tehran had dozens of crashes every night; the injured would be coming and going until morning. So long as they could sneak out of the wing unseen, a young man on crutches crossing the car park with a male friend would not be an obvious target—and anyone trying to maintain a low profile for Jabari could hardly throw a cordon around the hospital and check everyone's sex before letting them pass.

Martin steeled himself. He couldn't tell Omar to do the swap himself; it was clear which one of them was the better fit. Lurking half-naked in the women's wing of an Iranian hospital was not a risk-free proposition, but the truth was, he was more afraid of humiliation than any actual physical harm.

"Okay," he said.

Omar left them. Martin turned his back on Shokouh as they undressed. When he handed her his clothes it was impossible not to notice her breasts, but the sweater he'd worn was loose, and would be looser still on her; this was not a lost cause, not yet. She handed him her own trousers and manteau, and after a moment's hesitation he put them on; it was worth it for the warmth alone, and there was nothing blatantly effeminate about the garments to creep him out. In fact, he could have walked down any street in Pakistan dressed like this; it was almost the same as a unisex *shalwar kameez*.

Martin opened the door. Omar saw him and pressed his fist into his mouth, stifling a guffaw, but he regained his composure rapidly.

"Car keys," he demanded. Martin handed them over.

"My fe-riend will be-ring you ca-lothes," Omar stuttered, battling his way through the English tongue-twisters.

Shokouh picked up the crutches that were leaning against the sink. "Merci," she whispered.

"Bonne chance," Martin replied.

He closed the door and stood in the dark, listening to the sound of the crutches as she moved down the corridor, hoping the hospital's cleaners wouldn't start their shift before dawn.

3

"Guardian Council member Mr. Hassan Jabari," Behrouz translated, "left hospital today after recovering from injuries sustained in a car accident three nights ago. Police have interviewed the driver of the other vehicle, but found that nobody was at fault." He turned away from his computer screen to see how Martin was taking the press release.

"No appeal for witnesses?" Martin replied, struggling to concentrate. Their cramped office in the outskirts of Tehran sat directly over a bakery; three or four times a day the aroma wafting up from the ovens became impossible to ignore.

"Apparently not. I expect they got everything they needed from You-Tube."

Martin smiled. YouTube was blocked in Iran, but Shokouh's Paris interview, along with the anonymous bystander's movie of the crash scene, had been posted on dozens of other websites. Each time the official black list was updated to screen them out, the files turned up somewhere else. Internet download speeds in Iran were severely limited—by law, not by infrastructure—but in the past twenty-four hours Martin hadn't met a single adult Tehrani who had *not* seen both movies.

So far, though, the government hadn't blinked. Martin had phoned three different ministries seeking a comment, but nobody was willing to go on the record, not even to denounce Shokouh's words as slander. "Do you seriously expect an official statement every time a prostitute claims to have a politician as a client?" one bureaucrat had demanded incredulously.

"What about the movie of the crash site?" Martin had pressed him. "Doesn't that support her version of events?" Martin had briefly contemplated trying to track down the paramedics—whose faces were pixellatedout in the public version—but he'd decided he had no right to compound the dangers they already faced.

"If such a movie exists, it's a Zionist forgery."

"Can I quote you on that?" Martin had warmed to this conspiracy theory, but it needed a bit more work. Maybe Shokouh could be portrayed as a Mossad agent who had made the ultimate sacrifice, purely for the sake of embarrassing the Iranian regime. Or, as it turned out, not *quite* the ultimate sacrifice, which only compounded the embarrassment.

In the absence of a black ops extraction team with helicopters and night-vision goggles, Omar had managed to get Shokouh a doctored passport and a second fake husband—this one to escort her from the country and take the focus off her own documents. That she'd made it through the airport at all suggested that the "cousin" at the hospital had been acting for Jabari alone; VEVAK, mercifully, appeared to have dozed through the whole thing.

Martin's phone chimed. There was a message from Kambiz, a student he'd met in the run-up to the election; it read "Please go to Ferdowsi Square."

Downstairs, people were lined up outside the bakery for the lunchtime rush, men and women in separate queues. Some carried their stacks of flatbread from the serving window to a cooling table, compounding the olfactory lure. When Martin slowed down to savor the smell, Behrouz grabbed his elbow and tugged him through the crowd toward the alley where their car was parked.

They reached Ferdowsi Square just as the demonstration was getting underway. About thirty young men and women had gathered on a grassy traffic island around a statue of the famous poet. They were holding up signs, all bearing the same slogan: *haalaa entekhaab-e-taazeh!* Martin had no trouble reading Persian script when the calligraphy wasn't overly ornate—the alphabet was almost the same as Urdu—and in this case the individual words could not have been more familiar: *New Election Now!*

The signs themselves offered no English translation; though that might have made for wider coverage in the Western media, it would have opened up the protesters to accusations that they were British or American stooges. Nor was there any reference to Jabari to attract charges of defamation. But the slogan appeared to have hit the right note; Ferdowsi Square was one of the busiest roundabouts in the city, and most of the passing drivers were honking and cheering over the roar of the traffic.

Martin spotted Kambiz, but when their eyes met the young man looked right through him; Martin respected his wish not to be singled out as the reason a foreign journalist was here. There were no police yet, and only one other reporter—Zahra Amin, from the reformist weekly *Emkaanha*—but

Kambiz wouldn't need to be paranoid to worry that there might be inform- ers among the demonstrators themselves. Martin headed for the opposite side of the group to Zahra, to avoid having to compete with her for inter- views. He and Behrouz approached a young, plainly dressed woman and introduced themselves. Her name was Fariba; she was studying engineering at Tehran University. Martin asked her permission to record the interview on his phone; he no longer carried a separate audio recorder. She balked at first, until he showed her the controls and satisfied her that he would not be recording vision.

"You're calling for a new election," Martin began. "What was wrong with the one you've just had?"

"Two thousand candidates were banned from taking part," Behrouz translated. "That's not a fair election. People wanted to vote for many of those candidates, but they didn't have a chance."

"But isn't it too late to complain now? Wouldn't it have been better to protest before the election?"

"We did protest! We were ignored. The government didn't listen at all." As she spoke, Martin kept his eyes on Fariba's face and paid close attention to her tone of voice, letting Behrouz's unimpassioned words seep into his mind through a separate channel.

"So what conditions are you calling for, if a new election is held?"

"It must be open to anyone who wishes to stand. The approval of the Guardian Council should not be required."

"But isn't that role written into the Constitution?" Martin asked. "It can't be discarded overnight."

Fariba hesitated. "That's true, but the Guardian Council should make a commitment to do their job impartially and only disqualify real criminals, instead of everyone with different political ideas. That would be a gesture of good faith, a way of showing that they trust their own people. We're not children. They've put themselves above us, but they are not above us. They're ordinary people, no better than anyone else."

Martin knew better than to press her to comment directly on the Jabari scandal; that last oblique sentence would have to suffice. And while the West- ern media were, predictably, chortling over Jabari's indiscretion—Omar's fondest wish having been granted by everyone from CNN to *Saturday Night Live*—the political ramifications of the phrase *they are not above us* had a potential life that stretched far beyond Jabari's fifteen minutes of fame.

Martin thanked her, and went on to seek comments from some more of the demonstrators. He was halfway through his third interview, with a goateed accounting student named Majid, when Behrouz broke off in mid-sentence. A green police car had pulled up on the island, one side of the vehicle still protruding into the road, and three uniformed officers disembarked.

The senior officer was carrying a megaphone; he raised it to his lips. "You are instructed by the Chief of Police to move on," Behrouz translated. "This gathering is a distraction for drivers and a threat to public safety."

"We're big fans of public safety!" one demonstrator shouted in reply. "Drivers should keep their eyes on the road and their hands on the wheel at all times!" Majid and the others laughed, and Martin saw the two junior officers struggling to keep themselves from cracking up.

"You are instructed to disperse," the senior officer persisted. "This is a reasonable and lawful request." He didn't sound particularly vehement, or particularly confident that anyone would obey him.

"People like our signs!" Majid called back. "We're not distracting any-one." One of the cops came over and asked to check Martin's papers, but he wasn't belligerent about it, chatting matter-of-factly with Behrouz and trying out his English.

"I like Australia," he said, returning Martin's passport. "We beat you at football last year."

"*Mubaarak*," Martin replied. Congratulations. He'd long ago given up hope of finding a country anywhere in the world where it was safe to tell total strangers that he had no interest in sports whatsoever.

A small motorbike with a pillion passenger drove up onto the grass, closely followed by three more. The young men on the bikes wore dark glasses, army boots and green-and-brown camouflage trousers; some had full beards, but most were clean-shaven. Martin couldn't see any firearms, but at least two of the men were carrying batons.

"*Basij* or *Ansar-e-Hezbollah*?" he wondered aloud; both paramilitary groups had a habit of showing up at demonstrations. Martin was expecting Behrouz to answer, but it was the cop who replied, "*Basij.*"

Two of the Basijis strode to the front of the assembly. The policemen did nothing, but Majid went to join the ranks of his companions. Martin couldn't see Zahra anymore; there were too many people crowding the island. He switched his phone to video mode, hoping the battery would hold out.

"Put down the signs, you traitors!" one Basiji began. "We've had the elec-tion! The honest Iranian people have spoken. We don't need you parasites to tell us what to think." Martin heard the buzz of small engines yet again; more Basijis were arriving.

Some of the demonstrators began jeering angrily. There was too much for Behrouz to translate at once, and most of the fragments he offered sounded so idiomatic or obscure that they added nothing to the obvious body language. Martin tensed; he knew what was coming next. In Pakistan he'd covered protests that ended in gunfire, in bomb blasts, in visits to the morgue, but he hadn't become desensitized; none of that had inured him to lesser acts of violence. Before the first blow had even been struck a voice inside him was already screaming at the Basijis to stop.

Instead, they started: with fists, batons, boots. They were aiming for the placards, but they pummeled and tore at everything that lay in their path. The demonstrators were not outnumbered, but they were hemmed in on all sides. They were attempting to regroup to protect the women, and at the same time trying to hold on to the placards and keep them aloft as a gesture of defiance. The men being beaten on the perimeter were quickly becoming dazed and bloody, but it was hard for their comrades to pull them back from the front line without ceding ground.

Martin heard brakes squealing. He swung around. A tarpaulin-covered truck had stopped dead in the road, and for one terrible moment he had a vision of soldiers with automatic weapons piling out. But nobody emerged from the back of the truck, just the driver and two companions from the cab. They were solidly built middle-aged men, in work clothes, not uniforms, and they threw themselves into the fray with a grim, unflinching determination that reminded Martin of one of his uncles trying to separate feral cousins at a family gathering thirty years before. He filmed one of the men grabbing a baton-wielding Basiji under the arms and flinging him back onto the grass as if hefting a sack of potatoes.

In rapid succession there was a mosquito whine of more bikes arriving, angry shouting from the road, then another group of civilians joining the fight. Underneath his struggle to remain detached and simply record the details, Martin felt a mixture of admiration and dread. Most Iranians had no tolerance for seeing defenseless people being beaten, and they weren't shy about taking on thugs. But one punch-up on Ferdowsi Square would not settle anything. Unless someone within the regime came up with a political solution, people's frustration at the repression and hypocrisy they faced would continue to escalate—until the only possible response was a full-scale, bloody crackdown: 2009 all over again.

Martin could see nothing at ground level now but a scrum of backs and furious elbows, but someone deep within the pack, propped up by companions to a visible height, was still holding one of the placards over their heads. As Martin tilted the phone to capture the sight, a Basiji turned and glared at him.

"Hey, motherfucker! Hand it over!" He seemed to have learned English from one of Omar's DVDs—perhaps the mujahedin-friendly *Rambo III*. As the Basiji approached, baton in hand, Martin lowered the phone and looked around for an escape route, but between the vehicles parked on the roadside and the brawling mob spread across the grass, he was fenced in.

Behrouz caught his eye; in all the turmoil they'd become separated and he'd ended up about twenty meters away, near the edge of the square's ornamental pool. He held up his hand and Martin tossed the phone to him, half expecting it to end up in the water as punishment for his life-long neglect of ball skills. But Behrouz caught it, and without a moment's hesitation dashed out into the traffic and vanished behind an approaching truck. Martin froze, waiting for an ominous squeal and a thump, but the sound never came.

"*Khub bazi*," muttered the cop admiringly. The Basiji grimaced and spat on the ground, but did not give chase. Martin's heart was pounding. Behrouz had his own keys to the car, which was parked a few hundred meters away; he'd get the phone to safety, then come back.

Martin turned to the cop. "So, how do you feel when passing truck drivers have to do your job for you?"

The cop looked wounded. He held out his hands, wrists together. *We can't interfere. Our hands are tied.*

4

Nasim called in sick and prepared to spend the day at home, watching rumors and snippets of news ricochet between the satellite channels and the Persian blogosphere. She didn't have to go through the charade of making her voice sound pitifully hoarse and congested; the department's new personnel system made it as simple as choosing an option on her phone's menu, and for a single day's absence she wouldn't need a medical certificate.

The truth was, she really did have a cold coming on, which always happened when she was short of sleep, but normally she would have brushed off the symptoms and joined her colleagues in the lab. Her mother was more disciplined; she too had stayed up half the night, channel-hopping beside Nasim, but she'd still gone in to work. Her students needed her, she'd declared. Ordinary life couldn't grind to a halt just because there were people battling for the future of their country half a world away.

Nasim sat in the living room with her laptop beside her, listening for the ping of News Alerts while she cycled the TV between the BBC, Al Jazeera and IRIB. The Iranian government had ordered the country's internet providers to shut down all domestic accounts and coffeenets, but they had not yet disabled business access or international phone lines, so journalists and some bloggers were still getting news out. Nasim suspected that the government didn't really care; they were far more interested in keeping their own people in the dark than they were in fretting over international opinion.

IRIB, the national broadcaster, wasn't ignoring the unrest, but it was covering it as a kind of social malaise arising directly out of unemployment. The poor state of the economy was not an unmentionable topic, but the network's commentators blathered platitudes about the need for people to be patient and give the "new" Majlis time to address the problem.

Nasim had almost dozed off when a brief coda to IRIB's main news bulletin brought her fully awake. "Guardian Council member Mr. Hassan Jabari says his research into the drug problem has been misrepresented by malicious elements of the foreign media." Nasim thumbed up the volume. "Mr. Jabari issued a statement in Tehran this afternoon, describing a recent visit he made to an area of the city frequented by drug users, in order to gain insight into this tragedy. Having met one confused young man in urgent need of spiritual counseling, Mr. Jabari agreed to drive him to his own mosque, in order to obtain advice from the mullah there. Unfortunately Mr. Jabari's car was involved in an accident, and now his act of charity has been portrayed in some quarters as an act of immorality. Mr. Jabari stated that he would not take legal action against the slanderers, as his reputation among honest Iranians has not been affected by these lies."

Nasim experienced a strange sense of cultural dislocation. This sounded exactly like the kind of story a senator in Washington might try to spin, as an intermediate step between the initial flat-out denial and the inevitable, tearful press conference with spouse, booking into rehab and finding of Jesus. She tried to picture Hassan Jabari standing at a podium with his wife beside him, blaming everything on prescription pills, then announcing that he was off to Qom for six months to get in touch with his spiritual side.

The doorbell rang. Nasim ignored it, hoping it was an easily discouraged Jehovah's Witness, but the caller was persistent. She muted the TV and walked down the hall.

She opened the door to a smartly dressed middle-aged woman who asked, "Nasim Golestani?" When Nasim nodded, she went on: "My name's Jane Frampton, I'm a science journalist. I was hoping to have a word with you."

"A journalist?"

Frampton must have mistaken Nasim's expression of alarm for some kind of struggle to place her name, because she added helpfully, "You might remember me from such *New York Times* bestsellers as *The Sociobiology of The Simpsons* and *The Metaphysics of Melrose Place*."

"I... don't have much time to read outside my field," Nasim managed diplomatically.

"May I come in?"

"What is it you wanted to talk about?" By now her mother would have had the woman ensconced in the living room, sipping tea and chewing *gaz*, but Nasim considered hospitality to be a greatly overrated virtue.

Frampton smiled. "The HCP. Off the record, of course—"

Nasim replied firmly, "I'm sorry, that's not possible. You should direct all your questions to the MIT News Office."

"There'll be no comeback, I promise," Frampton insisted. "I know how to protect my sources."

"I'm not a source! I don't want to be a source!" Nasim was bewildered. Why would any journalist go to the trouble of tracking her down? She was all in favor of academic free speech, but a costly, politically sensitive project still awaiting funding was never going to get off the ground if every postdoc who hoped to play a part in it started acting as a self-appointed spokesperson.

When she'd finally convinced Frampton that she had nothing to offer her, Nasim returned to the living room and sat with her laptop on her knees, reading the latest blog entries. Jabari's statement was already being torn apart by dozens of expatriate Iranians, and even a few in-country bloggers had managed to get their own sardonic responses out onto foreign servers. As Nasim scrolled obsessively through the posts—all of them quoting the same tiny crumbs of information—she knew she was beginning to act pathologically, but she couldn't help herself. She wasn't contributing anything to the struggle; she could sit here reading blogs all day, endorsing some views and arguing with others, but nothing she did would change the situation on the ground in Tehran or Shiraz. She should have gone to work, taken her mind off the protests, and caught up with all the news when she came home.

She glanced over at the picture of her father on the wall, impossibly young, frozen in time. *What would he have expected of her?* Probably not to care about anyone's expectations. But when she followed her own instincts, ignoring her mother's sensible example, she ended up sitting here in a masochistic stupor, hitting keys like a trained rat, aching for a reward that could never be delivered.

The doorbell rang again. Nasim tore herself away from the laptop and opened the door this time on a gaunt young man.

"Can I help you?" Looking at the hollows of his face she could easily have imagined that he was going door-to-door begging for food, but he was wearing a designer-label jacket that probably cost as much as a small car.

"Are you Nasim?"

"Yes."

"I'm Nate Caplan." He offered her his hand, and she shook it. In response to her sustained look of puzzlement he added, "My IQ is one hundred and sixty. I'm in perfect physical and mental health. And I can pay you half a million dollars right now, any way you want it."

"Aha." Nasim was beginning to wonder if it was possible to overdose on cold remedies to the point of hallucinating.

"I know I look skinny," Caplan continued, "but I have no lipid deficiencies that would lead to neurohistological abnormalities. I've had biopsies to confirm that. And I'm willing to give up the caloric restriction if you make it worth my while."

Nasim knew what was happening now. This was why her contact details were supposed to be kept private, even while the Human Connectome Project remained nothing more than a set of ambitious proposals surrounded by a fog of blogospheric hype.

"How did you get my address?" she demanded.

Caplan gave her a co-conspirator's smile. "I know you have to be careful. But I promise you, I'm not setting you up. You'll get the money, and it will be untraceable. All I want from you in return is a guarantee that when the time comes, I'll be the one."

Nasim didn't know where to start. "*If* the HCP goes ahead, the first maps will be utterly generic. We'll be tracing representative pathways within and between a few dozen brain regions, and then extrapolating from that. And we'll be using hundreds of different donor brains, for different regions and different tracing techniques. If you really want to kill yourself and donate your organs to science, go right ahead, but even if I took your bribe and somehow managed to get your brain included in the project… you'd have no more chance of waking up in cyberspace than if you'd donated a kidney."

Caplan replied, more puzzled than offended, "Do I look like an idiot? That's the program *now*. But ten years down the track, when you've got the bugs ironed out, *I want to be the first*. When you start recording full synaptic details and scanning whole brains in high resolution—"

"*Ten years?*" Nasim spluttered. "Do you have any idea how unrealistic that is?"

"Ten, twenty, thirty… whatever. You're getting in on the ground floor, so this is my chance to be there with you. I need to put the fix in early."

Nasim said flatly, "I'm not taking your money. And I want to know how you got my address!"

Caplan's previously unshakeable confidence seemed to waver. "Are you saying the rabbit wasn't your idea?"

"What *rabbit?*"

He took his phone from his pocket and showed her a map of the area. A small icon of a rabbit wearing a mortarboard was positioned at the location of her house. When Caplan tapped the icon with his finger, an information overlay popped up, giving her name, affiliation and research interests. The HCP wasn't mentioned explicitly, but anyone in the know could have worked out that she belonged to a group that was hoping to be part of the project.

"You really didn't put that there?" Caplan asked, clearly reluctant to abandon his original hypothesis: that Nasim had inserted herself into a map of Cambridge sights and attractions as an inconspicuous way to solicit bribes from wealthy anorexics.

"Believe me," she said, "a bunny rabbit is not an accurate representation of my mood right now." She started to close the door, but Caplan held up one skinny arm and took hold of the edge.

"I'm sure you'll want to talk about this again," he said. "Once you've thought it over."

"I'm sure I won't."

"Just give me your email address."

"Absolutely not." Nasim increased her pressure on the door and he started yielding.

"You can always reach me through my blog!" he panted. "Overpowering Falsehood dot com, the number one site for rational thinking about the future—"

He pulled his hand free just in time to avoid having it squashed between the door and the jamb. Nasim locked the door and waited in the hallway, checking through the peephole until he gave up and walked away. She went to her room and summoned the Cambridge map on her own phone. Caplan's version hadn't been a hoax; the inane rabbit was there, exactly as before. Somehow it had been written into the map's public database.

Who had done this to her? How? Why? Was it a prank, or something nastier? She started mentally listing names and pondering motives, then caught herself. Instead of drifting off into a paranoid fantasy, she needed to gather some solid information.

Nasim took her phone and walked three blocks down the street. After a delay of a minute or so, the rabbit icon on the map moved to match her new position. She walked further, to a small park. Once the rabbit had caught up, she switched off the phone. Back in the house, she checked the map again, via her laptop. The rabbit was still in the park.

So nobody had disclosed her home address, as such—but her phone had taken it upon itself to broadcast her location in real-time to the world.

Using the landline, she called the department's IT support.

"This is Christopher, how can I help you?"

"My name's Nasim Golestani. I'm with Professor Redland's group."

"Okay; what's the problem?"

She explained the situation. Christopher sank into a thoughtful silence that lasted almost half a minute. Then he said, "You know AcTrack?"

"No."

"Sure you do. It's a reality-mining plug-in that learns about academic networking using physical proximity, along with email and calling patterns. Last semester we put it on everyone's phones."

The phones were supplied by the department to ensure that everyone had compatible software; Nasim just accepted all the upgrades they sent out without even looking at them.

"All right," she said, "so I'm running AcTrack. Is everyone else who's running AcTrack appearing on Google Maps?"

"No," Christopher conceded, "but you know Tinkle?"

"No."

"It's a new femtoblogging service going through a beta trial."

"*Femto*blogging?"

"Like microblogging, only snappier. It tells everyone in your network where you are and how you're feeling, once a minute. Tinkle are working on ways of extracting mood and contactability data automatically from non-invasive biometrics, but that part's not implemented yet."

"But why am *I* running it at all," Nasim asked wearily, "and why is it telling complete strangers where I am?"

"Oh, I doubt you're actually running a Tinkle client," Christopher said. "But on the server side, AcTrack and Tinkle are both application layers that run on a lower-level platform called Murmur. It's possible that there's been some glitch with Murmur—maybe a server crash that was improperly recovered and ended up corrupting some files. Tinkle does hook into Google Maps, and though it shouldn't be putting anyone on the public database, if you don't belong to any Tinkle Clan it might have inadvertently defaulted you to public."

Nasim digested this. "So what's the solution?"

"I'll contact the company that administers Murmur and see if they can get to the bottom of the problem, but that might take a while. In the mean time, you could try shutting down AcTrack; that won't take you off the map, but it should stop the location updates."

Following his instructions, Nasim interrupted the phone's usual boot sequence to enter a set-up mode where she could disable AcTrack. She checked the map again. The rabbit was still present—and still proclaiming her identity—but even though the phone was switched on, the icon hadn't moved from the park back to her house. She wouldn't get any more door-knockers.

She thanked Christopher and hung up. The whole bizarre episode had fractured her mood; the TV and the blogs had lost their hypnotic attraction. She paced the living room, agitated. People who might have sat beside her in a classroom fifteen years before were facing batons, water-cannon and bullets. The sheer fatuousness of her own tribulations made her life here seem like a mockery.

So, what was she supposed to do? Jump on a plane to Tehran and get herself arrested at the airport? She and her mother had departed illegally; they didn't even have Iranian passports anymore. And as far as she could tell, her adopted country was already following the best possible course: keeping its grubby fingers right out this time. And if they weren't, she doubted that the CIA was prepared to take advice from her.

The truth was, she had nothing to contribute. Whatever happened, it would all unfold without her.

Nasim picked up her phone and found the menu option for "I'm not as sick as I thought, I'm coming in after all."

Instead of the usual reassuring tone confirming success, there was a disapproving buzz and an alert popped up.

"AcTrack plug-in disabled," it read. "Unable to complete this function."

John Redland's group had the twelfth floor of Building 46 all to themselves. From her corner of the lab, Nasim could peer across Vassar Street at the Stata Center, an apparition out of a cartoon fairy-tale with its façade of tilted surfaces intersecting at vertiginous angles. As an architect's sketch or computer model it must have looked enchanting, but in real life this gingerbread house had developed all manner of leaks, cracks and snow-traps.

Nasim turned back to her computer screen, where a tentative wiring map for part of the brain of a zebra finch was slowly taking form. The map wasn't based on any individual bird, nor was it the product of any single technique. Some of the finches who'd contributed to it had been genetically engineered so that their neurons fluoresced under UV light, with each cell body glowing in a random color that made it stand out clearly from its neighbors; that was the famous Lichtman-Livet-Sanes "Brainbow" technique, developed at Harvard. Others had had their brains bathed in cocktails of synthetic molecules—tagged with distinctive radioisotopes—that were taken up only by cells bearing receptors for particular neurotransmitters. A third cohort had been imaged after selective labelling, with monoclonal antibodies, of the cellular adhesion molecules that bound one neuron to another. And a fourth set of birds had been subject to no chemical interventions at all, and simply had their brains peeled by an ATLUM—an Automatic Tape-collecting Lathe Ultra Microtome—into fine slices which could then be imaged by electron microscopes and reassembled in three dimensions.

Altogether, nearly a thousand finches had lived and died to create the map that lay in front of her. Nasim hadn't personally touched a feather on their heads, though she'd watched her colleagues operating, injecting and dissecting. None of the procedures carried out on the living birds should have left them in pain, and with decent-sized cages, plenty of food and access to mates, their lives probably hadn't been much more stressful than they would have been in the wild. Nasim was never sure exactly where she'd draw the line, though. If it had been a thousand chimpanzees instead, for a project equally distant from any urgent human need, she didn't know if she would have found a way to rationalize it, or if she would have walked away.

The map on her screen described the posterior descending pathway, or PDP, of the bird's vocalization system. The contributors had all been adult males, each with a fixed song of their own that was somewhat different from the others'. Redland had chosen the PDP for the sake of those two characteristics: it controlled a single, precisely repeatable behavior in each individual—the bird's fixed song—but there was also a known variation between the contributors thrown into the mix: no two birds sang quite the same song. Unless the team's mapping techniques could cope robustly with that degree of difference, making sense of anything as complex as the brains of rats who'd learned to run different mazes would be a hopeless task.

Nasim slipped on her headphones and linked the latest draft of the zebra finch map to a software syrinx, a biomechanical model of the bird's vocal tract. She had plenty of fancier, more quantitative ways to gauge her progress, but listening to the song these virtual neurons created seemed an apt way to judge success. The songs of the individual live birds had been recorded, and Nasim had heard them all; she knew exactly what the fast, rhythmic chirping of an adult zebra finch should sound like. As she tapped the PLAY button on the touchscreen, her shoulders tensed in anticipation.

The song was disorganised, weak and confused, more like an infant finch's exploratory babbling than anything a confident adult would produce. She glanced at a histogram showing a set of simulated electrical measurements; the statistics confirmed that they were, still, nothing like the signals measured by micro-electrodes in the brains of real adult birds.

The different mapping techniques complemented each other, each one excelling at revealing certain aspects of the neural architecture, but for the data to be meaningfully combined she needed to find common signposts that could be used as points of alignment. It was easy to build, say, a composite human face by locating all the eyes and noses in a thousand photographs, then making sure that you merged eyes with eyes, rather than eyes with noses. But for a thousand birds with a thousand different songs encoded deep in their skulls, the signposts were subtle aspects of the neural network, and they had to be coaxed out of the partial, imperfect data that each individual map supplied. Right now, it sounded to Nasim as if she were merging pitch from one bird with tempo from another, to produce a musical concoction that was not so much generic as puréed.

She steeled herself and plunged back into the computer code for the map integration software. The task was proving more difficult than she'd expected, but she did not believe it was hopeless. She was sure that once she found the right perspective, the right mathematical point of view, the signposts would become clear.

Nasim usually brought a packed lunch with her, but all her routines were askew today. By two o'clock her concentration was failing, so she went downstairs to the Hungry Mind Café. She bought the vegetarian ragoût and took it to a table where three of her colleagues were seated.

"How's the revolution going?" Judith asked her.

"There was a big demonstration in Shiraz yesterday," Nasim replied. "Ten thousand people, according to some witnesses. Not quite a general strike, but it's spread far beyond just students now."

"Have you still got relatives in Iran?" asked Mike.

"Yes, but I haven't really stayed in touch with them," Nasim confessed. When her father had been executed, her aunts and uncles on both sides of the family had declined to speak out against his killers, and Nasim had been so angry with them that she'd cut herself off from everyone, even before she and her mother had fled. Fifteen years later she was less inclined to judge them so harshly, but she'd never tried to rebuild bridges, and the blameless cousins she'd once played with were strangers to her now.

Hunting for a chance to change the subject, she gestured at the empty plates on the table. "Looks like you've all been here for a while. So what gossip have I missed?"

"Mike broke up with his girlfriend," Shen announced.

Nasim looked at Mike to see if it was true; he didn't seem too devastated, but he didn't deny it. "I'm sorry," she said.

"It was going nowhere," Mike replied stoically. "We were philosophically incompatible: she belonged to True Love Waits... I belonged to True Love Wilts."

"So how can we take your mind off this tragedy?" Nasim wondered.

Shen said, "Actually, we've been playing Thirty-Second Pitch. You want to choose one?"

"Hmm." Nasim's mind was blank, then she said, "Mike, you have thirty seconds to make yourself indispensable to… Amazon."

"Amazon?" He grimaced with distaste. "I'd rather work for the IRS."

"Twenty-five seconds."

"Okay, okay." He closed his eyes and took a deep breath. "I offer to write a psycho-linguistic compression algorithm for text. MP3s for the written word."

"Compression?" Judith interjected skeptically. "I don't think Kindle is facing bandwidth problems."

"Not compression for the sake of bandwidth," Mike explained, "compression to save the reader's time. Abridgement. Like Reader's Digest Condensed Books, but fully automated, and based on a rigorous scientific analysis of what readers will actually retain. With music, we *know* that it's safe to strip away certain sounds that are masked by others… so surely we can figure out what words can be omitted from a great slab of Melville or Proust without altering the impression that they leave behind. People are far too busy these days to indulge in rambling, discursive novels… but if they can feel just as Prousty in two hours as they would have in eight, every word lost is time found."

"*Moby-Dick* left no impression on me at all," Judith said. "I might as well have not read it. But other people can recite long passages from it verbatim. Doesn't that undermine the whole idea of compression?"

Mike hesitated. "No, it just means it will have to be tailored to individuals, based on a personal brain map. So who better for Mr. Bezos to hire than someone with brain-mapping experience?" He turned to Nasim. "I rest my case."

She smiled. "Well done. You're hired."

Shen said, "Can you improve their recommendations algorithm while you're at it?"

"Once they have your brain on file," Mike replied, "*everything* they do for you will be beyond reproach."

Nasim spotted Dinesh approaching, beaming ecstatically. He was carrying an opened envelope and a letter.

"I've got funding for HETE!" he exclaimed, waving the letter. "Lab space, equipment and ten people! For three years!"

"Congratulations!" Nasim glanced back at the others and caught a flicker of irritation crossing Mike's face.

Dinesh joined them at the table. "I can't believe it," he said. That was usually an empty protestation, but he sounded genuinely dazed. "It's really going to happen."

Mike said, "So you're just giving up on the HCP?"

Dinesh couldn't stop smiling. "What difference does this make to the

HCP? That will happen or it won't, it's not up to me."

Judith said, "Where's the money coming from?"

"Bill and Melinda—bless his shoddy, monopolistic software."

"Sure it's not the Turd Foundation?" Mike quipped lamely.

Judith scowled. "What are you, seven years old?"

Mike said, "Try laying some pipes. It's not rocket science." He rose from his chair and walked away.

Dinesh looked baffled. "What did I say?"

"He broke up with his girlfriend," Shen explained helpfully.

"I'll still be here for another two months," Dinesh said. "That's as long as Redland has funding for me anyway. It's not as if I'm jumping ship."

Nasim said, "No one's accusing you of deserting us." And it was absurd to be jealous of the funding he'd obtained when the HCP would require ten thousand times more.

HETE was Dinesh's dream project, which he'd been planning since his undergraduate days: Human Excrement Treatment Ecosystems. An ordinary composting toilet could deal with human waste *in situ*, but it was still far too expensive and finicky to be much help to most of the people who faced a chronic risk of disease from poor sanitation—let alone those caught in the aftermath of a flood or an earthquake. The aim of the HETE project was to develop a whole portfolio of microbial communities that could render human waste safe in almost any situation, with an absolute minimum of labor and no expensive infrastructure. Disease prevention was the first priority, but in most cases there would also be useful by-products, such as fertiliser, solid fuel or biogas. In the most ambitious versions Dinesh had sketched out, a single ecosystem would be capable of being pushed between three or four different equilibrium states simply by nudging the population ratios of the various microbes. That way, broken or partly flooded latrines in a disaster area could be reconfigured easily—perhaps even automatically—to focus on destroying pathogens as rapidly as possible, and then switched back into more productive modes when the emergency was over.

Shen and Judith excused themselves; they'd already overrun their lunch hour. Nasim asked Dinesh if he wanted to share her ragoût—it was more filling than she'd anticipated—but he was too excited to eat.

"My great-grandfather spent his entire life mopping out communal latrines," he said, "from the age of ten until the day he died. And there are still people doing the same job today. Human beings sweeping shit into drains that take it straight into the rivers."

"I *am* trying to eat," Nasim reminded him.

"Sorry. I know it's not a pleasant subject. I just want my own grandkids to be able to say that *nobody* is stuck with the same disgusting work."

"Yeah. I hope so, too."

"This is going to be a huge challenge," Dinesh admitted soberly. "The microbes living in our gut already outnumber our own body cells ten to one. Now we have to mimic and extend and improve upon that system, outside the body, in a safe, robust way. Dozens of species, thousands of genes, millions of interactions." He looked up at Nasim and smiled. "We'll need the best bioinformatics expert we can find."

"Aha." Nasim put down her fork. It seemed everyone was trying to ambush her today.

"Of course I'd have to follow standard procedures," Dinesh explained, almost apologetically. "I'd have to advertise the job and look at all the applicants. But from your experience here alone, I'm sure you'd leave everyone else for dead."

"Umm…"

Dinesh laughed. "I promise you, you won't need a face mask. You can sit in a nice clean office analyzing metabolic networks all day; nobody's going to ask you to dig pit latrines."

"Can I think about this?" she pleaded. Turning down a bribe from that idiot Caplan had been easy, because she'd simply had no power to give him what he wanted. But not only was Dinesh's project worthy, she couldn't even claim that it was beyond her ability.

Dinesh seemed to sense that he was losing her. He said, "I know the brain will always be sexier than the bowel. I didn't exactly run away from the chance to work with Redland myself. But if we're going to use technology to improve ourselves, this is the place to start: engineering *a second gut* that sits in the ground, banishing cholera and turning waste into fuel and fertiliser. Isn't that every bit as amazing as a brain implant, in its own way? You could even think of it as a rehearsal for the HCP—because some of the deep, underlying network dynamics is sure to be the same. It wouldn't be taking you far from your current path. It would all be experience; nothing you learned would be wasted."

With that, he ran out of steam; he just stopped and waited for her reply. Nasim couldn't argue with anything he'd said, and though she still felt somewhat flustered to be put on the spot, she could hardly blame him for asking. Every time he'd discussed the project with her in the past, she'd told him how much she admired the idea.

But she'd worked too hard to get where she was to risk taking a detour. It was one thing to say that, in principle, it was all good experience, but she knew what the competition would be like for the HCP, and she knew which projects would shift her résumé toward the top of the pile, and which would shift it toward the bottom.

She said, "You'll find someone else for the job. Someone who's as keen on the whole thing as you are."

Dinesh slumped against the table theatrically, trying to look suitably disappointed, but he was obviously still elated that the project was going ahead at all. "Ah well. If you'd said yes that would have been perfect, but it was too much to expect."

When he'd left, Nasim sat toying with the unappetising remains of her cold ragoût. How would it feel, she wondered, to know you'd been part of an endeavor that had saved a few million lives? Such a triumph was no foregone conclusion, of course, but now that she'd ruled out any part in it for herself it was hard not to feel a twinge of regret. Fate and distance had robbed her of her chance to rage against the ayatollahs; missing out on the war against cholera and dysentery had been her choice alone.

Still, the brain beckoned. Trying to turn a blurred jigsaw puzzle of snapshots from a thousand dead finches into something that could mimic their song was a very strange job, but she had to keep hoping that it would be good for something eventually.

5

Martin left his office at ten o'clock in order to cover the protest scheduled for noon outside the Majlis, but by the time he and Behrouz arrived at Baharestan Square the crowd already filled the street and they could get no closer than the Mosque of Sepahsalar, a hundred meters south of the center of the gathering. Martin's permit to travel to Shiraz had, unsurprisingly, come too late for him to cover the big march there the week before, but it looked as if the Tehranis were determined to outdo their cousins and reclaim the record for the biggest demonstration since the fall of the Shah. Police lined the street, and though they were heavily outnumbered and were not intervening so far, every one of the protesters would be aware of the bashings and shootings by militia in this very location, just three years before. Simply being here took a great deal of courage.

The Mosque of Sepahsalar also functioned as a madrassa, and Martin took the opportunity to buttonhole a few of the young men who were squeezing their way through the crowd to reach its gates. Most of these pious Islamic students turned out to be noncommittal, rather than angrily opposed to the protests. "The people have many legitimate grievances," one ventured. "I won't march with them, but they deserve to be heard." The uprising had become far too broad to be dismissed as a conspiracy of traitors and stooges; apart from a solid core of die-hard loyalists who refused to accept any criticism of the regime, many conservative Iranians had started to take a highly jaundiced view of the status quo. Once your children had been jobless for a decade, the streets were flooded with heroin and the guardians of morality had proven themselves to be hypocrites, what was left to fear from reformists who preached transparency and offered new economic ideas?

Certainly the demographics were changing: this crowd was dotted with gray-haired men in suit coats, and there were quite a few middle-aged women. Most of the latter declined to be interviewed, but Martin managed to get a quote from one woman who looked to be in her fifties. "I marched against the Shah," Behrouz translated, "because he shot his own people and imprisoned his opponents. Why wouldn't I march against thugs in clerical robes who think they can settle disputes the same way?"

Given that she was willing to speak so plainly, Martin decided to risk asking her opinion of Jabari.

She smiled. "Really, I don't care about that stupid man. It gives us all some encouragement to see a tyrant with his trousers around his ankles, but having seen it once we don't need to stop and stare."

Martin had been trying to wend his way through the crowd toward the Majlis as he fished for vox pops, but a steady stream of people were squeezing in from other directions, and he still couldn't catch a glimpse of the parliament's distinctive pyramid-shaped chamber. Whether or not the symbolism was intentional, the architectural heart of Iranian democracy was dwarfed and obscured by the tall, rectangular towers full of government offices that rose up beside it, so you could only see the thing itself if you were standing directly in front of it.

Still, he'd come within sight of the core of the protest, where placards and banners were thicker on the ground. The original slogan—*New Election Now!*—had been replaced by a single word: *Referendum!* That might have sounded tame to outsiders, or just plain cryptic, but no Iranian would be in any doubt as to what it meant. The 1979 referendum had approved the present constitution; to call for a new referendum was to call for a change in the whole system of government.

Martin's phone emitted a forlorn beep. He took it from his pocket, expecting to find that the battery was flat, but the message on the screen read NO SIGNAL.

He held it up to Behrouz. "What about yours?"

Behrouz checked. "Same thing. It looks like they've shut down the phones."

Martin felt a chill in the pit of his stomach. Blocking internet access had made it harder for the protesters to organize, but text messages and phone trees were better than nothing. Now the movement had lost all communications, just when it needed to be able to respond to events as rapidly as possible.

There was a squawk of feedback from a public address system, then a voice reached them, so distorted by the dodgy amplifier and overlaid with echoes from the surrounding buildings that Martin couldn't even make out his usual one word in three. Behrouz did his best to give a running translation, staying close to Martin and keeping his voice low to avoid annoying the people beside them, who were straining to hear the original.

The protest organizer welcomed the crowd and commended them for their courage, bringing an answering roar of approval: "*Balé!*"

"And because we are brave, we will be peaceful!"

"*Balé!*"

"And because we are peaceful, the people will listen!"

"*Balé!*"

"And because they listen, they will join us!"

"*Balé!*" The last cheer was deafening, and Martin felt an intoxicating wave of optimism sweep through the crowd. *A rush and a push and the land is ours?* The regime still had tens of millions of supporters, and loyal militias ready to deal with dissent just as brutally as they had the last time. But while part of his mind clung to those dismal facts, the sound of some hundred thousand people shouting in unison made him feel that anything was possible.

All of this was just a warm-up act; the unnamed organizer announced that a distinguished speaker would now address the gathering. Before the introduction was complete, Martin could hear applause breaking out closer to the podium.

"We welcome Mr. Dariush Ansari, founder of Hezb-e-Haalaa!"

As Martin scanned the crowd he spotted a handful of people whose greeting looked distinctly lukewarm, though there were not as many as he would have expected. Ansari's conciliatory foreign policy did not endear him to everyone who was simply weary of the regime, but he was the first politician to address one of these rallies, so perhaps people would give him credit for that. Thirty student leaders and more than two hundred demonstrators were already in prison; seven people had died in clashes with the militias. What he was doing carried no small risk.

"In the name of God, the compassionate, the merciful," Ansari began; the familiar words of the *bismillah* needed no translation. "I am honored by the invitation to speak here today, at this peaceful gathering of my fellow Iranians. I was in Shiraz last week—not to speak, only to listen—and I can tell you that whatever you read in certain newspapers, the people there were peaceful too. The shopkeepers whose windows were broken should send their accounts to the Ministry of the Interior."

That attracted some wry laughter from the crowd and even a few embarrassed smiles from the police, who had already formed a protective human chain in front of a long row of nearly identical establishments specializing in men's shoes. Martin wasn't sure that anyone would feel better to be reminded that they too could expect to be blamed for the vandalism of provocateurs; then again, maybe a bit of pre-emptive truth-telling would ease their frustration in the face of that inevitable libel.

Ansari continued in this unassuming fashion. He was no firebrand, but nor did he drone on interminably; Martin's attention had wandered for only a few seconds before Ansari had come to the point.

"If my brother is behaving in a way that troubles me, I might speak to a mullah and ask his advice. If I'm contemplating a business deal and my conscience can't decide if it's fair to everyone, perhaps a mullah can assist me. After all, it's his job to have studied the Qur'an and the Hadith, to have thought deeply about many complex moral questions, to have refined his ideas by disputation with his colleagues.

"But it is a very different thing to hand the mullah a machine-gun, an army, a prison, and tell him: if anyone questions your power, silence him. After more than thirty years, we have seen with our own eyes what the consequences are: the weight of all their weapons and privileges has dragged the mullahs down so they are no closer to God than anyone else.

"I believe the time has come for us to take responsibility for our own lives before God. The advice of true scholars should always be welcome, but let them live like scholars, not rule like kings. We need to prise open this closed system that protects itself from all possibility of change—"

Ansari broke off. Martin couldn't see what was happening, but the people who could were remaining silent and orderly, so it was unlikely that he'd been seized and dragged away.

After about a minute, Ansari spoke again. Behrouz translated: "I've been told that the President has just appeared on television and made an announcement. Mr. Hassan Jabari has resigned from the Guardian Council, because—I quote—'it is for the good of the nation to rob the disruptive elements and their foreign supporters of their dishonest ammunition.'" Behrouz winced apologetically; however pompous the original, he usually managed to produce less turgid English than that.

"Furthermore, the President tells us that he has appointed a senior judge to review all of Mr. Jabari's decisions when he was Prosecutor, as a guarantee against any hint of impropriety."

Martin contemplated this odd move. Bringing charges against Jabari would have been both embarrassing and unlikely to succeed; this would act as a sop to those conservatives who'd believed the accusations against him. Now an independent judge could reassure them that Jabari had not, after all, abused his earlier position to protect a secret cabal of sexual deviants.

"Finally," Ansari continued, "the President has declared that this must be the end of the matter. No complaint against the institutions of government, however fanciful, remains. So the people must leave the streets and return to their ordinary business."

An uneasy silence followed. Martin looked around at the faces of the demonstrators; no one was quite sure how to take the news. Deposing a member of the Guardian Council might have been seen as a great victory if it had flowed directly from a political dispute—say, a deadlock with a reformist Majlis. But Jabari had not been removed for frustrating the will of the people, and his replacement would be yet another conservative. The next election would see exactly the same kind of candidates disqualified as before. Nothing had changed.

Ansari broke the silence. "I must respectfully disagree with the honorable President. I say that many complaints remain—and they are not fanciful at all."

It was a simple observation, but the response was electric; the shouting and applause went on for at least a minute. If the announcement of Jabari's resignation had been timed to puncture the mood of the demonstration, that had been badly misjudged; instead, it had given everyone in the crowd a chance to affirm, with the vocal support of their fellow malcontents, that the momentum of the uprising was undiminished.

The organizer took the microphone and began giving detailed instructions for the march. After reminding everyone of the route, he added, "Most importantly, please obey the marshals wearing green sashes." Martin looked around and located a woman a few meters away, only now draping a broad strip of green fabric across one shoulder of her brown manteau.

They began to move north, toward Jomhuri-ye-Eslami Avenue. The marchers wouldn't expect any help from the traffic police, but the protest had been publicized well enough to deter most drivers from the route, and in any case, sheer force of numbers gave the pedestrians right of way. The density of the crowd kept their pace to a shuffle, and the afternoon heat was beginning to bite, but the atmosphere was upbeat, and the constant rhythmic chant of *ref-er-en-doom*—the English loan-word imported virtually unchanged into Farsi—was echoed playfully between different groups, breaking up the monotony and sparing people's throats.

Jomhuri-ye-Eslami Avenue was a broad, elegant street, with a stately row of fountains where it met Baharestan Square. It had been spared from the current spate of road-works that plagued much of central Tehran—all the flyovers and tunnels-in-progress that filled the streets with concrete dust, coating Martin's trouser cuffs and shredding his nasal membranes. Some of the upmarket clothing shops along the route were closed and shuttered, but others had banners of support in the windows, and a few had proprietors, sometimes even whole families, standing in the doorways waving and cheering. Martin thought back to 2003, when he and Liz had joined an anti-war march through Sydney, just before the invasion of Iraq. Given the outcome, that was hardly an encouraging comparison, but he wasn't reaching for a political analogy. It was simply that the measured, determined mood of the crowd, the steady rhythm of their advance, the whole texture of sounds and emotions, had been cut from the same cloth.

Martin felt a sudden ache of loneliness; he could not have expected Liz to be marching beside him here, but it would have been enough to be able to sit with her in the evening and say: *You know what I was reminded of today?* Now their shared memories meant nothing.

"Did you see that?" Behrouz asked him.

"Sorry, I was—"

"Her phone." Martin followed his gaze; the green-sashed marshal was using it to talk to someone. Martin checked his own phone; there was still no signal.

"Do you want to ask her about it?" Martin suggested. "If you can convince her we're not informers."

When she'd finished the call Behrouz approached her and made introductions. The woman gave her name as Mahnoosh.

She addressed Martin directly, in English. "I read some of your stories before they cut the internet."

Martin felt a twinge of self-consciousness; his reports were written for Australian readers skimming half-a-dozen foreign political stories over breakfast, not sophisticated Tehranis in the thick of the action. He said, "I hope you'll excuse any mistakes I made; I've only been here a few months."

She smiled slightly. "Of course."

"Do you mind if I ask you how your phone's working?"

"It's not going to the towers," she said. "Just direct to other phones."

"I don't understand."

She spoke with Behrouz. "We've set up a mesh network," he translated. "It doesn't rely on any infrastructure from the phone company; the phones just pass the data between themselves. Email, text messages, voice calls, web services."

Martin was impressed. No doubt the government would soon find a way to block the system—they were already jamming satellite TV—but for now the protesters had an unexpected advantage. "Can I plug into this network?"

Mahnoosh held out her hand and he passed her his phone. She inspected it for a few seconds then returned it. "Sorry, no. The best one is this—" She took her own phone from her pocket and showed it to him. The manufacturer's logo was one he'd never seen before: a triangle formed from three copies of the letter S.

"Who makes these?"

"Slightly Smart Systems," Mahnoosh replied, a hint of amusement in her eyes at the wonderfully self-deprecating name. "Indian software, Chinese hardware. But we made some changes ourselves."

Martin handed the phone back. He was surprised that Omar hadn't tried to sell him one, knowing how useful it would be. But since the night of the crash they'd been more circumspect in their dealings with each other; when Sandra Knight broke Shokouh's story in Paris she'd kept Martin right out of the picture, but the authorities would automatically have stepped up their surveillance of all foreign journalists.

They passed Cinema Europa, then Cinema Hafez. The Iranian stars gazed down coolly from their billboards, offering neither encouragement nor disapproval. Ahead of the marchers, a long stretch of asphalt was utterly deserted, empty of cars as far as the eye could see; even with the chanting crowd around him, Martin had a moment of end-of-the-world goose-flesh. Police were following the march, but they remained at the edges and he hadn't seen them administer so much as a provocative shove. Perhaps the authorities had decided to allow people to let off steam, unmolested, in one last show of defiance before Jabari's resignation was used to draw a line under everything that had come before.

Martin and Behrouz moved through the crowd, gathering quotes. "Jabari's resignation means nothing," one man opined. "It won't bring down rents. It won't give my son a job."

"But how would a referendum help the economy?" Martin pressed him.

"Not quickly," the man conceded. "But it would open the door to different ideas, not the same group holding power year after year. The hardliners call everyone else un-Islamic, but Ansari is not un-Islamic. I asked him myself, would he ban the headscarf in some places, like they do in Turkey. He said no, it's up to each woman if she wants to wear it or not."

Other people expressed similar views. They were tired of the stale, self-perpetuating clique that clung to power by wrapping itself in claims of piety. If throwing out the veto powers of the Guardian Council—or abolishing the Council entirely—was the only route to change, so be it. The voters themselves were perfectly capable of rejecting candidates who would harm the nation; as one woman put it, "We aren't infants who need the bones picked out of our food."

"*Rast! Injaa rast!*" Mahnoosh shouted urgently, raising her arms and gesturing. *Right, here!* She was steering the march off Jomhuri-ye-Eslami, into a side-street. She was not especially tall, but her voice carried, and her instructions were heeded and echoed back through the ranks. As the crowd squeezed into the narrower road Martin approached her.

"What's happening? I thought we were going straight to Ferdowsi Street."

Mahnoosh held up her phone, displaying an image of a train-carriage packed with militia, some of them carrying guns. A sign on the platform beside the carriage said Imam Khomeini Station—one stop south of Sa'di Station. If the marchers stuck to their original route, they would be approaching Sa'di Station just as the armed Basijis emerged from the Metro.

Martin exchanged a glance with Behrouz; did they want to break from the march and check out Sa'di? Martin was tempted, but then decided it was better to stay with the crowd and see how they fared.

He said, "So you've got a network of people with these phones... in all the Metro stations, on street corners?" Mahnoosh responded with an irritated scowl, as if to say: *Of course, but don't expect me to spell it out.*

She said, "Excuse me, I have work to do." She stepped out of the flow and stood at the roadside, shouting instructions, ensuring that nobody in her charge got confused and failed to take the detour. Martin made a mental note to try to get a copy of the picture of the carriage from her later. This wasn't the time to beg for it, but his editor would kill him if he didn't get that image eventually.

The detour, Saf Street, was reserved for pedestrians, so the marchers had no cars or motorbikes to contend with, just groups of startled shoppers and a couple of vendors selling balloon animals. After the run of men's shoe shops opposite the Majlis, this whole street seemed to be dedicated to women's shoes and handbags; the advancing crowd drove many of the leisurely window-shoppers through the doors of these establishments, possibly doubling the day's sales.

When they'd gone a few hundred meters Behrouz looked back and said nervously, "I hope there won't be people coming round that corner for another half-hour." The whole march would take a long time to flow through, and the Basijis could be at the intersection in as little as ten minutes.

Martin squeezed his way to the side of the road and climbed onto an electricity junction box. From this vantage he could see the crowd stretching all the way back to Jomhuri-ye-Eslami Avenue, but as he watched, the tail of the procession came into sight. He said, "Looks like the organizers have split up the march. They haven't just put a kink in the route; the people behind us must have been sent south." The Basijis would find no easy targets ahead of them, just a long deserted avenue.

"There'll be cops and informers tracking every move," Behrouz reminded him. "They won't make it obvious with helicopters, but they're still watching."

"Yeah." The cops had their radios; they didn't need Slightly Smart phones. Still, splitting up was better than everyone marching blindly into an ambush, and at least the Basijis had lost the advantage of surprise.

"*Chap, chap!*" Mahnoosh commanded them. Pedestrian-friendly Saf Street was coming to an end and the street ahead was narrow and full of cars. Martin tensed, expecting a heated confrontation between marchers and drivers, but after a short battle of wills, accompanied by a lot of honking and shouting, the crowd prevailed. A few drivers managed to reverse out of the way; others just stopped where they were and allowed the protesters to squeeze around them.

Martin stayed within sight of Mahnoosh, trying to pick a good time to ask her for an update on the militias. After a couple of minutes she motioned to him to approach again.

"We chained the gates at Sa'di Station," she confided, "but we didn't succeed to close Darvazeh Dowlat, and now half the Basijis are headed there." Darvazeh Dowlat was the next station up the line. If the marchers had kept going north they would have been heading into danger again.

"We couldn't go back to the Majlis?" Martin wondered.

"There's another group headed for Baharestan Station."

The street they were on ended at a T-junction with Sa'di Street, which ran between the two Metro stations; here, they were about the same distance from both. Mahnoosh called a halt, then instructed the marchers to leave their banners on the ground, cease all chants and disperse in groups of no more than three.

A young man behind Martin began objecting loudly, shouting that he hadn't come onto the streets just to surrender, but nobody else spoke up in his support, and his friends did their best to calm him down. It looked like most people felt they'd achieved a reasonable trade-off: having shown their numbers outside the Majlis and marched in defiance of the President's orders, they had not been cowed, but nor would they be reckless.

As the protest broke up, Behrouz said, "I want to find a pay phone and see if I can call my wife."

"Okay." Martin could imagine how she'd be feeling, with fresh denouncements of the protesters all over the TV and the mobile network disabled. He remembered when the army had opened fire on a demonstration in Peshawar and he'd left Liz wondering for hours if he was dead or alive. He said, "I'll meet you at the car in an hour." They were parked about three kilometres away, and Martin wanted to hang around a little longer and try to get that photo and some more background information from Mahnoosh.

Behrouz headed off. Martin looked around; Mahnoosh was nowhere in sight. He stood at the corner for a while, scanning the street, swearing under his breath. He'd lost her.

He decided to head south toward Sa'di Station; if he couldn't show his readers a train packed with Basijis, he might yet get a snap of them emerging from the Metro *en masse*. As he walked past shops and teahouses he could still see people around him that he recognized from the march; most had heeded the suggestion to break up into small groups, but there were also visible packs of young men—some of them dressed in heavy metal T-shirts, the uniform most despised by the regime—walking together, talking and laughing. It was easy to sympathize; there was something undignified about being asked to disown your comrades and slink away into the crowd.

Martin heard angry shouting from further down the street; he couldn't make out the words, but he had no doubt what was happening. A group of women with shopping bags walking ahead of him turned around and hurried away; at the same time he could see people running to join the fray. Part of him wanted to slip into the safety of a shop or an alleyway—*nobody would know, nobody would reproach him*—but he forced himself to keep walking. It suddenly struck him that he'd been far less timid in Pakistan, when it should have been the other way around: back then, he should have been thinking about Liz. But back then, whatever insanity he'd been swept up in, he'd always pictured himself *telling her about it*. Just having her to share his stories with had made him feel bulletproof; if nothing was quite real until he'd recounted it to her, how could the world ever intervene and break that narrative thread?

The source of the shouting came into sight: on the opposite side of the street, five Basijis were fighting with three young men, relentlessly swinging batons into flesh. One Basiji was brandishing an automatic pistol, ranting about traitors and pointing the weapon at anyone who came near, keeping a larger group of angry civilians at bay.

One of the youths in the center of the mêlée was swaying drunkenly, bleeding from a head wound, clearly in bad shape. Martin checked his phone, but there was still no signal. He looked around; a shopkeeper was standing in a doorway watching nervously. Martin mimed holding a handset and asked "Ambulance?"

"*Kardam,*" the man replied tersely: he'd already called. The landlines must be working.

Martin turned back to the fight and took some pictures. As he pocketed his phone he saw another, larger group of Basijis in the distance, coming north from Sa'di Station along his own side of the street. He was about to turn and begin his retreat when something else caught his eye: a green sash draped across the shoulder of a brown manteau. Mahnoosh was about fifteen meters from him, walking south.

Martin was baffled; he hadn't taken her for a martyr, deliberately putting herself in harm's way. Then he understood: she hadn't chosen to keep the sash on as a mark of defiance; she'd simply forgotten she was wearing it. She'd done her best to shepherd her section of the march to safety, then she'd walked away, alone, imagining that she'd become invisible, no more a target than any other woman in *hejab*.

Martin started walking toward her, trying to judge his pace so he'd reach her in time without drawing attention to either of them. The second group of Basijis were shouting slogans at the people they passed, but they were yet to start bashing anyone; Martin doused a shameful hope that they'd find some guy in a Rammstein T-shirt to keep them occupied.

Some of the people ahead of him were turning back, but Mahnoosh continued, undeterred. Why had she headed south at all, when she'd known what was coming? Maybe she'd wanted to see how things unfolded here—to bear witness to any violence, even if there was nothing more she could do to prevent it.

It could not have been more than thirty seconds before Martin was finally walking a pace behind her, but his heart was pounding as if he'd sprinted all the way. He spoke quietly in English without wasting time giving his name, trusting her to recognize his voice. "Please don't turn around. You're still wearing the sash."

For a second he wondered if his voice had been too soft—he hadn't wanted to attract curious stares from the shoppers around them—but then Mahnoosh reached to her left side and unclipped the sash, where it was fastened together near her waist. In a sequence of quick movements, she gathered up the swathe of material, sliding it lengthways across her shoulder until it was entirely in her hands.

When she'd stuffed the sash into a pocket of her manteau, Martin finally dared to look up to see if any of the Basijis were watching, but her deft maneuver seemed to have gone unnoticed. Then, just as he was contemplating turning around and heading north, one of the men met his gaze for a second, and he realized that he was too close now to flee without attracting attention. He was middle-aged, conservatively dressed, and even if his features marked him as a likely foreigner at least he wasn't toting a video camera. Far better to brazen it out than to act suspiciously.

He walked on briskly past Mahnoosh and into the oncoming Basijis, trying to prove his clear conscience by giving them no wider berth than he would have offered any other pedestrians, trying to channel the persona of a distracted foreign businessman who'd simply wandered out of his hotel at a bad time. There were ten of them, all with identical green batons, three with pistols. He could smell their acrid sweat. They'd been outmanoeuvred and humiliated, and even if they had no hope now of reliably picking protesters out of the crowd, it would not take much to be judged worthy of helping them work off their frustration.

One of them brushed against his shoulder. Martin said, "*Bebakhshid,*" and kept walking. He continued to the next street corner, then looked back. Mahnoosh had passed them too, unmolested. For a moment he considered approaching her, but with the streets full of Basijis it was still too dangerous; she was no longer marked as a protester, but she had no right to be talking to an unrelated, foreign man.

As Martin began climbing the stairs to his apartment, Omar's wife Rana appeared at her door. She greeted him politely, but it was clear that something was wrong.

"Have you heard from Omar?" she asked.

"No. Why, was he at the march?" Martin would not have expected to see him there; waving placards wasn't his style.

Rana shook her head. "But he didn't come home from the shop, and he's not answering the phone there."

"Maybe his car broke down?" The mobile phone service was still disabled; Martin was about to mention the mesh network he'd seen Mahnoosh using, but Rana would have tried that already if it had been an option. Perhaps the devices weren't thick enough on the ground to provide a connection out here in the suburbs.

He said, "Would you like me to drive to the shop and take a look?"

"Please, if you could. We'll come with you, *bizahmat.*"

"Of course."

Martin waited in the open doorway while she fetched her father-in-law, Mohsen, to accompany them; the whole family treated Martin warmly, but there was no question of him going anywhere with Rana alone. He felt a tug on his trousers; Omar's three-year-old son had grabbed hold of his knee.

Martin squatted down to greet him. "*Salaam, Farshid jan.*"

Farshid frowned. "*Baba kojast?*"

"*Namidunam,*" Martin confessed. "*Zud be khane miayad.*" He'll be home soon.

Mohsen and Rana appeared and the three of them headed for the car, leaving Farshid with his grandmother. Mohsen's English was as patchy as Martin's Farsi, but Martin worked out that he wasn't too worried yet: Omar had probably just been called away on business, somewhere with no access to a phone.

As they drove toward the city Martin scanned the radio stations for news.

The official news agency had already announced that twenty-seven people had been hospitalized after the march; the hospitals themselves refused to give out figures, and he could no longer guess whether casualties were being downplayed to exculpate the militias, or inflated in order to warn people off.

When they reached the shop it was locked and dark; Omar's car was still parked in the rear. Rana went inside to look around; Mohsen waited outside with Martin, leaning against the car, smoking. He had lost both legs in the war with Iraq; he had prosthetics, but he needed crutches to get around. After a couple of minutes Rana emerged, distraught. She spoke to her father-in-law, showing him a scrap of paper, then she explained to Martin, "He left a note inside the cash register. Someone arrested him, took him away."

"Who arrested him?"

Rana shook her head. "He didn't know who they were. Or he didn't have time to write it."

Martin didn't want to dwell on what would happen if VEVAK had uncovered Omar's role in getting Shokouh out of the country. "We could go to the police station, ask there," he suggested. He couldn't think of anything else to try; they'd be hard-pressed to find a lawyer at this hour. Rana repeated this to Mohsen, and he agreed.

The central police station was more crowded than Martin had seen it before, with a queue of anxious relatives spilling out onto the street and halfway down the block. There'd been no mass arrests at the march itself, and the brawls with the Basijis had not been widespread—the only explanation Martin could think of was that there'd been some kind of crackdown in the hours after the march, with hundreds of minor dissidents rounded up. He tried to find a positive spin on that: if Omar had been arrested for nothing more than a few indiscreet comments overheard by informers, the chances were he'd be released within a day or two, uncharged.

When they joined the queue the first half-dozen people ahead of them offered to cede their place to Mohsen; he politely declined, but they kept insisting until he accepted. Martin couldn't entirely fathom why he wasn't simply admitted to the head of the queue; it wasn't as if the dozens of people who were now content to remain in front of him were any less respectful of his status as a veteran. Perhaps it was a kind of trade-off, a gesture that showed respect without overstepping the mark into condescension.

Rana wouldn't lift her gaze from the ground, and she resisted Martin's attempts to distract her with small-talk and optimistic prognoses. He was trying to keep his own imagination in check; he knew what went on in Evin Prison, but nobody was going to round up and torture every last

Iranian who'd ever stocked contraband action movies. Only if they'd traced Shokouh's false passport back to Omar would he be in real danger.

Martin spotted a woman further along the queue speaking on a phone, though she was doing her best to hide it in her sleeve. As far as he knew the Slightly Smart phones weren't illegal, though perhaps they soon would be.

When she hung up the call, she turned and spoke agitatedly with her neighbor. Whatever the subject, it was not a private matter; within minutes Martin could see the news being spread up and down the line. Maybe the authorities had decided to charge Jabari after all; if his resignation hadn't been enough to win back conservative support, why not pull out all the stops and have a show trial, to prove that nobody was above the law?

But any mention of Jabari always conjured up at least a few wry smiles. Nobody was smiling as they heard this news.

The rumor finally reached Mohsen and Rana; Martin's Farsi had largely deserted him, but once he had heard Ansari's name mentioned he could think of only two possibilities.

"Have they arrested him?" he asked.

"No," Rana said, "he's been shot. They've taken him to hospital, but he's not expected to last the night."

6

Nasim hunched over her computer screen, gazing intently at a section of code from her neural map integration routines, blocking out thoughts of anything else.

No two zebra finches sang exactly the same song; no two finches had identical brains. So how could you use partial, imperfect images of a thousand different finch brains to build up some kind of meaningful composite?

On a gross level the same structures within the brain appeared in more or less the same anatomical locations, but as you zoomed in toward the level of individual neurons, the cues that counted most were the cells' biochemistry and their patterns of connections. The problem lay in keeping the notion of a pattern of connections from becoming meaninglessly vague, uselessly rigid, or maddeningly circular. If ten thousand cells of biochemical type A sent axons to ten thousand cells of type B, that certainly didn't mean that they were all interchangeable. But if you insisted that only neurons that were wired up to identical neighbors in identical ways could be treated as common features, there would be no matches at all. Worse, if you could only characterize every neuron by first characterizing the neurons to which it was joined, you ran the risk of pushing everything down a rabbit hole of endless self-reference. The whole endeavor was like trying to reconstruct the human skeleton from a thousand incomplete—and partly inconsistent—translations of "Dem Dry Bones" into unknown foreign languages. "The *fifflezerm's* connected to the *girglesprig*…"

Over the months she'd spent working on the problem, Nasim had tried all manner of high-powered statistical techniques and classification schemes from abstract network topology, but the approach that was finally showing signs of a payoff involved searching for distinctive sub-networks, not by their pattern of connections *per se*, but by their function. An engineer staring at a circuit diagram could group the components into various kinds of functional blocks—say, half-a-dozen that formed an oscillator, another half-dozen comprising a filter—without requiring an absolutely rigid, unvarying design for each of these meta-components. An oscillator was anything that oscillated; it didn't have to be a perfect match for the first one you'd encountered in a textbook. Similarly, if a group of neurons had the same general effect on their inputs as another group, it didn't really matter if there happened to be thirty-nine neurons in one group and forty-five in the other. "The same general effect" was easier said than defined, but Nasim had been refining the notion for weeks now, and she was convinced that she was finally closing in on a set of meaningful categories.

She tweaked a few definitions in her code and then started it running again. It would take a couple of minutes to process the full data set; she looked away from her screen and across the lab. Everyone was unnaturally quiet today; Redland was down in Washington, testifying before a House Select Committee on the mooted Human Connectome Project, and Judith had gone with him. The Committee had been holding hearings for a month, and Redland was just one of dozens of scientists who'd been called to give testimony, but the occasion of his trip had reminded everyone that their funding, and their future, lay in the balance.

The composite map appeared on the screen. Nasim was about to slip on her headphones when a mischievous impulse took hold of her. She pulled the headphone plug out of its jack, rerouting the computer's audio to its speakers. Then she fired up the software syrinx and ran the latest simulation of the finch brain's vocalization pathways.

The infantile babbling of her early trials had slowly been giving way to a more ordered song, but this time hairs rose on the back of her neck. The distinctive rhythms of an adult bird's call—the whole style, the whole structure—were finally present.

With the song still playing, she checked the simulation's virtual EEG. The waveforms were not an exact match to any of the biological recordings on file, but the statistics all fell within the population ranges. If she'd handed the traces to a neurobiologist, they would not have been able to pick the artificial one from the real.

Mike stepped away from his bench and looked around, annoyed. "Who took the bird out of the animal house?" he demanded. He was wearing a hairnet and something that resembled a plastic shower cap. "If I get droppings in my cell cultures, that's a month's work down the tube!" He finally homed in on the sound and turned to glare angrily at Nasim. "Where is it?"

It took her a moment to realize that he wasn't joking. She said, "No drop-pings, Mike, I promise."

Mike, Shen and Dinesh gathered around her desk and watched as she ran through a battery of further tests. She kept the syrinx warbling, trying to shake off the eerie feeling that she'd stitched together something grue-some from the corpses of the birds and could now feel the awakened result fluttering its wings in her hand.

Shen said, "We should play this to a female bird and see if she's attracted. A Turing test for zebra finches."

"No," Mike countered, "we should simulate a female's auditory centers, and see if *that simulation* is attracted."

"One program fools another program? How is that a test?" Shen de-manded.

"It's not a test," Mike agreed, "but it would be much easier for them to consummate the relationship."

Shen pondered this. "I think the Media Lab could put together some avian tele-dildonics faster than we could construct a purely software female capable of mating."

"Can we cut the Bride of Frankenfinch crap?" Nasim pleaded. "There's nothing in there but the vocalization PDP. If *that* can feel lust all by itself, then so can a Casio keyboard."

Dinesh said, "There's nothing in there that can feel lust, yet. But now that you can integrate maps from different imaging techniques, it would take us, what, eighteen months to do the whole finch brain?"

"Who's this 'us'?" Mike replied. "You mean the people who are actually sticking around to fight for the HCP?"

Nasim plugged her headphones into their jack, cutting off the speakers. "The recital's over," she said. "I have work to do."

At lunchtime, Nasim joined the others gathered around a widescreen monitor in the conference room, watching Redland give his testimony to the Select Committee. The session had taken place a few hours before, and the video had been posted on the web.

Redland stuck to the usual big targets: schizophrenia, autism, depression and Alzheimer's. The Human Connectome Project, he declared, would shed light on them all. This was almost certainly true in the long run, and it was a relatively easy goal to sell to the public, but Nasim still had her doubts about the wisdom of the strategy. It didn't take much reflection for people to start wondering if there weren't better, cheaper, faster ways to address those conditions. Mapping every corner of the brain would be a triumph of human self-understanding—with payoffs, eventually, that left the genome in the shade—but if you were going to spend billions of dollars and decades of hard work on that goal, selling it as a cure for some Affliction of the Month would only risk making the whole project seem like a bloated white elephant as soon as a drug came along to make that role redundant.

As Shen closed the playback window for the recording, he noticed a small image showing the site's live feed. "Hey, they're talking to Zachary Churchland!" He put the feed into full-screen mode.

Churchland was an octogenarian oil billionaire who had raised the possibility of funding his own brain-mapping project, in competition with any government effort. The press had started calling him "the Craig Venter of the HCP," but unlike Venter, he had no biotech skills himself. The neuroscientists advocating the HCP treated him with kid gloves, as they would any potential sugar daddy, but his professed motives could not have been further from their own statements about Alzheimer's and apple pie.

"Congressman, the ultimate goal of my project would be universal immortality," Churchland declared. His voice reminded Nasim of William S. Burroughs, a writer whose words had been sampled on one of her favorite dance tracks; she'd never sought out his books, suspecting they'd be rather straight-laced and stuffy, but he had such nice diction that she'd come to think of him as the epitome of twentieth-century gentility. "If there are public health benefits along the way, then that's well and good, but all of public health becomes a minor sub-problem when viewed in the light of the digital migration."

Congressman Fitzwaller, chairman of the Select Committee, pondered this reply in silence for a moment. He could hardly have been ignorant of Churchland's views unless he'd had his head in a paper bag for the last six months, but now that the man was there in front of him, in the flesh, giving testimony before this august body, he seemed not quite able to believe what he was hearing.

"Mr. Churchland, the scientists who have come before this committee have all been quite clear: the Human Connectome will not be a personal map of any one human's brain. It will not describe any individual's memories, or personality, or goals. Do you dispute that expert testimony, sir?"

Churchland made a sound that could either have been a sigh, or a sign of emphysema. "No, Congressman, I do not. I accept that a generic map is a necessary intermediate step on the road toward the mapping of individuals. Having reached that point, a great deal of work will remain to be done in order to achieve personalization. But to pretend that we will reach that point and then halt is simply absurd. We will continue. That is our nature."

Fitzwaller said, "What timescale do you anticipate for that development?

For what you call 'personalization'?"

"I am not an expert," Churchland replied, "but the people I have consulted on the matter suggest that it might be possible within twenty or thirty years."

"So this is not a development from which you would hope to benefit yourself, sir?"

"On the contrary, Congressman," Churchland replied crisply, "I am unlikely to see out the year, but upon my death my body will be frozen. If I do set up a trust to support this research, the deeds of that trust will expressly state that its goals include my own digital resurrection."

Fitzwaller looked down and shuffled through his papers with something of the air of a doctor reluctant to deliver bad news. Nasim could sympathize with his discomfort. She suspected that uploading *would* become feasible at some point in the future—perhaps by the end of the century—but to watch a dying man clutching at straws like this was just painful.

Fitzwaller said, "Mr. Churchland, do you really have that much faith in this technology? We are all grateful for the achievements and ingenuity of the medical profession, but surely there are limits to what mere humans can do."

Churchland reached off-camera and retrieved an oxygen mask, which he held over his mouth and nose for three deep breaths before replying. "Indeed, Congressman. And I would not wish to mislead this committee into thinking that I have definitely resolved to fund a project of the kind we are discussing. In fact, over the last month or so I have received some very persuasive representations from a group who believe that it might be at best inefficient and at worst highly dangerous to proceed in this fashion."

"Can you elaborate, sir?"

"I have been invited to fund an enterprise known as the Benign Superintelligence Bootstrap Project," Churchland explained. "Their aim is to build an artificial intelligence capable of such exquisite powers of self-analysis that it will design and construct its own successor, which will be armed with superior versions of all the skills the original possessed. The successor will then produce a still more proficient third version, and so on, leading to a cascade of exponentially increasing abilities. Once this process is set in motion, within weeks—perhaps within hours—a being of truly God-like powers will emerge."

Nasim resisted the urge to bury her face in her hands. However surreal the spectacle unfolding on the screen, there was, in retrospect, something inevitable about it. The uploading advocates who'd sold Churchland on an imminent digital resurrection hadn't lost their critical faculties entirely, but their penchant for finessing away any "mere technical problems" that might stretch out the timetable was, nonetheless, intellectually corrosive, to the point where the next step probably didn't seem like such a great leap anymore: hand-waving *all* practicalities out of existence, transforming the cyber-eschatologists' rickety scaffolding of untested assumptions into a cast-iron stairway to heaven.

Fitzwaller cleared his throat. "Mr. Churchland, it's not entirely clear to me how that matter is pertinent to the business of this committee."

Churchland said, "Rather than trust humans to perfect the brain-mapping technology that we've been discussing, I am leaning toward putting my fate in the hands of an artificial God, for whom such problems will be trivial. The Benign Superintelligence will rule the planet with wisdom and compassion, eliminating war, disease, unhappiness, and of course, death. I am told that it will probably disassemble most of the material in our solar system in order to construct a vast computer that will exploit all the energy of the sun. Perhaps it will spare the Earth, or perhaps the Earth will be reconstructed, more perfectly, within that computerized domain."

The camera caught Fitzwaller in the transition from bewilderment to revulsion. "'Rule the planet'? Am I to understand that you're contemplating funding a body that advocates overthrowing the lawful government of the United States?"

Churchland required more oxygen before replying, "Keep your shirt on, Congressman. There's no point fighting it, and the alternative would be far worse. Imagine if one of our country's enemies did this first. Imagine the kind of despotic superintelligence that Al Qaeda would create."

"Mr. Churchland," Fitzwaller said evenly, "does it not occur to you that most people on the planet would prefer not to have their affairs dictated by an artificial intelligence of any kind?"

"That's too bad, Congressman," Churchland retorted, "because I am coming to the view that we probably have no choice."

Judith stormed into the conference room and slammed her briefcase down on the table. For a moment Nasim assumed that she'd been watching the same feed, but then it became clear from her body language that she was oblivious to the sight of half the HCP's potential funding sprouting wings and flying away. She was livid, but it had nothing to do with Churchland's deathbed embrace of Bullshit Squared.

"Whoever's idea it was," she fumed, "*it really wasn't funny.*"

Nasim said, "Whoever's idea was *what?*"

"Can you think of a reason why *five* sleaze-bags would have hit on me this morning in Reagan Airport alone?"

"New perfume?" Mike suggested. Judith picked up the whiteboard eraser and hurled it at him; he squirmed sideways but it clipped his shoulder.

Dinesh spread his hands innocently. "How could that possibly be our do-ing? You think we're paying men to harass you, as some kind of prank?"

Judith took her phone from her pocket. "*Someone*, somehow, has signed me on to... PowerFlirt, or HookMeUp, or whatever the fuck it's called when total strangers get a message on their phone the moment I walk into sight—" She must have noticed the growing expression of discomfort on Nasim's face, because she loomed toward her and demanded, "What do you know about this?"

Nasim cringed. She'd thought Christopher in IT would have fixed every-thing by now, but she'd never got around to switching AcTrack back on and checking if her own problem had gone away—let alone following up the whole question of whether Murmur had made its system less prone to bizarre cross-infections. "I should have told everyone sooner," she confessed, flustered, "but I put the rabbit in the park and I just forgot about it."

Judith stared at her as if she'd lost her mind.

Shen said, "*Phwoar*. Isn't it called *Phwoar*? That's what I heard." He was sitting next to Nasim, and through the floor she could feel his chair reso-nating with a dull mechanical vibration.

7

Crouched in the dark recess behind the freezer-truck's compressor, Martin was wishing that he'd brought some music for the trip. He was wearing earplugs, but the relentless thumping of the compressor still seeped into his skull, and he was beginning to hallucinate snatches of songs emerging from the noise. In principle that might have been entertaining, but the songs were all terrible: soppy Bollywood love duets with doleful heroes and squeaky-voiced heroines; monotonous aerobics-class remixes of undeserved hits of the eighties; vapid punk-metal droning by airheads sporting novelty contact lenses. If he'd known before he'd left Tehran that there was so much bad music buried in his skull, he would have shoved a screwdriver up one nostril and done his best to scrape it all out.

Behrouz was wedged behind the other side of the compressor, and though it probably would have been safe for them to yell at each other while the truck was moving, Martin suspected that bellowing pleasantries and idle observations wouldn't have done much to help them pass the time. And being caught at a checkpoint playing "Twenty Questions" would just have been embarrassing.

Martin tried seeding counter-hallucinations, mentally dredging up a few bars of songs that he actually wanted to hear and hoping that whatever bizarre neural process was turning the noise into music would take the hint. "Infected" by The The should have been perfect, with a pounding rhythm that he could usually summon at will, but the compressor took it and mangled it into the Phil Collins version of "You Can't Hurry Love." Hunters and Collectors' "Run Run Run" morphed into Abba's "Dancing Queen." When The Smiths' "Rusholme Ruffians" became Elvis's "Teddy Bear," Martin decided to quit while he was ahead, but then the King himself devolved into a dire rockabilly act called the Stray Cats.

With no hope of an entertaining soundtrack, Martin was at a loss as to how to fill the hours. He didn't want to dwell on Omar—on what it meant, after a fortnight, that no authority would even acknowledge taking him into custody—so he devoted all his effort to *not* thinking about Mahnoosh. His brain fell for the ruse, and her face kept floating out of the darkness in defiance of his sham attempts to banish it. He'd seen her on that one day only, at the march, but whether through memory or imagination he had a vast library of snapshots of her in his head, already catalogued by mood: calm and reflective; mischievous; implacable—a thousand micro-expressions framed and accentuated by her no-nonsense olive headscarf.

The truck came to a halt and the driver shut off the engine. Refuelling, or yet another checkpoint? Under the emergency decrees all Iranians now required a permit to travel between cities; that had always been the case for foreign journalists, but Martin had never felt compelled to break the rules before, back in the days when it would have been easy. He checked his watch and guessed they were somewhere close to Ahvaz, which would put them within a hundred kilometers of their destination, but his phone hadn't been able to get a GPS signal since he'd crawled into the hiding place.

He heard the rear door open and someone heavy climb into the truck. A stack of crates was scraped across the uneven metal floor, as if unloading had begun, but the driver had assured them that there were no deliveries to be made along the way. Martin felt the floor vibrating under approaching footsteps; one instinct commanded him to move as far away from the intruder as he could, but instead he used his millimeters of freedom to slide his body in the other direction and brace himself against the thin sheet of rigid plastic that separated him from the cargo area. Something hard struck the partition: a baton, or maybe a rifle butt. There was a pause, then two more blows in rapid succession. Martin didn't flinch; his weight against the plastic kept it from buckling, absorbing the energy and deadening the sound of the impact. The cavity was meant to be packed with insulating foam; without his intervention it would have sounded hollow as a drum.

But did it sound like foam, or did it sound like flesh? He waited for an angry shout, an imperious command; a blade thrust through the plastic, or a bullet.

The floor vibrated again, the intruder retreated. The door swung closed.

After the truck had been unloaded in a noisy warehouse, the driver parked nearby and unscrewed the panels that concealed his extra cargo. Behrouz was released first, but he was still bent double and massaging his legs when Martin emerged, hobbling and squinting. He'd grown used to the smell of machine oil from the compressor, but it had been masking the cargo area's own distinctive scent of unwashed refrigerator. He glanced over at Behrouz. "I'll give you a hundred dollars if you can find me a hot bath in the next fifteen minutes."

Behrouz snorted. "What am I now, a tour guide? Don't be such a wimp, we've got work to do."

"That would sound much more convincing if you showed signs of being able to walk."

The nervous driver hurried them out of the truck onto a dark side-street, then took off with a deafening squeal of rubber. They were both wearing heavy coats and woollen hats, but away from the freezer they were over-dressed for a summer evening this far south. Abadan was on an island bounded by rivers, fifty kilometers inland from the Persian Gulf. To the west, across the Arvand River—renamed *Shatt al-Arab* once crossed—was southern Iraq; Basra wasn't far upstream.

Behrouz had brought a map of the city; he led the way to a truck-stop offering fast food and, most urgently, a toilet. In the restaurant, Martin slung his coat over his shoulder but kept the woollen hat on; in spite of the balmy weather many of the customers were wearing them, and though he'd always look foreign close up in good light, he still hoped that out on the street the right cues would prevent too many second glances.

The oil refinery was visible for miles, the vast complex lit up like a NASA launch site. Though it had been bombed into the ground by Saddam Hussein in 1980, it had been built up again after the war until it was once again the most productive in Iran, churning out nearly half a million barrels a day—when it was operating.

As they drew nearer to the complex, the streets became crowded; the picket line itself was still not in sight, but there were so many people coming and going—supporters bringing food and supplies to the striking workers, or people just wanting to witness the spectacle—that street vendors had set up half-a-dozen stalls. Martin saw a group of soldiers lined up in front of a government building, but they looked more uncomfortable than threatening.

Dariush Ansari had been born in Abadan, the son of an oil worker, and he'd worked in the same plant himself, briefly, as an engineer. His father had since retired, but his former colleagues had shut down the refinery for the funeral ten days before and they had not returned to work since. Ordinarily, Tehran would have sent in the army to deal with the pickets and bussed in workers from across the country, but someone in the regime must have grasped the fact that if they did that, it would end with the city in flames.

Half the people in the crowd were speaking Arabic; Martin's vocabulary was negligible, but he could easily distinguish it from Farsi. Many of the refinery workers were Arabic-speaking Iranians; whilst Ansari had not belonged to that ethnic group, he had been a local, and fluent in the local dialect—quite different from the Arabic studied in Iranian high schools— and his willingness to use it in speeches here had helped attract supporters. But rather than trying to inflame ethnic tensions, or demanding special treatment for the region, he'd focused on the benefits of a determined, nationwide assault on corruption and nepotism. People here knew that their wealth was being pilfered and wasted, but Ansari's answer had been transparency and equity, not separatism.

When they came within sight of the picket line, Martin saw that the usual *Referendum!* signs had been supplemented with photographs of Ansari and a new slogan that Behrouz translated as "Murderers, get lost!" That soldiers weren't tearing the signs from people's hands was no less amazing than if they'd borne the strongest profanities, given that this accusation and advice was meant for the government.

Martin took out his new phone and snapped some pictures of the pickets, trying to balance a fervent wish to avoid being seen by the soldiers with a fear that if he looked too furtive the people around him would take him for an informer. One young man did move toward him, scowling, but Behrouz stepped in and whispered an explanation that seemed to satisfy him.

He checked the pictures and queued them up for their long, tortuous journey to Sydney. Even back in his office in Tehran he was no longer able to use the internet; he had to print out his copy and fax it. He'd tried up-loading files direct to the newspaper's computer using a dial-up modem, but the government was degrading international phone lines to the point where the modems just kept hanging up; even the faxes he sent arrived peppered with static and were only legible if he used an absurdly large font. The conventional mobile service was now disabled across the country, and every major city had installed transmitters to jam the frequencies that had enabled the mesh network Mahnoosh had showed him at the demonstration in Tehran.

Slightly Smart Systems, though, had left one last option open: infrared. Their phones could pass data to each other by IR along a line-of-sight path, and whilst the government could interfere with the system in a limited space, such as a stadium or public square, in principle, they could no more jam it everywhere than they could flood the whole country with strobing blue disco lights.

The point-to-point bursts of IR carried email and news in much the same way as those services had worked in the days before the internet proper, when university computers had been linked up only sporadically via brief late-night phone calls, but in lieu of fixed landlines, the modern incarnation involved "polling" phones in the vicinity to discover which ones were in a position to exchange data. Before the restrictions on intercity travel had come in, Slightly Smart email had diffused across the country and over the borders in a matter of days; from Tehran, Martin had sent a test message to his editor and received a reply in four days, probably via Turkey. No doubt there would soon be government programmers working on ways to clog the whole system with spam—and plainclothes police strolling around arresting anyone who responded to their polling signal—but for now the benefits were worth the risk, and a crowd of Ansari supporters was a good place to start. Martin switched his phone to polling mode and parked it in his shirt pocket with the tiny lens of the IR transceiver exposed, leaving it to try its secret handshake on as many passing strangers as it liked.

As he looked around at the crowd, trying to judge whether it would be wise to attempt some interviews, Martin spotted the young man whom Behrouz had deflected earlier, returning with four physically imposing friends.

"You think we're in trouble?" he asked Behrouz.

"Who's this 'we,' *beegaané?*" Behrouz replied.

The first man ignored Martin and went straight to Behrouz, while the wrestling team hung back, looking stern and inscrutable.

"They'd like us to go with them," Behrouz announced.

"Is that an invitation to tea, or should I phone my embassy?"

Behrouz smiled. "It's up to you, but if you'd like to interview Ansari's brother, they can take you to him."

They walked for more than half an hour, heading into a maze of small, quiet streets far from the refinery. It was a poor neighborhood, but not an especially rough-looking one, full of car workshops, grocery stores and spice vendors. There were young children playing on the streets, and strolling teenagers who looked neither fierce nor fearful. Martin gave up feeling nervous; while it wasn't inconceivable that he was being set up, foreign journalists from obscure countries would have no value as bargaining chips in this purely Iranian game. He suddenly recalled the time a friend of Liz's had thoughtfully mailed her a DVD of *A Mighty Heart*, and he'd had to sit beside her in their apartment in Islamabad, watching Angelina Jolie convulsing with grief over the death of her journalist husband. Martin had given the movie four stars, and sent Liz's friend an email that won him a place on her no-Christmas-cards-ever list.

They arrived at a slightly shabby terraced house and were admitted by a wary doorkeeper who insisted on patting them down and examining their phones and wallets. There were other men lurking inside the house, but, encouragingly, Martin had yet to see a single weapon.

Karim, the young man who'd spotted Martin taking pictures, handed the two guests over to a middle-aged man who introduced himself as Mehdi and offered them tea and *halvaa*; it would have been rude to refuse, and Martin was grateful for the sugar rush. They sat on the carpet, shoeless and cross-legged, while Mehdi chatted volubly with Behrouz and politely enquired about Martin's health and family.

"*Hich zan nadaaram, hich baché nadaaram,*" Martin confessed: I have no wife, I have no children. Mehdi regarded him with a mixture of astonishment and pity.

"Your parents?" he asked in English.

"They both died a few years ago." Mehdi couldn't quite parse that, so Behrouz translated. Mehdi *tssked* and shook his head forlornly, momentarily as anxious and perplexed as if an orphaned child had turned up on his doorstep. But then he shifted his attention back to Behrouz and they started discussing football scores. There was a TV switched on in a corner of the room, tuned to IRIB's Channel One, which was screening reruns of a popular historical miniseries, *No Room to Turn*. Martin had heard claims that the show—which featured a love story between an Iranian student and a Jewish woman in Nazi-occupied Europe—was mere propaganda, portraying the endangered Jewish heroine sympathetically while caricaturing her Zionist relatives, but he'd yet to see enough of it to form his own opinion. In any case, it was a more enjoyable way to improve his Farsi than listening to Mehdi's match post-mortems.

After almost an hour there was a flurry of activity in the adjoining room; Martin hadn't heard the front door open, but apparently a small entourage had arrived, maybe through another entrance. Mehdi picked up the remote and turned down the volume on the TV. Martin managed to rise to his feet before Kourosh Ansari entered the room, alone.

Kourosh greeted Martin in English and Behrouz and Mehdi in Farsi. Martin said, "Please accept my condolences on your brother's death."

"Thank you." Kourosh had deep hollows under his eyes, and a few days' growth of beard set against a much longer mustache. "I heard him speak on a few occasions," Martin added. "He was impressive."

Kourosh murmured agreement.

There was an awkward pause; Martin wasn't sure whether it would be rude to get down to business immediately. He had never managed to get an interview with Dariush, and though that had rankled slightly, he'd understood why; the elder Ansari really hadn't had any reason to court a foreign audience. All Martin knew about Kourosh was that he, too, had studied chemical engineering. He looked to be in his late thirties.

Mehdi invited everyone to sit, then went to fetch more tea. "Do you work in Abadan?" Martin asked.

"No, in Esfahan," Kourosh replied, "but my job there is finished. I will work for Hezb-e-Haalaa now."

"In what role?"

"I have been chosen as provisional leader by the party's executive council. At present, we face some logistical problems with holding an election for the position."

"I can appreciate that." It was a minor, and possibly short-lived, miracle that mere membership of Hezb-e-Haalaa was not yet illegal. "So where do you see things going from here? The strike won't be tolerated indefinitely."

"Of course not." Kourosh hesitated. "But I'm still hopeful that the government will give some ground. They want to look reasonable; they want to be seen to be reacting to the people's anger. That's why they had Jabari resign."

"But how much more ground can they give? What are you hoping for?"

"A referendum within a year, to end the Guardian Council veto in time for the next presidential election."

Martin said, "Is that realistic?"

Kourosh ran a hand over his eyes. "I don't know. But I think it's the smallest thing that the people would treat as anything but an insult. How much Iranian history do you know?"

"A little." Martin fervently hoped that he wasn't about to be tested on the names of the Safavid kings.

"Abadan was once controlled by the British, by the Anglo-Iranian Oil Company. They refused to share their profits fairly—they wouldn't even give Iran the same deal as the Saudis received—but it was only a strike by the workers that gave the Majlis the courage it needed to nationalise the industry."

"A move that ultimately cost Mossadegh his job."

"Of course," Kourosh agreed. "Mr. Churchill persuaded Mr. Eisenhower that our Prime Minister was a dangerous socialist, and the CIA engineered their very first coup. But if they'd left him in place to rein in the Shah, we would not have had the mullahs taking power twenty-six years later."

"Perhaps," Martin replied. Mossadegh himself had been a far-from-perfect democrat, and the clerics of the time had had their own problems with him.

"Now I'm afraid we're facing the risk of more American meddling," Kourosh said.

"Really? Have they approached Hezb-e-Haalaa?"

Kourosh scowled. "Yes, but that's old news; my brother told them to keep their distance a long time ago. But now they're trying to start a new game. My friends in Iraq tell me there are plans to unleash the MEK and send them across the border."

The MEK—the Mujahedin-e-Khalq, the People's Army of Iran—was a nationalist group formed in opposition to the Shah. Its members had been pushed aside by Islamists in the 1979 revolution and ended up in exile in Iraq. Accepting the hospitality of Saddam Hussein while he'd engaged in a long and bloody war against their homeland had not been the best PR move in history. Though they claimed to answer to a kind of parliament-in-exile, they now had very little support within Iran, and since the 2003 invasion most of them lived in Iraq, in a strange twilight state, somewhere between refugees and prisoners-of-war.

"You think Washington would actually do that? Re-arm them and let them loose, just to make trouble?" The Bush administration had funded several armed Iranian opposition groups—including the MEK, and a Baluchi terrorist group called Jondollah—in the hope of eliciting a bloody crackdown from the regime that would serve as the pretext for an all-out war, but Martin thought those programs had been flushed down the chute with the change of administration. "You must have heard Obama acknowledge the CIA's role in the Mossadegh coup, in that speech in Cairo not long after he came to power? Reaching out to the Islamic world and announcing an end to American interventionism?"

Kourosh said, "I'm in no position to know if this plan has the President's blessing, or if some other arm of government has taken the initiative without his knowledge. But I can tell you exactly what would happen if the MEK came across the border: first, the Iranian Army would wipe them out with very little trouble, and second, the Iranian people would unite under the present regime and the reformist movement would be back in the wilderness for another twenty years at least. Not Hezb-e-Haalaa, nor anybody else, would try to exploit the situation for their own benefit. We are not traitors, and we are not idiots."

"Isn't the MEK still classified as a terrorist organization by the Americans?"

"Yes," Kourosh replied. "So of course they would do this quietly. That's why I prefer not to be so quiet."

Martin finally understood why he'd been plucked out of the crowd so eagerly; Kourosh wasn't interested in raising his celebrity profile; what he needed was a story that would embarrass the Americans into thinking twice—or dragging their rogue elements back into line, if none of this was actually coming from the top. *Brother of Slain Reformist Condemns US Backing for Terrorists* would get picked up immediately from his own paper's website and splashed all over the American broadsheets.

He said, "I can write part of this story, but I'll need to get messages to my colleagues in Washington and Baghdad to follow up on your claims."

"How long are you staying in Abadan?"

Martin glanced at Mehdi, who said, "You are my guest here tonight."

"Thank you."

Kourosh said, "When you've written whatever you need to send, pass it to Karim. We can get your email on a boat to Kuwait within a couple of hours."

"Okay." *Email on a boat* no longer sounded strange; at this point, Martin would not have been fazed by pigeons carrying flash drives.

Behrouz glanced at the TV, and Martin followed his gaze; the Supreme Leader was making an address to the nation. Mehdi turned up the volume and the four of them sat and watched the grandfatherly man with his black turban, white beard and round glasses.

Behrouz didn't bother translating; it had been a long day and Martin suspected there was nothing in the speech they hadn't all heard before. He managed to pick up the usual admonitions: do not take part in strikes or demonstrations, work hard to show your love for God and the nation, don't be fooled by the lies of the traitors and foreign enemies.

Just as Martin was tuning out, something in the speech caused Kourosh to stiffen with revulsion, then Martin heard jeers erupting from neighboring houses all down the street. He turned to Behrouz.

"He just thanked his beloved children, the Basijis, for showing restraint and keeping order across the country," Behrouz explained. Dariush Ansari had been shot in a motorcycle drive-by; if the killer had not actually been a Basiji, he'd been doing his best to imitate one. The police were investigating the murder, but so far nobody had been charged.

Kourosh left and Martin sat writing up the interview on his phone; the tiny virtual keyboard on the touch-screen drove him crazy, but it was still faster than using voice recognition, then correcting all the errors. It was almost one o'clock when he finished; he realized he didn't have PGP encryption keys for anyone but his editor, but she'd pass the story on to his colleagues almost as quickly as if he'd CC'd it to them himself.

He found Karim in the next room; the data jumped between their phones, then the young man went out into the night. Mehdi showed Martin to the guest room; as he lay down on a mat a couple of meters from where Behrouz was already sleeping he suddenly realized that he'd left his stupid woollen hat on all this time, even through the interview.

The next thing he knew, Behrouz was shaking him awake. Martin squinted at his watch, his eyes narrowed against the glare of the ceiling light. "If that's not four-thirty in the afternoon, I'm going to have to kill you." He had a pounding headache and a lump of undigested food in his gut; as he sat up he discovered all the places he was aching from being confined in the freezer-truck the day before.

Behrouz handed Martin his phone, which was showing an image of a very large crowd at the entrance to a building. The picture had been taken at night, and Martin didn't recognize the location. "What's happening?"

"That's the Ministry of the Interior," Behrouz replied, "just before midnight."

"Did they trash it?"

"I don't know; at the time this was sent it was surrounded, but not actually occupied. Three people had been shot, but the crowd still hadn't dispersed."

"News travels fast." This wasn't random hitchhiking; Hezb-e-Haalaa must have set up some kind of data relay, stretching between the cities. "Thanks for waking me."

"I've organized a ride back."

"Can we get coffee on the way?" Martin begged.

Behrouz looked dubious. "I said we'd be there by five."

As they hurried through the dark streets, it struck Martin that the only thing preventing Behrouz from doing both of their jobs was the fact that, as an Iranian citizen, he'd face much harsher penalties for writing a story that crossed the line. Behrouz's written English wasn't perfect, but a sub-editor could easily deal with the occasional minor blemish. And as for the supposedly greater journalistic impartiality of a foreigner, Martin had to admit that ever since he'd swapped clothes with Shokouh in the hospital his own claim on that virtue had been tenuous.

And Omar? What had Shokouh's rescue cost him?

Martin finally realized that they were heading back to the place where they'd been dropped off the night before. When they arrived, the same freezer-truck was parked there, waiting for them.

He turned to Behrouz. "Have you got any decent music on your phone?"

"Define decent."

"Nusrat Fateh Ali Khan?" Martin suggested hopefully. They'd never talked about music before.

Behrouz grimaced. "Do I look like a Sufi?"

"Do I? I can still appreciate *qawwali*."

"The Sufi-est thing I've got is Metallica," Behrouz replied pityingly. "The rest is hardcore."

"So after twenty-five hundred years of Persian culture—"

"Yeah, yeah. I already had that lecture from my grandmother."

Martin slipped the driver a hundred US dollars and they followed him into the back of the truck. He tried to get "Mast Qalandar" running through his brain, but by the time he'd been sealed in beside the compressor, "Enter Sandman" was already rising up from the noise.

8

Nasim had stayed late in the lab, running simulations for the finch paper she was co-writing with Redland, so it was almost ten o'clock when she arrived home. Her mother was in the living room, watching the BBC World News channel.

Nasim kissed her on the cheek. "Anything I should know about?"

"Did you eat?" her mother replied.

"Not really."

"I made *khoresht sabzi*."

"Oh, yum." Nasim could smell the delicate fragrance of the herbs; she went into the kitchen and opened the pot. "*Khoresht sabzi?*" she wailed. "When did chicken become a vegetable?"

"You should be happy," her mother protested. "I didn't use beef."

"I'm a *vegetarian!* I told you that! Have you ever seen a chicken photo-synthesize?" Luckily there was a pot of rice, too; careful examination with a fork revealed sultanas, but no fleshy surprises. The rice was still warm; Nasim spooned a small hillock of it—along with what remained of the crisp *tadigh* where it had browned on the bottom—onto a plate and carried it to the living room.

"One of my Ph.D. students is a vegetarian," her mother said. "He eats chicken all the time. Or maybe it's fish."

"If he eats chicken or fish he's not a vegetarian."

Her mother sighed. "You should be eating beef. Women need iron. You talk to biologists all day, you should know that."

"And you're an economist, so you should know that meat production wastes land, water and energy." She had given up meat only three months ago, but Nasim was already disgusted by the thought of eating flesh.

71

"Anyway, it's a personal choice. Imagine how you'd feel if someone tried feeding you pork."

"I ate bacon once," her mother confessed. "Accidentally, at a faculty party; it just tasted like fat drowned in salt. But the rule against pork is completely rational; the diseases of pigs are more communicable to humans. What diseases can you catch from *cows* or *chickens?*"

Nasim opened her mouth, then closed it again. She'd simply have to accept that she'd need to cook for herself from now on. "What's happening in Iran?"

"They've arrested someone for shooting Ansari."

"Really?"

"I recorded it." Her mother picked up the remote and hit a few buttons; the DVR began replaying the IRIB report.

The police had arrested a Palestinian immigrant, who had already confessed to the murder. His taped confession was played on air; he repeated no less than five times that he'd been acting alone, without assistance or encouragement from anyone. He'd been angry about Ansari's policy on Israel, so he'd bought an AK-47 from a drug dealer and ridden his motorbike to Ansari's house to make his opinion known. The police had also arrested the drug dealer, and were parading him as a kind of confirmatory witness.

Nasim didn't believe a word of it. If it had happened six months ago it might have been just barely plausible, but this was far too convenient.

It looked like no one in Iran had been appeased either; when Nasim switched back to the BBC, they were showing smuggled images of huge crowds outside half-a-dozen government buildings. If Jabari's hypocrisy had acted as a tiny seed for the superheated national psyche, just enough to make the simmering frustration visible, the murder of Ansari had brought everything to the boil. Ansari had not been a beloved national hero, just a calm, decent man with some modest ideas—but everyone in the country knew someone who had paid a high price for the crime of decency.

"Too many to kill," her mother mused, with a chilling tone of detachment. "If there were a tenth the number, they'd just mow them down and say they were all in the pay of foreign governments."

"However," the BBC announcer interrupted her, "this reformist sentiment is far from unanimous. Government employees bussed into Tehran from the countryside have been seen brawling with the protesters and disrupting their vigils. Commentators say that this is likely to be a more effective tactic than armed confrontation, whether by the security forces or the conservative militias."

Nasim felt her chest tightening with a familiar ache of helplessness. "Anything new about the MEK?" she asked; the last she'd heard on the subject had come from the White House that morning.

"The State Department, the Pentagon and the Iraqis have all chimed in with their own denials," her mother replied. "They insist that nobody in the MEK will be getting access to weapons, or a chance to cross the border."

"Do you believe that?"

Her mother frowned. "Now that it's been denounced by Ansari's brother and plastered all over the *New York Times*, I can't see them going through with it. But maybe the publicity will do some good: the UN should be resettling these people somewhere else, because they're never going to be safe in Iraq or Iran."

"Yeah." The MEK's base in Iraq, known as Camp Ashraf, held thousands of Iranian exiles, including women and children—not just would-be soldiers. Until 2009 it had been guarded by coalition troops, but since Iraq had assumed responsibility for the camp the situation there had become far more precarious. Pro-Tehran factions in Baghdad were constantly trying to deport the occupants back to Iran—and if international pressure precluded shipping people straight into Iranian prisons, the same factions could still do their best to make the camp's continued existence untenable. The MEK leadership certainly had a bloody history, and it was hard to know whether their renunciation of their old methods was sincere, but the whole community deserved something better than this desert limbo.

Nasim put her plate aside and curled up on the sofa beside her mother. It had been hard enough for the two of them, living illegally in Syria for three years, waiting for the UN to classify them as refugees and find a country willing to take them. They'd been cooped up in Damascus, in verminous apartments in the poorest neighbourhoods, sweltering in summer, freezing in winter. Their lives had revolved around evading the authorities, always having to move, or having to find the money to pay bribes to avoid being imprisoned or deported. Some schools had been willing to turn a blind eye to Nasim's status, but that had generally proved both risky and expensive, so most of her lessons had been at home. Sometimes her mother had found back-alley jobs sewing clothes, and Nasim had stood beside her sewing machine, passing her pieces of material; at the end of the shift their ears would be ringing so loudly that they couldn't hear each other speak. But she still met people who assumed that they'd simply jumped on a plane from Tehran to New York, where the mere mention of her dissident father had seen them naturalised on the spot, complete with bouquets and brass bands.

On the day they'd left Tehran, she'd wept twice as hard as on the day they'd hanged her father—because even after his death, she had felt she was abandoning him. She'd wanted to stay and fight, wanted to spit in the faces of his killers. That had been a meaningless, childish vision—and she would never forgive herself for the brutal accusations of cowardice she'd flung at her mother as she'd packed their suitcases—but even now, she couldn't simply cast those emotions aside.

She knew that above all else, her father would have wanted the two of them to escape the shadow of the ayatollahs, to find a safe home, to flourish. But she doubted that she'd ever stop feeling that she owed him something more.

9

On the fifth day of the siege of Evin Prison, just before dawn, saboteurs got in among the protesters long enough to burn down the chemical toilets. Surveying the resulting black-edged sculptures in melted plastic, Martin wondered if the end had finally come. People couldn't live like animals.

Within hours, though, shovels had been smuggled in from the surrounding suburbs and deep pits had been dug. Tents were commandeered, privacy was secured. By the time Martin confronted the inevitable and entered one of the reeking enclosures himself, the facilities were not just well-tested but adorned with graffiti, including some slyly vernacular English: "We honor Hassan Jabari for proving that a cock-up is better than a conspiracy."

Evin Prison sat on the line where the northern suburbs of Tehran gave way, abruptly, to the Alborz Mountains, some twelve kilometers from the city center. One minute there were crowded expressways, upmarket shopping malls and tiered apartment blocks in glittering white, the next there was barren rock sloping up into the mountains. Popular hiking trails began nearby, and a ski-lift wasn't far away, though it was definitely not the skiing season. At the bottom of the rocky slope sat the prison, its high gray walls topped with razor-wire, watchtowers rising from the cell blocks. To the west lay a shady green park with a teahouse and restaurant; those facilities were closed now, but the park itself had proved invaluable, with the trees offering shelter from the sun, and now the soft, excavatable ground saving the assembled masses from complete indignity.

Protesters surrounded the prison on all sides, but the bare rock behind it had proved the hardest to defend. For three nights running, the police had used water-cannon to force a retreat back down the slopes. But they

75

always ran out of water eventually, or their pumps ran out of fuel, and during the day the protesters rebuilt their barricades of metal drums and barbed-wire, and by sheer force of numbers pushed them up the mountain, driving back the police lines. Martin had watched from below as tear-gas grenades were smothered in drums of water or wrapped in fire-blankets, but never lobbed back to their senders. Apart from the sheer frustration of not prevailing, the police were offered no provocation: no stone-throwing, no swearing, no taunts.

The battles being waged in the suburbs around the prison were more complex, and it was hard to catch more than a few glimpses of the ebb and flow of territory, but the fact that supplies were still getting through demonstrated that the police had yet to form an impenetrable cordon between the protesters and their supporters. The authorities had cut off water to the drinking fountains in the park, but bottled water and a remarkable variety of home-cooked food were still finding their way in.

The prison itself was closed off now, but on the first day the guards had been only too willing to come out and interact. A line of protesters had stood at the main gate, and when ordered by a belligerent, near-hysterical officer to disperse, the first in line had replied, "My son is in your prison. He has committed no crime. I respectfully request that you release him now, or arrest me." IR links had ferried the man's words from a phone in his shirt pocket all the way to a PA system in the park, and from there they'd blared out across the expressway.

When he'd been arrested, the next protester had stepped forward. "My sister is in your prison. She has committed no crime. I respectfully request that you release her now, or arrest me."

The ritual had gone on for close to four hours; Martin had counted seventy-six arrests. Then, in the middle of the afternoon, the intake had ceased and the guards had withdrawn behind the gate. Either the beast had literally filled its belly, or someone in authority had decided that they'd made a mistake to play along at all.

Four days later, and still nobody knew what had befallen those seventy-six people. Rumors were rife, but Martin did not believe the worst: after surrendering themselves into custody, they would not have been lined up against a wall and shot. But the emergency decrees had eroded the already shaky protections of the legal system, and there'd be a strong temptation to portray the relatives of the dissidents caught up in the sweep as something far more sinister than anguished parents and siblings. Self-confessed spies and saboteurs would do nicely, and in Evin confessions generally came with bruises, or worse. With officials under stress and arguing among themselves, there'd be a perilous volatility added to the usual brutal machinery.

In the male ablutions tent beside the latrines there was a hefty pile of water bottles, but they were outnumbered by empties waiting to be refilled. Martin poured a little water into a basin, washed his hands thoroughly with soap, wiped some of the grime from his face and neck, then emptied the basin onto the ground outside. He itched to do more—literally, in places—but it was almost time for the noon prayers, which would put a big dent in the supply; it would have been selfish to make himself vastly cleaner than his own beliefs required.

Outside, he looked across the park and spotted Behrouz sitting on the grass near the boarded-up teahouse, his face in his hands. Martin called out as he approached; Behrouz looked up but didn't reply.

"Did you contact your cousin?" Martin asked him.

"Yeah." Slightly Smart email was still diffusing through the porous police lines and across the troubled city, but Behrouz had insisted that his wife not carry one of the incriminating phones, which in any case were in short supply. "He talked to Suri. She's fine. She's just worried." As he spoke, he picked nervously at a stain on his sleeve.

Martin sat beside him. "If you need to get out, get out. I think I can survive a couple of days without you."

Behrouz regarded him skeptically. Martin spotted Mahnoosh walking briskly through the crowd with a cardboard box full of smuggled essentials. "Do you need anything?" he asked.

"No."

"I'll be back in a second." Martin jogged after her, sliding open his phone's case as he went.

"You go through these very quickly," Mahnoosh observed as he handed her his dead battery in exchange for a charged one.

"Maybe," he replied, "but I'm not wasting them, I promise. I mean, I don't play games."

Mahnoosh said, "A man after my own heart."

Martin tried out the recharged battery on his old phone first; there'd been cases of people's phones getting fried, either by malice or some kind of inadvertent substitution. His old phone started up and gave the usual NO SIGNAL message, so he fitted the battery into his triple-S and waited to see if there was any data for him drifting through the crowd.

He made his way back to Behrouz, who was still looking despondent. "I'm serious," Martin said. "If you want to be with your family, just go. If they can get five shovels in past the cops, someone will be able to smuggle you out." In fact, he doubted that the police would be arresting deserters from the protest, but he didn't want to put it like that.

Behrouz shook his head. "Forget it. Everything's fine."

The muezzin began calling from the mosque in the exhibition center nearby; Martin could see the minaret from where they sat. Behrouz said, "I'm going to pray. I'll meet you back here."

"Okay." Martin watched the crowd gathering on the grass, spreading their prayer mats. The regime had a long history of denouncing opponents who claimed to be good Muslims as "hypocrites"—trying to inflate any political difference into a crime against Islam—but Jabari had rather robbed the word of its traction. In the face of defiance from hundreds of thousands of ordinary, moderately pious Iranians, there was a limit to how insulting they could be about their opponents' religious bona fides, and even their gentlest fatherly admonitions were no longer being taken very seriously.

Martin's phone chimed. No personal email had arrived, but he'd signed up to several newsfeeds. The system was being spammed, of course, but he'd only subscribed to digitally signed bulletins from a whitelist of trusted senders; all the node-clogging disinformation being churned out by VEVAK was slowing down the network, but for most purposes it was invisible to him.

There were reports from across the country on the previous day's Friday prayers; the phone's translations into English were full of grammatical errors—and a few surreal touches that probably came from bad guesses between homographs in the source text—but Martin still found them faster to decipher than the original Farsi. The gist of it was that more than a dozen clerics in Tehran and the other large cities had come out publicly in support of constitutional change. Two months before, that would have seen them thrown into prison; Martin wasn't sure that the more likely alternative these days wasn't assassination, but in any case there'd been an infectious wave of outspokenness. Once religious scholars were ready to attest that *velayat-e-faqih*—their role as guardians of society—didn't necessarily extend into every last corner of civil and political life, then the regime's position was demoted to the status of just one view among many, all equally compatible with faith and tradition. And once those same scholars were willing to suggest—however politely—that the regime might in fact have abused its power, *change* became not just a possibility worth contemplating, but a positive duty.

The list of strikes and vigils across the country now ran into the hundreds, and the general public were treating any outbreaks of looting and violence as entirely down to Basiji provocateurs. The police were stretched thin, but cars were not burning in the streets, and without the true anarchy needed to justify the harshest countermeasures, sending in the Revolutionary Guards against unarmed protesters would have risked an all-out civil war.

So the question was, how badly did the incumbents want to cling to power for its own sake? When the alternative was not Marxism, or a surrender to depraved Western hedonism, but a moderate, non-aligned social democracy that remained far more obedient to tradition and religion than, say, Turkey… was that a fate whose avoidance demanded tens of thousands of deaths and a country in flames?

It would have been nice to be able to put that directly to the President and his inner circle, but they just weren't giving interviews these days. So Martin sat on the grass and wrote it into his *Tehran Diary*, the five-hundred-words-a-day reward that his editor had given him for his serendipitous encounter with Kourosh Ansari. He was usually averse to such rhetorical flourishes, but in this case there was one saving grace: there was a chance that by the time the question saw print, his readers would already know the answer.

The first meal of the day arrived around dusk. As Martin joined the queue with Behrouz, he saw some people offering morsels to the feral cats that had been attracted by the shantytown's rubbish.

"Is that animal welfare, or are they testing it for poison?" Martin wondered.

Whatever travails the smugglers had faced, the plastic containers of stew they were dispensing were still warm. Martin hadn't realized how famished he was until he started eating. With a couple of pieces of flatbread to act as scoops, there was no need for cutlery, and the meal was gone in about two minutes.

"*Kheyli khoshmazeh,*" he declared approvingly.

Behrouz said, "Don't get too used to it, or you'll have to find yourself an Iranian wife."

Martin was tongue-tied for a moment; it wasn't Behrouz's style to be casually sexist. Had he noticed something? Martin tried to avoid protesting too much. "You don't think I can learn to cook like this myself?"

"Maybe you could," Behrouz conceded, "but it's a full-time job. Someone spent two hours just chopping the herbs for this."

"I think I can live with herbs from a packet."

Behrouz laughed. "Then why bother? Why not just give up and eat pizza?"

"There are limits." Iranian pizzas—though inexplicably popular with the local teenagers—were the worst Martin had tasted anywhere.

Later, they walked around the park trying to gauge the mood of the crowd. Everyone looked anxious and weary, but they'd all read the news about the dissident clerics; momentum was still going their way. Martin gathered a few quotes, but he didn't push it; people didn't want to be forced to measure and re-measure the situation, to keep spelling out the best and worst possibilities and calling the odds.

They came to a spot where one of the prison's watchtowers was in sight; Martin could make out two uniformed figures with rifles. A floodlight above them swept around automatically, illuminating the park and the protesters as often as it shone down on whatever grim courtyard was hidden behind the walls. Martin had an image of Omar sitting on a bunk, shadows of bars sliding across his cell in synch with the very same light. If they'd found evidence linking him to Shokouh's escape, surely they would have made it public and charged him. But then, if they suspected him but had no evidence, they would be trying to extract a confession instead.

"They hanged my uncle in there," Behrouz said. "In eighty-eight."

"Jesus." Martin was floored; this was the first he'd heard of it.

"I was only a kid, nobody told me much." As he spoke, Behrouz kept his gaze fixed on the ground. "But I heard my father and grandfather talking about it."

"Do you know why he was arrested?" There'd been thousands of extra-judicial killings in 1988; no trials, just a formulaic interrogation on political and religious matters, with wrong answers leading to death.

"He belonged to some kind of leftist group. They weren't killing people, or blowing things up—just publishing pamphlets against the mullahs. Actually, he'd been conscripted into the army, he was in Tehran on leave when they arrested him. No one really knew for sure what had happened for about a year. Then my grandfather heard that he was buried in a mass grave in Khavaran Cemetery. He was twenty-two years old when they killed him."

Martin said, "That's fucked." No wonder the place cast a pall over him. "Look, if you want to get out of here—"

Behrouz shook his head. "I can do my job. I'm only telling you so you'll stop asking me that."

"Okay." Martin got it now. "I'll shut up about it, and we'll both just do our jobs."

"Good."

As they walked on, Martin felt a surge of anger, but there was nothing to be done with it; the last thing Behrouz needed was to hear him ranting against tyrants.

"So if I'm hooked on Iranian cuisine," he said, "where exactly does a middle-aged, atheist foreigner start looking for an Iranian wife?"

Behrouz said, "Outside the divorce courts."

Martin woke from shallow, unquiet sleep to the sound of helicopters approaching. He staggered to his feet, reluctant for a moment to let the blanket he was wrapped in drop from his shoulders. The sound was coming from the direction of the prison, and it was accompanied by spotlight beams sweeping across the park; he counted six before one of them struck his eyes, blinding him to any more detail.

He crouched down and shook Behrouz awake. People were already gathering around the park's scattered trees; there was no sign of the kind of panic that would have ensued if anyone had actually seen a gun mounted behind one of the spotlights, and a part of Martin still refused to believe that the government would slaughter its own people *en masse*—even in 1988 they'd gone through an elaborate inquisitorial ritual, not just fired into an unarmed crowd—but what if they strafed the park lightly and killed a dozen protesters out of the thousands? Were they prepared to sell that, politically, as a necessary trade-off for the sake of restoring order? Were they ready to call the bluff of the majority of Iranians who'd stayed out of the fray so far, and say: Choose us—with a few unavoidable casualties—or back the traitors, and blame only yourselves when the streets are running with blood?

Martin joined the huddle of bodies in the shadow of the nearest tree. Under the circumstances, the whole idea of *shelter* was marginal, but anything was better than standing beneath a spotlight on open ground. He glanced at Behrouz, who was ashen; Martin knew better now than to offer any solicitous remarks, but he couldn't help feeling a twinge of guilt at the disparity between them. Though he was far from nonchalant about the situation himself, he was certain that if he'd had a young family it would have been ten times harder to be here.

As the minutes passed, it became clear that this operation was not a simple aerial assault on the protesters. The spotlights remained trained on the park, but the helicopters were keeping their distance and showing no signs of dispensing anything unpleasant: no bullets, no tear-gas, not even a blast of pressurized water.

The dazzle of the beams made it hard to keep watching the airspace over the prison, but Martin noticed a subtle shift in the illumination on the ground; the lights bathing the immediate area hadn't changed, but an adjacent region of the park had become darker. It took him a few seconds to make sense of that.

He turned to Behrouz. "I think one of them just landed inside the prison."

"Yeah."

"Meaning what?"

There was some angry shouting, and Martin saw people breaking cover and running across the grass to confer. Behrouz said, "I don't know what it means, but they think the prison's being evacuated."

"Okay." Martin considered this hypothesis. Anything was better than a hail of bullets, and maybe two could play the game of frustrating your enemy without bloodshed. There were plenty of inaccessible prisons out in the countryside—and even if they were full, it would have taken the government only a few days to assemble desert camps of huts ringed with razor-wire. If they plucked everyone out of Evin and deposited them in unknown or hard-to-reach locations, the siege would be deflated into an irrelevant farce.

Behrouz nudged him. "Look." Four men had picked up one of the concrete benches that were scattered throughout the park and were carrying it over their heads like an upside-down canoe. Martin supposed the concrete might offer a degree of protection from descending gunfire… but any safety advantages would be negated by the fact that the men were marching straight toward the prison itself.

When they passed out of sight behind a tree, Behrouz rose to his feet. "Come on."

Martin's skin turned to ice. "Are you crazy?"

"We don't have to get too close, but we should keep them in sight."

For one uncharitable moment Martin wondered if Behrouz was just trying to outdo him in the bravado stakes—as if the mere suggestion that he might have wanted to rejoin his family had wounded his pride. But that was unfair; what he was proposing was reasonable. Martin stood and followed him, zigzagging across the grass from tree to tree, wondering what an observer from above would make of them scuttling along in the wake of the concrete canoeists.

They stopped at the corner of the park; they had a tree to themselves and a clear view of the road that ran past the park and alongside the prison's perimeter wall. The men with the bench were already in front of the prison, twenty or so meters away. The wall itself blocked the line of fire from the watchtowers, but one of the helicopters was hovering directly above the prison gates. Martin couldn't imagine what the men's purpose was—unless they planned to use the bench as a battering ram, and he couldn't see that ending well.

Before the men reached the gates they stopped and rid themselves of the bench, depositing it on the ground in an upturned V. Then they turned and walked back toward the park.

"I don't get it," Martin confessed. "Do they think the prisoners are going to be moved by truck?"

Behrouz said, "The general population's about fifteen thousand, but even the thousand or so politicals would take an awful lot of helicopter trips. So maybe the helicopters are for the top brass, and the grunts and the prisoners will go by truck."

"Okay, but how is a *park bench* going to slow them down?"

Behrouz spread his hands; he had no idea.

Now that he was out of the direct glare of the spotlights, Martin could see the placement of the helicopters more clearly. Along with the one hovering above the gate, there were four lined up in a queue that stretched eastwards from the far side of the prison. As he watched, a sixth helicopter rose into sight and flew north, up along the slope of the mountains. Then the first in the remaining queue of four approached and descended inside the prison walls. It was like a taxi rank.

Another two groups of men came down the road, carrying two more benches from the park. Martin wasn't sure how many benches there were in total, but perhaps a large enough pile of them would constitute more than a trivial nuisance that could be moved aside in seconds. As they approached the prison gate there was a burst of automatic gunfire from the helicopter standing sentry; Martin flinched and the men stopped walking, but nobody appeared to have been hit.

He stared at the surreal tableau: the gray wall, the hovering helicopter, the eight men standing in a bright pool of light, holding up the benches like office workers warding off rain with newspaper umbrellas. Belatedly he lifted his phone and began recording.

The group at the front started walking again. There was another burst of gunfire, and one man collapsed. His comrades heaved the bench onto the ground, then two of them lifted the fallen man, who was able to put his arms across their shoulders for support, and they all began walking back toward the park. The second group took a few steps forward, then they too dropped their bench and retreated.

As the injured man approached the edge of the park, a man and a woman ran forward to examine him. There was a dark patch of blood on his right thigh, soaking through his trousers, but he was still conscious; one of the men pulled off his T-shirt and the woman tied it as a tourniquet around the injured leg. Martin knew there were medical students among the protesters, though he hadn't seen anything more than the most primitive first-aid supplies. He was torn between following the retreating group back into the park and retaining his present vantage point to see what the authorities' next step would be. He suspected that at any moment a couple of guards would emerge to move the pieces of the aborted blockade aside—and unless all the rules of the game had changed and the protesters were preparing to physically attack the guards, that would be the end of it.

A new sound intruded on the relentless drone of the helicopters. Martin turned to see a white Paykan tearing down the road beside the park, both front doors propped wide open. The car shot past him, heading for the prison; he raised his phone and framed it just as the driver—wearing a motorcycle helmet, a leather jacket and thick swathes of cloth wrapped around his knees and elbows—jumped from the car and rolled across the ground. The gunner in the helicopter opened fire, but Martin couldn't tell whether he was aiming for the car or the separated driver. In any case, the car kept moving straight ahead, struck one of the upside-down benches with its right wheel, veered sideways, and crashed into the prison gates.

Martin waited, tensed, half-expecting a fireball, but there was nothing; the car hadn't been packed with explosives, and any damage it had done had been from momentum alone. Bollards protected the gates from being rammed head-on, but the impromptu ramp had allowed a long run-up followed by a sudden sharp swerve. The driver had taken cover in the bushes on the side of the road opposite the prison; he'd probably not got off unscathed, but unless he'd caught a bullet, he was probably not fatally injured either. Before the sound of the impact had stopped ringing in Martin's ears, he heard a second car approaching. The helicopter left its post and flew rapidly toward the park; he grabbed Behrouz and pushed him flat against the ground, face-down in a mulch of decaying leaves, then stretched his arm out in what he hoped was the right direction and tilted his phone up.

He heard gunfire, then the roar of the car's engine shifting pitch abruptly as it passed. The second crash was far louder than the first. Martin was shaking; the helicopter was hovering very close to their tree—he could feel the downdraft, and a gentle rain of dislodged leaves. After a few seconds he drew his right arm in toward his body and thumbed the controls on the phone to play back the footage it had captured. He'd caught the second car slamming into the first and traveling four or five meters down the road as the two of them gouged an opening in the prison gates.

Martin still had his left arm across Behrouz's shoulder and he felt him move as if preparing to stand.

"Don't," he insisted, "it's right on top of us."

"So what's the plan?" Behrouz asked.

Having failed to defend the prison from damage, the gunner was probably suffering from a strong urge to compensate by firing at anything that moved. It was possible that the two of them were already visible through gaps in the branches above, but until someone screamed through a loudhailer that they should get to their feet with their hands in the air, playing possum seemed by far the best strategy.

"We wait for it to move," Martin said.

"Wait how long?"

"I don't know. It can't stay there forever." Martin pictured the helicopter hovering above the tree, the gunner sitting in the open bay. He'd be wearing night-vision goggles, but with any luck he'd be scanning the park and the road for approaching threats, not looking straight down.

A branch above them creaked perilously. Martin wondered if the downdraft could dislodge something heavier than leaves; apparently Behrouz had the same idea. He pushed Martin's restraining arm aside and rolled onto his back to see what was happening. When he failed to volunteer a report, Martin took a look for himself.

A man was standing in the tree, slowly edging his way out along one of the branches. He was steadying himself with one hand, carrying something in the other. Martin couldn't actually see any part of the helicopter chassis through the branches and foliage, but the downdraft and the spill from the spotlight gave him a good idea of its location: it was only a few meters from the top of the tree, and their arboreal companion was moving closer to it.

Behrouz said, "If the chopper pilot sees him, which way will it move?"

"Back toward the prison, so the gunner can get a better aim at him."

"But if we run in the opposite direction, into the park, we're going to be right in the line of fire, aren't we?"

"Yes," Martin agreed. "Good point."

"So we should run... sideways?"

"I think so."

Behrouz shifted into a squatting position, ready to move, and Martin did the same. He was still mesmerized by the man in the tree. He could now see that the object in his hand was one of the shovels they'd brought in to dig the latrines. Maybe he'd been hiding up there since nightfall, waiting to swing it into the face of the next Basiji saboteur who crept in to mess with the waste disposal arrangements.

The man brought one shoulder back, stood poised for a second or two, then flung the shovel like a javelin; Martin couldn't see his target, but there was a *thwack* followed by a deranged mechanical clatter. Behrouz ran one way, Martin the other, but the javelin thrower chose this moment to jump from the tree, landing on top of Martin and knocking him flat.

"Fuck!" He disentangled himself and looked up to see the helicopter spinning wildly, moving backward away from the park as it spiraled toward the ground. The shovel must have wedged between the tail rotor and its support, long enough to do real damage before the handle snapped and it fell away.

Martin clambered to his feet; he'd hurt his back and his right knee was giving him alarming signals, but he could just about walk. He couldn't see where the javelin thrower had gone, but a dozen men were running across the park, carrying tree branches and other improvised clubs. Martin watched anxiously as they neared the wounded helicopter; the pilot was struggling to bring it down safely, but it was rolling and pitching erratically as it descended.

It hit the ground with a thud about twenty meters away. The spotlight went out immediately, but as the men rushed in the main rotor was still turning. Martin waited for gunshots, but all he could hear over the engine was shouting. He looked around for his phone and finally located it a few meters away on the grass. He picked it up to start recording the scene, and it emitted a chime; the IR transceiver had come within sight of someone carrying fresh news.

Martin ignored the bulletin and kept filming, though he could make out almost nothing of what was happening in the shadows around the helicopter. The engine finally cut off, making it easier to hear the shouting, but apart from a general tone of belligerence this left him none the wiser. Then three uniformed men emerged from the mêlée, walking with their hands clasped behind their heads in front of a protester carrying an automatic rifle. Their captors made them kneel on the grass, then bound their hands with what Martin guessed were strips of webbing cut from harnesses inside the helicopter.

Behrouz approached. "Are you okay?"

"Yeah. You?"

Behrouz nodded. Martin handed him his phone. "Can you read this? I don't think I'm up to Slightly Smart translations right now."

Behrouz checked the newsfeed and said, "The Ministry of the Interior has been occupied. Seven officials have been taken under citizens' arrest." He held up the phone to show Martin a group portrait of sullen bureaucrats kneeling with bound hands, almost echoing the scene on the grass.

Martin looked over toward the prison. The taxi rank was empty now, with the last of the helicopters flying north across the mountains. He said, "They've evacuated the management, that's all." Maybe they'd never even planned to move the inmates; rather, the tide was turning so rapidly now that the prison officials and intelligence officers with the most to fear from the crowd's retribution had opted for self-preservation and a pre-emptive retreat.

They approached the group of men clustered around the helicopter. Martin spotted Kambiz, the student who'd tipped him off to the first protest in Ferdowsi Square; his jacket was torn and he was grinning nervously, managing to look both jubilant and anxious at the same time.

"What now?" Martin asked him.

Kambiz gestured at the helicopter. "They're trying to raise someone inside the prison on the radio. Now that VEVAK has run away, maybe we can negotiate with the remaining guards. We're not here to set thieves and murderers free. But anyone who hasn't even been before a court should not be in this place."

Martin said, "You've got one gun and three prisoners. What is there to negotiate with?"

Kambiz shook his head. "It's not about weapons. I wasn't even born when the Shah was toppled, but everybody understands that when something rotten starts to fall, you don't want to be standing where it will bury you."

Martin glanced up at the watchtower; the sentries there had a clear line of sight, but they hadn't fired on the men who'd captured the helicopter crew. Nobody wanted to be charged with treason by the present regime—but neither did they want to be charged with murder by their successors.

Half an hour later, the protesters sent a delegation of five people into the prison to negotiate face-to-face. No doubt there were things to be said that couldn't be spoken over an open radio channel. Martin passed the tense hours that followed interviewing some of the people who'd been involved in the bench/car maneuver; the injured man had already been evacuated, but the other participants turned out to be mechanical engineering students who'd rehearsed something similar in the countryside a week before—albeit not with live ammunition and a helicopter. "We wanted to fit remote controls to the cars," one of them told Martin, "but we couldn't get the parts without attracting suspicion." They'd bought half-a-dozen cheap Paykans from wrecking yards and left them in side-streets around the park before the siege had begun.

Just before dawn, the delegation returned. A deal had been struck in which the guards would continue to defend the cell blocks under the control of the prison authority—which held mainly convicted criminals—but they would not interfere with anything that took place in Evin 209 and 240, the political wings which came under VEVAK's control.

Behrouz translated the news, but when he'd finished he told Martin bluntly, "If you report that deal, you can have my resignation." If the regime survived, Martin doubted that his own silence would be enough to save anyone; someone on the inside would surely betray the prison guards to their brave superiors who'd flown off over the mountains. Then again, putting all the details down in newsprint would certainly diminish any prospect of a face-saving decision to let the guards' inaction go unpunished.

He said, "I won't mention it." He could find a circumspect way of phrasing things without actually lying. The protesters were still going to *storm the prison*, and the guards would still *tactically withdraw, to concentrate on keeping the most dangerous prisoners confined*. Nobody munching cornflakes in Sydney needed to know that certain choices had been made to allow all this to happen without bloodshed.

The sky was pale blue, but the sun was still hidden behind the apartment blocks of north Tehran as the protesters surged through the broken gates of Evin Prison. Martin let more than a hundred people enter before he even tried to elbow his way into the stream. If there was unexpected resistance ahead, he wanted to be close enough to the vanguard to witness it, but he didn't feel obliged to put himself at any unnecessary risk. This wasn't his revolution.

Still, as he and Behrouz passed through the gates and walked with the hushed throng between the gray cell blocks, Martin felt the history of the place weighing down on him. This was where the Shah's henchmen had imprisoned and tortured his enemies. This was where thousands of opponents of Khomeini had been hanged in mass purges. This was where labor activists, journalists, homosexuals, scholars, environmentalists and women's rights campaigners had been thrown into solitary confinement, beaten and raped. This was where Baha'i ended up, for the crime of believing in one prophet too many, or proselytizing Christians for the crime of believing in one prophet too few. This was where student leaders, after the protests of 1999, had had their faces pushed into drains full of faeces until their bursting lungs had commanded them to inhale, and where ten years later those who'd marched against electoral fraud had been beaten into surreal confessions that the true source of their treasonous passions had been the meddling of foreign puppet-masters and excessive exposure to the BBC. But he couldn't hold Evin's obscenities at arm's length as the aberrations of an alien culture. He had seen the American prison at Bagram, where innocent men had been battered to death; he had seen the detention camps in the Australian desert where refugees had lost their minds and slashed their bodies with razors. The toxic mixture of power and impunity was a universal human disease.

Martin turned to Behrouz, hoping they could exchange a few words that would puncture the solemnity, but the expression on his colleague's face was so stricken that he looked away again, not wanting to embarrass him.

The watchtowers were deserted now; if anyone was training rifles on the crowd they were well hidden. Martin had read accounts of the prison's layout by former inmates, but he hadn't committed the architecture to memory; he could only assume that someone who knew the place inside out was leading them to one of the political wings.

Section 240 was a squat four-story building with slits for windows. Apparently nobody had left a key under the mat, but Martin was too far from the doors to see exactly what was being done with crowbars, bolt-cutters and battery-powered tools in order to gain entrance.

When the main doors were opened the crowd surged forward, but not very far; inside the building there were more obstructions to be dealt with.

Behrouz said, "If every cell is this much work, it's going to be a long day."

Martin had read that there were about eight hundred. "Good practice for when you queue for your Metallica tickets."

When they finally managed to squeeze into the building they found themselves in a kind of foyer between the main doors and a deserted checkpoint with a barred metal gate. There was a glowering portrait of Khomeini on the wall beside a scroll covered in dense writing; Martin sounded out and translated a few words, until Behrouz put him out of his misery. "It's a kind of mission statement, committing everyone who works here to high ethical standards." His voice was thick with contempt. "It quotes some Quranic verses, but don't ask me to repeat them, because in the context I'd consider that desecration."

There was a sound of splintering wood. "*Keleedha!*" someone shouted excitedly; Martin didn't need that translated for him. People started passing jangling bunches of keys back through the crowd. A man in front of Martin offered him a bunch; Martin shook his head apologetically. "*Ruznaame negaaram. Momken nist.*"

Behrouz held out his hand and took them.

The protesters spread out, looking for the cells their keys would open. As Martin followed Behrouz to the crowded stairwell, he saw a woman ahead of them turn at the landing and he glimpsed Mahnoosh's face in profile. He felt a sudden ache of panic in his chest; he wanted to call out to her, to plead with her to be careful, but he was afraid that might sound presumptuous.

On the third floor there were two more metal gates that needed power-tools to break through; it was another twenty minutes before they were standing before the cells themselves. Martin raised his phone and snapped the scene: a row of identical doors stretching away down the corridor ahead of them, with no windows, just thin slits that appeared to be bolted shut. The place was shabbily clean, with a strong smell of disinfectant not quite masking an undercurrent of excrement. Even now, Martin could hear only faint, muffled shouting from a few inmates; the cells were almost soundproof.

The first key was matched, the first door swung open. A middle-aged man limped out into the corridor; he seemed dazed, unsure of what was happening. He was dressed in loose white clothes, barefoot; above his thick beard his face was covered in welts and bruises. He spoke with his liberators in a soft voice, with an air of puzzlement. Maybe he'd heard nothing of Jabari, of the strikes and marches. Perhaps he'd spoken to no one but his captors for years.

Martin held up his phone and started filming.

Behrouz said, "I'm going this way." He shook his keys and gestured at a second line of cells that started further to their right.

"Okay." Martin didn't follow him; he wanted to record what was happening, but he didn't want to thrust his camera into the faces of these fragile people. Another door opened in the corridor ahead of him; a tall, skinny youth, shirtless, with long red weals on his back, stepped forward nervously. As he talked with the protesters he was as quiet as the first man, but much more anxious, blinking and flinching away from anyone who came too close. Then he sat down on the floor outside the cell and cradled his head in his arms.

When the third cell opened there were shouts of jubilation; Mahnoosh was among the liberators here, cheering the loudest. After a moment Martin recognized the freed prisoner as a young man who'd been arrested on the first day of the siege; his face was bruised and one eye was swollen shut, but he was still wearing torn street clothes rather than prison garb. Some of his friends lifted him up on their shoulders and carried him toward the stairs.

As Martin turned to keep them in view, he heard a gun shot, very close. One of the protesters staggered, bleeding from the shoulder. Martin swung around, his ears ringing in the silence. A man with a neatly trimmed beard, wearing a pale green shirt decorated with the prison authority insignia, was standing a few meters away, in front of an open utilities closet.

The guard turned to Martin, shouting angrily, gesturing with his pistol. Martin raised his hands in surrender, but the guard kept screaming insults or instructions. Martin had no idea what he was saying, and the only response he could string together was an apology for his incomprehension: "*Ma'zerat mikham, agha. Farsi balad nistam.*"

The guard aimed his gun directly at Martin's head.

Mahnoosh called out urgently, "Put down the phone! He wants you to put down the phone!"

Martin tried to drop it, but his fingers wouldn't unclench. He wished he'd taken the keys when he'd been offered them.

The guard grunted and sagged to the ground. Someone had hurled a fire-extinguisher and hit him in the back. People piled on top of him, grabbing the gun and restraining him. Martin felt lightheaded; he sat on the floor and watched, detached from everything. The guard was taken to a newly vacated cell; the wounded protester was given a makeshift bandage and helped to the stairs. There was a hospital in the prison complex, Martin recalled. He wondered if they'd be willing to treat the man.

"Hey! Martin *jan!*"

Martin looked up to see Omar approaching, with Behrouz following behind him. His face was gaunt and he was walking with a limp, but he was beaming. Martin rose to his feet and stepped forward to embrace him, fighting back tears of relief.

"What happened? It looks like you lost twenty kilos."

"I did a hunger strike," Omar replied. "Looks like it worked. Twenty kilos and the walls come down; ten more and they would have made me President."

Omar wanted to phone Rana. The protesters had managed to force open two offices with working landlines, but there were already long queues for those, so they decided to try the floor below. As the three of them were walking down the stairs, Martin's phone emitted a chime he'd never heard before. He checked the display, and after a moment he realized that it was now showing an icon for the radio mesh network that he'd seen used at the Majlis protest. Someone must have found the local jammer and disabled it.

He showed Omar, who tried a few numbers, but the network was still jammed across most of the city. On the second floor one of the landlines was free; while Omar was making his call, Martin's phone managed another novel sound. Someone on the network was offering a streaming video feed.

He tapped the icon, and it expanded into a shaky camera shot of a TV screen tuned to an IRIB news broadcast. Martin gave the phone to Behrouz.

Other people around them were already cheering ecstatically. Behrouz scowled, struggling to hear more. Martin waited patiently; there was a loop of text running at the bottom of the screen, it would all be spelled out eventually.

Behrouz said, "The moderate clerics have won some kind of deal. There's going to be a referendum on the Guardian Council veto powers within three months, followed by new elections for the President and the Majlis before the end of the year."

That was it, *that* was the saving move. If the deal held, there would be no civil war, but no turning back to the status quo either.

Omar was sitting on the floor, the office phone in his hand, weeping with joy. Behind him was a huge gray filing cabinet that someone had tipped on its side, spilling VEVAK's meticulous accounts of their interrogations all over the floor. Maybe there hadn't been enough time to put everything through the shredders. Or maybe the fuckers had thought they'd be coming back.

Martin turned to Behrouz and held out his hand. "*Mubaarak.*" Behrouz shook it, but even as his expression of disbelief slowly melted into a kind of stunned acceptance, he wasn't ready to claim victory.

"Nothing's certain yet," he insisted.

"No," Martin conceded.

Behrouz smiled. "But it starts today. It might take us another ten years to be free—but it starts today."

10

Nasim stared glumly across the sea of dinner jackets and evening gowns, trying to think of a way to escape to her hotel room before someone made yet another hypocritical speech in praise of Kourosh Ansari, President-elect of the Islamic Republic of Iran.

She turned to her mother. "I can't believe I let you drag me down here. Half these people spent the last thirty years trying to get America to bomb their own country, just so they could go back and turn it into their own cozy little kleptocracy."

"That's unfair!" her mother replied. "A quarter of them at most. Anyway, that's just the old men; you should be thinking about their sons."

Nasim grimaced. "My idea of a romantic evening does not include a speech by Donald Rumsfeld at the Heritage Foundation."

"How many people have you actually spoken to tonight?"

"Am I allowed to count waiters?"

"Go and mingle." Her mother made a shooing gesture. "I didn't buy you that dress so you could spend the night whining in my ear."

Nasim left her and headed for the canapés. Amazingly enough, there'd been a vegetarian option, but it had been a quarter of the size of the other main courses and she was still famished.

As she stood at the buffet table trying to determine whether there was anything left that she could eat—other than garnishes—a voice beside her said, "Congratulations on your new President."

"Thank you." Nasim resisted the urge to add acerbically, "I do hope you'll let us keep this one." She turned to face the speaker; the painfully thin young man looked familiar, but it took her a few seconds to place him. "Are you stalking me?" she demanded. "Did you follow me to Washington?"

93

Caplan looked affronted. "Would you like to see my invitation? I'm a major donor to the Iranian-American Friendship Council."

"Since when? Three days ago?"

"Six, actually."

"Six? A real futurologist." Nasim looked around for hotel security, but there was no honest complaint she could make that wouldn't sound deranged and paranoid. "What exactly is it that you think I can do for you? Haven't you heard the news about the HCP?"

"Congress decided not to fund it." Caplan was stoical. "That's sad, but it's not unexpected. So there'll be no big, coordinated federal project, but I'm sure you'll still find grants here and there. I'll be setting up my own foundation to help with that, though of course I can't replace someone like Churchland."

Zachary Churchland had died three weeks before and descended into the frosty limbo of an Alcor cryonic vault. He had left the bulk of his estate to the Benign Superintelligence Bootstrap Project, having finally concluded that he couldn't trust his immortal soul to human hands.

"I heard someone's contesting his will," Nasim recalled. "Not just his widow; his first wife, too—"

"Third wife. Actually I'm helping her fund the case," Caplan explained smoothly.

Nasim stared at him. "How does someone get to marry Zachary Churchland, then end up needing *help* to fund anything?"

"A party in Las Vegas, a truckload of cocaine, and several professional athletes."

"I'm sorry I asked. But if she got nothing in the divorce, why would she be any luckier at the graveside? Or freezer-side."

Caplan smiled. "She won't be. But I found a lawyer who's convinced her otherwise, based in part on the Leona Helmsley case—you know, the woman who was ruled mentally unfit after leaving twelve million to her dog. The ongoing litigation should help keep the bequest out of the Superintelligence Project's hands for quite a while."

Pet dog, pet god; maybe the precedent would actually fly for a dyslexic judge. Still, Nasim was baffled. "Why should you care who gets Churchland's money? It's either Bullshit Squared, or the wives. It's lost to the HCP."

"No doubt it is," Caplan conceded, "but I don't want the superintelligence to come into existence before I'm uploaded. It's very important to me that I'm the first transcendent being in this stellar system. I can't risk having to compete with another resource-hungry entity; I have personal plans that require at least one Jovian mass of computronium."

"Really? I have 'personal plans' that require Naveen Andrews and a bottle of coconut oil, but I don't expect they're going to happen either."

Caplan was bemused. "Why are you so hostile?"

"I don't know," Nasim confessed. "Maybe it's because I've had enough experience of deluded fundamentalists to last a lifetime."

"Well, you're wasting your energy," Caplan replied loftily. "One way or another, everything I speak of will come to pass. You can either join us, or be left behind."

Nasim said, "Don't go crazy with those mushroom-stuffed vol-au-vents; I heard they can slash three per cent off the lifespan of nematode worms."

Back in their hotel room, Nasim's mother said, "I received an interesting job offer tonight."

"Someone wants to poach you?" Nasim was excited; it would have to be a big step up the ladder if they expected to lure her away from Harvard. "Who? Georgetown?"

"Kourosh Ansari." Her mother smiled at Nasim's expression. "He's looking for advisers to help plan the restructuring of the economy. In fact, his representative told me that he'd read *After Oil* as soon as it came out."

"Congratulations." Nasim was stunned. She'd certainly expected that parts of the diaspora would start trickling back to Iran, but even in those abstract terms she'd been thinking of a much longer time frame. "Have you decided what you'll do?"

"I think I'm going to accept the offer," her mother said. "There are no guarantees that they'll really follow through on my advice, but if I missed this chance to have some input into the reconstruction process I'd never forgive myself."

Nasim sat down on her bed; she picked up a pillow and held it against her chest.

She said, "I want to go with you."

"You mean come for a holiday? Of course!" Her mother beamed. "That would be wonderful!"

Nasim shook her head. "Not just a holiday. I want to go home. I want to live in Iran again."

Her mother sat beside her. "What about your work?"

"I don't know. That's all so uncertain now." The fact was, for a long time she'd been tacitly assuming that the HCP would go ahead. That would have meant a mountain of paperwork at the start, but the payoff would have been at least four or five years to focus on the science without further interruptions. Now it would be back to business as usual: begging for one small grant after another, never really being able to make plans that stretched beyond the next six months. "Maybe there's something just as challenging that I can do in Iran. Everything will be changing; there'll be a thousand opportunities."

"I'd come back and visit you, you know," her mother said. "If you stayed here. It's not as if we'd be apart all the time."

"I know." Nasim put an arm around her. "And I'd visit you too. Together we'd burn up all the oil in the world."

"So would that be so bad?" Her mother smiled. "I'm not trying to run away from you. But I don't want you destroying your whole career just because you don't want to be left alone here."

Nasim said sternly, "I'm not a child. This is a chance to rethink my plans. I spent so long hoping I'd be part of the HCP that I ended up with tunnel vision. Why shouldn't I think about trying something new?"

"All right," her mother agreed. "You can always come with me and take a look around before you make up your mind. Just don't burn your bridges straight away."

"I won't." Nasim embraced her. "So let's stop talking about me. We should be celebrating your new job!"

"What did you have in mind?"

Nasim looked around for the room service menu. "Just because the kitchen's officially closed, that doesn't mean they've run out of cake."

Later, lying awake in the dark, Nasim turned the decision over in her mind. The prospect of walking away from her brain-mapping work was wrenching, but it wasn't as if she was trashing her files and erasing herself from history. She'd already made some contributions to the field, and other people would build on them. She didn't have to chain herself to one project for the rest of her life just to keep the time she'd spent on it from being wasted.

She had always wanted to return to Iran. Now that her country was finally being reborn, she had to grab the chance to witness that with her own eyes, instead of watching everything unfold from a distance. All the frustration she'd felt at not being part of the uprising would be assuaged if she could at least be a part of the rebuilding.

She began drifting toward sleep. Her mind was still in turmoil, but she was going to have to get used to that. Going back would not be easy, but this was her time, this was her chance to reclaim the life that had been stolen from her. Going back would not be easy, but she knew now that she could not stay away.

PART TWO
2027-2028
۱۴۰۶

11

It was the day for Javeed to register for school, a week before classes began. Martin drove Mahnoosh to the shop early and the three of them sat in the back room unpacking boxes. Just the smell of new books always made Martin feel refreshed and optimistic; Mahnoosh was less romantic, and suggested that this was all down to traces of glue. Javeed's task was to crush the biofoam packing chips by hammering them relentlessly with his fists, and to complain at length about shipments that were cushioned with shredded newsprint or plastic bags full of air.

When it was time to leave, Javeed embraced his mother tightly, clinging for a few moments longer than usual. "*Azizam, azizam,*" she murmured reassuringly, pressing her face against his hair. "Don't worry, you'll love school."

"I know," Javeed replied cheerfully.

Martin kissed Mahnoosh. "See you this afternoon."

There was a long queue at the school; they had to fill in a form and then wait to have it processed. Martin didn't understand why they couldn't have done the whole thing online; he'd renewed his driver's license a month before without leaving home, thanks to a seamless process involving facial biometrics and a gadget that read the RFID tag in the card. Still, it was good for his son to see the school from the inside at least once before starting classes. When Javeed needed to use the toilet the woman ahead of them offered to keep their place in the queue, but Martin sent him on the small adventure of getting there and back by himself.

In the office, an administrative assistant sighted their collection of identifying documents and perused the registration form, ready to pass it through a scanner.

"I'm sorry, Mr. Seymour," she said, "you haven't written anything for the child's religion." She raised her pen, ready to correct this omission.

"He has no religion," Martin replied. "If the computer won't accept a blank, you'll have to write 'atheist.'" He saw a flicker of panic cross her face, but she recovered her composure rapidly.

"Forgive me," she said, "but I think you misunderstood the question. What it means is the religion of his paternal grandfather..." She gave Martin a frank, appraising look, then decided it was definitely worth adding, "or great-grandfather, or so on, as far back as necessary."

"Are you sure about that?" Martin had no wish to blow the matter out of proportion, but it would be good to know whether there was an official policy defining atheists out of existence, or whether he was just facing a flustered individual who didn't know how to handle this minor anomaly.

"When we ask if children are Kurdish or Arabs," the woman replied, "the fact is, they are all Iranians, and we simply mean the ethnic group of their ancestors. So it is completely logical and consistent to apply the same reasoning to the question of religion."

Martin had to admire the ingenuity of her argument. Most likely this woman had no discretion in the matter and she was simply trying to spare them all from the bureaucratic hell that would arise if the computer rejected their registration.

"My son's paternal ancestors were Christian," Martin conceded. The woman looked relieved and recorded his answer on the form.

"Which denomination?" she asked.

Martin honestly had no idea. "The Church of Saint Coltrane," he said. The woman started writing; when she paused halfway through he added helpfully, "*Kaf, vav, lam*—" She looked up. "I know how to spell Coltrane. I was just wondering whether you meant John or Robbie."

As they walked away from the office across a small playground, Javeed asked, "Why did you make that lady angry?"

"I don't think she was angry," Martin replied. "We just had to decide the right thing to put on the form."

Javeed looked skeptical, but he let it drop. "Where's my grandfather?"

"My father died before you were born. And my mother too." Javeed flinched a little; Martin had told him this many times, but it was starting to cut a little deeper. "They had very happy lives, so you shouldn't be sad for them."

"What about Mama's father?"

Martin steeled himself. "He's still alive. He's living in Tehran." Again, this was old news, but each repetition carried new weight.

"So why don't we visit him?"

"Because he's angry with Mama."

Javeed pulled a face, part incredulous, part anxious. "Still?"

"Yes."

"And her mama? She's still angry too?"

"Yes." That seemed to sting even more. Martin put a hand on Javeed's shoulder. "I know, it's hard not to be sad about that, but Mama's very brave about it, so we should be too."

Javeed turned to Martin, suddenly tearful. "If you get angry with me, will you leave me alone?"

"Ooh, ooh, ooh." Martin lifted him up and held him in his arms. "That's never going to happen. Never ever." Martin carried him all the way to the car, ignoring the growing twinges in his back. "Come on, no more crying. Remember what I promised you today? We're going to Uncle Omar's shop."

Javeed recovered instantly, all thoughts of abandonment forgotten.

As they walked from the car together Javeed tried to break free and run ahead, but Martin kept an iron grip on his hand. Ahead of them, three motorbike riders were pushing their way through the pedestrian throng, and though they never had a chance to build up much speed they were easily arrogant and inattentive enough to knock over a small child. As they passed, forcing Martin aside and almost into the gutter, he drew Javeed close to him and resisted the urge to stick his elbow into the face of the nearest rider.

Once the shop door had closed behind them he relaxed, and Javeed ran to embrace Omar gleefully. Then Omar's son Farshid started wrestling with him, lifting him over his head and turning him upside down. Javeed screamed with delight.

Martin greeted Omar. "Javeed just registered for school," he explained.

"Ah, so you're a big man now? Big scholar? Big sportsman?" Omar threw some punches at Javeed's upside-down torso; Javeed flailed back at him, emitting strange martial arts noises from one of his computer games. Omar turned back to Martin. "How's business, Martin *jan?*"

"Not bad. You know Iranians; they're never going to stop buying books. How's the shop?" Martin could only see half-a-dozen customers browsing the aisles, but whenever he'd been here at lunchtime the place was packed.

Omar gestured proudly at a new display of *cyber-ketabha*: two-hundred-sheet e-paper bundles with the look and feel of paperbacks. Each device could store a million volumes worth of text. "I already sold sixty of these this month." He beamed. "You're right, Iranians love books."

Martin feigned indifference and went to flip through a bin of old Blu-rays, marked down to clear. He lifted a disk out and held it up. "You know Vin Diesel's making a comeback?"

"Really?"

"It's called *The Chronicles of Kulos*. They're shooting it right now in the Negev Desert."

Javeed had managed to get free of Farshid and was now looking around the shop with a determined frown. "I promised he could choose something for less than fifty thousand tomans," Martin said. Omar scowled, offended. "Let him choose anything! You don't have to pay." Martin scowled back; he didn't doubt Omar's generosity, but he was struggling to instil some sense of restraint in Javeed.

Javeed was staring at a big cardboard pop-out display of various spin-offs from the *LOLCat Diaries* movie. The original lame tagline, "I CAN HAZ BLOKBUSTR?" had been ingeniously amended by the insertion of a caret mark pointing to the word "GAME"; layered in front of this was a cut-out image of a disheveled cat with its limbs splayed awkwardly, one paw on a joystick, bearing the caption "IM IN UR CONSOLE MESSING WITH UR WORLD." The distributors hadn't bothered trying to translate any of this; half the movie's dialogue had been dubbed into Farsi, but the rest had been left as a kind of anti-lesson in English. Martin watched with a sense of resignation; having caved in once over the movie itself, he now had nobody but himself to blame.

But Javeed didn't turn to him and inquire tweely, "I can haz LOLCat game?" Apparently the attractions of a contrivedly cute animal speaking a dialect of TXT from the formative years of the current generation of DreamWorks executives had a limited half-life, even for a five-year-old. Instead Javeed announced, "I want to try Zendegi!"

To his credit, Omar said nothing. Martin thought it over. He'd never been in *Zendegi-ye-Behtar* himself, but he'd read reviews; there was some good content, and plenty that was suited to children. There was Hollywood schlock too, if you really wanted it, but it wasn't compulsory.

He said, "If Uncle Omar's got time, and there are spare machines for both of us. If not, we'll come back another day. All right?"

Javeed caught the warning tone in the last sentence. He replied placidly, "Yes, Baba." Then he stood very still and waited for the verdict.

Omar led them upstairs. Eight of the spherical VR rigs—known rather grandly as *ghal'eha*, or castles—were inflated and opaque, but two were unoccupied. Martin found it a little creepy that the things blacked out when in use; it gave them an air of private peepshow booths, however innocent the actual content being conveyed. But then, it would have been even creepier to be standing inside one, blind to the world, knowing that anyone in the room outside could observe your every move. As they walked between the rows of occupied castles, Martin glanced down and saw a familiar logo on the base of one machine: a triangle with the letter S for each edge. How could he not love anything from Slightly Smart Systems?

First they had to sign on for the free trial; Omar took them to a desktop computer in a corner of the room and went through the formalities. Martin chose English and Farsi, and gave their real first names as identifiers; there was no requirement to supply a unique nickname.

"You want to look like yourself?" Omar inquired. "Or somebody else?"

Martin hesitated. Some protective instinct made him wonder if he should disguise Javeed's appearance, but from what he'd heard that didn't seem to be the usual practice. Omar showed Javeed a few predefined icons—including the dreaded LOLCat—but Javeed just became confused and indecisive. Martin said, "It's okay, we can go in as ourselves." If they were safe together on a public street, why would they need masks to be safe in Zendegi?

Omar had them take turns standing on a mark painted on the floor in front of the desktop; the cameras that snapped them from multiple angles were too small for Martin to see. They had to pronounce a dozen different syllables, then make faces expressing fear, surprise, joy, mirth, sadness and disgust. Javeed hammed it up mercilessly, but this wasn't like the wind changing and leaving you stuck with your ugliest countenance; the software could interpolate between the recorded extremes, rather than just spitting them back out at onlookers, unchanged.

Omar fitted them for gloves and wraparound goggles; there were small earphones built in, along with microphones and motion sensors. Then, with the goggles' screens flipped up, they walked to the centers of their respective castles, which looked like huge sheets of bubble wrap draped over the circular bases.

Martin turned to Javeed. "*Khubi, pesaram?*"

"*Balé.*"

Omar said, "Don't worry about the menu system, you can learn that later. If you want to get out in a hurry, just go like this." He made an emphatic thumbs-down gesture.

Martin said, "Thanks."

Omar grinned. "Enjoy the ride."

There was a faint hissing sound as the castles inflated around them, the limp plastic sheets rising up into a fishbowl shape; the walls had not yet turned opaque, but they already blurred the view. Martin raised a hand to Javeed while they still had clear sight of each other. "See you in Zendegi!"

Javeed looked slightly nervous now, but he called back confidently, "*Hatman.*"

When the raised circular rim was about as high as Martin's shoulders the aperture began to shrink as it ascended; a few seconds later he was inside an unbroken sphere about three meters wide. Near the edge of the circular base there was a thick hoop sitting over the sphere's translucent plastic; Martin guessed the hoop was held in place magnetically, so the plastic could slide freely beneath it, driven by rollers in the base. So far, the enclosure felt light and airy rather than claustrophobic; the vanished traffic sounds confirmed that the thing was soundproof, but the material wasn't airtight—they weren't relying on hidden machinery to keep them from suffocating, and a power failure would not be a big deal. Martin realized belatedly that "castle" probably meant something far less pompous than he'd imagined; the devices were actually very close kin to children's inflatable castles.

A woman's voice, speaking in Farsi, asked them to flip down their goggles. Martin complied—and saw an image that he could barely distinguish from the real translucent sphere he'd been looking at an instant before. He held up a hand in front of his face; the gloves were gone, and he could see the lines on his palms. If some crease in his shirt sleeve was improperly rendered he would never have guessed—and as soon as he wiggled his fingers and saw the correct response, the sense that he was *occupying* the image before him became unshakeable.

The sphere surrounding him began to expand, the floor spreading out and flattening as the wall receded. Then a small, circular aperture appeared in the wall, connecting Martin's bubble to another one beside him; within seconds, the structures had merged and he and Javeed were together inside a single dome.

Javeed laughed and ran toward him; Martin felt hairs rise on the back of his neck. The icon approaching him wasn't perfect—its gait was a little stilted, its facial expression not quite natural—but Martin felt more inclined to rub his eyes, as if his vision might be blurred from dust or tiredness, than to perceive the flaws as external. If not for the fact that his son appeared before him without goggles, he would have sworn that the whole thing was being done with cameras hidden inside the spheres. Well, no doubt there were such cameras, helping, but the overall feat went far beyond any kind of simple video link.

He took a few steps toward Javeed, and the knowledge that they were both stuck inside their separate treadmills—the spheres turning around them as they walked, like omni-directional hamster wheels—receded into irrelevance. Javeed reached out and grabbed at Martin's legs, then showed an astonished face very close to the most extreme he'd recorded; Martin felt nothing, of course, and saw his son's hands not quite making contact. Curious, he tried to lay a hand on Javeed's shoulder; just before he reached the fabric of the shirt the haptic glove produced a strange sensation, as if he were pushing through treacle. But the glove could exert no force to stop him, and when he persisted he understood why Javeed had looked so startled. As his real hand descended past the point where it would have made contact, his icon refused to portray his true motion; the result was a sudden, alarming conviction that his body was reeling forward uncontrollably. Martin retreated, and exchanged a knowing smile with Javeed. The lack of physical restraints made it easy to puncture the illusion if you wanted to, but that would defeat the whole point of being here.

Javeed held up his hand. Martin reached down and took it; the glove gave him the sensation of contact with skin, and its cues helped him avoid closing his hand too tightly—even though he was really holding nothing but air. And though there was no machinery to bear any of the weight of his son's arm, whatever Javeed was feeling seemed to prompt him to make the extra effort to keep his arm raised. It was a light, tentative grip that they shared, but unlike their other attempts at contact it was close enough to the real thing to be compelling.

"What now?" Martin wondered. As he spoke, the bright wall of the dome began to take on patches of definite color, as if the translucent plastic was being pressed very close to something. Or rather, close to many things: the patches of color sharpened into dozens of separate windows, looking out onto different scenes.

"Shall we go and take a look?"

Javeed said, "Yes," but he did not rush ahead. He kept his hand in Martin's as they crossed the dome, both of them working to maintain the delicate link.

The windows were tall and thin, and low enough for Javeed to see through easily. The first one they reached showed a grassy field at the edge of a forest. Children were running excitedly across the field, all of them boys, most at least a couple of years older than Javeed. The longer the two of them gazed at the window, the more sound from beyond flowed through, but even as the boys' shouting grew stronger, their words remained indistinct. With a shock, Martin realized that some of them were carrying spears. What was this, *Lord of the Flies?*

A winged tiger swooped down over the field, snarling and snatching at the children. Martin turned to Javeed. "I don't think this is for us." It was one thing to watch your character chased by a stylized monster in a console game, something else to flee breathlessly across the grass with a clawed beast bearing down on you.

Javeed looked hesitant rather than disappointed, as if wondering whether to argue just for the sake of it, but then he replied, "Okay."

They moved on to the next window. Some hundred meters away across barren terrain sat a low, sprawling building, its walls decorated with colorful abstract mosaics. There was no one in sight, and all Martin could hear was a faint buzz of insects. As he peered through the window, a caption appeared on the glass in both Farsi and English: *The Labyrinth*. Javeed tried sounding out the word, but both versions defeated him.

Martin told him what it meant, and Javeed said excitedly, "This one!"

"Are you sure?" Martin wished Omar had told him more about navigating the system; presumably there was some way to discover in advance whether there was a Minotaur lurking in this maze. "You think it will be fun?"

"Yes," Javeed insisted; he was growing impatient. "If we don't like it, we can just use our thumbs."

"That's true. So how do we get out?"

Javeed slipped free of Martin's hand and placed both of his palms against the window. There was a sharp click, as if he'd released the catch on some mechanism, and the window swung up like a garage door; at the same time, the section of the wall below it slid down until it was flush with the floor.

"You first," Martin said. Javeed walked straight through the narrow opening; Martin felt compelled to turn and go through sideways. He was glad it was already becoming second nature to treat every obstacle here as if it were real. There wouldn't be much point entering a maze on any other terms.

The bare gray rock between the dome and the maze sloped gently downwards; Martin was impressed that the platforms beneath their feet could tilt to accommodate this effect so seamlessly, and without the delays and noises he remembered from clunky sloping treadmills in the gym. There were no loose rocks or sudden shifts in height; at ground level at least, the landscape promised nothing that the technology couldn't deliver. Martin looked up at the clear blue sky and felt a surge of elation—followed immediately by a pang of unease. If Javeed got hooked on this at least he wouldn't end up as a couch potato. But then, if Zendegi wasn't even bad for his health, what excuse would there be to lure him away from it in favor of real adventures beneath real skies?

As they approached the maze, Martin saw how finely detailed the mosaic was, with blue and gold tiles as richly hued as any that adorned the mosques of Esfahan. The pattern was a complex system of intersecting grids and stars twisting across the surface. They walked around the building until they came to an opening in the wall—or rather, the mouth of a long passage whose own walls merged with the outer one. The passage was open to the sky; because the walls were so high, Martin hadn't realized before that the "building" had no roof. This was an outdoor maze, not a claustrophobic warren of tunnels.

There were words set into the tiles near the entrance: "Find the fountain, and change the world," he read. He laughed. "Okay, shall we go in and look for the fountain?"

"Yes!"

"Stay close to me. If we get separated, or there's anything happening you don't like, just give it the thumbs-down."

"Okay, Baba."

Martin searched Javeed's face for any hint of anxiety, then caught himself wondering what kind of subtleties might be lost along the way in the imperfect process that was painting the image in front of him. But his son's voice was being conveyed to him unchanged, and he'd sounded confident enough. "Okay, *pesaram.*"

They walked side by side into the maze. The sun was high enough and the passage wide, to keep the walls around them from plunging them into gloom. Martin kept glancing at the lush patterns of the mosaic, wondering if they might encode some kind of clue. If they did, it wasn't obvious, but at least there were no images of bull-headed monsters creeping into the design.

They came to their first junction. "*Raast ya chap?*" Martin asked.

"We should toss a coin," Javeed suggested.

"Hmm. I wonder…" Martin reached into his pocket; the gloves interfered with his sense of touch, but from the sensation against his leg through the material of his trousers he was fairly sure he'd gripped a thousand-rial coin. But when he took his hand out, Zendegi was either unable or unwilling to acknowledge the coin's existence. "No. Maybe next time we can find out how to get some local currency." He put the invisible coin back in his pocket carefully, not wanting to drop it into the sphere and trip up on it later.

"*Raast,*" Javeed decided. They turned to the right.

After a while Martin heard children's voices, shouts echoing between the tiles from somewhere not too far away. "Hey! So we're not alone."

"What if they get to the fountain before us?" Javeed's icon managed a near-perfect *it's the end of the world if I don't win* look.

"I don't know. Do you want to go faster?"

Javeed nodded enthusiastically. Martin started jogging, and Javeed ran to keep up with him. It was hard to accept, viscerally, that there could be no grazed knees from the rocky ground here—let alone the kind of tearful collisions with the walls that were almost guaranteed in the real world, when Javeed had friends over and they chased each other from room to room.

Martin didn't want to keep fretting about the downside, but he wondered if the mismatch between visual cues and physical consequences might stunt a child's instincts for dealing with obstacles in real life.

The passage turned left, offering them no choice this time. Martin heard footsteps and saw a child darting across an intersection twenty meters or so ahead of them; he or she was gone in an instant, but the voices were closer, and it sounded as if the child was a straggler chasing a group of friends. Javeed pumped his limbs harder, determined to catch up; Martin felt his own pace switch from effortless to distinctly sweaty.

They reached the intersection and turned right, the way the child had gone, taking them into a short passage that ended in a T-junction. Martin heard laughter that sounded very close, but the echoes made it impossible to judge the direction.

"Which way?" Javeed fretted.

"Right," Martin said firmly, for no particular reason. When they'd first gone in, he'd had some vague idea of using the keep-the-wall-to-your-right rule, which at least had the virtue that you wouldn't end up going around in circles. But he was beginning to suspect that their free trial would run out long before they solved the maze, whatever strategy they adopted.

They took the right turn, then the passage forced them left, then left again... into a cul-de-sac. Javeed stood at the wall, scowling; the set of his mouth wasn't quite authentic, but Martin recognized the signs of an incipient tantrum immediately. He leaned down beside him. "This is what mazes are for," he said gently, "to get lost in, to make mistakes."

"You said 'right'!" Javeed replied accusingly, utterly oblivious to Martin's suggestion that this setback could be acceptable, let alone desirable.

"So we'll go back to the same place and turn left."

"But we've lost them now!"

"Maybe. We'll see."

Javeed followed him out of the dead end, sulkily refusing to be hurried. Martin examined the mosaics around them, trying to commit the pattern to memory just in case there was some kind of visual cue marking the routes that led nowhere.

Back at the T-junction, they continued down the passage into the unexplored arm. It wasn't long before Javeed's disappointment had faded and they were running again—gloriously confused, if not quite lost. Martin kept hearing shouts and snatches of laughter, always children's voices. The sound of these elusive playmates made him want to whisper to Javeed, "Do you think there are ghosts here? Maybe this is a haunted maze, full of children who never found their way out." But he struggled to recall how old he'd been himself before such a notion would have elicited an enjoyable thrill, rather than sheer terror. It seemed wiser to err on the side of caution.

Then they took a turn and suddenly the children were all around them, coming in the opposite direction and almost colliding with them. There were more than a dozen, as real and unghostly as he and Javeed were to each other. "Not that way!" one of the girls scolded Javeed in Farsi. A boy added, "We went that way already, it's a dead end."

Javeed looked confused for a moment, but then he seemed to bond with the group in an instant, with no need for any adult nonsense: no exchange of names, no empty pleasantries, just a discussion of the matter at hand. The children barely acknowledged Martin, but that felt more like a kind of politeness than a deliberate rebuff; they simply weren't presuming that an adult stranger would want to speak with them, let alone be a part of their game. Martin wasn't comfortable letting Javeed out of his sight, though, so he tagged along beside him as the mob headed back down the passage, and some of the children attempted to explain to Javeed where they'd been so far and where they thought they were going. Martin couldn't work out if they'd been performing a systematic sweep of the maze, but he wasn't about to intrude with his own questions or advice. And Javeed was reconciled to the fact that he wasn't going to win any race now; it was enough that he'd been accepted into this group.

Martin let the boisterous chatter flow past him, just keeping an eye on Javeed and checking the mosaics for clues. When the group hit another dead end there were complaints and recriminations, but there was too much collective energy for anyone to start sulking, and no opportunity for disenchantment to lead to blows. Ten minutes later, Martin noticed a distinctive crowding of the mosaic's features that he'd seen twice before. Sure enough, a few turns later they reached yet another cul-de-sac. If he'd been alone with Javeed he would have stopped and explained the discovery to him, but as things stood he didn't want to interfere with the children's own plans. As they retraced their steps, Javeed chatted happily with the girl beside him, sharing his somewhat optimistic vision of school. "And I'm going to build a model plane, and then I'm going to build a car—"

"You can build a plane in Zendegi," she interjected, "big enough to fly in."

Javeed was speechless.

Martin could see the pattern on the walls growing simpler and more spacious, until they came to a junction where it was almost pared down to a sequence of eight-pointed stars sitting alone in a square grid; all the delicate complications and adornments had been stripped away. The children walked right past this signpost—but five minutes later their own haphazard strategy brought them back to it.

When they reached the end of the passage and took one last obligatory turn, they found themselves in a courtyard in the center of the maze. Directly in front of them was an octagonal fountain carved from white stone.

Shouts of triumph filled the courtyard. Javeed was ecstatic, jumping up and down with delight; Martin wished he could have lofted him into the air, though the way his back had been lately he probably should be grateful that it was impossible here.

"I want to throw a coin in the fountain!" Javeed said. Martin held out his empty hands. "They don't take our money here, remember?" No doubt that would be easily fixed once they had Martin's credit card details.

Some of the children were gathering around the fountain, searching for a hidden reward. Martin and Javeed joined them, but Martin was curious about more basic things than game-loot. Zendegi wouldn't play along if you insisted on trying to occupy the same location as a solid object, but what about water?

Martin said, "Try and splash me. See what happens."

Javeed hesitated, probably recalling the dose of vertigo he'd received when he'd tried to grab hold of Martin's legs. But he summoned up his courage and reached into the pool of water at the fountain's edge. From his expression it was clear that he felt *something*, but before Martin could ask him to describe the sensation, Javeed had taken him at his word and swatted some of the stuff in his direction. Martin blinked at the stream of droplets, unable to shut off the protective instinct. When he opened his eyes he put a hand to his cheek and felt moisture on his fingertips. Weirdly, he couldn't decide how convincing the sensation was in itself; the context told him what it should have meant, and his brain just accepted the whole package.

Javeed laughed and cupped some more water threateningly in his hand, but at the last moment he spared Martin and tipped it onto the ground instead. As it puddled on the gray stone, the hard surface fissured and disintegrated with a steamy hiss, then green blades of grass thrust their way up through the powdery residue.

Javeed shouted wildly, and soon all the children were joining in, scooping up water and dropping it onto the stone. Martin didn't want to rob the kids of any of their fun—and he felt a little self-conscious, too—but after a while he couldn't resist; he cupped some water in his hands and carried it to one of the few remaining patches that had escaped the transformation. That grass and stone felt the same beneath his shoes didn't really undermine his suspension of disbelief, and when he squatted down to check the texture with his hands it was downright eerie: when his fingertip made contact with a blade of grass, the sensation of gentle springiness created by the haptic glove's calibrated tickle was more than enough to bolster the illusion.

That was enough for him; Martin stood aside and watched as the children hunted for the spots they'd missed. Javeed kept crossing the grass around the fountain with handfuls of water that leaked through his fingers before he could find any stone to transmute, but he wasn't growing frustrated; everyone was having much too good a time.

A blue-and-gold butterfly hovered beside the fountain. Martin turned toward the sudden shouts of excitement and saw a whole swarm of them peeling off the courtyard's wall. Someone had splashed the wall, and unlike the change that had been wrought on the ground, this appeared to be self-sustaining; as the tiles of the mosaic became the scales of butterfly wings, their neighbours needed no extra dose of water to follow in their wake.

Javeed was open-mouthed with astonishment now; his face looked as if it had been pushed beyond the already overblown exemplar he'd given Omar. The walls of the courtyard disappeared beneath a tornado of butterflies that stretched up into the air; a few were flying across the grass, but the swarm as a whole kept its distance, preventing the spectacle from becoming oppressive. The children were shouting and squealing, but nobody seemed frightened. Martin went and stood beside Javeed and they watched in silence as the vortex of change ate its way through the walls of the courtyard and began devouring the surrounding maze. He looked up, afraid that the insects might block out the sky, but the funnel was broadening as it grew, the butterflies dispersing as they ascended.

As the maze disintegrated, the grass of the courtyard spread out to take its place; like a swarm of locusts in reverse the butterflies were transforming the once barren ground into lush greenery. But even more strikingly, the advancing horde left something intact: people. Apparently not everyone had managed to reach the courtyard, and now the stragglers were being liberated from the confusion of the maze. Martin saw one group of children leaping into the air, trying to catch the blue-and-golden insects.

When the butterflies reached the edges of the maze they flew off across the rocky desert, leaving behind nothing but an octagonal oasis centered on the fountain.

As calm descended, Martin could hear his heart pounding. He felt elated, but he was drained as well. He turned to Javeed. "You okay, *pesaram?*"

Javeed beamed at him. "That was fantastic! I want to do it again!"

Some of the children around them were already disappearing, literally fading into transparency as they departed. Martin said, "Not today."

"But we can come back tomorrow?"

"Not tomorrow."

"We have to come back!" Javeed was horrified, as if Martin had shown him this glimpse of paradise only to slam the gates shut.

"Don't get upset, I didn't say *never*."

"When?"

"Soon."

"*When?*"

"I don't know exactly. Give me time to think about it."

They headed back toward the dome. Martin knew they didn't need to return the way they'd come in order to exit from the game, but he was reluctant to yank them out of the experience abruptly.

As they walked across the grass, he spotted a man and a boy walking a few meters away to their left; the man raised a hand and called out in English, "Hi! How's it going?"

"Hi." Martin stopped and waited for them to approach. "I was beginning to think I was the only adult here."

"Me too." The man's icon had blue eyes and brown hair; he sounded like a native English speaker, but Martin couldn't place his accent.

"I'm Martin, this is my son Javeed. This is our first time in Zendegi."

The man said, "I'm Luke. This is Hassan."

Martin didn't offer his hand; maybe when he'd had more experience with the gloves the subtleties of the process wouldn't seem too daunting for a casual gesture. He turned to the boy. "*Salaam, Hassan. Chetori?*"

"*Salaam agha,*" Hassan replied shyly.

"Zendegi is great," Luke said, "but we're always famished afterward."

"Yeah, you can't fault it for a lack of exercise," Martin replied.

"What you need is a snack that's nutritious," Luke enthused, "*and* fun to eat!"

Martin stared at him. What were the odds that another man with a Western name and an Iranian son would be playing the same game at the same time? "You're not actually a person, are you?" he said.

Luke gazed back with a frozen smile, betraying no hint of offense. "I used to think that kebab-o-licious goodness could only come in a real kebab—"

Martin pointed his thumb to the ground, and found himself back in his castle. He flipped up the goggles' screens and saw the sphere opening up around him. Within seconds he could see Javeed for real.

"You okay?"

Javeed nodded, but said nothing. His posture had a hint of reserve that Martin knew was his punishment for failing to set a firm date for their return.

Martin left the gloves and goggles on the counter beside the desktop and they went downstairs. Omar was dealing with a customer, but Farshid was free and Javeed immediately began bombarding him with every detail of their experience. Martin stood and listened, feeling flat and a little disoriented; it was like coming out of a movie into daylight, or stepping off a plane from somewhere bright and exotic to face the same old mundane sights again.

Omar joined them. "What did you think?"

"It was good." Martin gave him a shorter version than Javeed's, which was still in progress. "I guess when you pay for it, you don't have to put up with the walking advertisements?"

"Yeah. You can get a discount if you let them bug you, but it's your choice."

Martin laughed. "That's a relief. It will be good to go back and be certain that everyone around us is real."

Omar's smile became equivocal.

Martin said, "What? Why can't I be sure of that?"

"It's not just ads," Omar explained. "They put in Proxies for fun as well. With some of the games there aren't enough real people playing, so they need to make up the numbers to keep it from getting boring. Or sometimes there are characters nobody wants to be—roles that are needed, but aren't very interesting."

"Okay." It made sense that some role-playing games would be padded out with grunts and cannon fodder, but Martin had never imagined that half the exuberant children splashing water onto stone in the labyrinth's courtyard could have been the same: software extras inserted to bolster the mood. "Won't that get confusing, though? What if Javeed thinks he's making a new friend?"

Omar shook his head impatiently. "You can always get Zendegi to tag the Proxies if you want to. But why spoil the fun? Maybe Javeed will play football in a stadium with twenty thousand people watching. Maybe you and twenty others will be real. Does he need to know which ones? When you take him to a movie, do you sit there pointing out which characters are real human extras and which ones are CGI?"

"Hmm." Martin could see the logic of it, but he still wasn't entirely happy.

Javeed had reached his third iteration of refinements and corrections in his story to Farshid. Martin put a hand on his shoulder. "*Bas, pesaram.* Say thanks to Uncle Omar, then come and help me make lunch."

Martin drove into the city with Javeed guarding the meal they'd cooked. Mahnoosh closed the shop and they sat on the floor in the back room, eating. Or rather, Martin ate and Mahnoosh tried to as Javeed regaled her nonstop with stories of Zendegi. By the time Martin had to go and reopen the shop, Javeed's plate had barely been touched.

"Don't worry," Mahnoosh said. "I'll reheat it at home."

Martin kissed them both good-bye. Javeed stood passively when Martin embraced him; if he'd been sulking he would have squirmed away, but this was his subtle freeze-out, where he declined to reciprocate affection, but also eschewed overt signs of hostility.

People of the Book was open until nine; Martin didn't mind the first few hours, but the evenings dragged. He'd given up hoping that they'd ever be able to afford an assistant to take the night shifts; the rent on the shop kept going up, and while their sales weren't falling, the numbers were flat. The only way to increase revenue would be to increase prices, and a *cyber-ketab*—with ten complimentary bestsellers pre-loaded—already cost less than five hardbacks.

Still, their customers weren't deserting them yet. As Martin was getting ready to close, an elderly woman in a headscarf approached the counter.

"Do you have *The Moor's Last Sigh?*" she asked.

"In Farsi or English?"

"Farsi."

Martin checked on the computer. "That's print-on-demand. I could run it off for you now, if you like."

"Please."

Martin tapped the screen and the machine behind him started humming. "Good choice," he told the woman. "It's my favourite of his. And it has the distinct advantage of never having been made into a song by U2."

She smiled nervously and looked around, as if she was afraid someone might overhear them. But she could have bought an electronic version in the privacy of her home if she'd wanted to. Instead, she'd chosen to walk out into the night and come back with an aromatic bundle of permanently inked pages, adorned with the name of the infamous apostate.

Martin put the book into a plain brown bag; it was warm as a freshly baked loaf. The woman paid cash. When she'd left, he stepped out onto Enqelab Avenue and pulled down the security shutters.

By the time Martin arrived home he was ravenous. Mahnoosh had eaten earlier, with Javeed, but she joined him anyway.

"How did things go at the school?" she asked, scraping the last of the *tadigh* onto his plate.

Martin recounted the glitch with the enrollment form, and Javeed's anxiety about her parents. "When I told him that your father had cut you off, he asked me if I'd ever do the same to him."

Mahnoosh's face crumpled in sympathy, but then her expression softened almost to a smile and she looked at Martin as if it all made perfect sense. "Zal and the Simorgh," she said.

"Sorry?"

"From the *Shahnameh*."

Martin shook his head. He'd known that Mahnoosh was mining a children's version of Ferdowsi's epic for bedtime stories, but he'd done no more than glance at the book himself.

"Zal is born with white hair, like an old man," she explained. "His father is so superstitious that he abandons him in the wilderness, but the Simorgh—a giant bird with a dog's head—finds him and raises him. Later, his father has a dream that the boy is still alive, and he goes into the mountains to ask his son's forgiveness and bring him back."

Martin bit back a complaint about the suitability of the story; would he have protested over "Hansel and Gretel"? But he could see how it might have planted an idea in Javeed's head that would have been rendered more real and threatening by a reminder of his grandparents' behavior.

"Are you sure they're never going to reconcile with you?" Martin still struggled to comprehend how anyone could maintain a feud with their own daughter for so long. "They must want to see their grandson."

"They have other grandsons," Mahnoosh replied. "I've been dead to them for twenty-seven years; one more grandchild isn't going to change that."

"What would?"

Mahnoosh pondered the question. "Maybe a pilgrimage to Karbala over broken glass, and a written renunciation of everything I believe in."

"If they're that fanatical, I guess you'd have to divorce me as well."

She shrugged. "They kicked me out twelve years before I'd even met you. And if you'd seen the band I was in back then, you'd know you just don't rate on the burning-bridges-with-the-parents scale."

"I can't believe you don't have video." Martin had seen a few still photos, but Mahnoosh had been unrecognizable. In fact, she'd looked disturbingly like Robert Smith. He knew there'd been an underground music scene in Tehran, but an all-female Goth-metal band called Unquiet Grave must have been several kilometers beneath the pavement.

"If your parents are a lost cause," he said, "there must be someone in your family who hasn't disowned you."

"Don't bet on it; my sisters are even worse!" She thought for a while. "One of my mother's cousins was okay, but I think she went to America, and anyway, I haven't seen her since I was a kid." She sighed. "Look, let's not make a big deal of this. Javeed has enough 'aunties' and 'uncles' and 'cousins' to spoil any child. I've never met my sisters' brats, but I bet he's luckier having Farshid around than any of them."

"Yeah." Martin put his plate aside. "So, what do you think about Zendegi?"

"Ah." Mahnoosh smiled. "I promised I'd go in with him next week, after school. To see for myself, before we sign up for a subscription."

"You'll like it," Martin assured her. "It's a lot of fun. Just… stay away from anyone who looks like some marketing software's idea of your trusted next-door neighbor. There's no danger that they'll talk you into buying anything, but it still feels awkward when you have to call their bluff and walk away."

After he'd washed the dishes and had a quick shower, Martin went to Javeed's room and stood at the foot of his bed. "*Shab bekheyr, pesaram*," he whispered—softly, but not too softly to be heard. Javeed's sleep was always disturbed by the sound of Martin coming home: voices and the clatter of plates from the kitchen, creaking floorboards, running water. If Martin failed to say goodnight before the house fell silent, Javeed would wake and call out for him.

Martin walked over to the bookcase beside the bed and picked up what he hoped was the right volume. Out in the light of the passageway he checked; it was the book of stories from the *Shahnameh*. He found "Zal and the Simorgh," and stood leaning against the wall as he read.

Upon spotting the infant Zal, who'd been left to die of exposure at the foot of the Alborz Mountains—the same mountains you could see from half the streets of Tehran—the giant bird had brought him back to her nest with the intention of feeding him to her chicks. Miraculously though, the whole family of predators had taken pity on him. In fact, the Simorgh turned out to be a soft touch, feeding her adopted son the best leftovers, and even giving him a few magic feathers as a parting gift when his repentant father came to take him back.

Nothing too frightening, and everyone was reconciled at the end. If Javeed was upset that Mahnoosh's own parents hadn't followed the script, Martin would just have to convince him that there were other kinds of happy endings.

12

Alerted by voices in Arabic and a whiff of expensive cologne, Nasim peeked out through a slit in the blinds just in time to catch sight of four men in immaculate suits strolling down the corridor past her office. Half-a-dozen more familiar figures hovered around them attentively, tripping over each other to ensure that the valued guests encountered no obstruction or inconvenience.

This was the third group of financiers to visit the premises in a month; nobody ever introduced Nasim to these men, but she gathered that they all came from wealthy Gulf States—the kind that had invested in solar-algal oil long before their fossil wells had run dry.

Nasim moved away from the window and sat at her desk, fidgeting unhappily with her notepad. She had no doubt that their guests had billions of rials to spare; the question was, could they be persuaded to send the smallest trickle in Zendegi's direction? The directors laid on the hospitality, the glossy demonstrations, the optimistic growth forecasts, but it was an open secret that their biggest competitor was growing faster.

In the last six months Cyber-Jahan had mounted a relentless campaign across the Middle East, poaching existing customers as well as signing up thousands who'd previously been uncommitted. Population wasn't destiny; after all, it was the Koreans who dominated the Chinese VR market, and they were also doing well in Japan. But Zendegi had never quite managed to pull off its own David-and-Goliath act; the days of stealing customers from its Indian rival were long gone, and now it was faltering even in its own heartland. Nasim couldn't see how they were going to hang on for another year without a very large injection of cash.

There was a soft tapping on her door; it opened before she had a chance to respond. Her chief software engineer, Bahador, slipped into the room and closed the door behind him. "Sorry, Nasim, but the boss told me to make myself scarce. He said I looked untidy."

"Untidy?" By any ordinary standards Bahador was perfectly well groomed, but perhaps the mere presence of the Giorgio Omanis was enough to render any less-tailored mortal shabby by comparison. Nasim gestured at the chair opposite her desk. "You'd better sit down and wait for the paranoia to pass." At least she had an office of her own, so she could close the door and draw the blinds; if she'd worked in the open plan area, she herself probably would have been banished to the ladies' toilets.

"So how's the tour going?" she asked in a low voice. "Did you hear anything?"

Bahador nodded and leaned forward. "When they came out of the *ghal'eha*, one of them said, 'There's nothing new here. We've seen this all before.'"

Nasim absorbed this news glumly. "I'm glad I wasn't asked to choose the demo suite; at least I can't get blamed for that."

Bahador scowled. "Screw them. We have better lighting effects than anyone else, better facial interpolation, better gait dynamics. Then they come here and complain that we're not hosting *completely different games*. No developer is going to write exclusively for us; the question is: Does the game look better, does it feel more natural, when it's running in Zendegi?"

"That's true," Nasim conceded, "but it's starting to look pretty marginal. So long as Cyber-Jahan has more customers, developers are going to release there first. And for anything with a strong social component, sheer force of numbers is going to make the experience better."

Bahador didn't reply. Nasim wished she could have said something to boost his morale, but she suspected that only a massive marketing campaign could save them now. Any advances in mere technical excellence would be like decorating the ballroom as the ship went down.

"If we had better Proxies," Bahador mused, "the numbers wouldn't matter so much."

"We *do* have better Proxies," Nasim protested. "We have the best biomechanical models in the world."

Bahador nodded impatiently. "But as you said, that kind of advantage is marginal. They *look* natural enough, but when it comes to behavior…"

"Behavior is a game-specific problem. It's out of our hands."

"That's my point," Bahador replied. "Maybe it shouldn't be out of our hands. If we could supplement the biomechanics with the best behavioural models—and allow developers to leverage the whole package for free—it wouldn't matter that Cyber-Jahan had the flesh-and-blood advantage.

Playing a game with ten thousand high-quality Proxies would actually be better than playing in a real crowd, because smart developers could tune all the interpersonal dynamics to suit the real players."

Nasim said, "Okay, that's a perfectly sensible goal—but we have no expertise in Proxy behavior. And we've looked into this before. The boss sent me on a head-hunting trip a few years ago: India, Korea, the United States, Europe; I went to about fifty campuses and start-ups looking for researchers we could hire, or technology we could license. But there was nothing that was really close to passing for human in anything but the crudest shoot-'em-up."

"Was that when you visited the Superintelligence Project?" Bahador had joined Zendegi a year later, but Nasim must have mentioned the trip to him before.

"Yeah. No AI there." She had spent a day at their Houston complex, curious to find out what they'd done with Zachary Churchland's billions once his bequest had finally made it through the Texan version of *Bleak House*. But the sum total of their achievements had amounted to a nine-hundred-page wish-list dressed up as a taxonomy, a fantasy of convenient but implausible properties for a vast imaginary hierarchy of software daemons and deities. The whole angelic realm had been described with the kind of detail often lavished on a game-world's mythical bestiary, but Nasim had seen no evidence that these self-improving cyber-djinn had any more chance of being brought to life than the denizens of the Dungeons and Dragons *Monster Manual*.

"That was five years ago," Bahador said. "The state of the art's changed; look at the viziers in *Palace Intrigue*, say—"

"They're not bad," Nasim conceded, "but we're never going to be able to acquire that technology exclusively for Zendegi. The game developers have no interest in picking a fight with Cyber-Jahan."

"So forget the state-of-the-art," Bahador suggested. "Hire the people who'll go beyond it."

"They're already working for the game developers! If we tried to poach Proxologists now, it'd mean a bidding war, and we just don't have that kind of money."

Bahador raised his hands in a gesture of mock resignation. "Okay, I give up. We're finished. I'll send my résumé to Bangalore and brush up on my Hinglish."

Nasim laughed. "If you really want to impress them, learn Kannada; that's the founders' first language."

Bahador glanced at his watch. "They'll be taking the guests to the board-room for tea soon. I'll be out of your hair in a minute."

"Maybe Cyber-Jahan will just acquire us," Nasim mused. "Wait for the stock to get a bit lower, then buy themselves a regional subsidiary."

Bahador said nothing, but he looked away, his body language suddenly reproachful, even wounded. Despite his own résumé joke, Nasim could tell that she'd crossed some kind of line. The two of them—along with a dozen of their colleagues—had worked like maniacs for the last four years to make Zendegi the most impressive VR engine on the planet. So how could she be so defeatist? How could she even think of surrender?

When Nasim arrived home she walked out to the balcony and peered into the bird cage; the four finches were sitting firmly on their perches, fast asleep. Clearly the local Tehrani subspecies had evolved to be oblivious to the sound of traffic. Their water tray was speckled with dead insects; it seemed unlikely that this would bother them, but she changed the water anyway, moving carefully to avoid disturbing the birds.

The lights had been out in her mother's apartment as she'd come up the stairs; it would have been nice to sit and talk with her, but it was after eleven, too late to disturb her. Nasim had eaten at the office a couple of hours before, but she couldn't face trying to sleep yet, so she sat in the living room and had her notepad stream a news summary to the wallscreen.

If she lost Zendegi, what would she do? It was not as if she'd be unemployable; the company was a household name, and even if it went down in flames people would understand the market forces involved, they wouldn't write off the technical staff as incompetent. The question was: Could she face something new?

Zendegi was the fifth job she'd had since returning to Iran, and the only one that had really suited her. She'd stuck out her first position—Online Outreach Director with Hezb-e-Haalaa—for almost six years, but in the end she'd finally had to admit that she was a bad match for politics. Everyone who'd been abroad in 2012 had suffered from martyr envy, but she'd lived through enough of the aftermath's mundanity and compromise to get over it. Iran was a democracy now, wobbly and imperfect but probably not doomed, and she'd lost any sense that she was personally responsible for shoring it up. If Zendegi was a frivolous indulgence, well, it was there alongside every other beautiful, forbidden thing that her contemporaries had risked their lives to regain.

"… has been tipped as a possible Nobel recipient for his work on bacterial colonies…"

Nasim gestured rewind-and-replay. The story was just a superficial thirty-second filler, but her knowledge-miner had correctly identified its subject as one of her former colleagues.

She watched Dinesh's smiling face as he deflected accusations of personal genius and attributed everything to his wonderful team. It wasn't news to her that HETE had been successful, but at some point she'd stopped paying attention. "Good for you, Dr. Bose," she muttered, sincere but still envious. She wasn't jealous of these snippets of fame; she just wished she could have steered her own life half as well. Dinesh had made good use of his personal obsessions—which might otherwise have been merely neurotic—by harnessing them to an admirable goal. Nasim couldn't believe that he'd spent a single day in the last ten years feeling bored and unfulfilled *or* guilty and self-indulgent. That was enough to make anyone want to smack him across the head.

A truck's horn blared close by, followed by a long, teeth-gritting squeal of brakes. Nasim went to the balcony and looked down at the highway; a near-miss this time, not a pile-up. It was enough to wake the birds, though. She stood in the dark listening to them chatter, wondering what they made of the strange racket that had roused them.

Back in the living room, the notepad had detected her absence and paused its display. Nasim made a throat-cutting gesture that blanked the screen, but instead of heading for the bedroom she sat down again.

She'd kept her gaze averted from another scientific endeavor, though it had attracted far more media coverage than HETE. If she was serious about exorcizing jealousies and regrets, she might as well go for the big one.

Nasim cupped her right hand beside her mouth to let her notepad know that she was addressing it and not just babbling dementedly to herself.

"Human Connectome Project," she said.

The map of the brain that appeared a heartbeat later was multi-colored and translucent, the familiar shape woven from a tangle of fanciful cables. Nasim had seen the emblematic image a few times before and dismissed it as eye candy, but now that she was actually paying attention she suspected that it was based on genuine regional connectivity statistics, with the glossy conduits rendered thick or thin in proportion to a tractographic count of nerve fibers between the different areas they linked. Like a schematic drawing of a metro system, it told something truthful in bright colors, even if it wasn't an engineering blueprint for the real tracks and stations.

She laughed softly; this wasn't so painful. Two months before, when the news of the first draft's completion had edged into her peripheral vision, it had filled her with a sense of uselessness and stupidity. If she hadn't succumbed to the naïve fantasy that her homeland needed her, she could have been popping champagne in Cambridge or Düsseldorf and cheering for the cameras; just one face in an anonymous white-coated crowd, but still basking in the glow of her small part in the collective achievement.

Now she felt just a wry impatience with her own touchiness and fragility. She was forty years old; if she couldn't get over a few bad career choices after fifteen years, that was pathetic. She'd forgotten an entire marriage in less time than that.

She navigated quickly past the gee-whiz bullet points, the byte counts trailing zeroes illustrated with comic-book stacks of Blu-rays reaching to the sky. *Yes, that's a lot of data you gathered, we're all very impressed.*

The paper that announced the draft map itself had appeared in *PLoS Computational Biology*; Nasim followed the link to it. There was one more blow for her ego waiting here; her own work on integrating data from multiple subjects and imaging techniques wasn't even cited in the references. She cursed the cheating bastards and skimmed back through the paper, looking for the evidence that would nail them. Whatever disappointments she'd brought upon herself, she still deserved this one tiny footnote in history.

Except she didn't. They'd used a different method entirely, statistical rather than functional, developed four years after she'd left the field. The final map they'd generated from their thousands of individual scans owed nothing whatsoever to her ideas about matching neural sub-circuits.

Nasim felt lightheaded now. She rubbed her eyes with the heels of her palms. If all the late nights she'd spent in Redland's lab had actually turned out to be irrelevant, maybe she should be grateful that she'd cut her losses and walked away. But if Zendegi was going down the tubes, and she hadn't even left one tiny smudged thumbprint on the HCP, what was left? After forty years, what had she accomplished? One bad marriage and two failed careers.

She stood up, her cheeks burning, refusing to sink into a heap of tears but still not able to laugh the whole thing off. Fretting about the HCP was useless vanity, but Zendegi's fate was real and pressing. She'd seen the boss after the money men departed, and he had not looked hopeful.

As she stared at the screen, her attention fell on a series of links leading off from the paper itself into the massive stores of data on the HCP's own servers. In the spirit of Open Science—and as a condition of some of the funding—all the raw scans that had been used to build the map were available on the web, along with the map itself. The HCP's first draft was not the final word; researchers around the world would keep adding more brain images and refining the results.

But even without fresh scans to contribute, anyone could come along and re-analyze the data.

Nasim read the whole paper. Every few paragraphs she had to break off to follow up an unfamiliar reference, or embark on a restless circuit of the room as she mulled over some technical detail, but after two hours she'd come to grips with everything.

They'd done it deliberately, she realized. They'd chosen a different way to combine the scans, not because her technique had been rendered obsolete by a superior method, but because they'd been aiming for a different kind of map. This draft would allow neurologists to diagnose pathologies more easily, and enable computational biologists to test many of their basic ideas. What it would *not* do, though, was give rise to a complete, working simulation of a human brain. It was, by design, too blurred, too abstracted, too generic. But that had been a choice. The same raw data, with different methods, might well yield a different kind of map, far more amenable to being treated as a blueprint.

There was no prospect of waking the dead; the individual memories and personalities of the subjects of the scans were unrecoverable. But their common attributes, their common skills, might not lie beyond reconstruction.

Other people, Nasim was sure, would already have thought along the same lines. Cyber-Jahan? Happy Universe? Games effects sub-contractors, like Crowds and Power? Anyone who was serious about building the best possible Proxies would have had two months' head start.

But she'd trained for this race, she'd written the book on it. She was rusty on the details, but she could be back up to speed in a week or two if that was what she wanted.

Out on the balcony, the finches were singing.

13

The plan had been for Mahnoosh to take Javeed to his first day of school while Martin opened the shop. The night before though, as Martin had been drifting off to sleep, Mahnoosh had turned and put a hand on his shoulder.

"We can open late just once, can't we?" she'd said.

"Yeah. That's a good idea."

As Martin shepherded him into the car, Javeed was as excited as he'd ever been. He'd been awake since five o'clock, checking and re-checking everything in his school bag, counting his colored pencils as if they were action figures. The impending novelty had even—finally—eclipsed the prospect of his return to Zendegi.

"I know *both* alphabets," he boasted, as Martin strapped him into the back seat. "Some kids don't know anything."

"Yeah, well, don't be too full of yourself," Martin warned him. "Maybe you're luckier than some kids. Your job is to help them catch up, not to make them feel bad."

"They should feel bad," Javeed retorted.

Martin scowled. "*Shaitan nasho!*"

Mahnoosh approached the car. She whispered to Martin, "I just phoned Omar about you-know-what, and he said he'd keep two *ghal'eha* free for us."

"Great."

Martin drove, blocking out Javeed's chatter and focusing on the road, leaving it to Mahnoosh to engage with him. The school wasn't much more than a kilometer away, and they planned to get into a routine of walking there, but today this would save them going back for the car.

124

It took them ten minutes to find a parking spot, but Martin wasn't going to drop the two of them off and circle back to pick up Mahnoosh, not today. When they finally reached the gate, the bell was ringing. They walked with Javeed across the playground, to the lines of boys and girls already forming outside his classroom.

Mahnoosh bent down and embraced Javeed tightly.

"Have you got everything, *azizam?*"

"Yes, Mama."

"I'll be back in a few hours. You wait for me here."

"Okay." Javeed squirmed a little, and she released him. Martin squatted down and kissed him on the cheek. "Have fun. I'll see you later."

Javeed went to join the line. Standing beside Mahnoosh, Martin reached over and took her hand. They waited until the teacher appeared and marched the two lines into the classroom. Mahnoosh waved, but the teacher had instructed the children to keep their eyes straight ahead, so Javeed didn't see her.

"Are you okay?" Martin asked her. The truth was he was feeling the tug of separation himself more keenly than he'd expected. For the first time in his life, Javeed would be going through something new without either of them beside him.

Mahnoosh scowled defensively. "Of course. Ah, we didn't take a photo!"

"Do it when you pick him up," Martin suggested. "That'll be better, because he'll have something to show you; he'll probably be waving a big drawing."

"The butterfly maze, I expect." All the classes had been led into their rooms now, and the parents were drifting away across the playground.

Mahnoosh said, "I'll drive you to the shop."

"Martin *jan*, are you awake?"

Martin opened his eyes. It was night-time; the unfamiliar room was lit by a lamp attached to the wall beside the bed. Omar was sitting on a chair, hunched toward him. Martin's mouth was dry and his head felt heavy.

"What?" he replied stupidly.

"You're in hospital," Omar explained; it must have been the lamplight, but he looked impossibly haggard, as if he'd aged a decade since Martin had last seen him. "You had an accident."

"Really? I don't remember." Visceral panic welled up in his chest. "Who else was in the car?" Martin swung his legs toward the side of the bed, but the sheet was tucked in so far under the mattress that he couldn't kick it free.

Omar reached out and restrained him. "Stay there, you've got a drip in your arm. I picked up Javeed from school. He's at my home, he's fine."

"Thank you." In the silence that followed Martin heard his own labored breathing; the sound didn't seem to belong to his body. "What about Mahnoosh?"

"She was driving."

"Can I see her?" Martin squinted at him, trying to read his face. "Get a wheelchair for me. We'll go to the women's wing."

"There was a truck," Omar said. "It went straight through the intersection."

"What does that mean?"

Omar's hand was still resting on his shoulder. He lowered his gaze slightly. "She died straight away. Nobody could help her."

"No." Martin knew this was impossible; Omar wouldn't lie to him knowingly, but the hospital bureaucrats could get anything wrong. "What if I was in the car alone? People just assume things. Did you ring the shop?"

"Martin *jan*, I saw her," Omar confessed. "They didn't know if you'd recover, and they needed someone to... say who she was."

Martin felt his body shuddering; he struggled to keep control. "I'm sorry you had to do that."

Omar made a dismissive gesture, muttering reflexively, "*Khahesh mikonam*." Don't mention it.

"You should go home," Martin pleaded. "It must be late."

Omar didn't argue. "I'll come back in the morning."

When Omar had left the room, Martin felt himself sobbing noiselessly. He closed his eyes and swam into the darkness of his skull, trying to catch up with her: looking for an afterimage of her face, a memory of her voice, any thread that he could follow. How could they have been torn apart when they'd been sitting just inches from each other?

He had touched her hand in the school yard, he remembered. He tried to grasp it more tightly, picturing the two of them together, trying to relive everything that had followed without being shaken free of her this time.

But the scene led nowhere, the blackness remained impenetrable. He didn't even know the last words they'd exchanged.

In the morning, Martin asked to see Mahnoosh's body. They removed his drip and catheter and an orderly took him in a wheelchair to the mortuary.

Her face was purple and swollen, barely recognizable; he gazed at it long enough to be sure that it was her, but he felt no urge to touch her, to speak to her, to hold her. This body was a kind of grisly portrait of the woman, captured at the scene of the crash; it proved that she'd been there as surely as a photograph, but that was all.

In the ward, a doctor came to see him. He'd had an operation to stem internal bleeding, and it appeared to have been successful, but rather than officially discharging him they were making special provisions for him to attend the funeral. "You need to bury your wife, Mr. Seymour, then come back to us after two days."

Omar came to pick him up. In the silent drive to his house, Martin struggled to prepare his words.

Javeed was waiting just inside the door. He flung his arms around Martin's leg and pressed his face against his trousers.

Martin lowered himself gingerly to the floor and embraced his son. He held him for a few seconds, then forced himself to let go; if he clung on too long he knew he would not be able to hide the fact that he was the one seeking comfort.

They were alone; Omar had gone on into the house, giving them privacy. "Where were you?" Javeed demanded.

"I was in the hospital," Martin said. "I got hurt, in the car."

"But where did Mama go?"

"Mama was in the car with me."

"Is she in the hospital?"

Martin didn't answer that. "You know, sometimes if you get hurt, it can be like you've gone to sleep."

Javeed nodded. "Total Knockout."

"That's what happened to me. The truck hit the car, it was like a big punch. I was knocked out for a day."

Javeed said nothing; in his games, no one was ever out cold for more than thirty seconds. "Mama got knocked out too," Martin persisted. "But she didn't wake up."

He took Javeed's hand. Javeed stared down at the floor and tugged on Martin's arm, swinging it back and forth, testing something rather than trying to break free.

"Farshid said Mama went to Paradise."

Martin hadn't been prepared for this, but he could hardly blame Farshid. Javeed treated him like a sibling, with no adult mystique, no power to bluff and delay. Javeed would have known that he knew something, and would have worn him down until he disclosed it.

Martin said, "No, Mama went to sleep and she didn't wake up. She got knocked out, too hard to wake up."

"Did you try to wake her?"

"The doctors all tried. But she couldn't do it."

"If she went somewhere," Javeed reasoned, "she would have told me first."

"Yeah, of course. She'd never just go away." Martin put a hand on Javeed's cheek and raised his face so they were looking directly at each other.

"But—" Javeed hesitated.

"What?"

"Is Mama dead?"

Martin said, "Yes."

Javeed's eyes narrowed. "She'll never get better?"

"No. She was hurt too much."

"But—" Javeed's struggle persisted a moment longer, then he gave up trying to untangle the impossible knot. He sagged to the floor and started wailing, "I want Mama!"

Martin bent over and cradled him in his arms. "I know," he whispered. "I do too."

Omar helped organize the burial. Martin was still barely functioning, and the only other funeral he'd arranged had been his mother's, almost twenty years before, in a country where he'd understood the culture inside out.

In her will, Mahnoosh had mentioned Khavaran Cemetery, where religious minorities and apostates were interred. Omar suggested that a proper Muslim burial might yet be attainable, to spare her family some distress, but a few hours later he'd changed his mind. "I spoke to her father," he told Martin. "They won't come, wherever it is."

Martin suspected that Mahnoosh would have shrugged this off, entirely unsurprised, but he still felt his fists tightening with anger. "What did he say to you?"

Omar shook his head. "Forget about it."

The funeral took place the next morning. Javeed had been clinging to him ever since he'd returned from the hospital, and Martin had been dreading even this brief separation. "I'm going to go and get some friends of Mama to come here to say good-bye to her," he explained. "I'll be a couple of hours. Is that okay?"

"Okay," Javeed agreed.

There were less than a dozen people at the cemetery. Martin had emailed Behrouz in Damascus, but his flight would not arrive until the afternoon. Along with Omar's family there were some old friends of Mahnoosh's, Farah and Yalda, their ex-husbands, and two relatives Martin had never met before, a mother and daughter that Omar had managed to track down.

When the gravediggers had lowered the coffin into the ground, Omar stood with upturned palms and recited a prayer in Arabic. Mahnoosh would have rolled her eyes—and whispered to Martin that for all of Omar's sweet hopes, the mullahs had consigned her soul irrevocably to hell—but she wouldn't have silenced him.

Martin had no eulogy prepared; everything had happened too quickly. "*Mahnoosh noor-e-ruzhayam bud*," he began. *Mahnoosh was the light of my days*. It was the truth—and he knew this was the way he was expected to express it—but even as he spoke he recoiled from the idea that he owed the people around him a single word on the subject. To speak about these things with anyone but her was not an affirmation of his love, it was a kind of debasement.

Surely he owed her more than silence, though? Whatever belonged to the two of them alone, he could still recount her virtues in the company of friends. "I never knew anyone so fearless," he said. "So honest, so kind." He stared into the grave, unable to continue; he felt as if someone were holding a gun to his head, forcing him to recite these flaccid incantations even though he knew they were just driving her away from him. Yalda stepped in, praising Mahnoosh's generosity and sense of humor.

Back at Omar's house there was a photograph of Mahnoosh propped up on a table, surrounded by flowers; it had been taken not long after Javeed was born—after six years of IVF—and Martin could see both the defiant light of triumph in her eyes, and a sense of humility and tenderness. It was a beautiful picture, but he wished he'd thought to dig up one of the disheveled twenty-year-old Goth to put beside it.

Rana and her mother-in-law, Nahid, had been cooking since dawn. Martin was enthroned on a couch in the living room, with Javeed beside him. The guests ate, talked among themselves, and came to him to offer their condolences. Martin was growing dazed and weary, and the effort needed to maintain even a minimal level of sociability made his head ache. Part of him longed to curl up on a bed in his own silent house with Javeed in his arms and let the blackness engulf them. But he didn't trust himself to fall that far and then emerge into the light again. At least all the irritating rituals and false notes served a purpose: like a concussion victim being slapped and prodded, he knew he should be grateful for anything that kept him from drifting away.

When Behrouz arrived, Martin was finally jolted out of his stupor; he hadn't seen his friend face-to-face for three years, and he couldn't just exchange a few desultory words with him then let his eyes glaze over.

Behrouz embraced him. "I'm so sorry, Martin." He bent down to kiss Javeed, who flinched away. "You don't remember me?"

Javeed shook his head.

"I had some adventures with your father when we were young. Once we saw a dragon fall from the sky; it almost landed right on top of us."

Javeed buried his face against Martin's side.

"How's work?" Martin asked. Behrouz was now a correspondent for the *Wall Street Journal*, which these days seemed to mean as much video journalism as prose.

"Not bad." Behrouz smiled slightly. "Business people might be the last paying market left for real news. If they're convinced that they're getting fearlessly objective information, they'll keep shelling out for it—while everyone else gives up caring and buries their head inside their favorite consensual reality."

Martin laughed softly, self-conscious but grateful for a few words of real conversation, a lifeline out of the pit. "You're not a fan of News Five Point Oh, then?"

"Don't get me started. HigherTribe is worse, but they're all pathological. What isn't filtered and spun is just invented out of whole cloth."

"Yeah." The replacement of journalism by rumor aggregators and group-think salons was a serious matter, but Martin's enthusiasm for talking shop was already beginning to falter. "How's Shadi?"

"She's in Canada; she's doing a Ph.D."

"Jesus. Everyone's kids got old so fast."

Behrouz smiled down at Javeed. "We had a head start on you. But you've still got the best part to look forward to."

Martin struggled to keep his composure. Mahnoosh should have seen Javeed growing into adulthood, studying, flourishing, making his own life. He didn't know where to direct his anger at the injustice of it. He'd heard people muttering about a court case; the truck driver was in hospital but was expected to be discharged soon. The man probably deserved to be imprisoned, but Martin wanted nothing to do with the process.

"How long are you staying?" he asked Behrouz.

"I have to fly out again tonight. I'm sorry."

"It's okay." Martin suddenly recalled that he'd be in hospital anyway; he was in no position to play host. He shook Behrouz's hand. "I'm glad you came."

Roused from his paralysis, Martin moved among the guests; Javeed clung to him, saying little. Mahnoosh's second cousin, Nasim, and her mother, Saba, had been at the cemetery, but Martin had barely registered their presence there. Saba, he now discovered, was a retired economist;

Nasim a computer scientist.

"I'm afraid we never managed to get in contact with Mahnoosh after we came back from the US," Saba lamented. "She was a teenager when we left Iran. But we had as much friction with the family as she did."

Martin said, "She mentioned you fondly, just a few days ago."

"Oh." Saba grew distraught; her daughter put an arm across her shoulders comfortingly. Nasim said, "I was ten when we left, and I have to admit that I didn't get on with her parents even then. If I'd realized that she was fighting with them too I would have tried harder to stay in touch with her."

Javeed looked up at her. "Are you fighting with my grandfather?" He sounded more intrigued than affronted.

Nasim looked at Martin guiltily. "Sorry, I shouldn't have—"

"It's okay."

Nasim addressed Javeed. "Not really fighting, but we weren't good friends."

"What brought you back from America?" Martin asked.

Nasim said, "My mother had a job with the Ansari government. I came back thinking I was riding the same wave, though I'm afraid I ended up with less lofty ambitions."

Martin had heard that story before. "I expect everyone who returned has helped the country in some way. So long as you're not sending out spam."

"Actually I work for Zendegi."

Javeed had lapsed back into shyness, so Martin spoke on his behalf. "My son's a big fan."

"Really?" Nasim turned to Javeed. "What games do you like?"

"I only went once," he said. "Mama was going to take me."

Martin said, "I'll take you again, as soon as I can."

Nasim dug her notepad out of her handbag and did something in a blur of thumb movements. Martin's own notepad chimed softly in response. "Use this certificate," she said. "Unlimited access; it won't cost you anything."

"I can't accept that," he protested.

"I insist," Nasim replied firmly. "It's done."

"Thank you." Martin looked down at Javeed. "Say thank you to Aunty Nasim."

"Thank you, Aunty," he said.

At dusk, Martin lay down beside Javeed in Omar's guest room. "I want to tell you something, but you have to promise you won't get upset."

"What?"

"Promise me first."

"I promise."

"I need to go back to the hospital tomorrow, so they can make sure I'm completely better."

Javeed did not look happy, but he struggled to keep his word. "I want to go with you."

"No, *pesaram*, you stay here with Aunty Rana. Or you can go to the shop with Farshid and Uncle Omar."

"But you won't come back!" Javeed was crying now, snot running down his face. Martin fished out a tissue and wiped it away. "Shh. Of course I'll come back."

"Everyone wants to leave me alone," Javeed sobbed.

"Don't say that." Martin forced himself to keep his voice steady. "You know Mama didn't want to leave you. She would have done anything to stay. And this is just… the doctors put some Band-Aids inside me for my cuts, and now they have to check that they're okay."

"They put something inside you?" Javeed sniffed, his curiosity piqued.

"Absolutely." Martin hesitated; would it frighten him more, or would it help him to understand? "They had to open me up to put them in." He lifted up his shirt and twisted to show the stitches along his side.

Javeed gazed at them unflinchingly. "Did it hurt?"

"No, I was sleeping. And now they need to make sure everything's okay. Like when you cut yourself: we always change the Band-Aid a few times, to make sure it's clean and the cut's getting better, don't we?"

Javeed pondered this explanation. "I want you to get better," he conceded.

"So I can go and see the doctor?"

Javeed said, "You can go."

In the darkness, Martin felt Mahnoosh beside them, close enough to touch. If he'd been alone with her he would have lost himself to grief, dancing with her memory halfway to madness.

But she wasn't a wild spirit, begging him to dash himself on the rocks beside her. He heard her voice calmly, in their child's slow exhalations. And she asked nothing else of him but to do what she could not.

Martin woke before dawn and managed to extricate himself without disturbing Javeed. Omar insisted on driving him to the hospital. As they parted at reception Martin tried to thank him for everything he'd done since the accident.

Omar cut him off. "What do you expect? You think I forgot who broke me out of prison?" Martin wasn't at his sharpest; he almost opened his mouth to protest that he'd done nothing of the kind before he caught the self-deprecating joke. Omar wanted no praise for what he perceived as ordinary decency.

Martin spent an hour sitting by his bed before a doctor appeared. His stitches were examined and the area palpitated; it was all over in a matter of minutes.

The doctor addressed him in Farsi. "There's something more we need to discuss." He'd told Martin his name, but Martin had forgotten it immediately.

"All right." Martin prepared himself for a lecture on post-operative wound care.

"After the accident you were bleeding. We did a scan in order to locate the source, and I'm afraid we also found a problem with your spine."

Martin laughed. "*That?* I've had that for years." He had never entirely recovered from being landed on when that man had jumped out of the tree during the siege of Evin Prison. "It's been treated as much as it can be, but I've been told it's not worth an operation on the disks."

The doctor glared at him reprovingly. "I'm not talking about a minor disk problem. I'm talking about a mass lodged next to your spine."

Martin didn't reply. He was tired, and he wanted to get back to Javeed. He couldn't understand why people insisted on putting needless obstacles in his path.

"At this point," the doctor continued, "we believe it's a secondary growth from a cancer in your liver. We need to operate immediately, to remove the spinal tumor and to try to resect the primary tumor."

"How long will that take?"

"Maybe four or five hours. We'll do it this afternoon."

"And then I can go?" Martin pressed him. Javeed would start fretting if he wasn't home by nightfall.

The doctor switched to English. "Have you understood what I've been saying?"

"Of course." Martin was offended. "What do you think I am, a tourist? I've lived here for fifteen years; my wife's Iranian."

"You have cancer, Mr. Seymour. We need to operate on your liver and your spinal cord. I can't say how long it will take to recover from the surgery."

Martin's skin tingled with fear, as if the gruff, middle-aged man seated in front of him had just brandished a knife in his face. It wasn't that he'd lacked the vocabulary to understand the message the first time, but for him, *sarataan* carried none of the terrible resonance of its English equivalent.

"I have cancer?"

"Yes."

"But it's operable?"

"The operation will help," the doctor assured him.

"How much?" Martin understood how absurd it was to demand certainty when he'd barely been diagnosed, but he couldn't keep his mouth shut. "Can you cure it? If you cut out what you've found then follow up with drugs and radiation, will that finish it off?"

The doctor said, "We'll see."

14

As Nasim sat waiting for Blank Frank to be rebuilt, she suddenly had a vision of herself standing at the edge of an aquarium pool, trying to persuade a two-hundred-tonne blue whale to swat a ball through a hoop with its nose. However smart the animal was, and however agile it could be in the open ocean, the real trick was finding a way for it to move without crushing everything in sight.

She'd managed to shoehorn the project into Zendegi's existing lease of computing resources from the Cloud; even so, the petabytes of data she was manipulating were almost choking the allocated racetrack memory. Paying for more storage wasn't an option; the boss had agreed to let her play around for a while to see if this wild idea panned out, but only if she could keep the whole thing from showing up in the accounts.

The model-building algorithm she'd used all those years ago on the zebra finch data did not scale well, but after she and Bahador had spent a fortnight trying to refine it, to no avail, she'd decided to plow ahead regardless. They needed some results to show to investors as soon as possible; elegance and efficiency could come later.

Bahador knocked and entered the room; Nasim had taken to leaving the door half open to spare him the formalities.

"We're getting a strong demand surge from the southeast Asian arcades," he said. "We're still below critical latency, but it's tight."

"Okay." Nasim gritted her teeth. "If you have to, just… kill all my stuff."

"Will do." Bahador departed as quietly as he'd come.

You could have argued with me, Nasim thought irritably. *At least gone through the motions, before accepting the inevitable.* She watched the progress bars from her half-dozen tasks inching toward completion. Normally she would have been delighted that so many Indonesians and Malaysians were starting their weekend with an hour or two in Zendegi, but the racetrack drives she was sharing with these gamers were the only place she had to hold the intermediate results of her calculations. If Zendegi needed the storage there was no question of saving what she had in an offline back-up; writing that much data to holographic dye cubes would take hours. She'd simply have to hand the space over immediately, tossing a day's work into the void.

The HCP had scanned the brains of more than four thousand subjects in unprecedented detail; most of the scans had been done on cadavers, but diffusion tensor imaging, which tracked the flow of water molecules along living nerve fibers, had also been employed. The full data set included equal numbers of males and females, but for the kind of composite model Nasim was trying to build it was worth analyzing the sexes separately, removing at least one source of variation; the more alike the brains' anatomy and organization, the clearer the final picture would be. She'd started with the males, because she knew that if she'd chosen females for the demonstration everyone would have demanded to know why. But the model-building algorithm needed to generate temporary data for every possible *pair* of scans. Even using just the male subjects meant dealing with close on two million pairings.

One task reached its endpoint, saving its results and freeing up its working storage and processor allocation. *Go see a movie instead*, Nasim begged the teenagers of Kuala Lumpur. *Just for tonight.*

She brought up a latency histogram. It was flickering at the edge of critical, with a small proportion of customers experiencing minor, sporadic delays between their actions and the changes they wrought upon the virtual world. Mere head movements were handled locally, within the *ghal'eha*; no amount of congestion within Zendegi's servers could disrupt the relationship between the user's gaze and the image rendered in their goggles. But the object descriptions being fed to the castles needed to be updated rapidly enough to maintain the illusion of a fluid, responsive world. A tranquil stroll across a Martian desert might not suffer from a few extra milliseconds of latency, but a game of virtual table tennis could go downhill very fast. And while the brain was good at filtering out brief perceptual glitches, once they crossed a certain threshold all it could do was encourage you to stop indulging in risky behavior for the sensorially confused—preferably after getting rid of the suspect contents of your stomach.

A second task finished. A third. Nasim peeked at one of the high-load games, looking down on a group of six hundred Indonesians who'd come together on a single, crowded battlefield to take on an army of leering demons. Along with their implausible rippling physiques, most of the good guys had magic charms and special powers—hard-won in gruelling quests, or stolen in battle, or maybe just bought with real money on the side. But nobody had signed up to play the spawn of the underworld; the enemy was entirely simulated. The game's designers had the mechanics of a certain style of swordplay down pat, and Zendegi's framework made the demons' motions anatomically plausible, but aside from threats to tear out their opponents' hearts they weren't much good at repartee.

Perhaps none of the boisterous young men and women playing *Minions of Eblis* really wanted an opponent who was anything more than a robotic caricature of evil—and encouraging the beheading of more empathetic characters was not on any sane person's wish-list. But in other games there were Proxies playing comrades and team-mates, guides and mentors, humble massed extras and world-shaking deities. Expanding the Proxies' repertoire far beyond the range of these glowering, tongue-poking puppets would see players flock to Zendegi just as surely as if their competitors' worlds had faded to black and white.

Nasim's fourth task finished. It took all the self-discipline she could muster not to message Bahador to hold off regardless, to give her ten minutes more, no matter what havoc it caused. Even a few dozen customers with nausea or vertigo would be too high a price to pay; word of such incidents spread quickly, even when it was all down to idiots who couldn't grasp the fact that they really *were* jogging after filling their stomachs with food.

The fifth task completed. Nasim glanced again at the *Minions* battlefield; the ground was soaked in green blood, the enemy almost vanquished, but if she remembered rightly, some of the demons had a habit of rising up and reconnecting their own heads. If she'd been feeling sufficiently ruthless she could have sought out the hidden levers that would keep these monsters down—but if news of her intervention ever got out, the stench would be worse than any number of *ghal'eha* full of vomit.

The sixth progress bar hit its endpoint and vanished. Nasim was dazed; she hadn't expected her luck to hold out. Now that the neural model had been rebuilt and safely stored, the vast digital scratchpad needed to create it was no longer required. She could test the end product at her leisure.

Bahador appeared in the doorway and asked hopefully, "May I—?" He must have been watching the race as closely as she had.

Nasim smiled. "Sure. Take a seat." Her desktop monitor had back-to-back screens; she switched on the flip-side and set it to mirror the main screen so Bahador could watch from his side of the desk.

Nasim took a few deep breaths. All the awkward maneuvering with cranes and slings to get the whale into position for each trial took so much time and effort that she sometimes longed for a little more rigmarole surrounding the test itself. But she'd automated everything and now she could invoke the whole complex set-up with a single gesture. She pointed at the icon on the screen and mimed tapping it.

Half-a-dozen windows opened in rapid succession. The largest contained what looked at first glance like a real-time MRI image of a living human brain. A second glance revealed that an awful lot of vital brain tissue was missing, so it was hard to see how the subject could possibly be alive. Nevertheless, regions of the scan were lighting up, displaying patterns of normal, healthy activity that any neurologist would recognize.

A male voice began to speak in English:

"It was the best of times, it was the worst of times, it was the age of wisdom, it was the age of foolishness, it was the epoch of belief, it was the epoch of incredulity, it was the season of light, it was the season of darkness."

The voice was faltering and flat. It might have belonged to an unenthusiastic, not-too-bright ten-year-old struggling to read aloud for his teacher, putting on a strange accent to amuse his classmates. The text-to-speech feature in the cheapest notepad was a model of perfect diction and clarity by comparison.

But this voice was not powered by a phonetic dictionary and a list of explicit contextual rules, assembled by lexicographers and linguists, then tweaked by comparison with millions of training sets. This voice was the product of nothing but the model-building algorithm's best guess at the detailed neural wiring of half-a-dozen regions in a hypothetical adult human brain: a brain that was the functional best fit to the two thousand males that had been scanned for the HCP.

"'The *epoch* of *incredulity*,'" Nasim echoed. "Not bad for a lowest-common-denominator vocabulary."

Bahador smiled nervously. "Can you push it a bit further? See if it stays on track?" The previous iteration had read as far as the second "times" before it ceased paying attention to the text and began emitting a disturbing, not-quite-random word salad.

Nasim fed in another piece of the sample text. The simulation had no hands to reposition a virtual page, no head to tilt to change its angle of view, but it could move its virtual eyeballs across a paragraph, and it was predisposed to read whatever fell within its visual field.

"It was the spring of hope," the voice continued. "It was the winter of despair. We had everything before us, we had nothing before us, we were all going direct to Heaven, we were all going direct the other way—in short, the period was so far like the present period, that some of its noisiest authorities insisted on its being received, for good or for evil, in the super..."

super… superlative degree of comparison only."

"One stutter," Nasim acknowledged. "After more than a hundred words. And all this with a skull full of empty space." She'd used a library of task-specific activation maps to select the regions of the brain to model—and in his present incarnation, Blank Frank possessed only the bare minimum needed to recite what was put in front of him. He had no ability to ponder the meaning of this quote from Dickens, to reflect on its imagery, to pursue its implications. He would not even recall the words a few seconds later; he possessed only working memory, a rolling present no deeper than it needed to be to parse a sentence. He could read a virtual teleprompter; anything more was beyond him.

As a proof of principle, though, he was spectacular. Every one of the two thousand male subjects scanned by the HCP would have acquired each word in their vocabulary under different circumstances. Over time, those words would have accreted vastly different associations. *Hope? Despair?* What kind of heart-breaking personal meaning had those strings of letters once carried for each of these men? Yet the algorithm had managed to peel away the tangle of idiosyncrasies and home in on the simplest common ground.

"So how do you teach him Farsi?" Bahador wondered. "Or Bahasa, or Arabic?"

"He's barely ten minutes old, and you want him to be a polyglot?"

"Won't he have to be, eventually?" Bahador insisted gently.

Nasim rubbed her temples, half-grateful, half-annoyed to be brought down to Earth so quickly. How close were they to impressing a potential investor? Back in Redland's lab her colleagues would have been awestruck, but winning over the Giorgio Omanis was another matter.

"How do we persuade a mob of jaded algae-barons—who don't even appreciate Zendegi as it is!—that a dim, monolingual zombie is the key to the next big thing in VR?" She thought for a while. "Maybe we just need to find the right metaphor. Why not sell this as 'strip-mining the brain'?"

Bahador looked uncomfortable. "Don't forget that we're talking about good Muslim boys; they might be partial to the occasional whisky, but any suggestion of grave-robbing is going to give them the heebie-jeebies."

Nasim scowled. "Organ transplants are perfectly acceptable in Islam, so I really don't see why—"

Bahador fixed her with an incredulous gaze. "You really think it's that simple? I'm not saying that if some cleric was persuaded to consider the matter for a decade or two you couldn't end up with a favorable ruling, but I wouldn't take it as given that anyone else will see this as cut and dried the way you do."

"The donors all gave unrestricted consent," Nasim said stubbornly. "That ought to be the end of the matter."

"Fine. So if you want an investor, find one who thinks the same way. You must have met a few godless American businessmen who'd think nothing of 'strip-mining' dead people's brains."

"I was a student!" Nasim retorted. "My friends were all students. Not everyone in America is a millionaire."

Bahador spread his hands. "Well, don't look at me. I'm the one who has to hide when the sheikhs come for tea." He glanced at his watch. "I'd better go keep an eye on the Indian surge if we don't want to lose the last of our loyal fans there."

Nasim nodded distractedly. When he'd left, she sat brooding. Personal connections weren't everything, and it probably wouldn't be too hard to get in touch with a few technology venture capitalists outside the company's usual circle of Arab and Iranian backers. Anywhere in East Asia, Europe or North America her track record at MIT would at least get her a hearing. But even if she could find potential investors with no ethical or cultural objections to exploiting the HCP donors this way, how many of them would see Blank Frank as anything more than a novelty act? A digital mosaic of corpse brains that read Dickens would look about as promising to most people as a car engine based on Galvani's twitching frog legs.

What she needed was someone at least as optimistic as she was about the technology's potential. Someone who'd listen to Frank's leaden recitation and picture a whole army of nimble, articulate Proxies rising from the same scans. Someone who'd convinced themselves long ago that the Human Connectome Project was destined to do more than help cure a few neurological diseases.

Maybe she should try the more conventional sources first, though, and leave Caplan as a last resort. She knew that he'd assembled a small empire of niche technology businesses, but she hadn't really followed his fortunes; she wasn't even sure that he still had money to burn. He could have squandered his inheritance on legal battles with the Superintelligence Project, trawling the world for homeless amnesiacs willing to swear that they were Zachary Churchland's love-child.

But the longer Nasim spent turning the options over in her mind, the more it seemed that her reservations were just excuses to spare her pride. She couldn't recall every word that she'd spoken to Caplan the last time they'd met, but she'd certainly spurned him comprehensively enough to make it awkward to come begging for his help all these years later.

Well, too bad. She couldn't afford to shunt her best prospect to the end of the list. She had a choice between wasting six months collecting polite, frozen smiles from a dozen cautious entrepreneurs, or going straight to the loose cannon who'd once tried to force half a million dollars into her hands on the strength of a rabbit icon on a map of Cambridge.

Nasim entered the boardroom and took a pair of augmentation goggles from the cabinet near the door. She spent half a minute fussing with the strap, trying to make the goggles fit comfortably; the room was equipped with the technology for the sake of impressing clients, but she rarely had reason to use it herself.

She sat at the empty conference table and waited.

Caplan came online punctually, appearing to be seated directly opposite her. Their two tables were apparently close enough in size for the software to decide to re-scale everything so they were superimposed exactly, which made for less visual fuss. Nasim had deliberately cleared the space where she'd expected Caplan to show up, and he'd shown her the same courtesy, but elsewhere around the table chairs from the two locations intersected haphazardly. The room he was in was a little smaller than hers, so his walls were ghosted around her to remind her not to step through them.

"You're looking well, Nasim," Caplan said mildly.

"You too." In fact, he barely seemed to have aged since they'd last met. Maybe the caloric restriction program was worth it after all, assuming this wasn't just vanity and software. Nasim was showing herself honestly enough; routine distractions had kept her from updating her conferencing icon for about eighteen months, but she was quite sure that this small oversight was not enough to make her look twenty-five.

"I read your proposal," Caplan said. "What you've achieved so far is impressive."

"Thank you." Nasim's mouth was dry; she'd already grovelled a little in the email she'd sent him, but she was steeling herself for a certain amount of retributive gloating.

"If I've understood you correctly," Caplan continued, "the main pay-off you see coming from this work is a set of stand-alone modules that your games developers will be able to call on, to assist them in programming a limited range of Proxy behaviors."

"That's exactly right," Nasim replied. "There are some aspects of so-cial—and even spatial—intelligence where humans still out-perform our best algorithms. If we can isolate a set of basic skills from the HCP data, then offer them up as a kind of library that developers can hook into with a minimum of fuss, that will benefit them enormously."

"But most aspects of the Proxies will remain the province of ordinary software?" Caplan pressed her. "Biographical details, long-term context, strategic considerations—"

"Of course," Nasim confirmed. "Even if we could construct a 'whole brain' model that included the neural dynamics needed to support long-term memory, and even if we could figure out how to wire a Proxy's notional back-story into that model... that wouldn't just be wildly ambitious, it would be inefficient and highly inconvenient. Developers need to have a simple database of facts about their non-player characters that they can manipulate as easily as the geographical database for the game world. Sure, they want certain responses to the human players to be more natural, but not at the expense of an ability to follow pre-determined scripts, or adopt explicitly programmed strategies. Trying to implement too much as part of the neural model would just make those things more difficult."

"Hmm." Caplan glanced down at some notes displayed on the table-top. "You mention reading players' facial expressions?"

Nasim gestured at her goggles; they'd be invisible to Caplan, but they both knew they were there. "In less than a year, these will be replaced by contact lenses. It won't be long before we routinely have an unobstructed view of players' faces."

Caplan said, "Sure, but don't you think human face-reading skills have already been surpassed by micro-expression analysis?"

"Perhaps," Nasim conceded. "But it might still be useful to developers to have something less forensic, for those times when they want a Proxy who seems attentive or sympathetic, rather than one who can beat you at poker or deliver a knock-out cross-examination in a murder trial. Anyway, that's only one skill out of dozens."

"Many of the other skills are verbal, though, aren't they?" Caplan pointed out. "I'm still not quite clear what the deal is with language."

"Ah." Nasim knew this was her weakest point, but she confronted it head-on. "Obviously the HCP data itself will only encode knowledge of English; that's the nature of the population they scanned. In the worst-case scenario, that *could* mean that we'd have to restrict our verbal modules to English, which we'd then license to VR providers with a large English-language customer base. Even so, that's a huge market, so we could expect a decent return in terms of revenue even if we couldn't use the same modules generally within Zendegi itself."

"And the less worse-case?"

"We could probably exploit English-based modules in non-English scenarios to some degree, just by feeding their input and output through existing translation software—just as we do for players who don't share a common language. But I'd hope we could do one better than that and train at least some of the modules to be bilingual."

"Expose them to huge data-sets and tweak them to give the right responses?" Caplan suggested.

"Yes."

"While hoping you don't obliterate the very skills that make these networks more useful than the dumb translator software that gets created the same way?"

Nasim replied, "Well, yes. We can only try it and see how it pans out. What else should we do?"

Caplan said, "Have you ever heard of *side-loading?*"

"No," Nasim confessed.

Caplan smiled slightly. "You didn't research me very thoroughly, did you? Just checked that I still had a pulse and a bank balance."

Nasim felt herself flush slightly, but took some comfort in the fact that her icon wouldn't betray her response. She said, "I'm sorry if I didn't dig deeply enough. I think I got distracted when I discovered that you owned an island in Cyber-Jahan."

"Doesn't everyone? They're so cheap." Caplan dismissed the matter with a wave of his hand. "Anyway... ten years ago I acquired a Swiss company called Eikonometrics." He slid a document across the table. Nasim glanced down; it was a report on the company's research over the last fiscal year. A soft blue glow at the edges flagged it as a file Caplan had put into their shared dataspace, rather than a physical stack of paper.

"They started out in subliminal image classification," Caplan explained. "They had a plan to harvest the brain-power of internet users by flashing up flowers and puppy dogs and road crash scenes just long enough to get a distinctive EEG signature. It was a very silly idea; some aspects of artificial vision might still be inferior to the equivalent human skills, but software caught up with the kind of results you could get on the cheap like that a long time ago."

"So why did you buy them?"

"Their business plan sucked," Caplan said, "but they'd gained some genuine insight into neural information processing, and they'd started branching out into EBLD—Evidence-Based Lie Detection. Polygraphs are about as reliable as witch-dunking, so it's not a huge boast to say that twenty-first century brain-scanning techniques have the potential to outperform them. You stick a witness in a PET scanner or MRI machine and see what parts of their brain light up when they discuss their testimony or view certain images. There was a fad for that in the teens, and Eikonometrics got some grants and did some interesting research. But then it became clear that in any practical context there were too many problems interpreting the responses—and most jurisdictions started ruling it out on privacy as well as technical grounds. That's when Eikonometrics shares hit rock-bottom, and I would have been crazy not to snap them up."

"Okay." Nasim was starting to get an inkling of where this was heading. "And side-loading… ?"

"*Side-loading*," Caplan replied, "is the process of training a neural network to mimic a particular organic brain, based on a rich set of non-intrusive scans of the brain in action. It's midway between the extremes: in classic uploading, you look at the brain's anatomy in microscopic detail and try to reproduce everything from that, whereas in classic neural-network training, what's available to you is just stimulus and response: sensory input and visible behavior, with the brain as a black box.

"In side-loading, you get to peer inside the box, even if you don't get to take it apart. You don't have the resolution you'd get by peeling the brain with an ATLUM, but you have the advantage that you can expose the living brain to all kinds of stimuli—words, images, sounds, tastes, smells—and see how they bounce around inside the skull. And it doesn't really matter how little external behavior is evoked if you can watch the pattern of *internal changes* rippling out from every stone you toss in."

Nasim said, "That all sounds fine in principle. But how far has it actually taken you?"

Caplan gestured at the Eikonometrics report. "Six months ago, we took a rat that had been trained to solve a particular maze. By observing its brain's responses to a barrage of random sensory cues, we managed to modify an initially unrelated virtual rat to run the same maze."

"Observing its brain *how?* Do you mean micro-electrodes snuggling up to ten thousand neurons?"

Caplan shook his head. "Not at all. Purely non-invasive methods: multi-mode MRI and surface electrodes."

Nasim was impressed now; this was more than she'd expected. "And with humans?"

"With humans," Caplan said, "the problem is that we don't really have a good generic virtual brain to use as a starting point. When the HCP published their results we started trying to construct one, but it looks as if you're doing a much better job at that than we are so far."

Nasim mulled over this frank assessment, sting included. The algorithm she'd used on the finch brains was public knowledge, but it wasn't so cut and dried that someone coming in cold could apply it to the HCP scans and expect to crank out a good result. So she had a head-start on the path toward something Caplan wanted, badly—but it would be a mistake to overplay her hand and imagine that this made her indispensable.

"So you think Eikonometrics can find a way to side-load languages into my Proxy modules?" she asked.

"I think it's worth trying," Caplan said. "I think it's your best chance. And there might be some other useful skills you could endow them with, the same way." He smiled. "Since I got your email, I've been giving that some thought. Suppose you could side-load motor skills from a few celebrity athletes: sign up the right soccer players and the Middle East is yours again. Add the right cricket players, and Cyber-Jahan is history."

Nasim was speechless. Motor skills were probably the simplest case imaginable—certainly less challenging than side-loading a second language. And Caplan was right: millions of people would vote with their credit cards to "play beside" their sporting heroes, captured with an authenticity that no celebrity-endorsed console game could ever come close to achieving.

The most she'd been expecting from Caplan was a modest cash injection, giving her a chance to pursue her research far enough to see if it could be commercialised. Instead, he'd just offered Zendegi a plausible route to market domination.

Nasim forced herself to reply coolly, "It seems we both have something the other could use."

Caplan inclined his head in agreement.

She said, "I'm going to have to discuss this with my superiors." If the Eikonometrics research was as promising as Caplan made it sound, Nasim was sure she could hook them on the sporting angle alone. "And there'll be a complex joint venture agreement to be thrashed out—"

Caplan said, "I understand. Bring on the lawyers! But don't run away and hide this time. Don't forget, you're at the heart of the deal."

Nasim laughed, but she regarded his bland, youthful icon with unease. Caplan would emerge with a substantial stake in the company, but this wasn't just about the cash flow that a synergistic marriage of their technologies could yield.

By setting up this meeting, she'd probably saved her job, her employer, her career... but no amount of commercial success with the Proxies would be enough for Caplan. She knew what the only worthwhile endpoint was for him—and she'd just agreed to harness herself to his cause.

15

Martin ran two kilometers on the treadmill. It took him fifteen minutes, and by the time he'd finished he was drenched in sweat—but then, that was the whole point of the exercise.

He grabbed a mat from a pile in the corner of the gym, put his towel over it and knelt down. He wiped the sweat from his eyes, then slipped on the goggles that were linked to the Physiotherapy Department's computers. When he looked down, his clothes had vanished from sight, along with much of his body: skin, fat, blood vessels, genitals, viscera. All that remained of him was muscle, bones and tendons. The towel beneath him was gone as well; he appeared to be kneeling on a transparent cushion that was supporting him over a mirrored surface that had replaced part of the gym's carpeted floor.

He moved his right foot in front of him, to the left, as he lowered his chest toward the ground, stretching out his left leg behind him to lie flat, while his right leg was bent and trapped beneath him. Looking down at his virtual reflection, he could see the piriformis muscle that crossed his right buttock at the back of his hip, helpfully highlighted in blue.

The operation to remove the tumor on his spine had impinged on a nerve in his spinal cord, giving rise to a month of excruciating pain. The pain felt as if it was in the muscle, though that had not actually been damaged at all: the pain there was a phantom, a false message. But his body didn't know the difference, and the muscle had clenched up tightly to protect itself against the perceived injury. Now that the nerve had settled down, that tightness had turned the original phantom pain into a self-fulfilling prophecy: the piriformis muscle really *was* the problem now. Not only had it been damaged by its own defensive response, by refusing to move normally it was pulling everything else around it out of shape. It needed to be coaxed back into its old routine, but after a month spent cowed and quivering, that was easier said than done.

Martin leaned forward as far as he could; the pressure on his right leg as he folded it against his body was transferred to the piriformis, stretching it a little. He kept the position for a count of twenty, then eased off.

Resting, he gazed down at the reflection of the back of his leg, at the inelegant network of fleshy ropes that had managed to tug itself so far out of balance that he was still taking painkillers just to sleep. There was something almost comical about the fact that the cancer itself had, so far, given him no pain, and the sophisticated drugs targeted against it had left him with none of the side-effects he'd been prepared to face, based on a lifetime of media images of people on chemotherapy. Instead, he just felt as if he'd been kicked in the arse by a donkey.

He leaned forward again, holding the stretch to thirty this time, trying to persuade the stupid muscle that its cringing was only making things worse. When he relaxed he scrutinized the result; he could have sworn that the bundle of blue fibers was already a few millimeters longer than when he'd started. But the imagery he was seeing wasn't likely to be that accurate; he didn't have magic MRI-vision, showing him his true anatomy in real time. It was all just an educated guess, a simulation cobbled together from a month-old scan and some postural cues extracted from ceiling cameras in the gym and the goggles' superficial terahertz view of his body. It could help him perform the exercise correctly, by looking for the same information as a human physiotherapist would, but that was it. He couldn't look down and search himself for new secondary tumors.

He did the piriformis stretch five times, then swapped legs and repeated the set; his left side was giving him no trouble, but the aim was to keep everything symmetrical. Then he went through half-a-dozen other lower-back exercises diligently enough, but with rather less zeal. They were all beneficial, and he didn't doubt his physio's advice for a moment, but it was hard to feel a sense of urgency over slightly stiff hamstrings; none of this routine was going to make a difference to the cancer, at least not directly, but if he could win back pain-free days and drug-free sleep, that would be both a victory in itself and a plausible boon to his overall health.

Martin showered and headed out of the hospital. He'd barely taken three steps along the road when a shabby white car pulled up beside him and a man in his twenties called out, "Taxi?" The car bore no company insignia; everyone in Iran was a taxi driver when they felt like it.

Martin nodded and got in the front seat; they agreed on a price to his home. After Martin replied tersely to his attempts to start a conversation, the driver cranked up the volume on his stereo, unleashing a track with a female vocalist who sounded like an Iranian Céline Dion interspersed with an insipid male rapper.

Martin tried to be stoical, but the song was too loud to blank out and too excruciating to ignore. "Please, would you mind turning that down?" he begged.

The driver didn't seem offended, but he held out his hand. "Extra service."

Martin said, "Forget it. Please stop the car."

The young man pondered this new request. "You should pay me for my trouble."

Martin was unmoved; they'd gone barely a hundred meters. "If you want flag-fall, get yourself a taxi licence. Just stop the car."

"You have to pay me!" the man insisted, outraged. "You want me to call the police?"

"Go ahead." Martin opened the door; the driver panicked and screeched to a halt, allowing him to disembark.

Martin slammed the door and walked away down Enqelab Avenue, trying to remember where the bus stop was. He paused and steadied himself against the side wall of a news kiosk, listening to the whine of motorbikes weaving through the pedestrians. He needed the treadmill to warm up before stretching, but it took away his energy for half the day.

He had to be patient. In six months, the perfect new liver being cultured from his own modified skin cells would be fully grown, ready to replace the tattered organ from which the primary tumor had been sliced. Ten years ago, stage four cholangiocarcinoma would have been a death sentence—and any form of treatment a gruelling ordeal—but Martin's weekly injections had no side-effects at all. Twenty-four hours a day, the artificial antibodies with toxins attached were bumping into the cancer cells strewn throughout his body and polishing them off, with no collateral damage. Nothing was certain—the metastasizing cells could always acquire resistance—but his oncologist said he had a thirty per cent chance of surviving five more years. Thirty per cent, up from zero with the old treatments.

Martin found the bus stop. At home, he set his alarm clock, then undressed and climbed into bed. The donkey-kick burned, but he wasn't supposed to take any more codeine before evening. He closed his eyes and pictured Mahnoosh beside him.

"I miss you," he whispered. He felt a twinge of guilt; sometimes it felt dishonest, or, perversely, like a kind of infidelity to summon up her presence.

"What's the problem?" she said. "I don't want to be forgotten."

Maybe not. Or am I just putting words into your mouth?

"As if I'd let you," she replied scornfully.

Martin suddenly recalled the night, not long after she'd moved in with him, when she'd been undressing for bed and he'd started chanting raucously, "Loose the Noosh! Loose the Noosh!" She'd thrown a bedside lamp at him and broken his nose.

She said, "Give me your hand."

She held it tightly as he drifted into shallow sleep, and when the alarm screeched three hours later, she still hadn't deserted him.

Martin was at the school five minutes before the bell. The other parents nodded to him, but didn't come too close; a few had tried to talk to him in the past, but there had always been a fundamental disjunction between the way they'd felt obliged to engage sympathetically with his family's tragedy, and the way Martin had preferred that they mind their own fucking business.

Javeed emerged from his classroom staring at the ground. When he finally looked up and saw that Martin was there, his expression of relief was haunted, provisional: this time his father had come, but there was always tomorrow. Martin fought against the instinct to smother him in reassuring promises: *I won't leave you, pesaram; you'll never be alone.* Even if he'd believed the words himself, why would Javeed take them seriously? His radiant mother had died without warning, in perfect health. What could his gray-haired, limping, jaundiced father possibly say to regain an aura of invulnerability?

Martin took his hand and they walked across the playground. "What did you do today?"

"Just stuff."

"Nothing exciting?"

Javeed didn't reply.

"Any pictures for me?"

Javeed stopped and unzipped his backpack. He took out a rolled-up sheet of what Martin always thought of as butcher's paper and offered it to him. Martin unfurled it to reveal a drawing in colored pencil.

A bird with a dog's head hovered over a nest on a mountainside; on closer inspection, it looked as if the nest was made of whole tree trunks. Inside the nest, a blond-haired boy stood stretching up his hands. The bird, the Simorgh, was holding a dead lamb in its claws.

"She brought him some food?" Martin asked.

Javeed nodded.

"So she's a friendly bird, she's not too scary?"

"She's friendly to Zal," Javeed agreed. "But he won't stay with her forever. His father comes and takes him back home."

"It's a good picture."

Martin rolled it up and Javeed stored it in his backpack again. Martin said, "No taxi today, we're going to catch the bus." Javeed was surprised, then he smiled approvingly. The bus to the city took a slow, complicated route, but they caught it so rarely that it still had some novelty value.

The journey took them past the bookshop; Martin cringed a little to see the crowds walking straight by the security shutters, not even able to window-shop. He was still paying rent on the premises, frittering away Mahnoosh's life insurance; he should make up his mind to reopen the place with an assistant, or try to sell the business. *People of the Book*. On the day they'd signed the lease, he'd insisted to Mahnoosh—with a straight face, for almost half an hour—that her own mildly ironic suggestion was a faint-hearted choice, and they really ought to call themselves *The Nicest of the Damned*.

When they reached their destination Martin apologized to Omar; they were half an hour late, and Omar always set aside two *ghal'eha* for them. "I wish you'd let me pay you what you're missing out on."

"It's once a week, it's nothing," Omar retorted. "Ah, here's the big warrior." He squatted down and kissed Javeed on the cheeks, then handed him a square of *gaz*.

"Where's Farshid?" Javeed asked anxiously.

"Helping someone carry a TV to their car," Omar said. "Don't worry, he'll be here when you're finished."

Martin and Javeed went upstairs on their own. They were becoming used to the mechanics of the process; after they'd put on their gloves and goggles, Martin held up his notepad to the two *ghal'eha* in turn. The machines read Nasim's certificate and made the connection to Zendegi; all he and Javeed had to do was step inside. As the rim of Martin's castle ascended, he saw one of their neighbors' spheres spinning furiously. Even through the sound-proofing he could hear a muffled trace of its inhabitant's rapid footfalls until his own bubble closed around him.

When Martin lowered the goggles' screens the bland white space of the castle vanished immediately and he was standing beside Javeed at the edge of a desert oasis. No gentle, staged transitions and no menus to deal with. They had made their selection on the weekend through Zendegi's website, sparing them all the preliminaries now.

Javeed gazed wide-eyed at the building that lay ahead of them in the distance. "King Zahhak's palace!" They'd seen pictures of the pale-brown mud-brick fortress when they'd chosen the story, but the sense of immersion, the knowledge that they'd stepped right into the picture, was already enough to render the sight far more vivid. In spite of the building material, the architecture was impressively crisp, with near-perfect scallops capping the walls above a series of narrow, slotted windows for archers. A cylindrical tower stood at each corner, with walls in exactly the same style; no fancy battlements here.

Javeed began striding across the sand, glancing toward Martin almost surreptitiously, as if he didn't want to be caught checking that his father was keeping up. They both wore white *dishdashas*, traditional Arab robes; this story came from the *Shahnameh* but it wasn't set in Persia. Martin had done more than enough treadmill work for one day, so he used a discreet hand gesture to tell Zendegi to amplify his steps. The result wasn't quite seven-league boots, but it enabled his icon to walk vigorously with almost no effort on his part.

The dusty trail leading into the oasis gave way to a broad, palm-lined avenue strewn with small white stones. Horses and camels rested on the shaded grass beside the road; streams rose from beneath the ground, feeding a series of shallow pools. Javeed, usually shy with strangers, called out, "*Salaam!*" to a group of older boys tending the animals, and they replied with friendly waves. Martin doubted that there were humans behind their welcoming smiles—who would choose to take on such a tiny role?—but he could still appreciate the warmth of their greeting for what it was, a part of the atmosphere. Nobody in a painting, a movie, a book, could ever be your friend back in the real world; that didn't render the whole exercise deluded or dishonest.

As they drew closer to the palace the streets filled with people and they found themselves weaving through a crowded bazaar. For their benefit, everyone around them was speaking Farsi—albeit without the usual modern colloquialisms, and in accents that sounded plausibly Arabic to Martin's ear, down to "w" in place of "v" and "b" in place of "p". Customers were haggling with traders for bolts of cloth, jewellery, fruit, grain, spices. Martin felt a pang of guilt at the sheer profligacy of the backdrop—surely software couldn't conjure all of this effortlessly; surely some human designer had slaved for days to get the details right?—but then he decided that it was probably all recycled, with a little tweaking, from one setting to the next. There were a thousand games and stories that would need a bazaar like this; once all the elements were set up, changing the faces and permuting the merchandise would probably be easy enough.

Javeed stopped, confused. "Where's the man who'll give us the job?"

"We have to go through the bazaar to the side of the palace. Remember?"

"He doesn't have an office here?"

Martin smiled. "I don't think so." Maybe it made sense that the king's elaborate domestic bureaucracy ought to have a recruitment center out in the bazaar, but the notes on the website had pointed them toward the palace kitchens themselves.

At Martin's urging, Javeed asked directions from a carpet merchant; they didn't have time to get lost in this maze. The woman's instructions led them past an unsavoury-looking garbage dump; it was mercifully incapable of sharing its aromas, but the buzz of flies alone was enough to turn Martin's stomach.

There was a bead-curtained doorway at the kitchen's entrance to keep out the insects without blocking the passage of air. Martin parted the curtain with his hands, wondering for a moment if Zendegi was tweaking the physics to ensure that not one bead brushed his face or shoulders and punctured his suspension of disbelief. The room was dim after the afternoon sunshine; when his eyes had adjusted he saw sacks of rice and legumes, and shelves stacked with earthenware bottles.

A harried-looking middle-aged man came through from an adjoining room. He introduced himself as Amir and greeted them politely, but it was clear that he expected them to explain their business without delay. Against all plausible cultural norms, it was Javeed he engaged with directly.

"We're looking for work," Javeed explained.

"Really? What can you do?"

"I can sweep the floors," Javeed said. "My father can carry things."

Amir looked dubious. "You have a strong back?" he asked Martin.

"Yes, sir." That might have been a bare-faced lie in the real world, but the morning's exercise had actually left him feeling flexible. If he was dealing with weightless provisions, he could probably lift enough to feed a small army.

Amir turned to Javeed. "And you're a hard worker? The new cook won't forgive a scrap of dirt on the floor."

"I'll do a good job," Javeed promised.

Amir made an elaborate pantomime of thinking it over, running his hand through his beard and scowling as if weighing up all manner of pros and cons, but this part of the story was pre-ordained.

"You'll need to start straight away," he said finally. "There's a banquet tonight, for the king and three hundred guests. The cook will expect to find everything spotless."

"Thank you, sir," Martin said. "You won't be disappointed."

He reached down and tapped the back of Javeed's hand.

"Thank you," Javeed added. Martin was glad that his son understood that Amir was no more real than the guides and assistants who smiled out from the screen of their home computer—but if they were going to take the story seriously, he expected Javeed to behave with courtesy—even if only to avoid acquiring bad habits.

Amir returned to his office, where he appeared to be agonizing over the accounts. Martin wondered if the plot generator stretched to the kitchen manager embezzling money to bale out his no-good, hard-gambling brother-in-law, but he wasn't about to hijack Javeed's crucial mission just to test the machinery at its margins.

Martin found the broom and handed it to Javeed. Even though the haptic gloves could exert no net force, the sensations they produced were enough to make light objects feel eerily tangible. As Javeed set to work, Martin didn't envy him; the floor was filthy, and sweeping up nonexistent dust and food scraps would be barely less tiring than doing the same thing for real.

When Javeed had finished in the storeroom, they moved to the preparation room, closer to the kitchen itself. Half-a-dozen kitchen hands—five teenaged boys and an older supervisor named Haidar—were plucking birds, gutting fish, and chopping and peeling vegetables. There were baskets for their waste, but most of it was ending up on the floor. The boys teased Javeed, calling him pipsqueak and dropping handfuls of feathers every time he thought he'd earned a brief rest. Martin watched his son's face; when the pressure started to get too much for him, he took the broom himself. When one of the boys, Ahmed, made as if to brush all his peelings onto a spot Martin had just cleared, Martin rebuked him sharply: "Show some respect and do your job properly." Ahmed looked to Haidar for support, but the man said, "Exactly. You should be busy enough without making trouble." Ahmed sulked for a while, but scooped the peelings into his waste basket.

Haidar addressed Martin. "I need you to bring in ten sacks of rice."

Martin handed the broom to Javeed. When he returned with the first four sacks on his shoulders—if he was going to play at being healthy there was no point taking half-measures—Javeed was gone.

"Where's my son?" he asked Haidar.

"Cleaning up the kitchen."

Martin peered through the doorway nervously, as if the ovens and pots full of scalding water could do Javeed real harm. He hurriedly fetched the rest of the rice, then slipped into the kitchen himself.

Javeed had swapped his broom for a cloth and was down on his hands and knees diligently scrubbing at an oily puddle. This from a boy with no compunction about treating a mustard bottle as a makeshift water-pistol then leaving the aftermath for others to deal with. Three assistants were tending to the stoves; the red reflected glow on their sweaty faces was enough to make Martin feel the oppressive heat himself.

"When's the cook coming in?" he asked one of the assistants, who was stirring the contents of a huge pot.

"Soon," the man replied brusquely.

"I hear he's impressed the king already. And he's only been here three days."

"He's a master of his art," the assistant declared haughtily. "Please, just do your job and stay out of our way."

With most of the pots now simmering gently, and the assistant cooks more fastidious than the kitchen hands, the mess in the preparation room soon became pressing again, and Haidar called them back to his domain. Javeed coped admirably, but Martin could see that he was growing tired. He made a hand gesture to summon up a private menu, invisible to Javeed, and shaved fifteen minutes off the story's overall running time. Javeed always pleaded for a full hour when they were making choices on the weekend, but Martin doubted that he'd feel too cheated by being spared a further dose of medieval toil.

A raised voice spilled out of the kitchen; someone was addressing the assistants in peremptory tones. "More heat, more water, more salt; I explained all of that yesterday. How difficult can it be?" The cook wasn't shouting abuse, but even his gentlest admonitions were followed by a crushed silence. Haidar and the kitchen hands lowered their eyes, their expressions hovering between cowed and reverential.

Javeed whispered, "That's him, Baba." He sounded a little fearful; Martin forced himself not to puncture the mood by grilling him on his resolve to continue.

"Yeah, that's him, all right," Martin agreed solemnly. Javeed knew that he could pull the plug any time he wanted; he didn't need endless prompting.

A skinny black-and-white cat ran across the room and into the kitchen, mewing plaintively. Martin heard the cook laughing, then calling to the cat, clicking his tongue. "You want some food?" he asked. "I doubt there's any to spare, but we'll see."

Javeed was standing in a corner of the room; Martin went and stood beside him. He caught a glimpse of the cat through the doorway, circling around expectantly as if following at the feet of someone who was making promising gestures. The cat began purring loudly, and a hand reached down and stroked its head, long, slender fingers scratching at its ears. "Tsk, tsk, tsk," said the cook. "What have we got for you, I wonder? *What have we got?*" The closer his patter came to baby-talk, the more Martin felt a chill down his spine.

The cat turned in ever tighter circles, rubbing its head against the long fingers. A second hand joined the first, stroking the cat's flank, seeming almost to urge it on as the cat moved faster, its shape blurring with speed, black and white patches melting into gray.

The cook's long hands caressed the whirling cat like a potter molding clay. The sound of its hopeful purring grew louder, pulsing with the pressure of the fingers against its skin. Then the hands squeezed the spinning body tightly, bringing it to a halt before withdrawing from sight. The blur of cat-fur froze into clarity again, but now its shape had changed: its tail and rear end had been replaced by a mirrored copy of its head and chest. The poor animal had been transformed into conjoined twins, with two hungry, complaining mouths in place of one.

The two heads grimaced and snarled at each other; their single body postured and feinted, but the animal was too unbalanced to fight in the way it was accustomed to and within seconds it had been reduced to a writhing, ungainly ring of fur, thrashing around on its side, snapping and clawing at itself.

The cook said coldly, "Plenty of food within your reach now," and kicked the brawling animal out of sight.

Martin looked around the room, but nobody showed any sign of having witnessed the abomination; they had all kept their eyes conveniently averted. For a moment he was close to real frustration and anger: *This "master of his art" is not what he seems, you fools!* But the whole point of the game was for Javeed—and himself, as the hero's sidekick—to be the only ones to understand. The cook was not a man at all: he was the demon Eblis in human form. His culinary skills were meant to seduce this weak-willed king; if the banquet was successful, Zahhak's display of gratitude to his impressive new servant would end in a transformation just as terrifying as the cat's, and vastly more fateful.

Javeed looked daunted; Martin touched his hand. "What are we going to do?" Martin whispered. "If Zahhak likes the food and he embraces the cook—"

"Feathers," Javeed announced. "We have to mix in some feathers."

Martin smiled. "Good idea." He'd been thinking of using a few handfuls of rotting waste from the garbage dump, but this sounded just as effective. It would also spare him any qualms about the wisdom of encouraging his son to spread dysentery.

Haidar and the kitchen hands finished their work: every pheasant had been plucked, every herb chopped, every vegetable diced. As Haidar surveyed the mess on the floor, he promised Javeed, "I'll put in a good word for you with the boss. I'm sure he'll want to keep you on."

Javeed tried to be polite, but he seemed to realize that there'd be something dishonest about assenting to this notion unreservedly. "I might be busy with a different job tomorrow," he confessed.

Haidar was a little taken aback, but his software could supply no sensible response, so he just bid them goodnight and left.

"Have fun, pipsqueak," said Ahmed, brushing a pile of aubergine skins onto the floor.

"I will!" Javeed retorted.

They were alone in the preparation room now. Martin helped Javeed finish sweeping the floor, but as they gathered up the last of the waste and carried most of it out to the dump, they kept one basket aside and filled it with the plucked feathers.

They stood by the kitchen doorway, listening, Javeed still holding his broom in case someone chanced upon them. Finally, the assistant cooks started carrying some of the dishes through to the banquet hall. The cook himself went with them, to watch over the serving of the meal and bask in the king's delighted praise.

Martin peeked into the kitchen. "Okay, it's empty! Quick!"

Javeed carried the basket of feathers past the long row of stoves; it might have been weightless, but he struggled with the sheer size of the basket, which forced him to hold his arms uncomfortably wide. There were only two pots still sitting on the flames, at the far end of the room.

Martin removed the lid from one of the pots and started scooping feathers into the stew. He felt them tickling his palm, and watched them sinking into the simmering liquid. "This is *so* disgusting," he enthused. It was almost impossible not to conjure up images of people pulling feathers from their mouths, grimacing with distaste. Maybe he and Javeed could sneak into the hall and actually witness that spectacle of discomfort. If no one was watching, Zendegi would gloss over all the details, which would be an awful shame.

Javeed tapped his free hand urgently. "Baba, they're coming back!"

Martin hurriedly replaced the lid of the pot. The footsteps were close; the doorway through which they'd entered was too far away. He looked around and saw the entrance to a small room; the door was already half-open. He grabbed the basket with one hand and Javeed with the other and led him into the room.

They stood behind the door. Beside them, metal pots and earthenware vessels were stacked on wooden shelves.

Two of the assistants entered the kitchen, grumbling, and left again—presumably carrying the last of the pots. Martin stuck his head around the door, just in time to spot the shadow of someone else approaching. He withdrew quickly.

"Zahhak, Zahhak, Zahhak!" the cook sighed dreamily. "All I want in thanks is one royal embrace." Martin had read the story in Javeed's book: when the king took the demon cook in his arms in gratitude for so fine a meal, his humble subject kissed him once on each shoulder—and from each shoulder, a snake grew out of the flesh. They were hacked off by the king's surgeons, but rapidly re-grew. The only thing that would appease them was a regular meal of human brains.

The cook whistled happily; from the sound of his footsteps he was practically waltzing around the room. Martin smiled down at Javeed. Soon there'd be shouts of outrage from the banquet hall, and a royal summons quite unlike the one Eblis had been expecting. No beheadings, though; Martin had even emailed Nasim to check that he'd ticked the right boxes to rule out that kind of violence. In the story, Eblis had simply vanished after conjuring up the snakes; confronted with failure, he could do the same.

The whistling stopped abruptly.

"What *do* I smell?" the cook said. "Pheasant blood, raw? When everything's well done?" He made a brutish snuffling sound. Martin glanced at the basket; they hadn't emptied it completely, and there was a residue of blood-caked feathers still sticking to the bottom. "The little pipsqueak left the floor clean, didn't he? No mess in sight. And yet…"

Three soft footsteps in their direction.

"And *yet*…"

Martin tensed, torn by conflicting urges. This was a fairground ride, a ghost train, nothing more. Did he want to smother Javeed, to cheat him of the brief, safe terror that every child craved?

"When is a door," the cook asked, switching to English, "*not a door?*" He'd lost his Arabic accent; now he sounded like James Mason in *Salem's Lot*.

Martin took Javeed's hand and met his eyes, hoping Zendegi could infer and reconstruct his look of reassurance, despite the goggles. He needed Javeed to know that if he was afraid, it was all right to flee—it was all right to give this make-believe world the thumbs-down and simply banish the monster.

"No takers? Really? But it's so simple!" Martin heard breathing just inches away, and a long-fingered hand appeared, clasping the side of the door.

"When it's ajar!"

The cook stepped into view, tall, smiling, reaching down toward Javeed. Martin tried to punch him, but he ducked aside effortlessly; as he did, Javeed slipped around the door. "Run!" Martin yelled after him, jubilant.

The cook rose up to his full height again, smiling at Martin unpleasantly. He was clean-shaven, which seemed like an odd choice for a disguise here, but maybe demons couldn't grow beards.

"Never mind," the cook said. "The pipsqueak's lost, but the father's twice the meal."

"Yeah, yeah," Martin replied. "I'm just the chaperone here, don't knock yourself out for my entertainment."

The cook's skin turned jaundice-yellow, his face haggard, his eyes hollow. Martin felt the donkey-kick aching in recognition; for a second he was back in the hospital gym, staring into a virtual mirror tuned this time to guess-his-future.

The demon's smile grew into a forest of pointed fangs as it bent down toward his shoulder. Martin feinted at its head; it drew back hissing like an angry viper and he quickly squeezed past it and around the door, then picked up the basket of bloodied feathers and swiped the edge across the demon's face. The yellow skin ruptured; maggots swarmed from the wound.

Martin turned and fled. If the thing caught up with him, infected him, *if Javeed saw snakes growing from his body—*

Luckily he'd already switched on his power boots.

Javeed was waiting at the doorway, urging him on, holding out a trembling hand toward him. "Baba! Quick!" Martin grabbed his hand and ran with him across the preparation room, the storeroom, never looking back, out into the light.

They fell onto the ground side-by-side, laughing hysterically. Martin didn't know when Eblis had given up the chase, but the ghost train hadn't beaten them over the head with its plastic monster. The game was just a game; it knew when to stop.

They rose to their feet and limped back towards the bazaar, cracking up again every few steps.

"Did you see his teeth?" Javeed asked.

"Gross, huh?"

"Worse than the man at the pizza shop. I wouldn't let him cook my dinner."

Martin clutched his stomach. He'd put no effort into running, but he was winded from laughing so much.

At the edge of the bazaar a crowd had gathered, watching a commotion in the distance. Dozens of finely dressed noblemen were streaming out of the palace and heading for their mounts. The banquet had been a disaster; the cook had been disgraced. Zahhak would not become the Serpent King who ruled over neighboring Persia for a thousand years.

"You changed the story," Martin said.

"Yeah." Javeed sounded dazed now; they'd known all along what they'd hoped to achieve, but success had never been guaranteed.

"*Mubaarak, pesaram.*" Martin squatted down beside him, then remembered that he couldn't hug or kiss him. "Well done! Let's go tell Uncle Omar and Farshid."

Javeed gave the thumbs-down and vanished, taking the scenery with him. Martin flipped up his goggles and waited for the castles to release them.

As they were coming down the stairs, Martin saw Omar and Farshid standing by the counter, staring intently down one of the aisles; when he'd taken a few more steps he could see the object of their interest for himself. A young woman dressed in brief shorts and a halter top was leaning against her boyfriend, one hand entwined in his, the other stroking his neck. Martin couldn't blame anyone for staring; to see a woman dressed like that, behaving like that, was still a rarity in Tehran—even if it could no longer bring fines or imprisonment. He remembered Mahnoosh elbowing him sharply a few times in response to his gawking when they'd visited Australia together; those public displays of skin to which he had once been perfectly accustomed had become alien, almost hypnotic.

Omar addressed his son in a low voice, but not too softly for Martin to hear. "If you want to fuck something like that, go ahead, they're begging for it. Just don't bring the garbage home to shame your mother."

Martin glanced behind him, but if Javeed had heard anything he didn't appear to have taken it in. Martin turned around and lifted his son up onto his shoulders; Javeed screamed and laughed, hardly believing it. Martin hadn't given him a shoulder ride for at least three years; the last time would be lost in the fog of infant memories.

The debt for the moment of joy was called in quickly; Martin sagged, the muscles of his lower back seizing up. Farshid rushed over to help Javeed down safely.

As Javeed briefed Farshid on his adventure, Omar approached Martin. "I'll get you a taxi."

Martin said, "We're catching the bus."

"Are you crazy? Farshid will drive you home. Farshid—?"

Martin raised a hand to cut him off. Omar got the message. "Okay, okay." He put a hand on Martin's shoulder. "*Khaste nabashi, baradaram.*" Literally, *may you not be tired, brother*—but it packed as much goodwill, encouragement and solidarity into three words as could possibly fit.

As they parted, Martin couldn't look Omar in the eye. He was ashamed of what he was thinking, but he couldn't stop thinking it.

I don't want you raising my son.

16

Every day for a week, in two three-hour sessions, Ashkan Azimi, captain of the Iranian national football team, lay inside an MRI machine and day-dreamed his way through a thousand fragmented matches. Some recapitulated highlights from his well-documented career; others anticipated games he'd yet to play, challenges he was yet to confront in reality. But whether the fragments struck old chords or required new improvisations, the chance to watch his brain making thousands of crucial split-second decisions illuminated Azimi's talent in a way that no amount of match statistics, video footage or biomechanical analysis could ever have equaled.

Caplan had sent five people from Eikonometrics' Zürich office to operate the scanner and supervise the side-loading process. As it happened, Azimi spoke perfect German—having played for Club Hoffenheim for two years—but the boss had insisted that Nasim watch over everything and ensure that there were no "cultural misunderstandings." Nasim didn't follow football at all, so it was Bahador and three other Zendegi programmers who'd collaborated with the Eikonometrics people on the scenarios to feed into Azimi's goggles as he lay in the machine. But maybe that was why she'd been chosen to babysit: she was the only member of Zendegi's staff who wasn't so star-struck that she'd spend the week begging the poor man for his autographed nail clippings.

Nasim's contribution had been to build a version of Blank Frank that focused on the cerebellum and visual and motor cortex, to act as a vessel for Azimi's physical prowess. Of course she only had to whisper his name into a search engine to be drowned in paeans to his leadership, his tactical genius, his modesty, his generosity, his sense of fair play—but those more abstract qualities would have to remain locked inside his skull. Quite apart from the technical issues, Azimi's management had drawn the lines very clearly: their client's personality was not for sale. Nasim had actually sat down with a lawyer and a consultant neurologist and negotiated a schedule to his contract that included a list of approved brain regions.

No matter. The prosaic truth was that in the context of a football match, conventional software could handle those "higher" aspects of behavior pretty well; human players might need to struggle with their egos in order to decide when to pass the ball to their team-mates, but for dumb software it was the easiest thing in the world to quantify and program. Nasim suspected that so long as the Proxy didn't bite an opponent's ear off or insult anyone's mother or sister, most people would simply transfer their impression of the real Azimi to his imperfect clone. After all, their hero had volunteered to stick his head in a fancy machine for a week; the result would be judged inferior to the original, of course, but people would reason that *something* of the man would have had to rub off. Motor cortex, schmotor cortex; half the population thought a heart transplant could make you fall in love with the dead man's widow.

Given the nature of the talents they *were* extracting, it was a shame that Azimi couldn't even stand on a treadmill and mime interacting with a ball. But no one had yet built an MRI scanner that could accommodate that, and after a seven-figure payment in Euros to their star, Caplan's budget didn't stretch to an attempt at being the first. Instead, they'd given Azimi an external view of a virtual body modeled on his own and he'd spent the first day just getting used to controlling its movements with his thoughts. Once that adjustment was complete, driving the puppet activated all of the brain regions they were trying to mimic. It no longer mattered that he was flat on his back; in his mind, he was there on the field.

With Azimi mostly lost in his reverie or chatting in German with the MRI technicians, Nasim was free to watch the side-loading process unfold. Blank Frank had started out with even less hope of kicking a goal than she had; whatever the average donor's talents had been, her reconstruction had been too crude to retain it. But with the MRI images as a guide, tweaking the connections between Frank's virtual neurons to bring their collective behavior into accord with Azimi's was like reverse-engineering a set of incremental improvements to a known piece of machinery—not trivial, but never entirely baffling either. With Frank already wired up in a generically human fashion, once Nasim had seen activity flash across the two brains she could often guess for herself where the changes would need to be made. The side-loading software could do better than guess, and it could do it a million times faster.

Gradually, out on the virtual playing field, Frank began imitating his mentor, clumsily and imperfectly at first, then with ever greater fidelity.

Azimi could spend only so much time in the scanner or his body would start cramping up and his mind would turn to mush. But Frank could keep re-absorbing the same lessons overnight, letting the software whittle away his imperfections while all the humans had gone home to sleep. Every morning Nasim came in an hour before everyone else and sat and watched "before" and "after" clips, summarising her student's progress.

She remembered a story her father had told her—a story, or a joke; there was no sharp distinction. A famous actor and a famous singer had been invited to the same party, and people kept begging the singer to perform his best-known song. But he wasn't feeling well, and he'd drunk too much wine, so he kept turning down their requests. Finally, the actor had taken pity on his colleague, and to spare him any further harassment had given the crowd his own rendition of the song—note-perfect, and indistinguishable from the singer's best performance.

The singer had turned to him in amazement and asked, "Where did you learn to sing like that?"

The actor had replied modestly, "I can't sing at all. But I have a talent for impersonation."

At the end of the week, Azimi and the boss gave a press conference in the boardroom. Nasim stood at the back and watched. Azimi wore his team uniform, adorned with sponsors' logos, and enough bling to asphyxiate and dice him if he'd still been under the scanner's magnets.

The boss announced that Zendegi had sub-licensed Stadium Legends, a Korean developer, to write the first work to make use of Virtual Azimi. They were on a tight deadline; the release was to coincide with Iran hosting the Asian Cup in less than two months.

Most of the journalists were sports-gaming specialists, and they followed the line the PR people had steered them toward in their press release, waxing lyrical about the joy Azimi's fans would feel when they could put on their goggles and play a match under his virtual captaincy. But then Gita Razavi—a "cultural critic" for *Generation 2012*—managed to squeeze a question in, and she seemed to be getting her cues from somewhere else entirely.

"Mr. Azimi, of course you've already tasted fame, but I wonder how it feels to be the first person on Earth to achieve an entirely new kind of immortality: a century from now, people might still be playing football alongside your Proxy."

Azimi smiled. "Of course I'll be honored if I'm remembered in any way at all after I retire, but I wouldn't call this computer game a form of 'immortality.' I'm not just a football player—I wrote a dissertation on Hafez. I am a son, a husband, I hope to be a father. This game has nothing to do with any of those things."

"So how would you feel if a Proxy could capture all those other aspects of your life?" Razavi persisted. "Do you think that might be a good thing—or do you think it should be prohibited?"

Azimi glanced at the boss, but then spoke for himself. "As I understand it, that's not even possible. I'm not an expert, but they tell me they can only copy a very small part of the brain this way. Anything more is too complicated for the technology."

Nasim was cheered; he'd actually been paying attention when she'd briefed him.

Razavi said, "Did you have any qualms when you learned that this project required the brains of two thousand dead men?"

The boss cut in. "We had no direct involvement with those donors, but the information they provided was offered up willingly to benefit all of humanity. This is nothing new; when a doctor makes use of a medical atlas, the truth is that it's only because thousands of people allowed their bodies to be dissected after they died that we have that knowledge at our fingertips. We should be grateful to those people for their generosity, and grateful to God for his glorious creation. And your lovely nose, Ms. Razavi, should be the most grateful beneficiary of all."

When the laughter had died down, another journalist took the opportunity to speak. "Mr. Azimi, what do you think will happen if the Kuwaiti team have access to this game? If they can play against you as many times as they like, won't that give them an unfair advantage?"

Azimi was prepared for that one. "In this game, my Proxy will be just one player. People can get together with anyone they like to make up the numbers—but with all due respect to both our fans and our rivals, any team they form will still fall a long way short of the Iranian national team."

"The advertising's come back on my photos," Nasim's mother complained. "I can't even look at my own wedding without someone trying to sell me haemorrhoid cream."

Nasim said, "I'll see what I can do." She'd just finished eating dinner and was finally beginning to unwind.

She switched on the TV and chose "photos" from the menu. Sure enough, even at the albums stage a sliding banner of slogans and links was superimposed over the bottom of each preview image.

Nasim put the TV into administrator mode. She launched debugging and monitoring software, followed by the client for the online photo manager,

Rubens. A decade before, she'd encouraged her mother to start using the free system. The interface was simple, the images were accessible anywhere, and everything was backed-up automatically to three separate locations.

The client froze. After staring at the debugger's window for a few seconds, Nasim understood what had happened. The server had figured out that the client was being monitored, and was refusing to talk to it. It wasn't going to co-operate with a snitch.

Nasim swore under her breath. When the ads had first appeared she'd managed to find a simple way to block them. That task had grown slightly trickier over the years, but now it looked as if the program's defenses had been ramped up substantially. She said, "This might have to wait until the weekend."

"That's no problem," her mother replied. "I never said you had to fix it straight away."

"All right." Nasim switched off the TV and started carrying the plates to the dishwasher. "But remind me again, or I might forget."

"I saw your press conference," her mother said. "On IRIB."

"Yeah?" Nasim hadn't seen anyone from IRIB in the room, though on reflection she wasn't surprised that they'd picked up the story. "How do you think it went?"

"You do know this is going to upset people?"

Nasim groaned. "Are you going to complain about the brain donors now? You're the one who wanted me to stay in the States and spend my whole career up to my elbows in gray matter." She closed the dishwasher and walked back into the living room.

"It's not the dead people's brains that worry me," her mother replied, "it's what you're doing with the live ones. People aren't going to be comfortable with that."

"'People'? Which people?" Nasim resisted the urge to tell her that if she had some ethical point to make she should make it, and stop hiding behind imaginary third parties. "We're not in a theocracy anymore, and I'm not going to be cowed into acting as if we were."

"No," her mother agreed, "we're not in a theocracy, but your fellow citizens are perfectly capable of voting conservatives back into power if they start to feel that their values are being threatened."

"Threatened by what? A small improvement in the state of the art for faking celebrities in online football games?"

Her mother shook her head impatiently. "Maybe not, but what comes next? I'm sure there are people who'd pay to be intimate with a Proxy of someone famous."

Nasim was bemused. Zendegi had its share of tame virtual pick-up joints—whose flesh-and-blood customers could always take things further elsewhere—but the board would have run a mile from any suggestion of facilitating cyber-sex. "So now you think I'm a pimp?"

"Oh, don't be obtuse!" Her mother glared at her. "But it's not in your hands how other people use these methods."

Nasim said, "There are already people peddling sex with virtual celebrities. I don't think they're looking to increase their level of *psychological realism*."

"Okay, put that aside. What's going to happen to workers whose skills can be transferred to computers this way?"

"You think we've made Azimi redundant?" Nasim replied. "He'll get a cut every time someone plays the game!"

"And you think ordinary people will get the same kind of deal?" her mother countered. "Let alone their colleagues who are put out of work without even being parties to the contract?"

"Automation's nothing new," Nasim said feebly. "Anyway... we're a long way from using this for anything more than novelty value. Don't expect a robot plumber anytime soon."

"Are you cheating your customers," her mother asked bluntly, "or are your claims about this technology real?"

"They're real." Maybe people would over-interpret the process, or ignore the fine print, but it was not all smoke and mirrors and celebrity fetishism. On a timescale of seconds, in a very limited domain, Virtual Azimi really had learned to act like the original.

"Then it will be improved upon," her mother said, "and it will be used in other ways. If you don't understand why some people might resist that, then I don't know what planet you're living on."

When Nasim went upstairs she had her knowledge-miner show her an updated news summary.

Nobody was rioting in the streets, burning Azimi's jersey for his crimes against nature, or Islam, or sport. On the contrary, fans were already signing up for a chance to play in the first demonstration match: one team captained by the real Azimi, the other by his virtual counterpart.

The story certainly had made an impact, bouncing around the globe within hours, but the reception had been mostly positive, albeit with some skepticism at the prospect that any real skills had been extracted from Azimi's brain. Comics had mined the news for its slight tinge of surrealism—an Egyptian sketch show portrayed their president engaged in a wrestling match with his virtual self—but so far, there'd been no rabid denunciations. As far as Nasim could see, most people were treating the process as scarcely more controversial than if they'd taped yellow markers to Azimi's joints and used motion-capture to insert him into the game.

In the dregs of the knowledge-miner's sweep was the news that the Benign Superintelligence Bootstrap Project had issued a video press release, with their public affairs officer, Michelle Bello, interviewing their director, Conrad Esch. The topical question addressed was whether the BSBSP had gleaned anything from the Human Connectome Project that might prove to be of more lasting significance than this brief spurt of interest in an online game.

Apparently, the answer was yes. By carefully studying the HCP data over the last few months, the Superintelligence Project had acquired vital clues that would allow it to construct a Class Three Emergent Godlet within five years.

"And when that happens, what can we expect?" Bello asked.

"Within two or three hours, the planet will be entirely in the hands of the Benign Superintelligence. Human affairs will be reorganized, within seconds, into their optimal state: no more war, no more sorrow, no more death."

"But how can we be sure of that?" Bello probed fearlessly. "Computers are capable of all kinds of errors and mistakes."

"Computers built and programmed by humans, yes," Esch conceded. "But remember, *by definition*, every element in the ascending chain of Godlets will be superior to its predecessor, in both intelligence and benignity. We've done the theoretical groundwork; now we're assembling the final pieces that will start the chain reaction. The endpoint is simply a matter of logic: God is coming into being. There is no disputing that, and there is no stopping it."

Nasim said, "Which of these reminds you most of a cat?"

Fariba examined the four photographs: the Eiffel Tower, a parrot in a cage, the Great Pyramid of Giza and the Empire State Building. A patch of light on the screen tracked her focus of attention as it moved from image to image.

"The pyramid most of all," Fariba said, "because of the thing Egyptians had for cats. Second is the bird, because it's a pet too, and because the cat might want to eat it."

Nasim gestured for a reset before the urge to say "thank you" or "good" or "correct" could start to nag at her. Four new pictures appeared: a bicycle lying flat on the road with some scattered groceries around it; a wilted flower; a wrecking ball swinging toward an apartment block; and a very young girl holding the hand of an old woman bent over in pain.

"Which of these pictures is the saddest?" Nasim asked. Fariba, with no memory of the previous test, contemplated the images for a few seconds before replying, "Maybe the bicycle. The girl with the grandma is stronger emotionally, but I'm not sure if its sadness and its sweetness should cancel each other out, or stand alone!"

Nasim gestured *reset* and *halt*, and turned to Bahador.

"I spend a few days playing football," he said, "and look what happens behind my back."

"A few days? It's been five weeks!" They'd had to fit water dispensers into the *ghal'eha* so all the Azimi groupies didn't dehydrate as they helped beta-test the game. "What do you think?"

Bahador smiled. "It's amazing. How many women did you side-load?"

"Twenty. Students mostly." Each recruit had lain in the MRI for ten hour-long sessions, going through a series of undemanding tasks: looking at pictures, reading short essays, listening to recorded speeches, answering simple questions. At night, the side-loading software had prodded and kneaded the inarticulate Blank Francine—assembled by Nasim from the HCP women—into her less tongue-tied Iranian cousin, Farsiphone Fariba: fluent in the written and spoken language, brimming with word associations, conversant with thousands of commonplace facts.

Fariba would never be mistaken for a philosopher or a poet. Conventional Proxies—which improvised around elaborate, branching scripts—could have far deeper, more convincing interactions with people, at least in situations for which they'd been tailor-made. But Fariba wasn't meant to do anything as a stand-alone system. Conventional software would still provide the back-story, goals, memory and context, but Fariba would make it a thousand times easier for developers to construct a flexible character who wouldn't lapse into embarrassing silence if the conversation moved beyond the range of possibilities envisaged in the script.

"Can you make a few different versions?" Bahador wondered. "With different weightings for the various side-loading subjects? That way the responses will always make sense, but they won't be the same for every character that uses the modules."

Nasim thought it over. "That's a good idea. For a composite Proxy it will still be the script that determines most of its personality, but it will be an added attraction if we can offer a kind of library of low-level variations." Developers could decide for themselves whether they preferred a particular character to associate cats with birds, or with pyramids. Even if nothing crucial hung on the distinction, that would give them more control over the tone of the game.

Bahador was dripping sweat onto the carpet; he'd just come from a game and Nasim had called him in as he'd passed her office on the way to the showers. "I should let you go," she said.

He looked down at his damp shirt. "Sorry, I must stink." He headed for the door. "What you've done is terrific. And so is the Azimi game. We're going to make a fortune!" He waited until he was out in the corridor before adding, "I expect a pay rise."

"Maybe when you start doing real work again," Nasim called after him.

She sat playing with the demonstration module. She'd already run rigorous automated tests on it, yielding no surprises or major problems—but there was something addictive about chatting away to Fariba in person.

"Which color here makes you think of warm weather?"

"If you could take only one of these items to a desert island, which one would you choose?"

"Which of the first three pictures tells a story that's completed by the fourth?"

The tests didn't always have a single right answer, but Fariba always managed a sensible response. She possessed no narrative memories, and no sophisticated beliefs—but all the words and concepts she'd acquired were wired together in a perfectly reasonable way. If she had no depth to her, she sounded less like a simpleton than an amnesiac who hadn't yet noticed her own plight.

The women who'd answered Nasim's advertisement had been happy enough with the modest payments they'd received for their work—and it hadn't exactly been arduous for them, once they'd grown used to the confined space of the scanner. Nasim didn't feel that she'd exploited them, that she'd pillaged their brains in return for loose change; their language skills, common sense and general knowledge, however vital, had hardly been rare commodities. Literally millions of Tehrani women could have done the same job equally well.

Nevertheless, a little more than raw vocabulary and dry factual knowledge had rubbed off. Sometimes Fariba exhibited quirks of phrasing that came straight from Asa, or offered witticisms that Azita would not have disowned. Sometimes she seemed as warm as Farah, or as acerbic as Chalipa.

So what was the bottom line? Fariba had no long-term memory, and no sense of herself. When Nasim reset her after every test, she lost nothing, because there was nothing to lose. Even if she'd run uninterrupted for an hour or a day, the passage of time would have left no mark on her. It would be crazy to start treating her as if she had interests, goals and rights.

But was she *conscious*—as much as the women who'd helped build her would have been conscious if, for a few seconds, they'd forgotten themselves and focused entirely on their simple tasks: thinking of a word, matching a picture?

Nasim wasn't sure. She was moving into territory where that prospect was no longer unthinkably remote; she had to tread carefully.

Still, at most it could only be a transient form of consciousness—with no conception of itself to underpin a fear of extinction. Splicing Fariba, and a thousand variants of her, into narratives in which they played no active part wouldn't bolster their fragmentary minds into something more substantial; that was just the illusion that human players would receive. The Faribas would still live—if they lived at all—in an eternal present, doing their simple tasks over and over again, remembering nothing.

17

"Dinner's ready," Martin announced for the third time.

"Okay!" Javeed had been in the bath for almost forty minutes, staging some kind of elaborate battle between the shampoo bottles. Martin listened for draining water, but all he heard was a resumption of missile sounds.

He walked into the bathroom and pulled out the plug. Javeed looked annoyed for a moment, but then he put down the blue conditioner that had been attacking the green vitamin enricher and stepped onto the bath mat without complaint. Martin handed him a towel and waited for him to dry himself.

Most of the bottles were Mahnoosh's; Martin would have thrown them out if Javeed hadn't kept using them as props. It had taken him three months to work up the strength to get rid of her make-up and clothes. He'd kept all her jewellery, still unable to face the task of deciding which pieces were just trinkets, and which Javeed might want to give to his own wife or daughter one day.

Javeed rubbed the towel vigorously between his legs, as if his unprotected penis required no lighter touch than his elbow. Martin had never quite stopped cringing when he saw this, but there was nothing to be done. He'd been caught unprepared when Mahnoosh had insisted on having their son circumcised—the day before she and Javeed left the hospital—because it was the "normal" thing to do. "What if he wants to marry an Iranian woman who isn't as tolerant of strange foreign customs as I am?" Islam supported the practice but attached no religious significance to it; Martin hadn't been able to use Mahnoosh's loathing of the mullahs as leverage. With no research on the medical pros and cons at his fingertips, all he'd managed in reply was, "What if he wants to clean the shower, naked, with something corrosive?" Thirty minutes later the deed had been done.

As they ate dinner, Javeed watched the football highlights on TV. Martin didn't feel obliged to feign interest, any more than he did with cartoons or wrestling, but he knew he'd feel a pang of jealousy when he heard Javeed excitedly discussing the results with Farshid. If he'd had more energy, perhaps he could have faked it, or even developed a genuine passion for the game. When he received his new liver, all these impossible tasks would become easy.

Javeed's homework was half an hour of handwriting practice, copying a series of words chosen to illustrate the different forms the same letter took in different positions. Martin sat at the table beside him, offering encouragement, but Javeed didn't need any help; his writing was already neat and precise, and he seemed to have grasped the concept of initial, medial, final and isolated forms just as easily as a child learning to write English grasped the concept of upper and lower case.

"Okay, bedtime. Clean your teeth."

Javeed didn't want Martin to read him a story; that had been his mother's job. He just wanted him to sit beside the bed until he fell asleep, and Martin was happy to oblige.

In the darkness, Martin's thoughts returned to the splinter he'd been digging at for weeks. When Javeed had been born, Omar and Rana had taken the request to be his godparents very seriously. Omar had brought up the subject of religion, assuring Martin that he was prepared to raise Javeed as a non-Muslim. With the one major sticking point out of the way, Martin had considered everything settled, and he'd never felt an urge to revisit the decision. The whole point of making such arrangements was to put the subject out of your mind: to contemplate the unthinkable once, as an antidote to all future morbid fretting over the consequences if the worst did happen.

He still believed that Omar was a good man, a good father, a good husband. Over the years Martin had heard him say foolish things about Arabs, Jews, Afghanis, Sunnis, black people, gays, women, and supporters of rival football teams—but everyone in the world talked shit sometimes, uttering outrageous, insupportable libels against some group of people. If Martin could have heard his own lifetime's worth of ill-considered utterances through someone else's ears, he was quite sure he would not have emerged as any kind of paragon of fairness and decency. Judging Omar for his lax self-censorship on issues Martin had been trained since childhood to treat as taboo would just be sanctimonious. And as for his crass remarks to Farshid about the woman in the shop, Martin was fairly sure that the rise of his own interest in women had coincided precisely with the point when he'd ceased caring about his father's opinion on anything. Farshid had probably been cringing inside and mentally humming a tune in the hope of blocking out every word. The only difference between an Iranian teenager and a Western one was that he'd been too polite to tell his father to shut up and stop making a fool of himself.

And yet... even if Omar's stupefaction in the face of changing public sexual mores really was close to harmless, and even if he could actually have befriended any of the people he'd derided in his loose-tongued moments just as easily as he'd befriended an atheist like Martin, that didn't really settle the matter. Martin wanted his son to share his own taboos. He wanted Javeed to be upbraided for repeating whatever bigoted, sexist drivel he brought back from the school-yard, not told, "I hear you!" or "Isn't that right?"

Was it wrong to want to have a lasting influence on his own son, beyond the color of his hair? Was it sanctimonious to want to pass on his own values? It wasn't about judging himself a better man than Omar. It was about not being erased from Javeed's life completely.

But where did that longing actually get him? What choice did he have? Behrouz did not have Omar's rough edges, but even if he and Suri had agreed to take Javeed, Javeed barely knew them. He'd be stuck in Damascus, a two-hour flight away from all his friends; learning Arabic would be the least of his problems. And any fantasy involving Australia had the same downsides multiplied tenfold. Martin hadn't stayed close to any of his cousins; Mark and his wife Rachel had come to Tehran for his wedding, but so far he hadn't even told them about Mahnoosh's death, let alone his own condition. Martin could just imagine the awkward silence if he phoned them, out of the blue, brought them up to speed on his dilemma, and then enquired as to whether their house felt empty now that their own three children had moved out.

Javeed stirred. "Mama! *Inja bia!*"

Martin said, "Sssh, it's okay." If Mahnoosh was beside them she was keeping silent; when he tried to drag her advice out of the aether, all he felt was a vague sense of concern and affection. To have known her for fifteen years was still not to know what she would have made of this mess. She'd gone along with the choice of Omar and Rana, but then, most of her other friends were divorced. Had the prospect of Javeed being raised by anyone but his own parents ever felt real to her? At least once she'd referred to Omar as a sexist troglodyte and Rana as a doormat. But Martin knew she'd loved them both, admired them both. Rana was quiet but strong; you didn't have to join a Goth band to stick it to the dictators.

When Javeed's breathing became slow and even, Martin left him. His back wasn't too bad, but he was trying to get off the painkillers completely, so he needed to stay up for a few more hours to exhaust himself before trying to sleep.

He went to the living room and switched on the TV. In his presence, at this hour, it defaulted to the local news channel—though he suspected that unless World War III had broken out there'd be no news all week that wasn't football, football, football.

18

The email read: "Could I meet you for lunch today? I know it's short notice, but it's important."

Nasim replied, "Lunch where? I'm a vegetarian." The prospect of having to locate a meat-free meal in Tehran was enough to make most people reassess their notion of "important." Online maps weren't much help; Nasim had stopped publishing locations herself, lest she lead anyone into false hope. Even the establishments where she'd succeeded on occasion were perfectly capable of taking their one suitable dish off the menu on a whim, or adding meat to the recipe without warning.

Martin responded in thirty seconds, "There's a place that does *kuku-ye-sabzi*, just around the corner from People of the Book."

Nasim had her doubts about how seriously they meant *sabzi*, but if she'd been too busy to accept the invitation she should have used an ironclad brush-off from the start. "Okay. Bookshop at one?"

"Great. Thank you."

When Nasim arrived at the shop, Martin was locking up and pulling down the shutters.

"You don't stay open at lunchtime?" she asked.

"I only open in the mornings myself," he said. "There's a student who comes in and does the evening shift, but I don't have anyone for the afternoons yet."

The place he took her to was a crowded juice bar with three tiny plastic tables squeezed between the wall and the serving counter, but the owner really did whip up a traditional herb-and-vegetable omelette without complaint—and without throwing in a handful of ground beef or diced chicken for "added flavor."

"How's Javeed?" she asked.

Martin took a while to reply. "He's still thinking it through, working out the implications. Every now and then he gets a fresh realization that Mahnoosh is really not coming back. Before his sixth birthday, we talked about it and he decided to let the day pass. He didn't want to celebrate without her."

Nasim tried to think of something encouraging to say. "I'm sure he's going to be resilient in the long run." Her mother had told her that Martin had cancer, but she had no intention of quizzing him about that. Most of their conversations since the funeral had revolved around Zendegi; she was only too happy to help provide the poor kid with some distraction.

Martin said, "Javeed's godparents, Omar and Rana, are wonderful people. So I don't want anything I say to be taken as a slight on their characters."

"Okay." Nasim shifted uncomfortably in her plastic chair. She had no idea where he was heading. She'd met the couple only once, at Mahnoosh's funeral, though her mother knew them through mutual friends.

"Omar already treats Javeed like a son," Martin continued. "I can't imagine anyone else caring more about his welfare. But some of Omar's ideas, the way he talks about women, about ethnic groups…" He trailed off. "You lived in the States for a while, didn't you?"

"About twelve years," Nasim replied.

"I think you understand what I'm saying. It's hard work to get all that racist, sexist garbage even halfway under control. Nobody really gets it out of their system. But that's no reason to give up and say it doesn't matter."

"Of course not," Nasim agreed cautiously.

"I don't want Omar raising my son," Martin said bluntly. "There are things that are important to me that he'll simply never accept—let alone pass on to a child with any conviction. I know I should be grateful that Javeed has someone like Omar prepared to look after him. But I can't make peace with it. I just can't. That's why I've come to you."

Nasim felt the blood draining from her face. *He was going to ask her to adopt the boy.*

"Martin, I—" She stopped, too flustered to say anything coherent. Mahnoosh had been her cousin, but she'd barely known her, let alone Javeed. If there'd been no one—literally *no one else* in the world, she might have been prepared to do this, but Martin seemed to be telling her that he wanted to toss aside his loyal and loving friends… just because she had a more Western sensibility?

Martin went on, "Last night I saw a replay of the football match in Zendegi between the two Azimis. Each team held the other to a draw." He laughed. "I was probably the last person in the world to notice what you've achieved, to appreciate how amazing it was."

Nasim was utterly confused now. Was he trying to flatter her? Praising her technical skills as if that had some bearing on her eligibility for this role?

"But once I saw that game," he continued, "I knew it was the answer. Javeed's happiest times with me these days are all in Zendegi. And I don't think he'd find it strange or frightening; I think he'd just accept it. I think it would make perfect sense to him."

Nasim said, "*What* would make sense to him? What is it you're asking me to do?" She thought she knew now, but having narrowly averted embarrassing them both with her first misunderstanding, she wasn't willing to take anything for granted.

"I want you to do for me what you did for Azimi," Martin announced calmly. "I want you to make a Proxy of me that can live on in Zendegi and help raise my son."

After forty minutes the owner of the juice bar started giving them dark looks. There were only so many banana milkshakes Nasim could bring herself to order for the sake of staying put, so they walked back to Martin's empty shop and sat in the small coffee lounge where patrons were invited to flick through their potential purchases.

"I have some money from my wife's insurance," Martin told her, for the fifth time.

"That's not the point," Nasim replied patiently. "It's not a question of expense. It's a question of complexity."

"I'm not asking for anything sophisticated," Martin insisted. "I don't expect this Proxy to deliver lectures on moral philosophy; I just want him to have the right gut reaction if his son starts referring to women as whores or Arabs as wild animals."

Nasim said, "If it were that simple, I could go back to the office right now and crank out an ordinary, scripted Proxy that flew off the handle in response to any list of triggers you cared to spell out. Do you honestly want something that crude?"

"Not *that* crude," Martin conceded.

"So do you really think that a Proxy whose only ability was knowing when to lay down the law—and who became tongue-tied whenever he was challenged to defend his views—would have any impact on your son at all? I'm not talking about high-powered philosophy! I'm talking about debating a six-year-old, or a twelve-year-old, with a more subtle response than 'Because I said so.'"

Martin was beginning to look deflated. He said, "I'm going to have to go and pick up Javeed from school."

Nasim said, "I'm sorry, Martin. You know if there's anything else I can do—"

"Thank you."

In the taxi back to the office, Nasim felt drained. She wondered how many other people had watched Virtual Azimi tenaciously holding his ground against the original—as if this proved them to be perfectly matched mirror-images—and concluded: *This is it, my chance to cheat death.* Well, if Azimi was hit by a truck, his widow would certainly receive royalties from the game for as long as it remained popular, but most people could forget about a Proxy preserving their earning capacity, let alone anything more personal. Maybe she should have told Martin that, while the match hadn't literally been fixed, Azimi would have been crazy to hammer his Proxy's team into the ground; that might have been good for his ego, but it wouldn't have helped anyone's bank balance.

Bahador spotted her as she stepped out of the elevator. "Did you hear about the cleric in Qom?" he asked.

"No—?" They walked together down the corridor; Bahador wasn't smiling, so Nasim decided that this probably wasn't the opening line to a joke.

"*Hojatoleslam* Shahidi. He just issued a statement denouncing Virtual Azimi as an affront to God and human dignity."

"An affront? Why?"

Bahador read from his notepad. "'God's gifts to us should be shared, and taught, and used freely to delight him, but they must not be made into commodities to be bought and sold.'"

Nasim rubbed her eyes. "Okay, but does he have any actual followers who'll boycott the game, or is he just another fat fart in a turban, hallucinating relevance and trying to make a headline?"

Bahador looked around nervously, as if he was afraid someone might have overheard her. "I don't know. I guess we'll find out."

"You didn't SocNet him?"

Bahador fiddled with the notepad. "He does have an UmmahSpace page, but it looks like most of his friends are sycobots."

"Hmm." It had been a while since Nasim's online outreach job, but anyone who didn't filter out interest-feigning bots was hardly going to be a formidable organizer. "I wouldn't worry about it," she said.

Nasim spent the afternoon in a videoconference with a developer who was using the Fariba modules in a new game called *Murder in Manolos*, a gossipy whodunnit set among North Tehran's Mall Princess cliques. Unlike *Virtual Azimi*, the novel technology would not be a selling point for the public; the aim was simply to get a smoother result for the non-player characters, with lower development costs.

There were a few technical hitches in the interface with the modules, but overall the project was going quite well. Nasim watched some demonstration runs; the Fariba-enhanced bit-players seemed at least as lifelike as anyone in an equivalent TV drama. She had added a feature to the library recently that had turned out to be invaluable, a routine called WTFquery(). When one of the Fariba modules generated some potential dialogue, before having the Proxy utter the words you could try out the whole exchange on another (non-identical) Fariba, and see if its neural response classified the would-be contribution as (A) a pertinent observation, (B) witty banter, or (C) a complete *non sequitur*. Screening out bizarre interjections from the Proxies that would have been the equivalent of stamping "idiot robot" on their foreheads did at least as much for their credibility as anything they actually said.

Nasim woke to darkness, certain that her father was in the house. Was he asleep in the spare room? Or had he got up to use the bathroom—was that what had woken her? She strained her ears, listening for his footsteps.

It took a few seconds for her conviction to fade. She could still see the two of them standing in the kitchen together, arguing about her work on the Faribas. In the dream, his hair had turned gray. That small touch had been enough to keep her satisfied, to make the whole scenario seem perfectly reasonable.

She checked her watch; it was just after three. Her alarm was set for five-thirty. She lay still, trying to clear her mind and let her limbs grow heavy, but after a few minutes she decided that it wasn't going to happen.

How much had she screwed up her life, she wondered, by trying to imagine her father's advice, his opinions, his disappointments, his praise? She was sure she would have stayed at MIT in 2012 if she hadn't felt compelled to return to Iran to prove that his struggle had meant something to her. But the problem hadn't been some nagging ghost in her head; the problem had been the silence. She'd *wanted* to live as if he were beside her, to cheat the murderers who'd taken him from her, but she'd never really mastered that act. Her own memories, her own love for him, her own judgment had not been enough.

So how could she leave Javeed to grasp at the same kind of shadows if there was any chance at all of replacing them with something more solid? She'd told Martin that what he'd asked for was impossible—but was that literally true? It would certainly be far more difficult than he'd imagined, but that was not the same thing at all.

She climbed out of bed; the room light came on slowly to avoid dazzling her as she crossed to her desk. It took her half an hour to cobble together a rough map of the brain regions that Martin's Proxy would need personalized in order to meet his goals. She had estimates of varying quality for the total amount of data required to differentiate each region in an individual from the crude average that Blank Frank represented.

That was a start, but there were still a lot of unknowns. The rate at which the best scanning techniques pulled *useful, distinguishing data* out of a subject's skull varied enormously, depending on how well the activity they were performing had been tailored for the region being mapped. It also tended to follow a law of diminishing returns: the better the Proxy became at mimicking the subject, the harder it became to home in on the remaining differences. But she could take the average rate she'd measured for the Faribas as a reasonable first approximation. Martin didn't know how long he had to live, but what if she assumed that he could manage, say, three hour-long sessions a week for a year?

Nasim re-checked her calculations twice, but she hadn't made a mistake. What he'd asked of her was not *necessarily* impossible. That was a long way from knowing that it could actually be done, but purely in terms of the information flows required it would not be like shifting an ocean with an eyedropper. Merely Lake Erie with a teaspoon.

It was afternoon on the US East Coast; Caplan kept strange hours, but he was usually awake by now. She emailed him: "Can you spare a few minutes to talk?"

The reply came back within seconds. "Sure."

Caplan preferred to meet in augmented reality, but Nasim wasn't set up for that at home, so they settled for plain audio. She lay on her bed with her notepad beside her and did her best to explain Martin's plight succinctly; she knew Caplan wouldn't have much patience for the details.

As it was, he interrupted her halfway through. "Why doesn't your friend just freeze himself? All cancers will be treatable in a decade."

Cancers, maybe; Nasim doubted that being frozen to death would be cured so quickly. "He has a son," she said. "That's the whole point. He wants to raise his own son, not come back when Javeed's an adult."

"Well, he can't freeze the kid," Caplan mused. "That would be illegal. Unless Iran has much more progressive legislation on these things than we have."

Nasim struggled to reorganize her tactics. How did you get through to someone whose entire world view had been molded by tenth-rate science fiction? Empathy for Javeed was out; Caplan probably believed that the only consequence of being orphaned at six was that you tried harder than anyone else to reach the top of your class in space academy.

She said, "Why did you buy Eikonometrics?"

Caplan didn't reply, so she answered for him. "To find out *how far* side-loading can go. You want to know if it can ever be a substitute for uploading: if you'll ever be able to reproduce the entire functionality of your brain without slicing it up and feeding it through an electron microscope."

Caplan said, "That's not the only question that makes side-loading interesting. But please go on, if you have a point to make."

"This is a chance to find out more about the limits of the technique," Nasim said. "You'll have a highly motivated volunteer, and a project that will force us to push the envelope."

"Motivated volunteers aren't hard to find," Caplan replied.

"Maybe not," Nasim conceded. "But the people who'd take the bait if you sprinkled some buzzwords around the net are your fellow wannabe-immortals, who'll expect perfect copies of their minds to wake up in cyberspace. Martin has no such illusions; he understands that the Proxy will have massive limitations. He doesn't imagine that we can make him live forever; he just wants us to use his brain to craft some software that can do a certain job."

"So when exactly did I become the Make-a-Wish Foundation?" Caplan protested irritably.

"This isn't charity," Nasim insisted. "It would yield valuable information for both of us." She was sure Caplan could see that; he was probably just annoyed that she was trying to set the agenda.

He said, "What would you tell your own staff, your own management?"

"That it's research that could lead to even better Proxies," Nasim replied. "Which is perfectly true. If this works, Martin benefits, Zendegi benefits, you benefit. If it doesn't, we'll probably still learn a great deal just from seeing exactly where things fail. So what's the downside?"

She waited, wondering if Caplan was going to make her swear not to turn Martin's Proxy into a transcendent being who would rob him of his rightful place as lord of the solar system.

He said, "If it doesn't work, are you prepared to clean up the mess? To put your botched creation out of its misery?"

Nasim was about to reply scornfully that the Proxy would be immune to any such need, but she caught herself. That was certainly the result she'd be aiming for: a devoted parent who lived in the moment, committed to his son's wellbeing, but no more capable of contemplating—or regretting—his own nature than Virtual Azimi or the chatty Faribas.

A failure, though, could miss that target in many different directions.

Nasim steeled herself. She said, "I'll spell out all the risks to Martin; in the end he's the one who'll have to decide the fate of anything derived from his own mind. But yes, if it comes down to it, I'm prepared to clean up the mess."

19

Martin had begun shaving his head three weeks before it was necessary, to give Javeed time to grow used to his altered appearance before he was confronted with the more significant change: the change in their routine. He'd been expecting a tantrum when he broke the news, so he chose the time and place carefully: at home, the day before their next visit to Zendegi, having just made their choices on the website.

"But I want to go to the shop!" Javeed screamed.

"Sssh. We'll still go to the shop, straight afterward. You can still talk to Uncle Omar and Farshid."

"But that's stupid!"

It was a fair complaint. If they were going to Omar's shop anyway, why not use the *ghal'eha* there?

"Aunty Nasim has a special kind of *ghal'e* that's easier for me to use, easier on my back. So she very kindly said that we could use that."

"I hate her!" Javeed proclaimed.

"No, you don't," Martin said flatly. "You hardly know her. Anyway, you don't even have to talk to her. We'll go there, we'll use the *ghal'eha*, then we'll go to the shop. Okay?"

"*No!* I want to do it *the proper way!*" Javeed's face contorted in anguish.

"Well, you have a choice: we can go to Aunty Nasim for Zendegi, then visit Uncle Omar in the shop, or we can just stay home and you can play for an hour on your console instead."

Javeed's face became a shade redder. "That's not fair!"

"That's the choice. Now do you want to help me cook dinner?"

"No—I'll help you throw it in the toilet where it belongs!"

Martin forced himself not to smile. "*Shaitan nasho.* And if you don't like

182

my cooking, that's all the more reason to help."

Javeed sat and wept as if the world were ending, but Martin hardened his heart. Javeed was too stubborn to reconcile himself to the new plan immediately, but while part of his insecurity obviously stemmed from Mahnoosh's death, Martin had no intention of letting that become a reason to indulge him on everything.

Within an hour, the tantrum had cooled into a long sulk. Javeed was not quite stubborn enough to start throwing food or breaking things and risk losing Zendegi completely.

After school the next day, they caught the bus to the small office block north of the city center that housed Zendegi's operations. Apparently most of the actual computers were elsewhere, scattered around the globe and leased as required. Nasim was waiting for them in the lobby; Javeed was aloof rather than downright rude to her, and Martin suspected that he just came across as shy.

On the fifth floor, Martin explained to Javeed, "My *ghal'e* is a special kind, like I told you, so I'll be in a room close by, but not right next to you." He tensed, prepared for an outburst, but Javeed just gave him a dissatisfied glare. When they reached the end of the corridor Bahador met them; he introduced himself to Javeed by waving a child-sized football jersey prominently signed by Ashkan Azimi. "*Agha* Ashkan told me I should give this to a friend of mine, but I don't know anyone in quite the right size." Javeed's eyes lit up with delight. He knew he was being bribed into compliance, but yesterday's complaints suddenly seemed petty.

Martin squatted down and kissed him. "Be good, *pesaram*. I'll see you in Zendegi."

Nasim led Martin to the MRI room. The scanner was far more compact than the older model in the hospital's radiology department—a machine that Martin had come to know all too well—but Bernard, the Swiss technician who operated Zendegi's version, had assured Martin that the magnetic field was an order of magnitude stronger. Martin had come in on three mornings the previous week to learn how to control his icon while lying flat on his back with his head immobilized in a padded helmet.

He took out his wallet, and removed his watch, his wedding ring, his belt and his shoes. He was wearing clothes that had been pre-checked and certified metal-free to save him from having to change for the scanner, but Bernard ran a detector over him quickly to be sure.

Nasim fitted the skullcap that would be used to take EEG recordings simultaneously with the multi-mode MRI; Martin sat beneath a UV light and watched in a mirror as the semi-permanent tattoos they'd given him revealed themselves with green fluorescence, to aid in the alignment of the cap. In order to limit interactions with the MRI's magnetic field and radio pulses, the skullcap's "circuitry" was purely optical, reading the electric field leaking out of his brain by observing its effect on tiny capsules of electrolytes incorporated into the tattoos.

Bernard swabbed Martin's arm with disinfectant and injected him with a mixture of contrast agents that had been magnetically polarized over-night in a special-purpose machine. You could image brain activity to a certain extent just by watching hemoglobin in the blood losing its oxygen to hungry neurons, and that was one signal they'd be looking for. But there were a dozen other processes that could be monitored simultaneously with modern machines—making the image sharper, more responsive and more informative—and extra chemicals with enhanced magnetic proper-ties were needed to render those processes visible. Bernard had sketched the details, but Martin had had too much else on his mind to take it in. It was sufficient to know that they were pulling out all the stops to gather as much information as possible.

Nasim passed him a pair of gloves and he slipped them on, then she helped him with his goggles; all of this equipment had been specially built for use in and around the scanner. He walked over to the MRI, lay down and wriggled around to try to find a reasonably comfortable position that allowed his head to sit in the custom-molded restraint.

"Everything okay?" Nasim asked.

"Yes, thanks." Martin's stomach was clenched with anxiety, but he'd al-ready asked all the questions he could think of the week before. Nasim had assured him that there was nothing he could do that would corrupt the side-loading process; even if he thrashed about and spoiled the scan, they'd just discard the bad data. There was no risk of it being used inadvertently and turning the Proxy's brain to mush.

"What if I have homicidal thoughts about my son?" he'd asked after one of the training runs. He'd been half-joking, but it had probably focused Nasim's attention more effectively than if he'd merely waffled on about his fear of exhibiting impatience or irritability.

"Does that happen often?" she'd inquired.

"No—but have you ever tried not to think of a pink elephant? Under threat of putting your only child in the hands of your evil clone?"

"Calm down, Dr. Jekyll. If you have any prolonged negative thoughts, let us know and we'll throw out the whole session. But if they're fleeting, I wouldn't worry. This machine isn't capable of churning out a second-by-second transcript of everything that passes through your mind; at best, we'll be able to discern your most persistent thought patterns and associations and train the Proxy to share them. But we'll be working hard to get enough information to do that. Brief mental tics will be right off the radar."

Nasim flipped the goggles' screens down, whiting out Martin's vision. The top of the cage she fitted over his head included a camera that would monitor his facial expression, just as it would be monitored in an ordinary *ghal'e*. He heard the servo motor sliding him into place inside the scanner. He was free to move his hands, but if he tried to raise them above shoulder-height he'd get a swift reminder of his actual circumstances.

"Are you ready for Zendegi?" she asked.

Martin said, "Yes."

Vivid blue sky. Yellow mud-brick buildings. Women in richly patterned scarves bustling past. Martin felt a tap on his hand. Javeed asked impatiently, "Baba, what's wrong?"

Martin finally gained control of his gaze and managed to turn his icon's head toward his son's voice without struggling against his restraints. "Sorry, I was just getting used to my *ghal'e*." He looked around. "So this is Old Kabul!" No time to make an entrance from the city's outskirts; they'd been inserted straight onto a busy street. A small boy leading a donkey loaded with gourds squeezed past them; he grinned at Javeed and greeted him with "*Salaam aleikum*." No doubt the phrase was wildly anachronistic, since they were meant to be in the pre-Islamic era, but Martin wasn't here to nitpick. They weren't planning to be too faithful to Ferdowsi, let alone historical fact.

"We need to get to Zal!" Javeed reminded him.

"Yeah—so what's your plan?"

"They don't know that the man in the prison is Zal," Javeed reasoned, "so you should tell them he's your son. Then they'll let you see him."

"Okay. So we have to find the prison. Who should we ask?"

"Hmm." Javeed didn't want to entrust a random passer-by with this vital query, so they made their way along the crowded street. People could be heard touting wares from all directions, but the hubbub was not unpleasant; compared to the car horns and motorbike engines of downtown Tehran it was bliss.

Javeed spotted a pomegranate seller. He tapped Martin's hand and whispered, "Buy something first, to make him happy."

Martin smiled and obliged. He mimed reaching into the money-belt beneath his *kameez*; he'd remembered to pre-order coins on the website the day before. When he'd bought the fruit he addressed the trader respectfully, "Sir, my oldest son has gone missing, and I heard he was arrested this morning due to some misunderstanding. I need to visit him, but I'm a stranger in this city. Can you tell me where I'll find him?"

The man expressed his sympathy and offered detailed directions. Martin struggled to commit them to memory; he should have ordered a pen and paper along with the coins. But Javeed appeared to have taken it all in; he set off briskly down the street, turning to Martin to urge him to catch up.

"I told you Afghanis were friendly," Martin said, tossing the pomegranate onto the ground. The week before, one of Javeed's schoolmates had pointed out an Afghani boy in another class and declared that his parents were sure to be murderers and the child himself a shameless thief.

"That man wasn't a real person," Javeed replied.

"That's true," Martin conceded. "But I've been to the real Kabul and met plenty of real people there."

Javeed scowled impatiently; this wasn't the time to talk about such things. Martin tried to relax; if he started thinking about all the pernicious nonsense he wanted his Proxy to be prepared to counter, he'd end up hijacking every Zendegi session for community service announcements. He had to trust Nasim to extract the same abilities from subtler cues.

They threaded their way through the crowds, past merchants selling clay pots, okra, lentils, whole butchered sheep. Martin couldn't fault Javeed's memory or sense of direction; he showed no signs of confusion or hesitation. In less than five minutes they were outside the prison.

It was an imposing, fortified building. As he pounded on the gate, Martin found himself recalling Evin, and the siege. A man with a thick black beard opened the gate a crack and eyed the callers suspiciously.

Martin repeated the story he'd told the fruit-seller.

"We have three hundred prisoners," the warder replied. "How will I know your son?"

Martin assumed that Zal was sticking to an alias; being known as the visiting prince of Zavolestan might have got him released, but it would also have risked sparking a war. "His hair is white, like an old man's. But he's young, less than half my age."

"I know the one," the warder replied. "He was caught creeping into the palace stables."

You don't know the half of it, Martin thought. "He was just looking for a place to sleep," he said. "We're strangers here, I and my two sons." He gestured at Javeed. "The boy misses his brother. Can't you let us see him for a few minutes?"

The warder sniffed viscously, then hawked and spat on the ground. He opened the gate and let them through.

Three buildings with ominous barred windows faced into a central courtyard. The warder led them across muddy ground; Martin found himself skirting the puddles as if his new virtual self, lacking contact with the dry floor of a *ghal'e*, couldn't help taking the threat of discomfort more seriously.

It was dim inside the prison building; it took a few seconds for Martin's eyes to adjust. Two rows of cage-like cells stretched out ahead of them on either side, each containing half-a-dozen grimy inhabitants. There was no furniture at all, just some straw on the ground and a bucket for each cell that Martin was glad he couldn't smell. In spite of himself, he couldn't help searching the prisoners' faces, wondering about their treatment and when they'd be released.

The warder led them toward a cell near the end of the right-hand row. "Hey, stable-boy! Your father's here for a visit!" A white-haired youth turned, a shocked expression on his face. His real father, Sam, was off fighting a war in Gorgsaran. Out of the warder's line of sight, Javeed raised a finger to his lips: we won't give away your secret, so don't give away ours.

Zal walked over to the edge of his cage. "Welcome, Father. Welcome, Little Brother. I'm ashamed that you're seeing me this way."

"I'm sorry it's come to this," Martin said. "It's my fault for not putting a roof over our heads."

The warder left them. They drew closer to Zal and he asked in a low voice, "Who are you? I'm sure you weren't in my expedition."

"We're simple Persian travelers," Martin explained. "We heard about your plight and wondered how we could help."

"You must keep silent," Zal insisted. "If Mehrab learns that Sam's son was inside his palace, visiting my beloved Rudabeh, no good will come of it for anyone."

"Do you want us to take a message to your entourage?" Martin suggested. They were camped on the outskirts of the city. "You must have been missed by now."

Zal shook his head. "If my companions learn my fate, it will be hard to restrain them. And if they enter the city and free me, that will make trouble that will not be easily undone."

Javeed said, "Why did you sneak into the palace?"

Zal sighed. "Imagine a woman as slender as a cypress tree, with a face more lovely than the full moon."

"But couldn't you just ask her father to let you marry her?"

"I will! I must!" Zal replied fervently. "But first I need to write to my own father, to persuade him that this match is auspicious. And then my father must find some way to win over the Persian King Manuchehr, to convince him that this alliance will not lead to tragedy. Mehrab is the grandson of Zahhak, the monster who brought death and sorrow to Persia for a thousand years! I cannot condemn Mehrab for his ancestor's crimes—or in the same breath I would have to renounce my beloved—but nor should I misjudge the struggle I'll face to gain my father's approval and Manuchehr's blessing."

That Javeed had supposedly derailed Zahhak's infamous career in an earlier encounter didn't seem to faze him; if he'd been able to change the whole history of the *Shahnameh* there'd be no framework for the stories left standing.

"Then how can we help you?" Javeed asked.

Zal stood in silence, pondering the question. Then he squatted down to bring his face close to Javeed's.

"Tell me, are you a boy who can come and go from a place unseen?"

"Yes," Javeed replied confidently.

"Are you a boy who can be trusted with the most prized of my possessions?"

"Yes."

Zal hesitated, rocking back on his heels nervously. He wiped his nose on his filthy sleeve; his commoner's disguise was very authentic, to the point where Martin had trouble picturing Rudabeh letting him into her room at all.

Zal made his decision. "In my tent outside the city," he whispered to Javeed, "there is a small bag made of plain brown cloth, with nothing to distinguish it or draw attention to its value. But if you can bring it to me without anyone knowing what you've done, I will throw open my treasury to you. You will have emeralds, diadems, five golden thrones, a hundred Arab horses adorned with the finest brocade, fifty elephants—"

"Elephants!" Martin saw Javeed's happy face, captured in Omar's shop before their first session, rendered at full strength for the first time in months.

"Listen carefully," Zal said. "We are camped on the southern bank of the river, a short march east of here. There will be two sentries standing guard, but we are not at war, so they will not be too serious in their task, and they will not be watching the river. Sneak in through the rushes, then make your way through the camp. My tent lies furthest to the south. The brown bag is beside my sleeping mat. Bring that here, and all my hardship will be lifted. Do you understand?"

"Yes."

"Can you do this for me?"

"Yes."

Zal reached through the bars and grasped his hand. "Fortune has favored me with an ally such as this. God protect you, Little Brother."

Javeed was silent as they walked back toward the courtyard. Zal had been his hero even before Mahnoosh's death; Martin was beginning to worry that the whole encounter might have been too intense.

"What are you thinking, *pesaram?*" he asked gently.

"Can we get an island?" Javeed replied. "To keep the elephants?"

"Ah. We'll see."

The warder let them out through the gate; Martin handed him a coin in the hope that it might make him more amenable upon their return. On the street, Martin found his bearings by the sun; he was assuming it was morning, and when they caught sight of the Kabul River it was on their left, so they were definitely heading in the right direction.

"See the mountains?" Martin said.

Javeed looked up across the river at the craggy brown peaks. "Yes."

"When I came here in real life it was winter, so they were covered in snow. It was beautiful, but the weather was freezing."

"That's when you were a reporter?"

"Yeah. Twenty years ago."

"And there was a war here?"

"Right. There was war here for more than thirty years."

Javeed absorbed that in silence, but Martin knew he'd keep turning the revelation over in his head. He remembered more of what Martin told him than Martin remembered himself.

The closely packed houses and shops soon gave way to small fields. The river, usually narrow, was swollen with the summer's melted snow; as it turned toward the dusty track they were following, Martin spotted a cluster of lavishly decorated tents a few hundred meters ahead. Three horses were visible, tethered to stakes, but there was nobody in sight. Maybe the sentries were having a siesta, but however vulnerable the apparently unguarded camp looked, Martin didn't want to risk marching straight in rather than following Zal's advice.

"That's the expedition," he said.

"Where are the elephants?" Javeed asked anxiously.

"Back in Zavolestan, I expect. Don't worry, I'm sure Zal will keep his word."

They turned off the track and headed for the riverbank. As they approached, Martin regarded the thick, reedy vegetation with dismay. That the rushes couldn't actually scratch their skin raw—or even register as tangible to any part of their body save their hands—offered a certain consolation, but it wouldn't stop the plants impeding their movement almost as effectively as the real thing.

Martin went first, pushing the springy plants aside with his hands, clearing the way for Javeed to follow close behind him. The plants weren't quite as tall as he was, so he walked with a crouch to keep himself hidden, grateful that at least his knees were spared the effects of doing that in an ordinary *ghal'e*. After a while he felt he'd settled into a successful rhythm, and he tried to crank up the speed—but Zendegi was having none of it: *the same, only faster* didn't compute. At first he could make no sense of this; he couldn't believe that the reeds were so heavy or stiff that a faster pace would require superhuman effort. Then he peered down at the mud and saw it adhering to his sandals as he lifted his feet. He couldn't feel the burning in his calves that might have come from pulling himself free of such sticky ground over and over again, but the bottom line was that Zendegi wouldn't let him operate his body as if these forces were of no consequence to him.

Perhaps they should have come closer to the camp before taking this arduous detour, but Martin had been paranoid about being spotted, and it probably wouldn't help if they modified their plans now.

After five minutes Javeed lost patience. "You're too big and noisy!" he complained. "Zal didn't say for you to come. Let me go by myself!"

Martin did not like the sound of that, but when he looked across the dispiriting expanse of marshland that still lay ahead of them, he finally noticed the fine network of gaps that a smaller body could slip through. Every third step he took was accompanied by the sound of reeds springing back into place, but with a little bending and swaying of his own Javeed could simply pass between them, almost in silence. Being lighter, he sank less deeply into the mud. And once he reached the camp his size was sure to offer similar advantages.

"All right," Martin declared reluctantly. "Just remember—"

"If I'm scared, thumbs-down," Javeed replied. "Don't worry, Baba, I'll be okay."

Martin turned aside and let him dart ahead. Within half a minute he'd vanished from sight.

Standing alone in the mud, Martin struggled to keep his thoughts from turning self-consciously to the Proxy. It was as if the invisible apprentice who'd been peering over his shoulder all this time, silently observing everything he did, now deserved some form of acknowledgement—and a concise lecture on some fine points of parenting to supplement all this long-winded teaching by example. But that wasn't how it worked. And since all the Proxy could do was *mimic* Martin's thoughts—not receive them, like telepathic messages—the very last thing it needed was reflections on its own creation that might risk transforming its mind into a hall of mirrors.

The proper subject for contemplation was Javeed, the proper mood a celebration of the fact that they could still spend time together. But in the life Martin had once imagined for them this journey would have been a mere rehearsal, whetting their appetite for the real thing. It was hard to swallow the claustrophobic vision of his health declining to the point where they could rule out actually traveling anywhere: not Afghanistan, not Australia, not even the ruins of Persepolis with the other tourists. Just Zendegi, over and over again—with his body laid out flat, as if he were already in the morgue.

He cut off that line of thought and tried to focus on his memories of the real Kabul. He pictured the crowded city of twenty years before; thousands of refugees expelled from Pakistan and Iran had found their villages too dangerous to return to, and had ended up living in bombed-out buildings in the capital, trying to survive the winters with broken roofs and the only fuel whatever dead trees could be found in the city's parks. He'd met one family—Ali and Zahra and their four young children—not too far from the bend in the river where Zal's imaginary party was camped. When Javeed was a little older he would need to hear their story, to hear who'd survived that winter and who hadn't.

Insects hovered over the mud. The sun was almost directly above now; Javeed was taking too long to return. Martin's thoughts snagged on a complication: the Proxy needed to be ready to make the right judgment, not only for the six-year-old Javeed, but also for the ten-, the twelve-, the fifteen-year-old—for however long it continued to be invoked. It would have no power to form long-term memories, or be shaped by its experience of watching him grow up; it had to work out-of-the-box with Javeed at any age. The last thing Martin wanted it to do was to treat his teenage son like an infant.

And he was supposed to prepare for that... how? By mentally prefacing every action with a conscious acknowledgment that it might not be appropriate at some time in the future? Well, he'd just done that. Back in the here and now, Javeed was a small child, and he'd either got lost or been caught. That he hadn't pulled the plug on the whole simulation meant almost nothing—least of all that he didn't need help.

Martin pushed through the rushes as fast as he could. It was only when he drew close to the camp that he attempted a degree of stealth; he was prepared to risk detection, but so long as they remained in Zendegi he wouldn't lightly throw away any chance they still had to succeed.

He crawled the last few meters on his knees and elbows; easier than in real life, maybe, but the concentration it took to manipulate his icon through the reeds felt almost as draining as any physical task. Charmingly, the game's designers hadn't failed to allow Zal's party a place where they could feed fertiliser to the river's algae: a tent had been set up backing onto the reeds, and it was sheer luck that Martin spotted it in time to avoid getting too close to its output plume. He crawled up beside the tent, then rose into a squat, partly sheltered as he peered into the camp.

Just out of sight, a man spoke, his voice at the edge of patience as if he'd been repeating the same question for a while. "Are you a spy, or a thief? *Which one is it?*"

"No!" came Javeed's plaintive reply. "I just wanted a job to feed the elephants."

Another man laughed. "Do you see any elephants?"

"No, but you could take me to Lavosestan."

"*Where?*"

The first man said, "He's a crazy little thief. Do you know what we do to thieves who don't tell the truth?"

"I'm not a thief!" Javeed retorted. "I'd never take anything—unless someone told me to."

"Really? So what were you planning to take? And who is your master who told you to take it?"

"No one!" Javeed insisted. "I just wanted to see the elephants."

Martin forced himself to keep some perspective. Javeed wasn't having an easy time with his captors, but he didn't sound desperate yet. His priorities were not hard to guess: an attempted rescue that blew their whole mission would not be acceptable.

Martin crept into the camp, steering clear of the interrogators, hoping he hadn't become disoriented and really was heading south. He wasn't sure why there were so few people around; maybe they'd already sent a search party into the city, looking for Zal after he'd failed to return from his latest night of passion. The whole arrest scenario had been cooked up last weekend by the game's software; the original story of Zal and Rudabeh had been a mixture of politics, family obligations and romantic swooning, loaded with proto-Shakespearean possibilities, but of limited interest to a six-year-old.

Helpfully, Zal's tent was distinctly more ornate than the others; Martin could have sworn there was real gold thread in the design, or at least... whatever. A reddish-brown stallion was tied up right by the entrance; it regarded Martin irritably, and as he tried to squeeze past it, it began to neigh. Martin put a hand on its flank. "Sssh. Stay cool, buddy, and you might get to play Rakhsh in the sequel." That promise seemed to do the trick, or maybe it had caught a trace of its master's scent on the intruder and deduced that Martin was here with Zal's blessing.

He ducked into the tent. The silk brocade and *khatam* knickknacks were almost enough to blind a non-princely eye, but Martin scrabbled around beside the sleeping mat until the plain brown bag materialized from the clutter as a kind of absence of decoration that refused to go away. It was about the size of his hand, sealed with a knotted drawstring; it made no sound when Martin shook it, and when he squeezed it gently he felt nothing but a slight rearrangement of its contents beneath the material. Definitely not a dagger, nor lock-picking tools. Maybe a rolled-up piece of parchment?

Martin lifted his *kameez* and stuffed the bag down the front of his *shal-war*. The fabric bulged slightly, but the *kameez* would hide that. Whatever cultural specifics might plausibly be ascribed to this mutated version of a medieval poet's tale of a much earlier time, Martin was fairly sure that the game's rating precluded anyone patting down his groin.

The stallion snorted haughtily as he emerged from the tent, not quite betraying him, but making it clear that he was there only on sufferance. He moved quietly back the way he'd come, glad now of the mud on his clothes.

Then he stood at the edge of the river and bellowed, "Javeed! *Pesaram! Koja'i?*"

The reply came back instantly: happy, relieved, not quite tearful. "Baba! *Inja hastam! Inja bia!*"

Martin strode toward his son's voice, oblivious to everything else around him, barely noticing the member of Zal's retinue approaching him before the man stepped directly into his path.

"Who are you?"

"Forgive me, sir; I've been searching for my son." Martin looked past his interlocutor; Javeed was standing on a patch of bare ground between two men. One of them had a scimitar in a scabbard strapped to his back; Martin's skin tingled with fear and revulsion, but he had to trust the game to have kept the threat abstract and muted. If anyone had waved a blade in Javeed's face—

"That's not an answer."

Martin forced himself to focus on the man blocking his way. "We were in the river, fishing; our boat struck a rock and went down. My son and I became separated. I swear, until now I was afraid he'd drowned."

The man regarded him suspiciously, but a flicker of compassion crossed his face. Martin was sure he wasn't human, but he wondered if he was one of the new-style Proxies that Nasim had mentioned, boosted with fragments of neural circuitry. *Are you a dumb cousin of the thing I'll leave behind?* Martin wondered. *Just human enough to react with real emotion to the idea of a drowned child?*

The man with the scimitar said, "We thought he was a thief. Why didn't he speak the truth?"

Martin said, "Sir, I apologize, but sometimes he goes crazy from the sun. His mind runs away from his work; all he can talk about is elephants."

The third man laughed. "Elephants in 'Lavosestan'? He's got too much imagination to be a fisherman."

Martin tried to appear deferential, though part of him was having trouble resisting the urge to grab a fallen tree branch and start clubbing everyone who continued to stand between him and his son. "As you say, sir. But he's done no wrong, and we need to go back and drag out the boat while there's still a chance to find it."

The two men closest to Javeed exchanged glances. "Very well," said the one with the scimitar. They stood aside; Javeed ran to Martin and took his hand.

As they walked out of the camp Javeed said, "I thought you weren't coming. I thought you were going to leave me there."

Martin's heart was pierced, but he forced himself to speak calmly. "I'd never do that. You know I'd never do that."

Javeed said mournfully, "What will we tell Zal?"

"It's not what we'll tell him, it's what we'll show him."

"Huh?"

Martin produced the bag, making as a big a show of it as he could. Javeed was enraptured.

"*You got it!* What's in it? What is it?"

"I didn't look inside. That would have been rude."

Javeed flapped his arms and grimaced with impatience. "Give it to me! Let me look!"

"Not a chance!" Martin replied. "I'll give it to you outside the prison, but only to carry, not to open. It's Zal's business what's inside."

All the way back into the city, Javeed kept begging for a peek, but it soon turned into a game; he was teasing Martin, he didn't expect to get his way. Martin was giddy with relief; Javeed hadn't really felt abandoned, and the delay in freeing him had been worth it in the end.

"We should bring lunch for Zal," Javeed suggested.

"Good idea." They bought some apples, grapes and pomegranates from the man who'd told them the way to the prison, then some cooked ground beef wrapped in flatbread from another shop.

At the prison, the warder seemed to have forgotten his previous bribe. "One visit a month! By royal decree!" He started to close the gate, determined to follow the letter of the law until Martin reached into his money-belt and came up with a handful of amendments and exceptions.

As they entered the cell block, Zal was standing near the edge of his cage. "Father! Little Brother! What have you done? I don't deserve this feast!" They passed him the food and he shared it out among his cellmates.

When the warder left, Javeed approached the bars. "We got what you asked for," he whispered, holding the bag discreetly by his side. The other prisoners averted their eyes as the contraband changed hands.

"Truly you are worthy of my praise and gratitude," Zal said. "Half of all I have is yours."

Javeed shook his head. "Just the elephants."

Zal smiled. "As you wish, Little Brother." He stepped back and unknotted the drawstring of the bag, then he pulled the mouth wide and drew out a golden feather.

Martin caught a flash of unease on Javeed's face. "Are you okay?" he whispered. They both knew what the feather meant, what it would bring.

Javeed nodded.

"We can go now if you want to. We'll sort out the elephants on the website."

"I want to stay," Javeed said. He added, barely audibly, "I want to see it."

"Father, do you have a flint with you?" Zal asked Martin.

When Martin shook his head, one of the other prisoners produced a small gray stone that had been hidden in his clothes. He handed it to Zal, who clasped him gratefully on the shoulder.

Zal struck the flint against a bar of his cell, holding the feather in the same hand. "Thanks to God and King Hushang, for the gift of fire." Martin saw the spark, but nothing followed. Zal repeated the motion a second time, a third. Finally, the feather caught alight.

White smoke wafted across the prison. The feather blazed with an intense light, but remained unconsumed. The inmates stood and watched the flame, then one by one their knees buckled and they fell to the ground, asleep.

A voice echoed through the building, tender and outraged, loud enough to shake Martin's teeth. "What is this injustice? Who has put my own sweet child in a cage?"

The Simorgh stood at the entrance from the courtyard, filling the doorway, stooped to fit. Its dog's head alone was half the size of a man; its muscular raptor's body, adorned with shimmering metallic feathers, was squeezed into the confined space—but rather than making it look trapped and trammelled, this only concentrated its power.

Martin touched Javeed's hand and they backed away slowly toward the prison's far wall. However many Brownie points they'd earned with its foster-son, they did not want to be standing in this creature's path when it decided to move.

Zal knelt and lowered his face. "My beloved protector, I am ashamed to ask for your help. You see with your own eyes where my carelessness has brought me. But I must find a way to marry Rudabeh without turning her family against mine. Give me this chance to salvage my fortune, and I will not disgrace myself again."

Martin looked down at Javeed; he was not unafraid, but he was utterly engrossed. Javeed's hair was a few shades lighter than that of the average Tehrani; nobody had ever spurned him because of it, least of all his parents, but that didn't seem to be the point. And whatever resonance he'd found in the story of Zal's childhood, he seemed to have taken consolation in the idea that his hero's abandonment had gained him a strange kind of love and protection, more fierce, more powerful than the human kind he'd lost.

The Simorgh charged, a blur of flowing muscle and outstretched talons wreathed in gold. Javeed flinched, emitting an involuntary whimper. Martin said, "Enough," and brought them out.

He waited in the whiteness for the motor to free him, then he heard Nasim pull off the cage. He flipped up the goggles himself.

"Everything okay?" Nasim asked. Martin wasn't sure if she'd watched the whole session, but in any case he wasn't in the mood to start analyzing the implications for the Proxy of all the choices he'd made.

"Yeah. I'll see you tomorrow morning."

"Right."

Martin shed his hi-tech attachments and reclaimed his belongings. He walked to the *ghal'eha* room where Javeed was waiting with Bahador, already wearing his signed Azimi jersey over his school clothes. Martin squatted down and embraced him tightly.

"*Mubaarak, pesaram.* We'll get an island for those elephants as soon as we get home."

They took a bus to Omar's shop. Martin had told Omar the same half-truth he'd told Javeed: that Nasim had equipment that was easier on his back. Omar had not made a big deal about it, and he greeted them as warmly as ever.

As Martin stood listening to Javeed recounting his adventure for Omar and Farshid, he thought: this is it, this is how it will be. Exactly the same scene, even after I'm gone: Javeed returning from his weekly session in Zendegi with his father.

Omar, Rana and Farshid would love and protect him, but he would not have lost his old life, his old family, completely. Even Mahnoosh would still be there beside him, in the Proxy's echoes of Martin's memories of her.

It was stranger than Zal's story, but it could still come true. All he had to do was immerse himself in the side-loading process—and hang on long enough to be sure that it worked.

20

Nasim walked past the protesters in silence. For the first few days she'd tried taunting them, hoping to get a violent reaction recorded on the building's security cameras that would force the police to intervene and move them on. But she had to admit that they were disciplined; even her suggestion that their favorite mullah belonged on the same bonfire as all the rest had raised barely a snarl. They'd studied 2012 and they'd learned from the winning side: the only route to popular respect was through restraint.

The crowd outside Zendegi's offices grew larger every day; this morning Nasim reckoned it was close to a hundred. Shahidi had found out about the Faribas and had wisely shifted his focus to them; by going quiet about Virtual Azimi he was no longer asking anyone to make the impossible choice between football and piety.

His supporters had adopted a curious slogan, repeated on all their placards: OUR SOULS ARE NOT FOR THESE MACHINES. A prohibition, rather than a flat-out denial of the possibility. Why couldn't they simply have scoffed at the prospect of machines ever possessing "souls"? That was the current Vatican position, which left *their* amateur philosophers with no controversy to fret over. Shahidi himself certainly hadn't said anything implying that Proxies modeled on fragments of human brains should be seen as human, but nor had he explicitly denounced the ambiguous slogan. He wanted it both ways, benefiting from the sly nod toward the most backwards, superstitious notions that would classify the Proxies as a form of forbidden "sorcery," while at the same time declining to make the claim—no doubt preposterous, and even blasphemous, in most of his colleagues' eyes—that a piece of software ever *could* have a soul.

Martin arrived for his ten o'clock solo session. He was punctual as always, but he was looking increasingly frail. He was no longer working in the bookstore, and Nasim had managed to persuade him to accept payment for his time here; though Zendegi would not be mining his scans for fragments to incorporate into games, there was still the possibility that their research would ultimately lead to commercial benefit.

As Nasim fitted his EEG skullcap, she said, "Do you think you could come for two hours tomorrow?"

"Of course." Martin hesitated. "So there's a problem?"

"The network's not converging as quickly as I'd hoped," she confessed. "More data can only be a good thing."

"Okay." Martin met her eyes in the mirror. "Two hours is fine, starting from tomorrow. Make it ten hours a day if you have to."

Nasim smiled. "I promise you, you'd go crazy long before ten."

When he was in the scanner, she went to her office to monitor the start of the data collection.

Martin's sessions with Javeed were crucial, but they did not yield anywhere near enough data. Even his current interactions with his son relied upon neural circuitry that could not be clearly resolved during the events themselves; for the Proxy to have any chance at all of handling a decade's worth of future encounters, the side-loading needed to have a much wider base.

So when Martin was alone, Nasim fed him a barrage of words, images and micro-scenarios to reach the places that no amount of children's *Shahnameh* could reach. Scripting hours of hand-tailored stimuli every week would have been impossibly labor-intensive, but Nasim had set up an automated feedback process that started with some not-quite-random imagery and then homed in on material that was seen to activate the regions that required more detailed mapping, shining spotlights into those corners of his skull from which the Proxy most needed to pick up extra cues. There was nothing so crude and literal as questionnaires about Martin's values and opinions, or rehearsals of imaginary conversations with an older Javeed; for all that Martin would have tried to respond sincerely, it would have taken superhuman self-control for anyone to behave naturally under those conditions. If he had wished to leave behind a video message for his son to view on some future birthday, he could have done that easily enough; the whole point of the side-load was to burrow deeper. The best way to do that was to deal in fragments, resolving Martin's mental landscape with the finest granularity possible before trying to re-create it in the Proxy's responses.

Nasim watched the images Martin was currently seeing, captioned for her with source information: shops in Islamabad, a Pakistani taxi, a Karachi street stall selling newspapers and cigarettes. Amputee children in a refugee camp in Quetta. Nobody could yet make video transcripts of dreams or memories, but the feedback process wallpapered these sessions with a kind of photo-library substitute for a visual autobiography.

Mahnoosh's face appeared; it was the same photo of her that had been on display at the funeral. When Nasim had explained the process to Martin, he'd insisted that she include his wife's image in the initial set and let the software decide if it was useful. Apparently it was.

Nasim closed the window, discomfited by the sense that she was intruding, even though Martin had more or less given up on the idea that anything in his skull could remain private. The neural activation map from the MRI showed that the process hadn't gone off the rails: the data being gathered was certainly more targeted than anything they would have obtained from Rorschach blots and white noise, or random imagery and audio fragments. Whether it would be sufficient to reach their goal remained to be seen; at this stage, if she'd dropped the Proxy into any kind of test scenario it would have made the first Dickens reading seem like a triumph of sophistication.

The version of Blank Frank she'd started with approximated far more of the brain than anything she'd built from the HCP scans before—but that didn't make it any more functional from the beginning, it just exposed all the flaws in the construction process more acutely. It was like the difference between making a toy car out of poorly molded plastic, and trying to do the same for a ten-thousand-gear timepiece that calculated eclipses and the phases of Venus; the first might actually move, clunkily, straight from the mold, but the second was guaranteed to seize up. It was going to take a staggering amount of polishing and fine-tuning to make all those wheels turn smoothly, let alone adapt their motions to Martin's private cosmology.

Bahador knocked and entered the office without waiting for Nasim to reply. He said, "We're being hacked."

Nasim followed him back to the programmers' room. Khosrow, Bahador's deputy, was compiling a list based on complaint reports coming in from the arcades. Nasim stared at the summary, shocked and dismayed. It had already crossed the two thousand mark.

A dozen of the screens around them showed specific environments that the intruders had managed to corrupt. One of the senior programmers, Milad, was examining an instance of *Minions of Eblis*. It had been infiltrated by a squadron of World War I biplanes, which were dropping balloons full of something brown and sticky onto the demonic battlefield.

"What's that supposed to be?" Nasim asked. "*Napalm?*"

"Hyper-treacle," Milad replied, struggling not to smile at the sight of the brown goo dripping all over their customers' icons. "It's a highly viscous fluid, defined with its own custom equations of motion—which are chewing up resources big-time, because they're deliberately difficult to compute. It's been used in other attacks, like Happy Universe in 2023, though obviously this is a refined variant or it would never have been accepted into our object queues."

"Great." Nobody would actually *feel* the stuff as it clogged up their virtual hair and drizzled down their faces—unless they got it on their hands—but apart from looking ridiculous in front of their comrades, the players were stuck with the fact that Zendegi was treating it seriously as part of their environment. That was a recipe for kinaesthetic dissonance: if you ran into a patch of hyper-treacle it couldn't forcibly impede your real feet, but if it glued your icon to the spot while *you* kept physically running, you either lost all sense of immersion in the game world, or you started to feel as sick and confused as if your inner ears, your visual system and your proprioceptive faculties had decided to go to war over their mutually exclusive theories of your body's motion. For a few million years prior to the existence of virtual reality, this had been a very good indicator that you'd eaten something you'd be better off without. People were soon going to have some very real fluids sloshing around their *ghal'eha*.

Nasim said, "So why aren't we pulling it out of the queues?"

"I'm trying to find a way to automate that," Milad replied. "On an object level, it's masquerading as demons' blood, and on superficial queries the two are completely indistinguishable. It's only its custom behavior and appearance when it's actually rendered that reveal its true identity. So to filter it out, I'm going to need to set up something that works from its final appearance."

"Okay." Nasim stepped back and left him to it while she tried to make a judgment about the bigger picture. If each corrupted game was going to take ten or fifteen minutes' worth of programming to deal with, she'd have no choice but to shut everything down for the day, forfeiting several million dollars in fees. Then again, maybe Milad's filter would be adaptable with some minor tweaks to all the other intrusions—but she didn't have long to determine how realistic that hope was. Thousands of customers were already signing out and demanding refunds, while the hard cases who hung around pretending they could "play their way through" the anomalies would be a PR and litigation nightmare when their steely dedication turned out to be the perfect emetic.

"What's happening with *Virtual Azimi?*" Nasim asked Bahador. He pointed to his own display, which showed a football field invaded by sheep. There weren't enough of the animals to hem the players in and stop them moving completely, but they'd certainly brought the game to a halt. The human players were standing around swearing, or fruitlessly trying to chase the sheep away; the animals were responding with skittish swerves that might or might not have been behaviourally accurate but certainly looked maximally frustrating. Virtual Azimi and the other Proxies were so confused by the whole turn of events that they'd all adopted their emergency strategy of sitting on the grass, holding their ankles and wincing as if they'd been injured.

"So have you got someone dealing with the sheep?" she asked.

"Arif," Bahador said. He added, deadpan, "His father's a butcher, he'll know what to do with them."

This was the game where they had the most to lose, but there might be a chance to salvage the situation. Nobody would try to run straight through the animals as if they weren't there, so at least there was no prospect of dissonance and nausea.

They walked over to Arif's desk. "How are things looking?" Nasim asked him.

Arif was staring at a properties window showing the responses the sheep objects were giving to a list of standard queries. "They're camouflaged as Proxy players," he said. Hardly *camouflaged* to human eyes, but the whole programming environment was based on protocols in which objects "told" Zendegi about themselves, rather than requiring the system to examine them in detail and reach its own conclusions. Zendegi would have ground to a halt if every pebble and blade of grass had to be drawn and inspected to confirm its true nature before being accepted as being what it claimed to be.

"Okay," Nasim replied, "so they need to be filtered based on their appearance. Maybe you can adapt what Milad's doing—?"

Arif turned to face her. "I've got a better idea. Can I use the Faribas?"

"The Faribas?"

"They do 'what's wrong with this picture?' almost as well as a human inspecting the same scene. If we use enough of them, we can show them every environment of every game in progress and have them point out the anomalies directly to an automated object filter."

Nasim thought it over. "Some of the fantasy games have all kinds of jokes and anachronisms," she said. "The people we side-loaded for the Faribas weren't in on the jokes; they would have classified them as anomalies."

Arif gazed at her in disbelief. "At this time of day, that's less than one per cent of what's running! We can shut those games down and give people refunds. It's no reason not to salvage all the rest."

He was right. Nasim said, "Okay, go ahead and try it."

As Arif set to work, Bahador said quietly, "It's disturbing, isn't it?"

"Being invaded by sheep?"

He shook his head. "The prospect of spawning a few thousand slaves like that."

Nasim didn't reply immediately. The truth was, she shared his disquiet to a degree, though it didn't make much sense. She'd convinced herself that there was nothing wrong with the Faribas popping in and out of existence all over Zendegi, whispering advice to the scripted Proxies in dozens of games, whenever the Proxies' behavior was too difficult to humanise by other means.

"They're not slaves," she said. "They've learned how to do a microscopic part of what a human does. If a factory worker guides a robot arm through a sequence of moves, does the robot become as human as the worker?"

"No," Bahador replied, "and I don't think the Faribas are human either. But it's still eerie, churning them out by the thousands."

Nasim said, "What difference does it make, whether it's one or a thousand?"

Bahador spread his hands in an admission of uncertainty. "Maybe none at all; I don't know. If I were sure that I knew the right way to think about this…" He trailed off, but Nasim could guess where he'd been heading. If he'd been certain that the Faribas were conscious, he would have been out on the street with Shahidi's followers. If he'd been certain that they were not, he would have applauded Arif's idea without reservation.

Arif worked quickly; the necessary hooks to the Fariba modules were all in place already, he just had to tie them together with a few other systems. When it was done, he tried out the anomaly-recognizer on an instance of the *Virtual Azimi* game; the sheep all flashed red, and nothing else was targeted. Then he quickly added code to purge the selected objects.

He turned to Nasim. "Can I—?"

"Yes, of course."

Arif ran his program. The sheep vanished. The human players began to cheer and applaud; the Proxies looked around, found nothing unfamiliar, and decided to stop feigning injuries.

Nasim said, "Launch it on everything."

Arif was taken aback. "*Everything?* No more tests?"

Nasim glanced at her watch. "We've lost at least three-quarters of a million dollars already. I'm willing to bet that this is going to make things better, not worse."

Arif didn't have personal authorization to launch so many processes at once, let alone the kind that intervened in every single game across Zendegi. Bahador and Nasim both had to sign off on the move—and an automatic notification of their action would be passed further up the hierarchy.

As she waited to be summoned to the boss's office to explain what had happened, Nasim took some comfort from checking a sample of the games on Khosrow's list. *Minions* was back to its usual uninhibited gore-fest; the biplanes had fallen victim to their own blatant absurdity. Nasim didn't ask for details of the symptoms that had afflicted all the other games, but as she flicked from environment to environment it occurred to her that some anomalies might have been subtler than sheep or treacle bombs.

Still, if they were subtle enough to be missed by the Faribas, maybe they'd be subtle enough for the players themselves to continue to the end of their session without even noticing that anything was amiss. As various games finished, the corrupted instances would be discarded; Bahador had had three people checking through back-up files, and he was sure they had reliable versions of all the major games. As new groups of players came online, they would start afresh with a safe copy of the program. There were a few games on Zendegi that ran continuously, supposedly twenty-four hours a day, but their fans were used to occasional reboots.

All in all, they'd been lucky. Arif and the Faribas had saved them from a crippling debacle that could easily have been ten times worse than the losses in revenue and prestige they'd already suffered.

Nasim's notepad buzzed; she was wanted upstairs. She knew that the good news wouldn't be enough when she still couldn't answer the hard questions: Who had done this and why? How had they broken through Zendegi's defenses and defeated all of the elaborate cross-checks that were meant to guarantee the integrity of every game?

And given that they'd managed to do all that once, how could they be prevented from doing it again?

It was after one in the morning when Nasim arrived home. She went out onto the balcony to refill the finches' food trough and change their water. Her ex-husband had given her the original breeding pair as a kind of joke, after she'd told him she missed her old research. At least Hamid had had a sense of humor. Unfortunately, the same perennially light-hearted attitude had extended to his relationships with other women. Nasim certainly hadn't wanted someone who'd smother her with possessiveness and earnest declarations of undying love, but with Hamid she'd erred in the other direction.

She sat in the living room, trying to organize her thoughts and unwind enough to catch a few hours' sleep. The board had held an emergency meeting and approved her plan to bring in an external security consultant to analyze the day's breach and try to prevent recurrences. Proud as she was of her staff's response to the crisis, she knew they didn't have the specialist knowledge required to find the source of the problem and permanently shore up the barricades.

As to whether the breach had been the work of Shahidi's supporters, Nasim remained openminded. She had already underestimated them once, and it would be too glib by far to assume that they could not have resisted painting self-incriminating slogans all over Zendegi's landscapes if they'd had the chance. As far as she'd been able to determine, they organized their protests with phone trees, where every direct link involved face-to-face friendships and genuine trust—a strategy that was invisible to SocNet's analysis, but wasn't wildly different from some of the techniques that had brought down the theocrats in 2012. Hacking into Zendegi would have taken much more than a dash of resourceful political recycling... but Nasim was making no more assumptions. Let the consultants work it out.

She had her notepad disgorge its latest news summary; she expected to catch still more flak, but before she could switch off for the night she needed to feel that she'd run the gauntlet and taken all the punishment on offer. As it turned out, jokes about the intrusion were still flitting around the globe, but most of them were remarkably gentle. Perhaps that wasn't so surprising; the pranks themselves had generally been witty and good-natured, and while it was embarrassing to have been hacked at all, the swift response meant that Zendegi hadn't been made to look spectacularly incompetent. A few hundred customers—out of hundreds of thousands in the affected games—had suffered some short-term nausea; a few dozen *ghal'eha* had needed scrubbing out. The company's share price had fallen, but not dramatically.

When she'd fast-forwarded through all the variants of the "Sheep Stop Play" story, her knowledge-miner served up something from a completely different vein. The *Wall Street Journal* had just published an article on Ei-konometrics' new product range: a set of trainable software modules for automating production lines and call centers.

"One worker in a semi-skilled job of this kind—and across the globe, there are five hundred million jobs in this category—can teach the software everything it needs in order to take over the work of tens of thousands of his or her colleagues. Of course, we're not talking about ambulatory robots gathering around your office water-cooler; the work must already be physically constrained, as in a suitable factory process, or entirely computer-mediated, as with call centers. An Eikonometrics spokesman declined to comment on the prospects for software able to climb the next rung up the skills ladder, but a source close to the company indicated that the financial services industry would be the likely next target."

Nasim had known that something like this would be coming eventually, but she still felt blindsided, and cross that Caplan hadn't bothered to warn her a few days ahead of the announcement. Five hundred million jobs at stake, and Zendegi had pioneered the technology… That didn't rule out Shahidi's supporters as the hackers, but it certainly extended the list of suspects.

Five hundred million? Nasim couldn't quite process the idea that the methods she'd shared with Eikonometrics might throw half a billion people out of work. There were several perfectly truthful footnotes she could append to that stark claim in the hope of rendering it more palatable: conventional software probably would have automated most of the same jobs within a decade or so, regardless—and someone else would have adapted her finch paper's methods to the HCP sooner or later if she hadn't done it herself.

But she was the one who'd made the technology work, and brokered its fusion with side-loading. She'd saved her own job, and those of her own employers and colleagues; she'd reaped the benefits for herself and the people around her. If those on the losing end of the same transformation were angry, what did she expect? That they'd take a suitably stoical attitude and spare Zendegi from any backlash… because someone else almost certainly would have screwed them over in the same way, eventually?

In all her years in exile, what she'd wanted most of all was to join the fight she'd been forced to flee—to spit in the faces of the murderous fanatics who'd killed her father and ruined her country. And ever since her return, she'd been itching for a rematch. She'd wanted the theocrats to stagger to their feet again, for the sheer pleasure of watching them bloodied again, brought down again.

But the war she'd actually found herself in was nothing like her father's struggle. Perhaps not many people would subscribe to Shahidi's medieval view of side-loading, but there were other reasons to feel disquiet about the process—some of them indisputably solid and real. The killjoy cleric who didn't want the workers playing football with their hero's Proxy was enough of a political animal to put that point of contention aside and find common cause with everyone whose job was at risk. This was not going to be a simple matter of watching one more crazy mullah brought down by people with saner priorities.

Nasim switched off her notepad. It was after two, and she knew that if she didn't get four hours' sleep she'd be useless in the morning. She had an appointment with the security consultants, and she needed to be sharp or they'd have her signing off on all kinds of expensive placebos.

21

"Congratulations, Mr. Seymour. Your new liver is ready."

Dr. Jobrani turned his computer screen so Martin could see the photo that had been emailed from the organ bank. Even obscured by a maze of translucent scaffolding and immersed in a yellow-tinged nutrient bath, it looked encouragingly healthy and whole. It was miraculous enough that a slab of meat this large could have been grown from a few dozen cells extracted from his own skin; that the result was also an intricate maze of chemical factories and energy stores was positively surreal. And even if the whole liver-in-a-bottle process wasn't quite as flawless as advertised, Martin had seen enough scans of what remained of the organ he'd been born with to be pretty sure that this hydroponic version would be a trade-up.

"Now it's just a matter of scheduling the surgery," Jobrani explained. "I managed to get them to pencil you in for a slot early next month. Once you've signed the paperwork I can send you to the surgeon for the final checks, and we can make it official." He rubbed his hands together enthusiastically, then started pecking his way through his computer's menus, hunting for the right form to print out.

Martin hadn't seen his oncologist in such an ebullient mood before, perhaps because this was the first time he'd had anything like good news to offer him. Two weeks earlier, he'd had to tell Martin that the tumor-specific markers in his blood were showing an increase. The cancer was developing resistance to the antibody treatment; that had not been unexpected, but it was happening earlier than they'd hoped. The new liver could certainly prolong his life, but the resurgent cancer would probably still take him within a year.

Martin said, "What are the risks? Of the surgery?"

Jobrani stayed focused on his menus. "It's best if you discuss that with the surgeon. Just let me find this form."

"I'm not sure about the date," Martin said. "Can't we make it a few months later?"

"Later?" Jobrani stopped typing and looked at Martin. "Why would you want to do that?"

Martin had been preparing himself for this conversation for some time. In his imaginary rehearsals, his white lies had always emerged smoothly and persuasively, and he'd won the day without too much fuss.

He said, "I want to spend more time with my son before I risk the transplant. If I die on the operating table—"

Jobrani scowled. "That's nonsense! You know that the state of your liver is the only reason you have no quality of life now. It's true that you could die in surgery—but if you survive you'll have ten times as much energy, for at least another six or eight months. Every week after the transplant will be worth ten weeks of the kind of life you have right now—and twenty of what you'll be like if you push back the date much further."

Martin looked him in the eye. "Forget about quality of life. Can you swear to me that my chances of surviving six more months from today are greater if I have the transplant? That the odds of dying during the operation are less than the odds of dying from the lack of it?"

"If you postponed the surgery for six months," Jobrani replied, "your chances of dying in the theater would triple. At least triple."

"Okay. But that's not what I asked."

Jobrani had no interest in sanctifying Martin's bizarre request with actual probabilities. "You're not being reasonable, Mr. Seymour. Do you really think your son benefits from seeing you this way?"

Martin said, "There are things that I need to resolve. Things that are important to me. I can't take the chance of leaving them unfinished."

Martin was on the verge of pulling something out of the freezer to microwave for dinner when Rana turned up on the doorstep with an enormous bowl of hot stew.

He invited her in, then went through the ritual of *ta'arof*, refusing the gift three times before finally accepting it. Rana insisted that she couldn't possibly join them—she would be eating with Omar and Farshid when they got home—and though she also insisted that Martin and Javeed should feel free to start immediately, it would have been unbelievably rude either to hurry her out of the door, or to begin the meal in her presence.

So Martin put the fragrant dish in the kitchen and the three of them sat nibbling on pistachios.

"You should come and stay with us, Martin *jan*." Rana looked around the living room appraisingly; she almost seemed disappointed that there were no clumps of dust or obvious traces of vermin in sight. Martin was still perfectly capable of keeping the house clean.

"You're very kind," he replied, "but honestly, we're doing fine here." Javeed, whose idea of heaven would've been having Farshid on call to entertain him twenty-four hours a day, glanced at Martin, but managed to keep his mouth shut.

Rana smiled regretfully. "Well, the offer's always open. You and Javeed would be welcome as our guests, any time."

"Thank you." Martin didn't doubt her sincerity—and he could forgive her for scanning his house for signs of incipient Widower's Squalor—but he wasn't ready to let the last traces of structure in his life start melting away. He'd finally given up on the shop and put the business on the market; if he lost control over his own domestic routines he'd have nothing.

"So how is everyone?" he asked. He hadn't visited Omar's home for a while, nor discussed his family, and it turned out that after six years on a waiting list, Rana's father-in-law, Mohsen, was about to have new prostheses fitted: fully functioning mechanical legs that he'd be able to control by thought alone. Javeed listened in amazement to Rana's sketch of the process: they'd already implanted electrodes in Mohsen's spinal cord and he'd spent two months practicing with virtual copies of the limbs, fine-tuning the interface in preparation for the real thing. Martin was surprised that Omar hadn't mentioned any of this.

Rana left, and they wolfed down the stew. Though Martin did not forget to take the medication that helped with his impaired digestion, he ate so rapidly that he got stomach cramps anyway, and Javeed spent the rest of the evening teasing him about his greediness and bad manners. Laughing made the cramps worse, which only egged Javeed on. When Javeed finally climbed into bed, Martin sat smiling in the darkness, clutching his side.

Just after midnight Javeed woke, crying for his mother. Nothing Martin did comforted him. Finally, at his wits' end, he brought an electronic photo frame loaded with pictures from the Australian trip he'd taken with Mahnoosh the year they'd married. Martin had never got around to showing them to Javeed before, and something about the unfamiliar images fascinated and calmed him. It was as if this evidence that his mother's life extended far beyond his current knowledge of her gave him back a small part of what he'd lost: a sense of her continuing, a sense of a well that would never run dry.

When Javeed fell asleep, Martin went back to his own bed and tried to conjure up Mahnoosh beside him. All the hours he'd spent in the scanner reliving his memories of her had robbed him of any hope that he could be surprised by some long-forgotten incident, but that wasn't important now. All he wanted was her presence, even if it was utterly familiar; even if it offered nothing new.

But the darkness remained blank, the pillow uninhabited. He'd wanted her to haunt the Proxy's thoughts the way she'd haunted his own—so was that the trade-off? Was that how it worked? At his behest, had she already acknowledged the succession?

Martin paid the taxi driver and walked slowly past the protesters, who seemed to regard him more with curiosity than malice. Who was this sick old man visiting Zendegi day after day? He was surprised that they didn't know yet; that they hadn't guessed, or got the news from an informer on the inside. After all, he was here to commit a sin that made Azimi's whoring of his God-given talent about as serious in its blasphemy as a love potion or a lucky charm.

Inside, he willed the elevator to fail; if he had to take the stairs he could spin that out for at least fifteen minutes. But the door sprung open and the usual insufferably cheery woman's voice asked him in Farsi to state his destination. Martin let her cycle through English, French, Arabic and back to Farsi before responding.

Nasim was caught up in a meeting that had run into overtime; Bernard helped Martin prepare for the scanner. "How long are you planning to stay in Tehran?" Martin asked him.

"It was going to be six months," Bernard replied. "I've been training some local staff to use this machine. But I might be staying on; I've met someone I like."

"Congratulations. But you should take him back to Europe, to be safe."

Bernard was surprised. "You're kidding, right? I thought no one had been prosecuted for years."

Martin said, "If it's still considered political suicide to take the laws off the books, I wouldn't treat them as defunct."

Bernard adjusted Martin's goggles and gestured for him to approach the MRI. "I think I'll take my chances," he said. "If we go back to Europe, in three months I'll be wearing a wedding ring."

Martin lay down in the machine. His body was rigid; he took a few deep, slow breaths. He closed his eyes before Bernard flipped down the goggles. His fists clenched; no gloves today. The motor whirred.

Bernard said, "Martin? Can you open your eyes please?"

Reluctantly, Martin complied. The goggles were feeding him street scenes of Sydney in the eighties, accompanied by snatches of music and news. Hunters and Collectors sang "Carry Me," the vocals as raw as an open wound. Tim Ritchie on 2JJJ introduced The Residents' eerie, pulsing electronic version of "Jailhouse Rock." Whatever its faults, the machine had certainly learned how to take him back.

Martin tried to relax and follow the cues as the state premier, Neville Wran, floated in front of him, waffling gruffly about nothing comprehensible. Martin couldn't recall having any particular opinion of the man. State politicians just made him think about trains—train drivers' strikes, trains coming to a halt in the middle of the night. Once he'd been traveling home from the city, close to midnight, and the train had stopped on the bridge over the Parramatta River for forty minutes, for no apparent reason, with no explanation. He'd looked out over the dark water and thought about diving in and swimming to the shore, just to put an end to the waiting. The memory was vivid; he could see red paint flaking off the carriage's old-style, manually operated doors. He could have jumped out; there'd been nothing to stop him. But he hadn't been quite foolish enough. In fact, he hadn't really been tempted at all.

And he'd been back to that carriage a dozen times already under the scanner's gaze. Was it something he desperately needed the Proxy to remember? Had it been a great defining moment for his world view, his moral framework? No. So why was he wasting time thinking about it when every second he had left was precious—and every second in this machine doubly so?

Now the goggles showed Midnight Oil on stage at Selina's nightclub. Martin could almost smell the spilt beer and acrid sweat... *but so fucking what?* No doubt something in his head lit up at the sight of this performance; he'd been there on the night, or one very like it. But he was just spinning his wheels, deepening the ruts memory had carved out by pure chance. The machine didn't know how to take him anywhere new from here. It knew it needed more from him, but it didn't know how to find it.

The machine seemed to reach the same conclusion; it gave up on the nostalgia trip and started showing him photographs of strangers. An old man stood in the ruins of a house; the style of his clothing and what remained of the building made Martin think of the earthquake in Kashmir. A woman with a dark blue, lace-trimmed headscarf held the hand of a young girl in a pink floral dress, on a crowded street somewhere in Indonesia or Malaysia. Individuals, couples, families; each image persisted for just a second or two. Though Martin couldn't help noticing clues as to where and when the pictures had been taken, Nasim had reminded him many times that this wasn't meant as a trivia quiz, a tool to boost the Proxy's general knowledge. The aim was far more abstract: the images were like flashes of light, positioned at random in a vast space of possibilities, and the record of his brain's responses was like a collection of shadows of a single complex object, cast from many directions. If the Proxy could be sculpted so it cast the same shadows, that would help strengthen its resemblance to him.

The metaphor was imperfect; the real process was neither as simple nor as passive as that. But it did include a hint of one potential pitfall: a thousand acts of illumination from the same direction would reveal no more detail than a single flash. Nasim and her colleagues did not understand the process well enough to know in advance which images would be freshly revelatory and which would tell them nothing new. The only solution was to throw so many different scenes at him that the unavoidable dilution of their effectiveness would be overcome by sheer force of numbers.

Martin caught himself being distracted by these meta-thoughts and forced himself to attend more closely to the images themselves. Two boys in a parched rural landscape prodded an ants' nest with a stick as their dog looked on dubiously. Two tearful women embraced on the steps of a courthouse. A drunken youth swung a punch at another man outside a nightclub while a woman sitting awkwardly on the pavement looked up at them, scowling. Martin struggled to keep his eyes open; he succeeded, but it felt like a superhuman task. A frail-looking child rode alone on a merry-go-round, seated on the back of a red horse with a garish green saddle. An elderly woman gazed sadly at a framed black-and-white portrait of a uniformed man. It was like being trapped in a never-ending Benetton advertisement. Martin thought about the contents of his freezer; Rana had brought them a meal the night before, and if he bought two more frozen meals on his way home he'd be fine until the weekend. Then he and Javeed could go to the bazaar together, and cook something in the afternoon. He loved chopping fresh dill; the scent was exhilarating.

Nasim said, "Martin, we're taking you out."

The goggles went blank; Martin waited for the servo to withdraw him from the scanner.

When his face was uncovered he sat up and turned to Nasim. He said, "I'm sorry, I know I lost focus. I didn't get much sleep last night; maybe I just need some more coffee."

"I don't think coffee will do it," Nasim replied. "Even when you're attentive we're getting nothing useful now. The rate's been trailing off for days."

Martin felt a chill of fear. "You're not giving up?"

"No, of course not!" Nasim sighed. "This is my fault; I should have been on top of this sooner, but I've been a bit distracted by the inquisition."

Apparently the investigation into Zendegi's breach had been generating resentment and discontent among the staff; Bahador had made some acerbic comments about a return to Khomeini-era paranoia the last time he'd bumped into Martin.

"We've pushed the current methods about as far as we can," Nasim continued, "but that's not the end of it; it just means we have to change tack."

Martin said, "Okay—but how close is the Proxy to completion right now?"

"It's improved a lot over the last few weeks," Nasim assured him. "Quantitatively, statistically, we can show that. But at this point it's not…"

"Foster parent material?"

"I'm afraid not."

"What about mind-the-kid-while-I-duck-into-the-shops material?"

Nasim smiled uneasily. "We've got some way to go, but I'm not discouraged. We always knew this wasn't going to be easy." Martin appreciated the way she declined to point out that she'd originally told him it would be impossible.

"Is there still a chance we could complete this in six months?" he asked. "If you find a new approach, that might even be faster than the old one, mightn't it?"

Nasim didn't answer him directly. "Give me a few days," she said. "Take a break from the scanner. I'll talk to the people at Eikonometrics who've been working on some other side-loading projects. Between us, I'm sure we can come up with a better way to pick your brains."

"We won't want the books!" The man, Reza, laughed as incredulously as if Martin had offered him a good deal on a blacksmith's forge. "We'll take over the lease, but forget about the stock and the business. We want to use this space for a gym."

Martin resisted the urge to throw Reza's derisive laughter back at him. "A gym? *Here?*" He gestured at the shop's display windows stretching from floor to ceiling, just centimeters back from the pavement packed with pedestrians and motorbikes.

"Exactly!" Reza replied enthusiastically, as if Martin had been congratulating him on his visionary plans. "We're taking more space upstairs and next door, but we need this place for the windows. We put the hot women just behind the glass. Free advertising."

Women exercising, on display on Enqelab Avenue. Reza must have caught the hint of skepticism on Martin's face, if not the undertone of dismay, because he declared with cheerful optimism, "This is a new country. Anything is possible."

They used the real estate agent's website to organize the transfer of the lease. Martin had three weeks to vacate the premises.

When Reza left, Martin put an advertisement online for his print-on-demand machine, then emailed the three students who'd worked for him in the past, to see if any of them could come in and do shifts for the closing down sale. He composed some posters on the office computer, then printed out versions proclaiming fifty, seventy-five, and ninety per cent off. He taped the first set to the windows.

Then he found an empty packing box and took it to the English language section. Javeed would have ten million electronic books to choose from, but Martin still wanted to pass on something from his own century. From the novels he picked out *The Grapes of Wrath*, *Animal Farm*, *Catch-22*, and *Slaughterhouse Five*; from non-fiction, *The Diary of Anne Frank*, *Down and Out in Paris and London*, and *The Gulag Archipelago*. He was tempted to go on and fill the box to its rim, but once he started fretting over omissions he knew there'd be no end to it. Javeed wasn't going to a desert island, and the weightier Martin made this package, the greater the risk that actually reading the books would seem like a daunting or oppressive prospect.

Would the Proxy have anything worthwhile to say about these works? Martin wasn't sure that he remembered enough himself to discuss them in any detail. But anyone risked seeming like a lightweight to a teenager who'd just read Solzhenitsyn; it would be absurd to set the bar too high. Martin would be satisfied if the Proxy could share a laugh with Javeed at the mention of Major Major or Milo Minderbinder and bluff his way convincingly through the rest.

He stood by the sales counter and looked around the shop; in a strange symmetry, it had begun to smell of wood and glue, the way it had smelled when the carpenters had first been putting in the shelves.

Was there anything else he should set aside? He already had Mahnoosh's bookshelf at home, stacked with her favorite works in Farsi; he wouldn't know what to add to that. He taped up the box and wrote Javeed's name on it in big letters, to be sure it wouldn't get thrown out by mistake if something happened to him suddenly.

As he was putting the packing tape back in the storeroom, his notepad chimed.

The message from Nasim read: *I think we've found something worth trying.*

"Martin, this is Dr. Zahedi." Nasim stepped aside so they could shake hands.

"Pleased to meet you," Martin said. His mouth was dry. Nasim had answered most of his questions on the phone, but he was still feeling anxious.

Dr. Zahedi gestured at a chair in the corner of the MRI room, partly hidden behind a movable screen. "Take a seat, please," she said.

Nasim said, "I'll give you some privacy."

Dr. Zahedi took Martin's blood pressure and listened to his heart. He gave her the physicians' access code to his online medical records and she flipped through his scans and pathology reports in silence. It occurred to Martin that Bernard had never logged the injection of his exotic contrast agents in these records—and if Dr. Zahedi logged what she was about to give him, he'd have a lot of explaining to do to his oncologist.

"The drug Ms. Golestani has asked me to administer has moderate sedative and disinhibitory effects," Dr. Zahedi explained. "It's been approved at much higher doses as one component in a regime used for general anesthesia, but the dose we'd be giving you today would be less than a tenth of that."

Martin said, "So there's no chance I'm going to... stop breathing, or have a heart attack?"

"The chances of any adverse side-effects are extremely low," Dr. Zahedi assured him. "Even with your impaired liver function, I'm confident that you won't be in any danger. But I'll be here throughout the session, to be absolutely sure that nothing goes wrong."

"Okay." Having gone out of his way to avoid the risks of surgery, Martin had a claustrophobic sense of his choices narrowing. But he was not going to be paralyzed and cut wide open; he was not going to be breathing through a tube. He would be taking *one tenth the dose* of *one component* of a general anesthetic.

"The other aspect of the protocol that requires your consent is the use of an infrared laser to induce mild pain," Dr. Zahedi continued. "This will be applied only to one finger, and the power will be well below the threshold that could cause tissue damage. There will also be a limit imposed on the number of times the laser can be used in a given period; I've been asked not to disclose the details, to avoid the possibility that it could reduce your aversive response. But I'm satisfied that there's very little chance of psychological trauma."

Martin said, "I'm sure I'll be fine." Nasim had already explained the logic behind the finger-zapping. The drug was intended to make him more suggestible, more responsive to the images he was shown, but at the same time it would put him at risk of wandering off on a mental tangent. Eikonometrics had found that Rhesus monkeys on the same drug could be induced to keep focusing on a barrage of less-than-riveting images by inducing mild pain whenever their attention wandered. If that had got past an animal-experimentation ethics committee, Martin was willing to give it a go.

He signed the consent forms. When Nasim rejoined them and asked if he had any questions, he said, "Tell me once more that this isn't going to make the Proxy permanently stoned."

Nasim smiled; they'd been over this already. She said, "Giving you a drug that changes some activity patterns in your brain means we're gathering data that's only *directly* comparable to the Proxy's activity if it's also been subject to the same changes. So we will, in effect, need to 'drug' the Proxy while we train it to match your responses. But that's still going to bring the Proxy's neural wiring closer to yours—with benefits that will persist when it's operated normally."

Martin thought he *almost* understood, but Nasim, seeing the lingering doubt on his face, took one more shot.

"Think of it this way," she said. "A method actor wants to play you in a movie, so he takes you to a bar and gets you tipsy, so you open up more than you otherwise would. All he's seeing is what you're like on alcohol, so naïvely you could say that all he's really gained is the power to imitate you in that particular state. But of course, it doesn't really mean he's going to play you as a drunk in the movie. It just means he's got some dirt on you that helps him to play you better, sober."

Martin said, "So basically, all this technology is a substitute for Robert De Niro and a bottle of Jim Beam?"

Dr. Zahedi administered the injection. After a few seconds, Martin felt… pleasant. Untroubled. He sat smiling faintly while Nasim fitted the skullcap and goggles and led him to the MRI.

Before she flipped the goggles down, Nasim pushed something that looked like a thimble over Martin's right index finger. She said, "If you really can't stay focused, just take this off. But if you do that, it's the end of the session."

"Okay. I understand."

When everything was in place, the servo-motor whirred. For the past few weeks Martin had experienced a sinking feeling as he slid into the machine for his solo scans, but the drug certainly took the edge off that.

The sequence of photos that had been interrupted in his last session resumed from the beginning. Martin gazed at the old man in his earth-quake-ravaged house; he was sure he'd felt sympathy for his plight before, but this time it was as if a physical barrier that had been standing between the two of them had been erased. Not only was the man's presence more vivid and compelling, Martin found himself examining the scene as if he genuinely had a role to play, a stake in the outcome, an ongoing connection. Where would the man get food, water, shelter? What had he been through? Who was he mourning?

After a couple of seconds the man was gone, but Martin ignored the image in front of him and kept pondering the implications of the quake. His arm jerked involuntarily, as if he'd touched the edge of a hot plate and pulled his hand away before registering what had happened. Then he felt the painful jab of heat on his finger. He was prepared to believe there was no permanent damage, but the laser certainly delivered more than a tickle.

He'd lost his chance with the second image, but when the third appeared—a young Iranian couple strolling in a park—he gave it his full attention. Immersed in the scene he felt a glow of paternal warmth, as if he might have been standing before Javeed and some future daughter-in-law. Unfortunately, that glow outlasted its allotted time, and he was punished accordingly.

After that, he made an effort to prepare for the cycle: engage, react, disengage. It had to become automatic. Monkeys could do it; how hard could it be? He managed three successful immersions in a row before overshooting and burning his finger again.

Then four immersions, then… it must have been twenty minutes later that he stopped to reflect on how well he was doing. Keeping up the pace had been hard at first, but once he'd got into a rhythm—

Contemplating the task instead of performing it won him another stinging rebuke. Martin didn't make the same mistake again. He cut short a hopeful vision of this cascade of brighter, sharper flares penetrating the fog-bound backwaters of his brain and lost himself in the flood of images, treading water in an endless present.

22

"We believe it's an inside job. The question that remains is: inside *where?*"

Jafar Falaki, of Falaki Associates, reached across Nasim's desk and handed her his interim report. Ominously, the usage meter on the side of the USB stick read "2.7 terabytes"; Nasim decided that a brief oral summary might be helpful.

"So you can't rule out Zendegi's staff," she said, "but you can't rule out any of our providers either?"

"Exactly."

Nasim had been hoping that Falaki would identify some simple, foolish error that she or one of her colleagues had made, leaving Zendegi vulnerable to intrusions by any sufficiently resourceful stranger. Having found the hole in their defenses they could have worked out how to plug it, and that would have been the end of it. It might not have told them who the intruder had been, but then, it would have left them with no urgent need to know their enemy's identity. The embarrassment of having to admit to some shoddy programming would have been worth it. Anything was better than having to deal with full-blown industrial counter-espionage.

"So where do we go from here?" she asked. "We have thirty-seven providers in our pool, all with impeccable reputations, all audited and certified as thoroughly as..."

"As thoroughly as each other?" Falaki suggested. "The standard industry protocols are valuable, but they're not a watertight guarantee of anything. What you really need to do is put pressure on them to install third-party hardware monitoring."

Yeah, right. The major providers of Cloud computing took security very seriously, allowing independent auditors to perform snap inspections and random integrity tests. But yanking thousands of processor chips right out of their sockets and forcing them to talk to their circuit-boards through extra hardware that watched and verified their every move would not only be hugely expensive; in some of their customers' eyes it would amount to a stark admission that there really was a problem demanding that level of overkill. For one company alone to adopt those measures would be commercial suicide. For the whole industry to adopt them, all at once, would require a miracle.

"We don't have the clout to make that happen," Nasim said bluntly. "If we banded together with all the other high-end users, we *might* be able to start negotiating the introduction of hardware monitoring… maybe ten years down the track. But pointing the finger at thirty-seven companies and saying 'The blame lies either with one of you, or with us' is not going to cut it. They're not going to invest millions of dollars to fix a problem that might have nothing to do with them, when they can pass the buck between themselves—or even better, pass it right back to us."

Falaki said, "I understand. It's the ideal solution, but we're not living in an ideal world."

Nasim turned the USB stick over in her hand. Most of the report's weighty appendices would be automated analyses of log files, software settings, and hardware tests for Zendegi's own equipment. Falaki's team had scrutinized everything from personal notepads—her own included—to the company's workstations. They'd found no evidence of an external hacker gaining access, but then they'd found no evidence of impropriety by any of her staff either.

"So short of hardware monitoring, what's the next best thing?" she asked Falaki.

"Software overseers," he replied. "Every process you run in the Cloud gets twinned with a supervisor process that watches its back—preferably from the vantage point of a different provider. It's not foolproof and it's quite expensive; maybe a fifty per cent resource increase if you don't want your customers to experience lags."

"But it would make life complicated for whoever's screwing with us?"

"Absolutely," Falaki replied. "And it would make it far more likely that we'll either end up with evidence against them, or succeed in blocking them out completely."

"Unless they're geniuses who can subvert anything."

Falaki smiled. "No one has magic shortcuts for every possible challenge. Even if one of your providers is completely corrupt and is messing with your processes more or less at will, we can still make it very costly for them to do that *and* look innocent."

"More than it costs us?"

"I believe so," Falaki said carefully.

Nasim was doing her best to put off imagining sharing this news with the board. A fifty per cent increase in their computing outlays would be painful, but it would be money well spent if it led them swiftly to a lone saboteur. At the opposite extreme, though, if Cyber-Jahan had decided to play dirty, the prospects could be very different. A company like that would have the expertise and resources to bleed Zendegi from two wounds at once—customer losses and expensive countermeasures—and to keep it up for months, even years.

She held up the memory stick. "I *will* read this, I promise, but we might as well get as far as option three."

"All right." Falaki cleared his throat. "This only pertains to the possibility that a member of your own staff is involved, but you might want to consider it, for peace of mind."

"Go on."

Falaki said, "I sometimes find it useful to bring in another firm, run by an old business partner of mine, that employs some skillful interrogators. They could interview your staff and pursue the issue more robustly than we've been able to so far."

Nasim stared at him, waiting for his earnest face to crack. She wasn't used to being teased by people she barely knew—it had taken Bahador a year to start including her in his office pranks—but maybe this was Falaki's way of defusing tension in a stressful job. "Skillful interrogators" was a common euphemism for a very specific kind of person in post-2012 Iran: former VEVAK agents who'd had the connections and resources to cushion their fall.

Falaki gazed back at her blandly. He was serious.

Nasim said, "I think we might pass on that."

Martin had been taking the disinhibitor for nearly a week before Nasim finally found the time to sit down and review the effects of the drug. There'd been an initial rise in the number of new synapses being characterized, but that much was almost inevitable; for a major pharmacological intervention to have revealed nothing new would have been as strange as if the shift from winter to summer had left the pedestrians of Tehran traipsing out identical routes through the city—making no tracks to hitherto unrevealed parks or outdoor cafés.

Even beyond that anticipated surge, though, the drug had continued to pay off. Before, the barrage of images had been sending Martin rapidly into a glazed, unresponsive state, almost independent of the details of the content being shown to him. Now, each new image elicited a fresh response; Nasim could see the splash of activity in every scan.

They had long ago dragged Martin up and down the highways of his life, engaging with every significant biographical event, every ethical concern, every strongly held belief and esthetic preference. But that had not been enough to map the whole landscape—to delineate the topography that kept those highways from tumbling away into the void. What made any given human brain entirely distinct from another came down to details that were far too minor to be recounted by the subject, too minor even to be of interest to them, too minor, in fact, for any sane person to tolerate having to contemplate them, hour after hour, day after day. Only by shutting down the parts of Martin's brain that were choking on the sheer quantity of minutiae had it become possible to start gathering the information they needed.

Now the side-loading software had massaged the Proxy into a form that mimicked virtually all of Martin's fragmentary responses. If the data kept coming through at the current rate, within a month or so they'd have the Proxy in a stable state, ready to test in short scenarios.

Ready for a conversation.

Nasim cleared all the scans and histograms from her screen and sat contemplating the endpoint of the process. A child could take comfort from just about anything: a stuffed animal, a cartoon character, a mythical figure in a storybook who lived out the same plot over and over. The imprisoned Zal that Javeed had been so delighted to encounter had been nothing but a set of branching script fragments.

But Martin was not Javeed's cartoon hero. He could not be replaced by a clip library of favorite scenes. Either the Proxy would capture the actual dynamic between them, or it would be useless.

The question was, could it be enough without being too much? When she'd built the blank receptacle for the side-loading process, Nasim had used the best functional maps available, but every choice had involved a trade-off. Every region she'd omitted risked robbing the Proxy of something it would need for its task; every region she'd included risked burdening it with goals it had no power to achieve and desires it had no power to fulfill.

So could the Proxy come close to re-creating the way Martin would have spent an hour in Zendegi with his son—answering all of Javeed's questions, sharing all his jokes, vanquishing all his fears—and still not know, or care, precisely what it was itself?

Nasim had done her best, but the only way she'd know for sure on which side of the line she'd fallen would be to ask the Proxy, face to face.

23

"Do you get along with birds?" Shahin asked.

"Of course!" Javeed replied. "I even met the Simorgh once."

"The Simorgh?" Shahin laughed. "Well then, an eagle shouldn't trouble you one bit." He took a strip of leather from a small pail sitting on the ground beside him and wrapped it around Javeed's right hand. "Hold your arm up, boy." Javeed complied. "A little higher," Shahin suggested. "I want to be sure he can see you way down there."

Shahin whistled, and took a piece of rabbit meat out of a second, covered pail. Martin heard the swish of wings before he spotted the eagle approaching, descending from a nearby cypress tree. Javeed flinched slightly as the bird came closer; he turned his face aside, but he managed to keep his arm motionless. When the eagle alighted on his leather-bound fist, it found itself unable to wrap both feet at once around this tiny perch. Martin feared that it might sink its talons into the unprotected skin further up Javeed's arm—and though his gut reaction was all about the nonexistent threat of pain and injury, the risk of the bird puncturing the illusion of its own physicality seemed real enough. But instead, it managed a kind of balancing act, shifting from one foot to another as it gobbled the rabbit flesh that Shahin dangled in front of it as a reward. Javeed wouldn't feel its weight pushing his arm down, but the glove could probably manage a convincing impression of those four long, muscular toes clenching and unclenching.

They had come to the estate of King Kavus in the hope of accompanying him on his latest folly. Javeed loved all the stories of Kavus, and in the bowdlerised children's version they were harmless enough, but Martin had balked at exposing him to detailed immersive depictions of the king's bloodthirsty military misadventures. Against the advice of Zal and countless

221

others, Kavus had invaded Mazanderan, the land of demons and sorcerers, where his army had engaged in mass-slaughter—in the original, blithely hacking into unarmed men, women and children. The White Demon, protecting his land and people, had blinded Kavus and his soldiers and rounded them up as prisoners, whereupon Zal's son, Rostam, had embarked on a quest to rescue the vain young king. This had involved slicing witches in half, pulling the ears off innocent bystanders and ultimately cutting out the White Demon's liver and using his blood as a balm to restore Kavus's sight.

Kavus's repentance over the Mazanderan fiasco had proved to be shallow and insincere; he remained bloated with pride and immune to good counsel. But after scouring Zendegi's catalog of *Shahnameh* scenarios, Martin had finally found a Kavus story that was free of acts of evisceration, and he'd managed to talk Javeed into accepting it in lieu of the bloodier alternatives.

"Now you feed him," Shahin told Javeed. "Reach behind your back and I'll pass you the meat." Martin watched nervously as Javeed accepted a strip of raw pink flesh, holding it gingerly between his thumb and forefinger. He brought his arm in front of him and quickly raised the meat toward the bird, releasing his grip as it seized the flesh in its beak.

"You're doing well," Shahin said. "Now we'll put the hood on."

Javeed looked to Martin for support; Martin smiled encouragingly. Shahin handed Javeed the leather hood, showing him how to hold it stretched out across his fingers and bring it over the bird's head without alarming or annoying it. The hood had an aperture for the beak and nostrils and was loose enough to cover the eyes without touching them, but Martin still found it extraordinary that birds of prey really could be trained to accept these strange encumbrances.

At Shahin's prompting, Javeed crouched down and slowly moved his hand and its passenger toward the wicker cage that sat beside them. Despite its blindness, as it approached the open door the bird deduced what was happening; it gave an irritated shrug and made as if to spread its wings and take flight. Javeed emitted a startled grunt, but he kept his hand steady and after a moment the bird allowed him to continue.

Shahin said, "Touch your hand to the side of the perch." Javeed did this, and the bird felt its way onto the wooden perch inside the cage. Javeed withdrew his arm and closed the door.

"Well done," Shahin said. "You're a fast learner." He turned to Martin. "If you and the boy can get a dozen of the king's eagles caged by noon, I'll take you on as assistant handlers."

Martin glanced at Javeed. "We'd better get to work then."

The empty cages were stacked nearby. Armed with a pail of rabbit meat and Martin's imitation of Shahin's whistling, they strode through the cypress grove, trying to lure the birds down, taking turns to offer their clenched fists as perches. Martin knew that the game wouldn't make their task impossible—no matter what the real outcome would have been if two inexperienced strangers had sought to round up someone else's hunting birds!—but nor did it give them an entirely easy ride. The first two birds came to them without much trouble, but the third one they spotted ignored Martin's whistling for three or four minutes, only to swoop down unexpectedly, knock over the meat pail and return to the trees with an unearned treat in its beak.

Javeed was undeterred; in less than a minute he'd located another bird, and this one turned out to be better behaved. When it landed on Martin's fist it stared into his face, blinking and examining him curiously. Martin doubted that anyone had side-loaded a golden eagle, so its behavior could only be surface-deep, but he couldn't help feeling a degree of affinity for the creature. He was on his way from the biological sphere to the digital, and in his new home this counted as native life.

When the twelve cages were full, Shahin approached them with three burly helpers. "Good work! Now we need to get these quickly to the king's pavilion. He's determined to set out while the sun is high."

Each of them carried two cages through the grove. Javeed gripped his pair by wrapping his hands around the bars at the side; the cages were too tall for him to lift them from above. Martin doubted that anyone, let alone a six-year-old, could have borne the torque on their wrists that would have come from trying to carry the cages this way, but Javeed was smart enough not to mistake a game in Zendegi for a lesson in correct load-handling techniques.

Shahin led the way to a grassy field where Kavus's "pavilion" stood waiting. Its base was a circular platform some fifteen meters wide, constructed from a lattice of woven fibers similar to those used to make the bird cages. In the center was the royal tent; the fabric of its walls was lavishly embroidered in gold and violet, and the open flap revealed a plushly cushioned and similarly decorated throne.

Spaced around the platform, just in from the rim, were dozens of identical wooden rods, all vertical, standing about two meters tall. Near the base of each rod a length of rope lay coiled on the platform.

Martin and Javeed had not been the only ones busy in the grove; Shahin and the others had already gathered at least thirty eagles, and their cages stood on the ground to one side of the pavilion. Martin started laughing; he couldn't help himself. A part of him simply couldn't believe that Kavus's deranged scheme would succeed for one second, even in Zendegi.

Javeed was annoyed. "Don't, Baba!" he whispered. "You'll make everyone cross with us."

Martin said, "Sorry. You're right." He glanced at the young man behind him, whose face was glistening with sweat, as if he really did feel the weight of the birds he was carrying. The man remained silent, but frowned slightly, in a manner that seemed to advise caution more than it expressed disapproval. Kavus was not a popular ruler, but the throne itself still commanded respect; only the most experienced generals and learned sages were entitled to question the king's plans, and then only with the utmost tact and diplomacy. A commoner giggling derisively was beyond the pale, and Martin wasn't interested in spending the next hour rotting in a dungeon.

They deposited the cages near the others; some of the newly arrived birds fluttered their wings and rose briefly from their perches, as if to protest their treatment. Martin caught himself wondering what they were "used to"—how often they hunted with Shahin and the king, how often they were caged—as if such questions had answers.

Shahin addressed his workers. "We've brought forty-eight of the king's finest eagles, as he commanded. Now watch me carefully; this is what you must do next."

Shahin squatted down and opened one of the cages, reached in and touched the foot of the hooded bird with his leather-clad fist. It moved obligingly onto his hand and let him carry it slowly out of the cage. He walked over to the rim of the pavilion and squatted again to bring the bird close to the ground, then with his other hand he lifted up the rope that was lying coiled near one of the rods. Four strands of rope were anchored to the platform, and between those fixed ends it had been knotted and woven into an elaborate harness. Shahin slipped the harness over the bird, stroking it behind the head to calm it. Then he lowered and tilted his hand, encouraging the bird to step off. The bird took a few steps across the surface, then felt the harness grow taut. It fluttered its wings a few times, irritated by this strange new impediment, then became still, resigned to the vagaries of its fate.

Shahin turned to face them. "Don't stand there idly; follow my example. The king will be here soon!"

Javeed threw himself into the task and Martin left him to it, working separately in order to get the job done quickly but staying close by. Javeed had already grown confident with the birds, in spite of their daunting size, and every time Martin glanced at him he looked focused and assured. Did it matter that real falconry took years of training and that these birds were following a script that simply forbade them from turning feral and scratching someone's face off? Javeed wasn't doing any of this in order to go hunting with tribesmen in Kyrgyzstan. The game-tasks still took patience and persistence, and even weightless, the birds demanded fine motor control from their handlers to stop them getting skittish. Martin resolved to stop fretting; Javeed wasn't in danger of forgetting the stubbornness of flesh-and-blood creatures, the sharpness of real talons, the recalcitrance of the animate world. He shouldn't start confusing Javeed's situation with the Proxy's; it was not his son who would soon be confined to Zendegi.

Shahin and his helpers worked faster than the newcomers; their "experience" made that plausible enough, though it occurred to Martin that at another level it was down to the fact that the birds didn't need to waste time trying to bluff these non-humans into taking them seriously. In any case, their speed was welcome; Martin had tethered just five birds—three less than an equal share—when Shahin called out to everyone to move aside. The birds were all in place, and the king was approaching.

The royal party arrived on horseback, with the king accompanied by flag-bearers, guards and courtiers. Kavus himself wore a jewelled crown and carried a mace encrusted with rubies; Martin suffered a momentary Liberace flashback.

The riff-raff stayed clear as the king inspected the pavilion and its tethered birds; three advisors walked behind him, offering obsequious praise after every royal remark.

"I see that the clouds betray a favorable motion of the air," Kavus opined. "What could be more auspicious?"

"Lord of the World, your wisdom is greater than that of all your ancestors combined."

Though lines like that weren't too far from Ferdowsi, everyone was hamming it up; Martin saw that Javeed was smiling in disbelief at these pompous gits, notwithstanding his earlier dousing of Martin's own display of disrespect.

"Would you trust this man to design an aircraft?" Martin whispered.

"No way."

Martin patted his empty money-belt. "And I forgot to buy us parachutes."

Javeed said, "If you get scared, just give it the thumbs-down."

"Okay."

One of the king's advisers approached Shahin and spoke to him quietly.

Shahin passed the news on to his staff. "The king has called for my service, and I am to bring the two lightest of my apprentices." Javeed was a shoo-in, obviously, but Martin was preordained to be a passenger too, which might have explained why his three competitors were all tall and solidly built. He didn't even need to point out that he'd lost ten kilos in real life since his icon was snapped.

Kavus seated himself on his royal throne and a flunky closed the tent flap so His Majesty wouldn't have to watch the staff carrying on untidily around him. Martin and Javeed followed Shahin onto the pavilion, where they set about priming the aircraft's engines: hooking pieces of rabbit meat onto spikes that protruded from the forty-eight rods, just out of reach of the tethered eagles. Javeed was too short to reach the spikes himself, so his job was to carry the pail of meat and hand chunks to the two adults. The birds, still blinded, did not react to the meat, but at the sound of approaching footsteps some of them chafed against their constraints, tugging on the ropes in random directions as if to signal their annoyance to their captors.

When the preparations were complete, Shahin spoke with the adviser, who approached the royal enclosure.

"Lord of the World, Jewel of Persia, your good fortune brings justice and happiness to all your people."

Kavus emerged from his tent and gazed up into the sky. "No human before me, however great their birth and station, has dared attempt this feat; none after will have the courage to repeat it." He looked down and stretched out his arms toward the gathered observers. "The glory of this day will be burned into your memories, as the image of the sun sears your vision." They bowed their heads in agreement, then began retreating to a safe distance.

The advisor remained on the platform; now he signaled to Shahin to proceed. Shahin directed Martin and Javeed to two different starting points, separated by a third of the platform's circumference, then took up a position himself equidistant from both of them.

Kavus thumped the shaft of his mace against the wicker floor and cried out, "Now I join the angels!"

They began unhooding the eagles.

The first bird whose sight Martin restored paced the floor irritably for a few seconds, then feinted toward his hand as if to bite it, but once it noticed the meat dangling above its head it flapped its wings and rose into the air as far as the harness would allow it.

When the ropes grew taut, though, it seemed to grasp the nature of its situation perfectly, because it gave up struggling and returned to the floor. It knew it couldn't reach the meat; there was nothing to be done but wait for the humans' next bizarre, capricious action.

Alarmed, Martin looked to Shahin. His bird was on the floor too, but he was encouraging it with a series of nods and grunts; perhaps these were signals used in hunting. After a few seconds, Shahin's bird heeded the cues and flew up toward the lure.

Martin turned to see what Javeed was doing; he was already mimicking Shahin. Martin felt weirdly self-conscious; the noises were embarrassing enough coming from Shahin, and his own attempts would surely sound sillier: all this, in the presence of royalty. But the Lord of the World would be even less pleased if his precious sky-pavilion toppled over on the grass, unbalanced by one tardy peasant.

Martin faced the eagle again and tipped his head skyward, grunting and snorting. The eagle blinked at him bemusedly. What was it waiting for—should he mime taking flight himself? If it had been a seagull he might have flailed at it with his hands to drive it off the ground, but his instincts warned against trying that on a raptor. He looked back at Javeed, whose bird was airborne now; it was straining against the harness as if the hunk of rabbit flesh just beyond its reach were a pigeon fleeing across the skies. Now there was an idea for Kavus's next version: harness some actual living prey, and maybe take-off would proceed more smoothly.

Javeed made a guttural noise. "Like that, Baba!"

Martin imitated him. Nothing. He tried again, deeper in the throat, while flicking his head up encouragingly; finally, his eagle took flight, and when it reached the end of its tether it remained aloft. Maybe you had to be a native Farsi speaker for the right sound to come easily.

The three of them moved around the pavilion, unhooding the eagles and encouraging them to persist in their futile attempts to reach the lures. Martin still had the most trouble persuading his birds that they should mush like sled dogs, but Shahin and Javeed waited for him; if they'd raced ahead at their own pace that would have risked unbalancing the whole structure.

When Martin set his tenth bird in motion, the pavilion lurched and began to weave across the grass like a hovercraft with broken steering. Apparently the combined effort of thirty golden eagles—according to the game's fanciful notion of their power—was enough to overcome the weight of the craft and its passengers; with friction all but banished, the imperfect cancellation between the horizontal thrust from the variously inclined tug-ropes was enough to send the pavilion skittering in all directions. The field was wide and there were no obstacles nearby, but the earthbound observers wisely mounted their horses and retreated further from the action.

Javeed was beaming with delight. "Hold on to the rods!" Martin warned him; Javeed nodded and took hold. Martin wasn't sure if it was entirely logical—nothing Javeed did could actually support him in his *ghal'e*; holding thin air wouldn't help him stay upright when the real floor beneath his feet tilted—but it was a good habit to cultivate regardless, and it could certainly affect what the game did to his icon. Martin was feeling slightly queasy from the visual cues alone; if anything, the fact that he could feel himself lying flat on his back, motionless in the scanner, exacerbated his discomfort as his eyes told him he was zigzagging across the grass. But it was worth it just to see Javeed so happy. If the worst happened, Martin decided, Bernard would probably manage to stop him choking on his own vomit.

Kavus was standing in front of his tent, trying to appear regally composed even as he swayed like a sailor on a storm-tossed deck. His adviser, who'd wisely gripped the side of the tent, looked as sickly as Martin felt.

Shahin called out, "Come on, get to work! The next three together!"

Martin unhooded his eleventh eagle; it regarded the mad, sliding world around it with a look of doleful avian stoicism. "On the count of three," Shahin shouted. "One. Two. *Three!*"

Martin grunted at the bird and flicked his head. It rose from the platform, and when its tether snapped tight the pavilion's motion suddenly became smoother. Martin peered over the edge. Before, they'd been scraping the grass, brushing against every second tussock; now they were clear of the vegetation, half a meter or so above the ground and still rising.

"Again!" Shahin urged them. Martin hurried to unhood the next bird. "One. Two. *Three!*"

They quickly brought the last of the eagles into play. By the time Martin had a chance to look around again they were higher than the treetops—which was lucky, because they were drifting straight toward the cypress grove.

"The Lord of the Earth becomes Lord of the Sky!" Kavus proclaimed modestly. "Ten thousand generations will not see the equal of this feat!"

"Lord of the Earth... Lord of the Sky," his adviser mumbled. The poor man did not look well.

The pavilion passed over the grove, safely clear of the highest branches. Martin took a step towards Javeed, then he felt the platform tilting and retreated. Though Javeed was lighter than his two fellow bird-wranglers, Kavus and his adviser must have been far enough from the center to help maintain the balance. But the luck—or contrivance—that had granted them a level ascent meant that any change now was risky. If they moved at all, it would have to be coordinated very carefully.

"Try looking through the floor," Martin called to Javeed. Javeed glanced down, then squatted and peered through the latticework. Martin had his icon adopt the same posture, discordantly aware for a moment that his real back and knees remained unbent. He could see straight down into the treetops, and as they drifted along he spotted a small, unguarded bird's nest with three speckled eggs, built on a forked, swaying branch. He felt a sting of resentment; however well-researched the details, there was some-thing demeaning about seeing the natural world through so many layers of mediation—rubbing his face in his rapidly dwindling prospects of ever encountering such a thing in the wild for himself. *Would he ever go hot-air ballooning with Javeed in the real world?* It wasn't beyond hope. Maybe after his transplant, if everything went well.

For now, though, this was what he had to make do with. Better to savor the details than resent them: for his own sake, for Javeed's, for the Proxy's.

Javeed called out to him excitedly, "Baba? Did you see the eggs?"

"Yeah!"

The eagles carried them higher, and the wind—or some persistent differ-ence in strength between the birds—drove them further across the land. The king's estate gave way to ploughed fields, then pristine woodlands. Martin wasn't sure exactly where in Iran they were supposed to be; Kavus was a figure out of myth, not history, and if the *Shahnameh* had ever named his seat of power it had slipped from Martin's memory. It wasn't important. Wherever they were, Javeed was ecstatic, gazing down at the landscape from the edge of their glorious, impossible contraption.

"Baba! See the river!"

"Yeah, it's beautiful." Sunlight glistened across the silver thread. "Hey, see the dark spot near the bend in the river? Now it's crossing the water—"

"I can see it."

"That's our shadow."

Javeed looked up at him to see if he was teasing, then looked down again. "Ohhh!"

When they rose into a thick bank of clouds and the air turned to fog around them, everyone started laughing with delight, even Kavus and his motion-sick courtier. When they emerged, the land beneath them was hidden. They drifted through a surreal world where massive shapes that, in the distance, seemed as solid as carved white rock melted into swirling tendrils as soon as they drew near. Martin barely spoke now; he needed only to exchange a glance or a smile with Javeed to make the connection, to convey everything.

See that cloud that looks like a dog's head?

Yes! And Baba, see the one behind it, like a nose with snot coming out one side?

They continued to ascend, and the world of giant sculptures flattened out into a blanket of torn gray fleece. Through every tear was a glimpse of the desert far below.

Then in the distance, rock punctured the blanket. The peak of a mountain broke through the clouds.

"Mount Damavand," Shahin declared.

"Mount Damavand," Kavus echoed, "where noble Feraydun imprisoned the Serpent King Zahhak, pinning him with iron stakes to the walls
of the darkest cave. But as we rise above Damavand, so I rise above even
Feraydun's glory."

"Lord of the World, there have been none to equal you," the advisor
declared, without much conviction.

The pavilion was starting to list. Shahin addressed the adviser discreetly.
"The birds are tiring. It's time to return."

The adviser spoke with Kavus. Kavus shook his head angrily. "I am lord
of every animal and bird; these eagles will do as I bid. I have come this far,
and now the angels await me." He raised his face to the sky and spread his
arms triumphantly. "See!"

Martin followed his gaze. There was high cloud above them, with the
sun behind it; dazzling beads of light shone through the cloud where it
thinned.

Shahin lowered his face in deference, then spoke to his apprentices. "We
need to keep the birds striving, we need to urge them on. When you see
one flagging, go to it, encourage it, assure it that it will receive its reward
when the trip is done." Martin wondered how he could have missed the
whole "useful phrases in the language of eagles" seminar.

Suddenly the platform tilted, with Martin's side dropping half a meter. Everyone but Kavus had been holding onto something; the king staggered but
caught himself. One of Martin's birds had simply given up. He approached
it and began repeating the grunting and nodding that had worked before;
it cocked its head skeptically and stayed exactly where it was.

The platform tipped again, this time on Javeed's side. Martin watched
Javeed moving toward his own protesting eagle. "Keep holding the rods!"
Martin urged him; they were close enough together that Javeed could always
grab the rod ahead of him before releasing his grip on the one behind.

"Okay," Javeed replied, a little irritably, as if he already had enough to
think about.

"I'm serious," Martin insisted. The game couldn't test their actual grip
strength—nor would it take it upon itself to prise their fingers loose, whatever the notional forces on their bodies might be—but Martin suspected
that it would distinguish very sharply between "Look, Ma, no hands!" and
more prudent strategies.

Javeed squatted in front of the bird and tried to get it flying again, but
he had no more luck than Martin. Martin called to Shahin, "Can we give
them some meat from the pail? Maybe that will restore their energy, enough
to continue."

Shahin looked dubious, but then he said, "Try it." The pail was beside him; he bent down and gave it a shove that sent it sliding toward Martin. Martin managed to intercept it before it went over the edge; he took out a strip of pink flesh and offered it to the troublesome bird.

The bird grabbed the meat and gulped it down. In an instant, Martin's side of the platform dropped again; the bird's two neighbors had seen it being fed and had decided to follow the same strategy.

"No, no, no!" Martin wailed. He tried desperately to get the first bird flying, but it ignored him completely.

The platform began lurching ever more erratically, as one eagle after another joined the strike. Javeed was laughing; he knew the end of this story and he didn't seem to care if his own father hastened the disaster. Martin looked over at Shahin, but even the master was having no luck.

Kavus cried out angrily, "I am Lord of the World, Lord of the Sky, lord of every living creature! Only God himself is above me. *I command you to carry me to the sphere of the angels!*"

The pavilion dropped through the clouds. About twenty of the birds were still in action, which was enough to slow their descent, but not to halt it. The desert was getting close, very fast. At least they wouldn't drown, like Icarus, but it wasn't going to be a soft landing.

Martin caught Javeed's eye. "Hold on tight, *pesaram*."

Javeed mimed straining against the two rods he was holding, to prove that his hands could not be dislodged. "Are you scared, Baba?"

"No. Are you?"

Javeed looked down past the edge of the platform. "Zendegi won't hurt us."

An updraft caught the pavilion and set it tumbling. They were upside down, hundreds of meters above the desert, hanging by their wrists. Martin heard Javeed bellowing, but all he could see around him were wings and ropes; the birds had been panicked into flight, and as they tried to escape downwards they were only hastening the fall.

The roll continued, righting the platform. Martin's skin was icy from shock; he looked around for Javeed.

Javeed had not let go. His hair and clothes were disheveled, but he was wearing a wide-eyed roller-coaster grin. Martin emitted a brief, involuntary sob of pure relief.

None of the passengers had been dislodged, though they all looked several shades paler than before; even Kavus had had enough sense to grab hold of the royal tent, which now sported a magnificent tear along one side. The birds were bedraggled—some with feathers coming loose from their wings, some awkwardly tangled in their ropes—but about half of them were now straining upward, offering some hope that their efforts would break the fall. Martin braced himself, tensing his muscles, sharing a smile of anticipation with Javeed.

The sound of the platform snapping apart and the thick cloud of dust rising up around them almost made up for the fact that the crash itself was imperceptible. Martin stepped off the platform, his hands trembling. He made his way through the white dust to Javeed, whose *ghal'e* would have shaken with a more convincing thud.

"Are you okay?"

Javeed nodded; he was beaming, untroubled. He put his hand in Martin's. "That's the best thing we ever did!"

As the dust settled they saw Shahin tending to the birds. At first Martin thought he was merely untangling them from the rope, but then it became clear that he was releasing them from their harnesses completely.

When Kavus realized what was happening he was outraged. He screamed and gesticulated at the adviser, who approached Shahin and struck him across the face. Shahin froze and stared at the ground.

He said, "Lord of the World, forgive me, but we have no food for the birds." The strips of meat that had been spiked on the rods as lures were all gone. "They can't carry us home on empty stomachs. The most we can hope for now is that they will hunt for themselves."

Kavus composed himself. "Rostam will come to my aid," he declared. "Word will reach him in Zavolestan that his lord requires his assistance. He will bring food and wine, fifty slaves, fifty horses, and fifty golden cages for the royal hunting birds."

Martin said, "And that will take… how long?"

Kavus blinked at him in disbelief, too startled even to be angry. For his Master of Birds to address him directly was already a staggering impertinence, but for this worthless apprentice to speak his mind loudly and freely—*to question his lord's understanding of their fate*—was like something from a dream.

Martin turned to Javeed. "I know you'd like to meet Rostam, but I think he's a couple of days away at least."

Javeed looked out across the desert; there was not so much as a wisp of dust on the horizon. "We'll see him next time." He gave the thumbs-down, and everything vanished.

Martin lay in the scanner, waiting for the motor to bring him out.

24

Nasim had begun making a habit of spending half an hour with her colleagues in the programmers' room every morning. Falaki's investigation had left everyone feeling like suspects, and she didn't know a better way to raise morale than sitting down with people, asking them to talk about their work, and making it clear that she appreciated their efforts. No one could yet rule out the possibility that the breach had originated in this room, and she would have been negligent to pretend otherwise, but that did not mean the whole place had to descend into paranoia and resentment.

Milad had been showing her a new interface for developers to tap into the social instincts of a set of composite, male, multilingual side-loads—there were so many different types of modules now that Nasim had given up inventing nicknames for all of them—when every monitor in the room sounded an alarm and opened a window into the same environment. Every complaint coming in from the arcades now triggered this response; Nasim had decided it was better to be safe than tardy. Most of the alarms were trivial matters that were only passed on when the arcade staff were inexperienced: personal disputes between customers, or basic misconceptions about the way the system was supposed to work. And even the majority of genuine programming glitches had nothing to do with Zendegi and simply needed to be forwarded to the appropriate game developer.

This complaint was not trivial, though, and it could not be palmed off on someone else. In the ballroom of the starship *Harmony*—home of a popular science-fictional soap opera of the same name—handsome, epauletted, anthropomorphic aliens were turning into excrement. And they were not merely melting into pools of suggestive goo that might have raised a snicker but could have been something else entirely; they were morphing into stick

233

234 • Greg Egan

figures built of soft brown cylinders flecked with undigested roughage.

"Arif!" Nasim shouted. "Launch the Faribas!" Some of the post-colonic gingerbread men were running around the ballroom, trying to embrace people. The thumbs-down escape had been disabled; why every customer didn't just whip off their goggles, Nasim couldn't guess—unless it was pure shock—but stampeding party-goers had formed a crush at the exit and the first dreadful hug was clearly only seconds away. Nasim averted her eyes; she was already having trouble keeping her breakfast down.

"Arif?" She walked over to his cubicle.

"They're not working!" he exclaimed. "The Faribas! I'm showing them the environment, but the modules are just… frozen—unresponsive."

Nasim said, "Grossed out?"

"What?"

She risked a brief peek at the ballroom, then looked away again; brown smears on tablecloths and ballgowns lingered on some fold of her visual cortex that was going to need scrubbing out with disinfectant. "How many people could sit staring at *that*," she said, "and calmly point out all the anomalies?" The Fariba modules had included all the basic human visual responses; they would hardly have needed specialized training to acquire this one. Every donor to the HCP would have averted their gaze—and if their eyes had been pinned open and forcibly locked on the nauseating scene, they would have done their best to blank it out, to stare right through it. The Faribas had no power to turn their eyes away, but they could still mentally disengage and refuse to sift through this sewer.

Arif pondered the unexpected obstacle. "Maybe I can route all the objects into separate environments and show each of them to a separate instance of the Faribas. Then we can eliminate anything that grosses them out—without them having to spend time telling us exactly where it is in the original scene."

"How long will that take?" Nasim glanced at another part of his screen; six thousand complaints had now been registered. Hundreds of games were affected, including *Virtual Azimi*.

"Five minutes. Maybe ten."

"Go!"

Arif started typing. Nasim watched him, agonized for thirty seconds, then went to Bahador. "Shut us down."

"Are you sure?" He looked at the *Harmony* window through a gap in his fingers. "Oh my God. Now it's *kissing*—"

Nasim reached over his shoulder and tapped the icon to start the shutdown. The touch-screen needed both of their thumbprints; all the confirmatory steps were taking forever. When the ballroom scene finally blanked out, Nasim slumped against a partition.

She closed her eyes and tried to think calmly about the situation. Within half an hour they could restart from back-ups, and Arif's improved filter would be ready if they needed it. One Fariba *per object* would cost a lot to run, though. In any case, they'd be refunding all their customers for the outage, and most of those who'd witnessed anything like the *Harmony* attack would never be coming back.

Nasim composed herself and walked to the front of the room, where she could see all the programmers at once. Arif was still typing, his eyes locked to his screen, but everyone else looked dazed. This was the first time in a decade that Zendegi had been shut down completely.

"I'm sorry," she said, "there was no choice this time; we had to retreat. But this isn't over. Cyber-Jahan tried to muscle in on us; Shahidi's tried boycotts and intimidation. But we're not going to be cowed by anyone—"

Her notepad buzzed.

"Excuse me." She took the device from her pocket—expecting an angry summons from the boss, but half-daring to hope it was a message from Falaki informing her that his supervisor processes had paid off and pinned down the hackers.

The message was from an anonymous sender, and it consisted of five English words:

"Care to discuss a truce?"

Beneath this curt offer was a link to a site in Zendegi.

Nasim stepped into the *ghal'e* and watched the walls rise up around her. She hadn't been inside one of these machines for years; she'd grown used to a God's-eye-view of the games, not a participant's. When a voice from the interface told her to flip down her goggles she muttered an obscene reply under her breath; she hated being prodded. She'd go in when she was ready.

She'd talked it over with Bahador and Falaki, and they'd decided to restart just enough of Zendegi to enable the meeting to take place immediately. Everyone else would remain shut out; Nasim and her host would have the system to themselves. If the meeting ran on too long, Bahador wouldn't let Zendegi bleed money by delaying the full re-launch, but this way some of the tracking would be simpler. There was no guarantee that they'd be able to locate the physical source of the hacker's virtual presence, but it was worth doing what they could to improve the odds.

Okay, you want a truce? Here are my terms: Zendegi changes absolutely nothing, and you get six years in prison for commercial sabotage.

Nasim flipped down the goggles.

It was dusk. She was standing, alone, in a motionless Ferris wheel gondola, high above an amusement park. She could hear tinny music, and people talking and laughing in the distance below her. The *Wiener Riesenrad* was not as popular a virtual postcard as the Taj Mahal or the Great Pyramid of Giza, but it cost next to nothing to keep it on file.

Below her, people milled around the stalls of the amusement park; all of them Proxies, of course. There was nothing to stop the hacker arriving on the ground among that virtual crowd, but given that the link in the email had pointed specifically to this gondola there didn't seem much point waiting anywhere else.

"Nasim Golestani?"

Nasim turned around. A clean-shaven middle-aged man, dressed in old-fashioned Western clothes—coat, tie, fedora—stood in the adjacent gondola, some ten or twelve meters away.

"I'm Nasim," she replied, in English. "What should I call you?"

"Rollo." He spoke with an American accent.

"Pleased to meet you, Rollo." Ah, Iranian civility; her mother would be proud. "Would you like to join me here? I promise I won't push you out."

"I'm fine where I am, thank you."

"As you wish." The wind blew gently across the park, rattling the huge machine, but Nasim's default auditory settings put clarity above realism; she'd have no trouble hearing his voice.

"I'm sure you've already guessed who I represent," Rollo said confidently.

Nasim hesitated before replying, but she couldn't see what she'd have to gain by bluffing. "I have no idea. Honestly." If he was an emissary of *Hojatoleslam* Shahidi, he had a strange way of showing his adherence to Islamic tradition, and why anyone from Cyber-Jahan or the Chinese labor unions would be into fedoras and Ferris wheels was beyond her.

"The CHL," Rollo declared.

"I beg your pardon?"

"The Cis-Humanist League."

Nasim refrained from groaning. "Okay, I get it: *cis,* not *trans.* I'm not what you'd call a Latin buff, but I did a year of organic chemistry."

She waited for Rollo to say something more, but he seemed momentarily taken aback, as if he'd been expecting a very different response.

"So you're 'on the side of humans,'" she said. "You're... pro-technology? But you're opposed to the crazies, the transcendence cults?" He didn't contradict her. "Great. Welcome to the club. I'm quite partial to my own species myself."

Rollo looked positively wounded now. "You haven't even read our manifesto, have you?"

"Strangely, no," Nasim confessed. "Seeing as I'd never even heard of you until twenty seconds ago."

He shook his head in disbelief. "The arrogance is breathtaking! You march right into territory we've been mapping for decades, and then you turn around and tell me *you have no idea who we are?*"

Nasim spread her hands. "What can I say? Fire your publicist." She caught herself; she was letting her hostility get the better of her. This man might be a self-important prick who thought everyone in the universe read his blog rants, but he *had* just brought Zendegi to its knees. A computer-savvy anti-Caplan. Maybe if she locked them both in a room together they'd annihilate each other.

"I'll make it simple for you then," Rollo said. "Item seven of the manifesto: *No consciousness without autonomy.* It's unethical to create conscious software that lacks the ability to take control of its own destiny."

Nasim said, "Exactly what 'conscious software' do you have in mind? Do you want Virtual Azimi to have voting rights?"

"Of course not," Rollo replied impatiently. "We only targeted that game to hit you in the wallet; it's obvious that Virtual Azimi can't be conscious. But that's where we draw the line: no higher functions, no language, no social skills. You don't get to clone a slice of humanity and use it to churn out battery hens."

Nasim was starting to feel off-balance; after steeling herself for the prospect of negotiating with a theologian who solemnly believed in angels and djinn, she was having to do some recalibration to focus on an adversary so much closer to her own philosophical territory.

"*None* of the side-loads can be conscious in the human sense," she said. "They have no notion of their own past or future, no long-term memory, no personal goals." Martin's Proxy would inherit some of his narrative memories, but she was hoping Rollo had no knowledge of that project.

He said, "So if I scooped out enough of your brain to give you amnesia and rob you of all sense of identity, I'd be entitled to do what I like with you? To treat you as a commodity?"

"I'd say the major ethical problem there is that you'd essentially be killing me," Nasim replied. "But nobody had their mind wiped to make the side-loads. The HCP donors were already dead, and the people we scanned are all still living their own complete, fulfilling lives, irrespective of anything that happens in Zendegi."

"And if I copy you exactly," Rollo countered, "atom for atom, and then mutilate your duplicate, *then* it's acceptable?"

Here we go, Nasim thought, *hypotheticals about matter transmitters. The golden key that unlocks every philosophical quandary.*

"Nobody gets *mutilated* when a side-load is made," she said. "We build them up from nothing, we don't hack them down from some perfect, fully functioning virtual brain."

"I know that," Rollo replied, "but the end product is still the same. And you don't even know exactly which mental processes you have and haven't excluded! I've read the patent applications, with all their talk of functional mapping, but don't kid yourself that it's down to some kind of fine art, where you can pick out a subset of abilities precisely—let alone guarantee that they'll all fit together into some kind of stable entity. If you want to make something human, *make it whole.* If you want to enable people to step from their bodies into virtual immortality, perfectly copied, with all their abilities preserved and all their rights intact… go ahead and do it, we have no problem with that."

"That's fifty years away, at least," Nasim said, "maybe a hundred."

Rollo shrugged. "No doubt. But if you want to put humanity into a cheese grater and slice off little slavelets to pimp to the factories and the VR games, well… then you've got a war on your hands."

Nasim looked away. Part of her wanted, very badly, to start blustering about his imminent capture, but she had no idea what the prospects of that were, and in any case a bout of premature triumphalism wouldn't win her any favors.

"You might find the factories harder to breach than Zendegi," she said. "They'd probably go for in-house computing rather than the Cloud. Especially now."

"Of course," Rollo said. "And sabotage is not our preferred option anyway. We'll be campaigning hard to outlaw side-loading everywhere; smearing shit over your customers is just a short-term tactic. Eventually you'll find a way to block us out, and even if Zendegi and Eikonometrics go bankrupt in the process, your intellectual property will just end up with someone else. But we're starting early, outside the law, because it's the only way to nip this atrocity in the bud: to slow the growth of the practice by making it clear—from the start, to everyone—that doing things this way will attract a penalty."

"Atrocity?" Nasim scowled. "If you're such a warrior for the rights of conscious beings, stop pissing around with Zendegi and go derail a massacre somewhere."

The lights on the Ferris wheel snapped on; some of the Proxies beneath them clapped and cheered.

Rollo looked back at Nasim calmly. "So you're happy with your games modules; your conscience is clear. Fine. But do you really think it will stop there? If there is no law, if there is no line drawn, what makes you so sure that it's not going to end with software that even you'd call conscious? With no rights and no freedom. It might not require anything that sophisticated to churn out shoes or notepads, but what about aged-care services? Or child-minding?"

Nasim's skin crawled at his use of that phrase, but she still didn't believe that he knew about Martin.

"Every time you attack us," she said, "we use tens of thousands of side-loads as part of the defense. How does that grab *your* conscience?"

Rollo betrayed no surprise or anguish, but his icon wouldn't necessarily display every emotion that crossed his flesh-and-blood face. After a while he said, "That's disgusting, but it's not going to change anything."

He looked down at the Proxies. "How long will it be before the process is so cheap and simple that you're using side-loads in every crowd scene? Computers are never going to rise up and enslave us, like the idiots in Hollywood portrayed it—or rescue us, like the idiots in Houston believe—but you'd happily send our most human-like mind-children straight into a hell of meaningless servitude and fragmented consciousness that we built for them all by ourselves."

Nasim said, "The only thing that's going to come close to hell for side-loads is if we have to keep using them to screen out your shit."

Rollo met her gaze. "These are our terms: you can keep Virtual Azimi and anything else that's limited to vision and motor skills, but you have to announce an end to the use of all other side-loads. If you don't make the promise within seven days, and honor it within another seven, the attacks will resume."

Nasim nodded curtly, to signal understanding. She felt a grudging respect for him, for at least setting conditions that were probably survivable; the deadlines weren't impossible, and with the sports Proxies untouched Zendegi could still remain afloat. She said, "It's not my decision, but I'll pass on the message."

Rollo held out his hand and turned his thumb down. The whole postcard vanished with him.

Nasim removed her goggles and waited as the wall came down around her. When she picked up her notepad from the table beside the *ghal'e* Falaki called her immediately.

"We couldn't trace your visitor," he said, "but I do have some good news."

"Go on."

"We've got solid evidence from the supervisors of a process being corrupted at one specific provider. I've already passed the log files on to their security people."

"Which provider?" Nasim asked.

"The FLOPS House."

That was in Europe somewhere. Nasim took her notepad away from her ear to glance quickly at the screen; the machine had already matched Falaki's words to an address book entry for the company, in Holland.

"It's very likely that this wasn't the only site breached," Falaki warned her. "Still, it's a start."

"Absolutely." If it was an inside job from within the FLOPS House, there was a chance of seeing at least one of the saboteurs arrested. Grab a thread of the conspiracy and good police work might unravel the whole thing.

"What do you know about the CHL?" she asked Falaki. He and Bahador had been monitoring the whole encounter.

"They haven't shown up on our radar in the past," he admitted. "I've set some things in motion, but right now we have nothing on them that you won't get from ordinary public searches."

"Okay."

Falaki wasn't expecting anything back from the FLOPS House for at least twenty-four hours. She thanked him and hung up the call.

Nasim set her own knowledge-miner sorting through the Cis-Humanist League's net presence; it was mostly text, and mostly on untraceable torrents. Rollo had been exaggerating slightly when he said they went back decades, but they'd been in various fora for fourteen years. Maybe Falaki would manage to trace the group's origins to some founders who'd been less careful about protecting their identities in the days when their agenda had been a lot more abstract.

Nasim needed to speak to the boss, but she lingered in the *ghal'eha* room, trying to decide exactly how she'd brief him. This wasn't necessarily a fight to the death for Zendegi; their enemy had offered them terms of surrender that wouldn't cripple them. And she could already see the comedians on Bloomberg: "Ever had a shit of a morning?" Swiftly stopping the attacks—and appeasing Shahidi as part of the bargain—might be the only way to keep the share price from going into freefall.

Accepting the truce need not mean the end of their current growth spurt. Zendegi had yet to sign up a star Indian cricket player, but equally, Cyber-Jahan had failed to convince anyone that their latest version of motion-capture—spiced up with myoelectric recordings and marketed as "Muscle Memory"—was a serious rival to side-loading. The Indian equivalent of Virtual Azimi could still belong to either one of them.

If they renounced more sophisticated side-loads though, that would be the end of the *vision splendid*, where every game developer released a special version first, exclusively for Zendegi. And Martin was not anyone's idea of a sports star; the board would pull the plug on his side-loading immediately.

The boss would want a transcript of her conversation with Rollo, but there was no way in the world that he was going to view the whole VR recording. So she might be able to get away with spinning her impression of the encounter, making the offer of the truce seem less trustworthy—and making him want to dig in his heels against the extortionists.

Nasim closed her eyes and tried to see the way forward. It had been thirty years since she'd felt a strong urge to pray to anyone or anything, but for a moment she came close to begging for a miracle…

Not from God, but from the Dutch computer crime squad.

25

When the day finally came to vacate the bookshop, Martin had had insomnia for three nights in a row. Arash, the softly-spoken commerce student who'd helped him sell the last of the stock, did most of the work disassembling the removable fixtures. The new occupants had agreed to deal with the remaining shelving when they remodelled; they'd get to sell the wood as scrap as compensation for the inconvenience of having to smash the joints apart with sledgehammers.

Just before noon, the buyer for the print-on-demand machine dropped in and took it away. There was nothing left now but empty shelves and a pile of mystifying, Ikea-like components that might have been the parts for anything from a bedroom suite to a set of kitchen benches. Arash had a friend with a small truck coming by in the afternoon to take them to a recycling center.

The office computer sat on the floor. Martin turned to Arash. "Do you want that? It's only two years old. I don't have time to sell it myself." His voice sounded hollow in the carpetless space. He kept seeing Mahnoosh standing beside him in the same empty room twelve years before.

Arash did *ta'arof* and refused three times, but finally agreed. Martin shook his hand.

"Thanks for all your help. Especially these last two weeks."

"Don't mention it."

"I'd better call a taxi." Martin wanted to grab an hour or two of sleep before he picked up Javeed. As he pulled his notepad out of his pocket, his hand started shaking and the thing ended up on the floor. "Jesus!"

Arash bent down and picked up the notepad. He said, "Do you want me to get a taxi?"

242

Martin's right hand was still flapping uncontrollably. He grabbed hold of it, feeling like Dr. Strangelove, but then the left hand joined in too.

"I'm sorry," he said, "can you do that for me?"

"I can get one on the street," Arash suggested, moving toward the door.

"I'd prefer a real one, if it's not too much trouble."

Arash made the call. Martin's hands finally stopped moving of their own accord, but his legs felt unsteady; he walked over to the wall and sat down on the floor. Dr. Jobrani had given him a list of warning symptoms for declining liver function. Wrist tremors were near the top of the list.

Arash returned the notepad and hovered anxiously. Martin said, "It's okay, I'm not having a heart attack."

His hands were steady now. He made a call himself. "Omar *jan*, I'm sorry, but is there any way you can pick up Javeed from school?"

"Of course. I'll send Farshid." Omar paused. "What's happening?"

Martin said, "I need to go to the hospital. Can you tell Javeed there's nothing to worry about?"

"I'll tell him. Do you want me to bring him there later?"

"I'm not sure. I'll give you a call when I've seen a doctor."

"Okay."

There was an awkward silence. "That's my taxi now," Martin lied. "*Khoda hafez.*"

"*Khoda hafez.*"

Arash was looking worried. "Should I call an ambulance?"

"No." Martin made a brief call to Dr. Jobrani's message service, describing his symptoms and saying he was coming in straight away.

He was beginning to feel lightheaded. The taxi arrived, and Arash helped him in. The driver played something loud and ugly on his music system, but Martin didn't have the energy to complain, and after a while his attention was wandering so much that he didn't really care.

He found himself sitting in a chair in the emergency waiting room, with no memory of having entered the building. When he turned and looked around, the woman behind him frowned disapprovingly, as if she suspected he was in some kind of self-inflicted drug haze. He drifted off again, then realized someone was examining him in a different room.

"Hey! Hey!" The doctor, a young man Martin had never seen before, was patting his cheek gently. "Can you try to focus, Mr. Seymour? Have you been taking any drugs not recorded on your file? Tranquilizers? Sleeping pills?"

"No." Martin looked around the room. "I don't know how I got here."

"I think you have some swelling," the doctor said. "I'm going to get you scanned as soon as possible."

"Swelling in my liver?"

"In your brain. Ammonia in your blood can cause some types of brain cells to enlarge."

"I didn't drink ammonia," Martin protested. *Ammonia in the blood?* It sounded like something only an alien could have. "Am I dying?" He was too spaced out to feel much fear at the prospect, but how could he say good-bye to Javeed in this state?

The doctor squeezed his shoulder reassuringly. "You're not dying, you're just disoriented. We'll have you fixed up in no time."

A nurse wearing an olive headscarf held a paper cup of water to his lips. Afternoon sunlight reflected into his eyes from something glinting on the far side of the room.

"Huh?" he said.

"Wait a second." The nurse rearranged his pillows and tried again. This time water entered his mouth. He could feel the sunlight on his cheek now. He had a line in his arm. It was nice of her to give him fluids by mouth when he had a line in his arm.

Martin slept fitfully. When he woke, he could see the ward reflected in a window, hiding the darkness outside. He felt terrible, but he felt whole again. Everything since the bookshop seemed unreal; he knew the gist of what had happened, but he wasn't sure he'd actually been present for any of it.

A nurse strode past his bed. "Excuse me? Can I make a phone call, please?" he asked her. As he spoke, the taste in his mouth and the smell of his breath made him nauseous. His belongings were probably in the drawer beside the bed, but he didn't trust himself to get to them unaided.

"It's two in the morning," she said, approaching.

Martin covered his mouth with one hand, trying to spare her from his nuclear halitosis. "I have to tell people where I am."

The nurse waved her notepad at his bracelet to access his records. "Your designated contact, Mr. Omar Rezaee, was informed of your admission earlier this evening."

"Oh. Thank you."

When she'd left, Martin thought this over for a while and decided it wasn't enough. He swung his legs out of the bed and managed to open the drawer without pulling the intravenous line from his arm.

"I'm fine, Omar *jan*," he whispered into his notepad. "Tell Javeed I'm fine. I'll call soon." He had the machine send his words as a text message. Then he climbed back into bed and sank into a dreamless sleep.

In the morning, Dr. Jobrani came to see him. Martin had to bite his tongue during the examination; he was tired of strangers touching his body, however respectfully, however necessary it was.

"So do you want the transplant now?" Jobrani inquired tartly. "Or have you decided to be the first human being who tries to live without the urea cycle?"

"I want three more days," Martin said.

Jobrani snorted. "You'll be waiting more than three days for a theater. Probably ten."

"I want three days out of the hospital."

Jobrani collapsed his stethoscope into an oversized pen with a Pfizer logo and slipped it into his pocket. "I want world peace and a holiday in Tahiti."

"I'll buy you a ticket for the replica in Dubai. Two days. Please, it's important."

Jobrani was unmoved. "What do you want to do? Finish writing your memoirs?"

"Something like that." More like checking the proofs. "What are my chances of surviving the transplant?"

"Now?" Jobrani thought about it. "Fifty-fifty."

Martin said, "And there's nothing you can do to give me a few days out of here that won't involve the same level of risk?"

"Nothing I can justify medically."

"I'll pay the full cost," Martin said. "You won't have to lie to my insurance company."

"There's an implant we could put in with keyhole surgery," Jobrani conceded reluctantly. "No general anesthetic. We might still nick a vein and kill you, but probably not."

"And this implant will keep me healthy?"

"It should keep you conscious, and a notch above bed-ridden; it substitutes for some of the liver's functions, but not all of them. It's what we would have used if you'd reached this point and there hadn't been a perfectly good organ waiting for you."

"How much will that cost me?"

"Five million."

"Rials?"

"Tomans."

A toman was ten Iranian rials. Five million tomans was about ten thousand US dollars; Martin still had enough of Mahnoosh's life insurance to cover it. He'd wanted to leave that money for Javeed, but his own policy would pay out soon enough.

Martin said, "How soon could I have it done?"

Jobrani struggled with his notepad's interface, frowning and cursing

246 • Greg Egan

under his breath. "If you can pay in advance, we can do it tomorrow afternoon."

"Fine." Martin took his own notepad from the bedside table and transferred the money.

Javeed would be in school. Martin called Omar and let him know how things were going; Omar said he'd bring Javeed in to visit in the afternoon.

Martin lay back and closed his eyes for a few minutes, trying to build up the strength for one more call.

He was surprised when Nasim answered; given all the problems Zendegi was facing, the most he'd been hoping for was her voicemail.

"I won't be able to come in tomorrow," he said.

"Are you all right, Martin?"

"Not really," he admitted. "This is crunch time; no more scans. You need to build the Proxy with whatever you've got."

Nasim was silent for a while, then she said, "Okay. I can do that."

"What sort of time are we looking at?"

"I'll do a provisional build overnight," she said. "Then I'll test it myself sometime tomorrow. But then I'll need you to come in and..."

"Give the final verdict." Martin had interviewed his own potential replacements for most of his journalistic postings; if he looked at it that way it might not be so strange.

Nasim said, "When will you be able to do that?"

"I'm in the hospital right now, but they'll be letting me out soon. I'll give you a call in a couple of days."

"All right."

"I saw the news," Martin said. "I'm sorry you're having a hard time."

Nasim laughed. "Don't worry about it. Whatever else is going on, we're going to make this happen."

When Martin put the notepad down and looked up at the ceiling, violet bruises moved across the white plaster in waves.

26

Nasim spent the day reading reports from Falaki's team and passing her summaries up the chain of command. With three days remaining to the first of Rollo's deadlines, the board had decided to hold off making any decision until it was clear how the investigation in Holland was panning out. An act of capitulation that resolved Zendegi's problems might make the stock market happy, but a timely arrest could do the same without eroding the value of the company's intellectual property. The security experts at the FLOPS House were working diligently through the log files Falaki had sent them, as well as their own staff access records, and they were hopeful that they'd soon identify the culprit. Certainly everyone was confident that an outsider could not have done the deed.

The total number of customers using Zendegi was down twenty per cent on the same time slots the week before, but there had also been tens of thousands of people joining up; perhaps they were hoping to witness some entertaining mayhem if there was another attack. The first breach had certainly been more amusing than repellent, so anyone who'd missed the whole punitive escalation angle might be expecting something diverting that would let them hold onto their dinner. Nasim knew that Happy Universe had long included a kind of ritualised breakdown of the usual game-world boundaries, where selected environments could sporadically gatecrash each other just to stir things up. But she wasn't about to kid herself that the cis-humanists' assault would lapse into a kind of harmless anarchist theater.

By the time she'd cleared her in-tray of everything pressing involving the extortionists, it was nine in the evening and no one else was in the building. She went to the tea room and microwaved one of the vegetable lasagnes she kept in the freezer there; she sat eating in the empty room, giving herself fifteen minutes away from her desk and screen. She didn't feel ready for the task that lay ahead of her, but she knew that if she went home now she'd get no sleep at all, and only have to face the same thing, twice as tired, the following night.

She'd prepared a test environment for the Proxy weeks before: a simply furnished antechamber where in the future—if all went well—the Proxy would be brought up to date with developments in Javeed's life before it stepped through into a different space to meet him. It would be her job to deliver these briefings, but she would not enter the environment through a *ghal'e*; her own sense of immersion was not important, and software could move her icon for her while her webcam supplied facial data.

Back in her office, she set the test in motion.

A wide-angle view of the antechamber appeared on the screen. The walls were paneled with oak, and two plush red sofas stood on either side of each of the two doors. The Proxy entered through one door, emerging from a world of featureless whiteness resembling the inside of a closed *ghal'e*. Its icon was being moved for it involuntarily at first, but as it woke to find it-self in mid-step it took the reins easily enough. It was using the same form of puppetry Martin had used when he was lying in the MRI, but starting it flat on its back would only have encouraged it to brood on its strange condition as it struggled to recall how to get its icon upright.

Nasim's icon was seated on one of the sofas by the second door. The Proxy turned to face her, smiling in recognition, and the screen switched to her point of view.

"Nasim?" the Proxy said. "What are you doing in Zendegi? Where's Javeed?"

"You'll see Javeed soon," she said. "I'm just here to bring you up to speed."

The Proxy frowned slightly, but then it seemed to grasp what she meant. It waited patiently for her to say more.

"It's 2030," she said. "Javeed's nine years old now; his birthday was last week."

"Okay." The Proxy beamed at her, apparently unperturbed by the realiza-tion that he must have been woken more than a hundred times already. Certainly the neural activity maps in the corner of the screen revealed no stress, no fear, no hostility.

"His icon's been updated," Nasim continued, "so don't be surprised by how tall he's become."

"No, of course not." The Proxy gestured at the door. "What's he into now? Still the *Shahnameh?*"

"Close: elephant racing."

The Proxy laughed. "How? How can he sit on an elephant in Zendegi?"

"Most of the *ghal'eha* now have something like a retractable mechanical bull," Nasim explained. "There's a geodesic frame to support it, and it folds up out of the way when it's not needed. The shape's variable, so you can feel like you're riding almost anything: a motorbike, a horse, an elephant. Or you could just be sitting on a motionless chair."

"That's amazing," the Proxy said. "*Elephant races!* Javeed will be over the moon."

Nasim said, "Does the situation bother you?"

"What situation?"

"The fact that Martin's been dead for more than two years," she said bluntly.

The Proxy's face showed nothing but sympathy. "How's Javeed coping?"

"He's all right," Nasim replied.

The Proxy said quietly, "I hope I've been some help."

Nasim wasn't comfortable responding to that. "What's your relationship to Javeed?" she asked.

"Relationship? I'm his father. Javeed is my son." The Proxy's expression was mildly quizzical; the neural maps still showed no distress, no anxiety.

"If Javeed's your son, what should I call you?"

The Proxy was amused. "You know my name: Martin Seymour."

"But Martin's dead," Nasim insisted.

"From cancer," the Proxy replied. "Liver cancer. We all knew that was coming."

"So how can you be Martin, when Martin's dead?"

The Proxy roared with laughter. "I get it now: you're just screwing with me, to see my reaction. You know how I can be Martin, Nasim. You of all people know how."

Nasim kept her nerve. "And that doesn't bother you at all? How you're here? Who you are?"

The Proxy regarded her with good-natured bemusement. "Why would it bother me? Martin is dead. I'm here in his place. Wasn't that the whole point?"

Nasim restarted the Proxy and pushed it harder. This time, she claimed it was 2040; she had her icon aged to make the lapse seem more real.

"Javeed's nineteen," she said. "He's engaged to be married." She hesitated. "I expect it's hard for you, knowing that you'll miss your son's wedding."

The Proxy remained sanguine. "I'm sure he'll show me the video. I never expected to be there in person, like a ghost trapped in a wallscreen; the truth is, I never thought he'd keep me around this long at all. But if he still wants my advice, I'm happy to keep giving it."

Nasim said, "Maybe he doesn't want your advice, but he doesn't know how to stop waking you. Do you think it's easy for him to shut you down and walk away?"

The Proxy replied, with just a trace of irritation, "Don't take offense, Nasim, but that's something I'll discuss with Javeed face to face."

Nasim soon lost any sense of reticence; she had an obligation to be as thorough as she could, to test her creation almost to destruction while Martin was still in a position to judge the results. She restarted the Proxy again and again, announcing different ages for Javeed, trying different ways to provoke it into angst. In her darkest moments she had feared that she might have been creating some mewling, pitiful thing that would chafe against its limitations, obsessing over its lack of embodiment, its imperfect memory, its truncated sense of self. But the consequences of its neural deficits appeared to have turned out exactly as she'd hoped: the Proxy seemed incapable of missing the things it lacked.

How much of this equanimity was down to her choice of ersatz neuroanatomy, and how much to Martin's own clear-eyed acceptance of the imperfect deal he was buying into, Nasim couldn't say. But the result was about as far as it could have been from a tortured abomination, screaming that if it couldn't have real wind on its face, real hope for its future and real memories of its past it should be wiped from the face of the Earth. Confronted with stark reminders of its nature and every kind of stress short of outright sadism, it remained simply grateful for its chance to outlive Martin and keep watch over his son.

Nasim continued the tests until dawn, then she took a break to grab a quick shower, change her clothes and gulp down some coffee. Then she sat and worked her way through another dozen permutations. It was beyond her power, beyond anyone's, to know how the Proxy would respond to every conceivable piece of news that the coming decades might bring, but when she pushed the envelope the results tended more to laughter than to tears.

"I'm afraid Javeed's become a follower of Shahidi," she declared. "He doesn't want to see you anymore."

The Proxy's shocked silence dissolved into guffaws. "Nice try, Nasim, but we agreed that if Javeed doesn't want to wake me, no one else will. I'm guessing Martin's still alive and you're just putting me through my paces before he signs off on me."

Nasim replied provocatively, "And does it worry you that one of us might reject you?"

The Proxy snorted. "I'd be worried if the two of you *weren't* doing some heavy-duty quality control before you unleashed me on my son."

"So far," Nasim assured it, "you've come across as remarkably stable. But how do you feel when I tell you I'm about to shut you down, leaving you with no memories of our conversation?"

"You'll remember what we've said," the Proxy replied. "That's enough. And when I'm doing my job for real, Javeed will remember; that's more than enough."

Nasim halted it.

Looking back, her night's labors seemed surreal. Even after hours of dialogue, she couldn't decide if the Proxy was genuinely conscious—in spite of its deficits, in spite of its crippled sense of self—or if it was just an accomplished actor: a brilliant mimic who felt nothing at all, but knew Martin's responses inside out.

She was certain of one thing, though. Even if Rollo was right and the Faribas were like battery hens in hell, this was one side-load who wasn't facing a life of voiceless suffering. Either Virtual Martin felt nothing, or he felt exactly what he claimed to feel: love for his son, acceptance of his limitations, and contentment with the purpose for which he'd been brought into existence.

As to whether he could fulfill that purpose, it was up to Martin now to decide.

27

"When are you coming hooooome?" Javeed demanded, pulling free of Rana's grip and walking over to the monitor beside Martin's bed.

"Don't touch that," Martin warned him, "or the nurse will beat me up."

"When?" Javeed repeated.

Martin said, "Tomorrow night I'm going to come and stay with you and Aunty Rana, then after a few nights I'll come back to hospital for my new liver. Then after a few more nights we'll both be back in our own home. How does that sound?"

Javeed ignored all the obfuscatory details and cut straight to the point. "Why don't they give you your liver now?"

"It's not quite ready," Martin lied. "That's why I've got the little one until then." He moved the sheet aside and showed Javeed the tiny, neat scar left by the keyhole surgery. "The one that the robot put inside me."

Javeed still didn't quite believe him about the robot, even though Martin had shown him images from the manufacturer's glossy website.

Rana said, "It's taking them a long time to grow your liver. A whole child can be born in nine months!"

"An adult liver weighs as much as a newborn baby," Martin claimed, fairly sure that this was neither true nor relevant. All he needed now was for Dr. Jobrani to walk in while his visitors debated the reasons for the organ's tardy arrival. "Anyway, I'm lucky they can do it at all."

"Thanks to God," Rana agreed. "You'll be out soon, as healthy as ever. Like Omar's father with his artificial legs. You should see him, Martin: he's like a young man again." This was clearly intended as a form of encouragement, but Rana seemed to mean it sincerely.

"Yeah?" Martin smiled. "Well, he waited more than forty years, so I don't have anything to complain about."

Rana glanced at the clock on the wall and addressed Javeed. "Say good-bye to your father. We'll go home and have some dinner."

Javeed approached the side of the bed and Martin kissed him. "Thanks for coming, *pesaram*. I'll see you tomorrow." He turned to Rana. "Thanks for bringing him. I know he's a handful."

"*Khahesh mikonam.*"

"I'm not a handful!" Javeed protested.

"No, he's been good," Rana said, almost convincingly. "It's a pleasure to have him." She rose from her chair.

"I'll see you tomorrow," Martin said. "*Khoda hafez.*"

"*Khoda hafez.*"

When they were gone, Martin took his notepad from the side of the bed and returned to the Zendegi website. He'd narrowed down his list to three scenarios, but he wanted to make a definite choice for the following day so he could fall asleep knowing there'd be one less thing to deal with in the morning.

In Zendegi, a great many people spent a great deal of time pretending to fight and kill each other, and Javeed had shown no signs that he would buck the trend. For all that Martin had tried to steer him away from battle scenes, the chances were that within a few years the attraction would prove irresistible. Martin had gone through that phase of his childhood fencing with sticks and shooting water pistols; there had been no technology around to make his opponents fountain blood and spill viscera. That magic had been confined to the movies, with the most graphic material out of his reach—though at twelve he'd managed to sneak into *Jabberwocky* and found himself in heaven.

He was hoping there'd be time for several different test runs before the transplant, but with Zendegi's health looking as precarious as his own, he needed to be prepared to make a judgment as quickly as possible. So if he wanted to see the Proxy jump through hoops, there was no point starting with any but the highest, and no point sparing the flames.

Nasim collected Martin from the hospital and drove him across the city. She seemed nervous, but it was clear from her demeanor that the optimistic verdict she'd given him after her own tests had been genuine. The Proxy had not disappointed her; the only thing she feared was that Martin might not feel the same way.

It was half past seven when they arrived, but despite the chilly morning Shahidi's supporters were out in force. Martin had only been following the politics sporadically, but he'd heard Zendegi's side-loads being lumped together with a whole grab bag of permissive and un-Islamic trends. The respectable conservative line went like this: Nobody wanted the corrupt mullahs back, lining their pockets and throwing their enemies into prison, but the pendulum had swung too far and a correction was desperately needed. A vote to rein in immodesty and blasphemy would be the antidote to extremism, dealing with popular discontent before it exploded into a violent backlash.

In the MRI room, Nasim fitted Martin's skullcap. Bernard was having a day off; his trainee, Peyman, was operating the scanner. There was no need for contrast agents; they would not be collecting side-loading data today. The only reason Martin was here and not in a *ghal'e* was that controlling his icon mentally, via the scanner, would spare him from fatigue and allow him to fake a few futuristic tweaks to the system.

Nasim said, "Don't get alarmed if the Proxy doesn't show up for a few minutes; it's hard to say in advance how long I'll be talking to it."

"Okay."

"Feel free to kill the game any time you want to, or to keep running it for as long as you like. The scanner's yours for three hours if you need it."

"Thank you."

Nasim flipped down his goggles and fitted the cage over his head. Martin waited for the whir of the motor that would carry him back into Zendegi.

The dying embers of a campfire lay in front of him; an orange light was breaking on the horizon. Martin stretched his arms out, feeling his way into his new body; the hands and forearms that came into view belonged to a giant, but the skin was as smooth and unlined as a child's. Zal's son Rostam had been preternaturally huge; only the Simorgh's intervention—in which the bird had offered detailed advice on the herbal drugs to use for a Cae-sarean—had allowed Rudabeh to give birth to him and live. But Rostam's son Sohrab was even more prodigious; the *Shahnameh* had him playing polo at three, shooting arrows and throwing javelins at five, and leading a conquering army at the age of ten.

Martin turned away from the dying fire. He was standing on a slight rise; below him, embroidered tents and horses draped in silk brocade carpeted the desert as far as he could see. Around the tents, soldiers were finishing their meals, completing their ablutions and tending to their mounts. He could remember when a crowd scene like this would have needed a Hollywood budget and an hour's worth of computations to render each frame; now it was being done in real time for his eyes alone. Or his, and one other pair.

As he surveyed the camp, the soldiers who glanced his way quickly lowered their gaze in deference to their ten-year-old general. He had asked Nasim to modify the way he saw the Proxy, retaining some resemblance to his own appearance but changing a few parameters to break the spell; it would be hard enough playing his own peculiar role without the distraction of a mirror-image of his true self standing in front of him. The preview she'd emailed him had seemed workable—and it had looked so much like one of his uncles that Martin had decided to call it privately by the same name. His Uncle Jack had died twelve years before, and Martin had not been close to him since childhood, but borrowing his identity felt less strange than picking a name at random.

When the white-haired man clad in armor strode toward him up the rise, Martin started to have second thoughts about his choice, but it was too late for that. Javeed would see the same icon as he'd seen from their very first trip together, so Martin did his best to let the sense of familiarity overwhelm everything else.

"Javeed?" Jack broke into a grin of delight and disbelief. "I thought you might outgrow me one day, but this is ridiculous!"

"Welcome back, Baba." Martin stepped forward and reached down to take his hand.

Jack was speechless for a moment, overcome with emotion. Martin tried to appear affectionate, but also a little blasé; the experience was meant to be anything but new to him. For Jack, every time would feel like the first time he was seeing his son again after his death. But Martin understood why Nasim had insisted that it be this way; not only had the side-loading process been pushed to its limits to get this far, she hadn't wanted to curse the Proxy with a sense of its own life in time.

Martin drew his hand away. "Does it help if I tell you that it always helps when I tell you that you always get over the shock?"

Jack burst out laughing. "Absolutely!" He looked away, fighting back tears. "Ah, *pesaram.* I wish—" Martin knew how the thought ended: *I wish your mother could have seen you like this.* But Jack passed the test and kept silent; Javeed didn't need that wound torn open, week after week.

"What's happening at home?" Jack asked him. "How are Uncle Omar and Aunty Rana?"

"They're good," Martin said. "The shop's still going well. Umm… Uncle Omar's father died last year."

"I'm sorry. What happened?"

"He had a heart attack." Martin underplayed it, as if to say: *It was sad, and I'll miss him, but he was a very old man,* trying to appear neither anguished nor untouched.

Jack seemed to be on the verge of pressing him for more, but then he caught himself; whatever need there'd been to discuss the death, that conversation would have happened long ago. "How's Farshid?"

"He got married. He's got a daughter now."

"That's great. Are they living with you and Omar?"

"Yes." Martin hesitated. "I don't think his wife likes me very much."

Jack said, "Maybe she's just a bit jealous, because you and Farshid are so close."

Martin didn't reply and Jack let it drop. "What about school?" he asked.

"School's okay. I'm getting good marks in Farsi and English. And I'm the third fastest runner in my grade."

"*Mubaarak!*"

Martin spread his bulky arms. "But today I think I'd make a good wrestler."

Jack laughed. "So you're Sohrab?"

"Yeah. Do you remember the story? Rostam was hunting along the border with Turan, and one night his horse went missing. While he was looking for Rakhsh he hooked up with Princess Tahmineh, but all he really cared about was his horse; he didn't hang around to look after the kid."

Jack smiled uneasily; perhaps he knew that this tale of parental neglect turned out rather less happily than that of Sam and Zal.

Martin said, "Don't worry, Baba, you're not playing Rostam. I made up a new character, an adviser from Princess Tahmineh's court who travels with her son as a kind of guardian."

"A kind of guardian," Jack echoed. Maybe the demotion stung a little, but it was better than the fate in store down the line for Sohrab's father.

A bearded Turani nobleman approached Martin and bowed low. "My lord, the sun is risen and your soldiers await your instructions." Martin wanted to laugh—just as he and Javeed had once giggled at Kavus and his sycophants—but he stayed in character: twelve-year-old Javeed playing the revered boy-general Sohrab.

"Today," he replied portentously, "we take the White Fortress."

"As you command, my lord."

Martin paid almost no attention to the troops gathering behind him; there were trumpets sounding and orders being shouted, but he trusted the game to handle the logistics without his oversight or supervision. He wasn't here to hone his nonexistent skills as a military commander, or to fret about rivals rising up to overthrow him; this whole vast army was just an elaborate backdrop, a part of the landscape.

He and Jack rode out across the desert side by side, ahead of the tide of horsemen and the camels following with the army's provisions. Nasim would have explained to Jack how Javeed could be riding his mount in a *ghal'e*, while Jack would be controlling his own icon in essentially the same way as Martin was.

Alone with Jack, Martin didn't push the arrogant prince persona; he treated his surrogate father warmly as a co-conspirator with whom he was happy to break the frame. Javeed, Martin hoped, would soon get used to the memory problem and find a way to talk to Jack that satisfied them both. It would be frustrating to have to repeat himself, but he'd also have the power to set the agenda.

"Farshid's daughter is called Nahid," Martin said, "like his grand-mother."

"How old is she?" Jack asked.

"Nearly one."

"So how do you feel about having a little niece around?"

Martin said, "She's nice sometimes. When she's not screaming."

"She must keep everyone busy," Jack said.

"They're always fussing over her," Martin complained.

"Well… she's a baby, she's helpless. She needs to be watched closely; she still has to learn everything about the world."

"Yeah."

"Think about all the fun you had with Farshid," Jack said. "Then think how happy Nahid will be if she has someone like you to look up to the same way."

"Hmm." Martin didn't want to play Javeed as a pushover, but he didn't have the stomach to take the resentment to a pathological extreme: threats to run away from home, or thoughts of harming the child. Jack was doing a reasonably tactful job so far; good enough, surely, to provide a kind of safety valve. Whenever Javeed felt his whole adopted family was against him, he'd always have his dead father's ear.

They rode on in silence for a while, but Martin could see Jack watching him out of the corner of his eye. It was impossible not to feel moments of dizzying empathy for Jack's position, to imagine how painful the ache of love for Javeed would become from across that strange horizon. But Martin wasn't here to offer him emotional support in some bizarre co-parental bonding session—least of all when any words of encouragement he provided would vanish from Jack's memory long before they could be any real help. And if Jack's task weighed heavily, as it surely did, at least the weight could not accumulate. When the alternative was losing contact with Javeed completely, Martin did not believe it would be too much to bear.

"The White Fortress!" Jack announced, pointing into the heat-haze, proving that he'd been paying the game world far more attention than Martin had. In real life, Martin had never ridden anything larger than a donkey, but Sohrab's horse responded to his urging and galloped ahead; Jack was left in the dust, though when Martin turned he could see him catching up.

Sohrab had been born in the town of Samangan, on the border between Persia and its neighbor Turan. When his mother had finally explained his lineage to him, he'd decided to gather an army from Turan and march on Persia to seize Kavus's throne for his absent father, and then claim Turan as his own. His campaign did not end well, but Martin was content to sample the relatively upbeat beginning; the twelve-year-old Javeed might be into swordplay and gore, but epic tragedy was unlikely to hold much attraction for him for several more years.

As he drew nearer to the white stone building, a smear of dust appeared in front of it. A lone Persian soldier was riding out to confront the invaders.

Jack caught up with Martin, his horse covered in sweat. "Do you really want to start this war?" he asked. "What if you sent a message to Rostam first? What if you told him who you were and asked for his advice?"

Martin rolled his eyes. "Stop trying to play peacemaker! This is what Sohrab *does!*"

"Okay, *pesaram*." Jack laughed to cover his nervousness; he had no way of knowing if he'd tested Javeed's patience by pushing the same line a hundred times before. "Well, at least I can tell Princess Tahmineh I gave you some advice."

Martin could make out their enemy now, as his armor glinted in the morning sun. He urged his mount forward; the thought of the coming confrontation turned his stomach, but a boy who had never seen a real act of bloodshed would not be so squeamish.

The two adversaries came to a halt within shouting distance. The Persian soldier was tall and solidly built; in real life Martin would have given him a very wide berth, with or without the presence of lances. The man's beard was flecked with gray; he had survived a few decades as a warrior.

"I am Hejir!" the Persian called out to him. "I serve Kavus, Lord of the World. Tell me your loyalty and your intentions."

Martin smothered his conciliatory instincts and followed the script. "I am Sohrab, loyal to my own proud lineage, and I've come to take the crown from that fool."

Hejir recoiled in disgust. "I can still smell the milk of your mother on your breath! Turn back, or she'll be washing your body in her tears."

"Can it be true that you've heard nothing of the glory of Sohrab? No man who had would dare to face me alone!"

"Kavus will have your head as my tribute," Hejir replied. "Your body I will bury here in the dirt."

Jack had caught up; Martin turned and motioned to him to stay back.

Martin called out, "Surrender now, and I'll spare your life. Cling to stubborn pride, and I'll give no quarter."

Hejir raised his lance. "Return to Turan while you still have the breath for idle boasting. It is no shame for a child to flee from a warrior."

Martin leaned forward and commanded his horse to charge.

The desert streaked past him jerkily, like something shot on a hand-held camera, but the signals from his motionless, horizontal body turned the whole thing into a strange, smooth swoop, as if he were an eagle descending down the face of a cliff. Hejir was charging too, flying up to meet him. As they approached, Martin fumbled with his lance; his gloves made it tangible but he had no reliable sense of the geometry of the encounter. Hejir struck him squarely in the chest; Martin's weapon didn't even make contact.

As they separated, Martin looked down; his armor was dented, but there was no other damage, and he had not so much as shifted in his saddle. Hejir looked formidable to Martin's eyes, but baby-faced Sohrab was a giant, too heavy to be dislodged by the force of any ordinary blow.

Martin brought his horse around. He could see Jack approaching in the distance. Hejir was circling back towards him; his lance had snapped, but he'd drawn his sword. Martin would have leaned over and vomited if there'd been any way to get the stuff out of his throat, but he had to appear suitably exhilarated for Jack's sake. He was a high-spirited boy with a stick for a sword: Javeed with his shampoo-bottle missiles, six years on. He thought of Javeed's face after Kavus's flying pavilion had gone into a spin. That was the look he wanted: a pure, innocent thrill.

Hejir was closing with frightening speed, already gripping his sword with both hands. Martin contemplated throwing the fight, simply letting himself be knocked down and injured; that in itself would be a test for Jack to witness, and other tests could follow in later battles. But he didn't have time for the luxury of slowly building up his nerve. He raised his lance and focused all his attention on the impending encounter. Hejir was committed to coming close enough to strike a blow, but their weapons were no longer evenly matched, and their bodies never had been.

The lance struck Hejir and threw him from his horse. Martin wheeled around and saw the Persian soldier flat on his back, his sword far away in the dust. Martin dropped the lance and dismounted, unsheathing his own sword and striding toward his enemy. As Hejir rose to his knees Martin swung at him like a child playing with a plastic toy; the gloves did their best to imbue the steel with a sense of real weight, of real consequence, but the task was beyond them.

Hejir twisted to avoid the blow, but this was the end game: he was disarmed, and the giant loomed over him. He bowed his head.

"I am bettered," he said. "I beg for your mercy."

Martin said, "I told you, no quarter." He swung the weightless sword again; his gloves shuddered as he parted Hejir's head from his body. Blood gushed richly from the dead man's neck, spilling onto Martin's legs and feet. He stared down at the corpse, dazed and sickened but clinging to one certainty: he had to be prepared for Javeed to do something like this. Everyone who cared for him had to be prepared.

"You worthless piece of shit!"

Martin turned; Jack was approaching on foot, his horse a few meters behind him. "You fucking worthless piece of shit!" He tore the metal helmet from his head and threw it on the ground; his face was contorted with anger and disgust.

"Baba, it's just a game," Martin pleaded.

"Are you my son?" Jack raged. "Is this what that fucker Omar did to you?"

"Baba, I'm sorry—" Martin stood his ground as Jack walked up to him and started flailing impotently with his fists at Sohrab's giant body.

Jack sank to his knees. "Is that what I taught you? You couldn't help yourself, even when he begged for his life?" He clawed at the dirt. "What am I, then? What am I doing here?" He struck his head with his fists, distraught.

"Baba, no one's hurt, it's just a game," Martin insisted. He shared Jack's revulsion at what they'd both witnessed; he had known full well the feelings that his act would provoke. But he was sure he could have held his own response in check for Javeed's sake; he could have stood back from his anger and found some gentler rebuke than this.

Jack gazed up at him wretchedly, cursing and ranting incoherently. Martin could see the helplessness in his eyes; he knew he'd gone too far and he wanted to stop. But the part of him that could do it wasn't there. Maybe he still felt the ghost of it, like a phantom limb, but it had no purchase on reality, no power to change his course.

Martin said, "I'm not Javeed. This is just a test."

Jack emitted a blood-curdling sob; his whole body shuddered with relief. But he still hadn't won back control: he kept cursing Omar, cursing

Javeed, cursing himself.

"I'm sorry," Martin said. "I screwed up, I'm sorry."

Jack looked down and shook his head impatiently. He didn't want a post mortem, he just wanted to be done with this.

Martin stretched out his hand and erased him.

28

"There was a family I met in Kabul," Martin said. "Ali and Zahra. They had four children; three girls and a baby boy."

They were sitting in the MRI room. Peyman had made himself scarce. Nasim said, "Go on."

"They were from a small village in Bamyan Province. They'd been living without papers in Iran for three years, but they got caught in a sweep and sent back across the border. It wasn't safe in their village, so they ended up in Kabul.

"I met Ali on the street. It was winter; he was selling firewood—smashed-up furniture from garbage dumps, mostly. He invited me to his home and introduced me to his family; I interviewed him and his wife. I didn't have a photographer with me, so I made a time to come back the next day.

"When I returned… some people from the group that Ali had fled in Bamyan had found him, a few hours before. They'd cut off his head, in front of his family. In front of his wife and kids." Martin covered his eyes with one hand. "I didn't see it happen, but I saw what it did to them."

Nasim was silent for a while, trying to think of a way through the impasse. "There are a couple of things we could try," she said. "I could go back and find all the images we showed you that triggered that memory, and then rebuild the Proxy omitting your responses to them. Or we could put in some kind of filter, so the Proxy gets shielded from anything similar that happens in Zendegi."

Martin looked up at her, incredulous. "Filtering his memories or censoring his experiences isn't going to fix this. The Proxy should have been able to remember what had happened and talk about it with Javeed, calmly and sanely. If we just pluck it out of his head, or shield him from anything that reminds him of it, then what about the next thing that makes him go ballistic? The problem doesn't lie with his memories; it's the fact that he doesn't have the capacity to deal with them."

Nasim said defensively, "I did tell you that there'd be limitations." She had certainly included all the brain regions normally associated with impulse control, but given that the Proxy was, by design, incapable of forming all of the same perspectives as the original, there were always going to be situations where it was not going to behave the same way.

"I'm not blaming you," Martin replied, without rancor. "You explained everything. I didn't listen."

Nasim shifted in her chair. "So what will you do?"

"Javeed will live with Omar," Martin said. "There was never any choice about that."

"Can you talk to Omar?"

"I have to." Martin laughed and wiped his eyes. "But how do you tell someone who's offered to spend the next ten years raising your son that you've got a list of subjects on which you'd prefer that he kept his mouth shut? How do I do that without poisoning our friendship—and poisoning him against Javeed? Maybe I can slip it into some notes I hand him, just after the list of Javeed's allergies."

Nasim said, "You've been friends for fifteen years. Surely you can talk to him about anything now?"

Martin regarded her with bemusement. "Is it like that for you? No boundaries at all?"

"Well, not exactly," Nasim admitted.

"I've never been that close to Omar," Martin said. "Ever since I arrived in Tehran he's gone out of his way to help me, but even now it's still like we're... guest and host. We can kid around about things that don't matter, but we don't criticize each other—that would be crass and ungracious. And after all these years of mutual tact, I don't know how to change the rules without making it feel like a slap in the face."

Nasim didn't know what advice to give him. "You'll find a way," she said.

Martin spread his hands: *maybe*. "Thanks for trying so hard with the side-load," he said. "I hope the research still tells you something useful." He stood.

"I'll give you a lift home," Nasim offered.

Martin shook his head. "I'll get a taxi. You must have other things to do."

"Let's not do *ta'arof*. I cleared my diary for the morning; I'll give you a lift."

They rode in silence most of the way. Nasim felt helpless; a part of her was still hunting for ways to salvage the project, to patch over the difficulties and make everything work. She knew that it was pointless, though. Whatever she proposed now, Martin was not going to change his mind.

When they reached the house, she walked with Martin to the door. "After the operation, if you're not able to cope with an ordinary *ghal'e*, I can still organize time in a scanner."

Martin said, "Thanks, but if the transplant's successful I should be in much better shape. Actually, I'm planning some trips with Javeed. There's only so much *Zendegi-ye-Behtar* I can take."

"Okay." They shook hands. "Good luck," she said.

Nasim was halfway back to the city when her notepad buzzed. The call was from Falaki: too much to deal with while she was driving, so she found a side-street where she could park and call him back.

"There's good news and bad news," Falaki said.

"Please don't make me choose."

"I'll start with the short version then," he said. "We know pretty much what happened at the FLOPS House. But we don't know who did it, and we don't expect to find out anytime soon."

Nasim digested that. "Okay. How did they do it?"

"It was a chip hack. The FLOPS House found a rogue processor in one of their servers; that's what enabled everything that happened to you there. But it looks as if the chip would have covered the tracks of whoever steered the attack, so we can't expect to get reliable evidence as to who that was."

Nasim stared out into the traffic. "They can't find out who had physical access to the server?"

"The processor doesn't seem to have been put there by someone tampering after the server was installed," Falaki replied. "It looks as if it's been there since the machine was built."

"So they got hacked chips *into the supply line?*" Nasim had only ever heard of that being done before by major crime syndicates.

"It looks that way," Falaki said.

"Have the FLOPS House cleared all their hardware?"

"Not yet; they're working their way through. That could take them a month or more. The data we had on the breach helped them narrow down their first tests, but for a comprehensive sweep there'll be no shortcuts."

A month or more? But it was worse than that; if the cis-humanists had introduced their own custom chips into the manufacturer's stock, there was no reason at all to think that only one provider was affected. Even if Zendegi stopped doing business with the FLOPS House, if they tried to push ahead in defiance of Rollo's deadline, there was no guarantee that they'd be safe from a further attack.

"There is an upside," Falaki said. "If you want to start negotiating hardware monitoring with the providers, this is the leverage you need."

"You could be right," Nasim conceded glumly. "But that's still going to take five years."

"Of course," Falaki agreed.

"And in the meantime?"

"In the meantime, I'd say the least risky approach would be to give these people what they want."

Nasim knew that this advice made sense, but it was still hard to swallow. "Did you find out anything about the CHL's founders?"

"There were five people who played a central role in the early discussions on the net," Falaki said. "Some of them must still be active on the same issues. We've passed the names on to the Dutch police, and they'll liaise with the authorities in the relevant countries. But we've got no evidence at all of criminal activity by any of those individuals. Don't expect to see them rounded up and questioned; at best, some jurisdictions might add them to surveillance lists."

"I see."

When she'd hung up, Nasim sat watching the cars stream past her, trying to psych herself up for the call to the boss. Zendegi would not go down the tubes; Virtual Azimi would keep them afloat. The act of capitulation stung, but she would probably get to keep her livelihood.

As she turned the notepad over in her hands, she felt her fingers shaking. She could still see the expression on the Proxy's face as it struggled to bring itself under control: the horror at reaching out for the strength it needed from a part of its mind that simply wasn't there.

Nasim spent an hour and a half with the boss, mapping out Zendegi's retreat. She had already started Bahador and Arif working on contingency plans, searching for ways to ease the transition for those games that used the Fariba modules and the other higher-level side-loads. For some of the games a fair approximation of the linguistic and social skills the Proxies were calling upon could be achieved with conventional software; Zendegi could license and adapt off-the-shelf modules and substitute them for the side-load versions. In other cases there would be no workaround, and they would simply have to pay penalty clauses to the developers.

It was an expensive, demoralising mess. Nasim tried not to over-interpret the understandable chill coming her way, but it struck her that once she'd overseen the clean-up, she'd make a convenient scapegoat. For the simplest cases, her expertise at exploiting the HCP data had now been entirely automated, so Zendegi and Eikonometrics would have no trouble generating new side-loads without her. Everyone was grateful for Virtual Azimi, but everything she'd done since had turned out to be a liability.

As Nasim walked back to her office she glanced again at the small orange triangle on her notepad, a flag from her knowledge-miner. She had ignored it during the meeting because the triangle denoted a subject she had categorized as minor, peripheral; the breaking news would not be an arrest at the FLOPS House or a fresh proclamation from Shahidi. But the color code implied that other measures of significance had lifted the story's ranking to the top of the queue: the world at large was taking it seriously enough to outweigh her own judgment on the topic. It was the kind of unsettling combination that might have arisen if a singer whose career she'd been following with mild interest had just been unmasked as a serial killer.

She sat at her desk and streamed the report to her monitor. There'd been some kind of terrorist attack in the US overnight. Three trucks packed with fertiliser bombs had destroyed a think-tank in Houston; mercifully, the place had been empty, so no one had been killed. Nasim stared at the helicopter shots of smoke rising from the charred concrete, still unsure why the story had registered on her personal radar.

Then she saw the reporter at ground level, interviewing a witness outside a coffee shop close to the site of the bombing, and a chill crept up her arms. She had been in that coffee shop herself, half a decade before, when she'd traveled to Houston as part of her tour to scout out AI technology for Zendegi. The "think-tank" to which the reporter kept referring was the Superintelligence Project.

29

The night before the transplant, Martin couldn't sleep. There was a weight pressing down on his chest, and when he closed his eyes it only grew heavier.

He looked across the guest room at Javeed's sleeping form. The electronic picture frame sitting on the bedside table glowed softly, still showing photos from the Australian trip. Javeed had grown attached to these images of his parents' exotic past.

Living with Javeed in Omar's house felt like a taste of the future, a preview of life after death. The last time they'd been guests here had been straight after the accident, but this was different: Javeed was almost settled now. Everyone accepted him as part of the family, and he slotted in unselfconsciously with no awkwardness or shyness. If anything, Martin worried that he might come across as too sure of his place, but no one seemed to mind, and that was better than him spending the next ten years feeling constantly beholden to his hosts, mortified by every fingermark he left on the walls. Rana had no interest in pretending to be his mother, but she treated him exactly like one of her nephews. Martin had no doubt that she would have preferred an easier intermission between raising Farshid and the arrival of grandchildren, but she would take her promise to Mahnoosh very seriously, and she would never let Javeed feel unwelcome or unloved.

For six days, Martin had been waiting for an opportunity to talk to Omar, but there was always someone else around. Worse, he still didn't know what he'd say. Sometimes his worries turned to white-hot panic, as if Omar might be scheming to induct his son into a cult of murderous Aryan supremacists, an Iranian Ku Klux Klan. Sometimes the whole thing shrank into insignificance, as if it were just a neurotic tic, a laughable fastidiousness over language.

Lying in the dark, watching the photos cycling beside Javeed's bed, Martin wasn't even sure how much of his fear was about his son's future and how much was about his own death. He had seen his parents die, peacefully, and the world had not come to an end. He had witnessed the violent deaths of dozens of strangers, and the world had not come to an end. The only thing that could be done for the dead was to protect and care for the survivors. But would he have been so blind, for so long, to the impossible trade-offs that the Proxy had entailed if he'd been thinking only of Javeed? He had not merely wanted Javeed riding through Zendegi with a trusted companion to watch his back and offer good advice; he had wanted to *be* that companion. Even with his thoughts dissolving into fog each time they parted, it would have been a kind of survival.

Martin heard someone walking through the house; he recognized Omar's throat-clearing cough. He climbed out of bed and opened the door; he could see light spilling into the living room from the bathroom. He walked to the kitchen in the dark, filled a glass with water and stood drinking.

The toilet flushed and Omar emerged, sending a shaft of light through the adjoining rooms. Martin didn't turn but the light stayed on and he heard Omar's footsteps approaching.

"Martin *jan*, are you all right?" Omar whispered.

"Yeah."

"Do you need anything?"

Martin shook his head. "I can't sleep, that's all."

Omar hesitated, perhaps wondering if he should press his guest to be more forthcoming. Then he said, "Wait."

He walked back to the bathroom and turned out the light, then he switched on a small lamp in the living room. He approached Martin again. "Come and sit here. We can talk for a while."

Omar ushered Martin into Mohsen's armchair, then sat on the couch beside it. He was wearing an Iranian national football team jersey and tracksuit pants. Behind him on the wall was a painting of Imam Ali; a yellow light shone through the clouds around the Imam's green turban while chains of flowers and ornate calligraphy filled the bottom of the frame in the foreground.

"You're worried about the operation?" Omar asked.

"Just a bit."

Omar *tssked*. "Everyone is praying for you. It will be all right."

"The surgeon's good, but the patient's not so great."

Omar reached over and squeezed Martin's forearm. "Come on, don't talk like that."

Martin said, "Can I ask you something?"

"Sure."

"I don't want to bring back bad memories…"

Omar frowned, but he was puzzled, not warning him off. "It's okay, you can talk about anything."

"When you were in Evin," Martin began, pausing to look for some sign that he was overstepping the mark, "why didn't you tell them about me?"

Omar looked confused; he rubbed one eye with the heel of his hand. "Tell who what?"

"When you were being questioned," Martin persisted, "why didn't you give VEVAK my name? Nothing too bad would have happened to me; I would have just been deported in the end. It might have made it easier for you, if you'd given them something."

Omar stared at him blankly for a second. Then he laughed softly, mindful of the house full of sleeping people. "You mean, about the hospital? Why didn't I tell them that the only way I got that faggot out of the hospital was because some crazy foreign journalist gave me his clothes?" He looked down, shaking his head with mirth. "Do you think they would have believed that? They would have been sure that I was lying, and they would have beaten me even harder." He leaned back on the couch, one hand over his mouth, trying to control himself. "It's lucky they didn't arrest you. If you'd tried to tell them the truth about standing in the cupboard in ladies' clothes, they would have beaten you black and blue."

Martin grinned back at him as if he shared the joke. The truth was, he felt a mixture of relief and humiliation. He was glad that Omar hadn't actually suffered needlessly to protect him, but he felt like a fool for holding the wrong idea for so long.

Omar seemed to sense his discomfort; he became serious. "I'm not laughing at you, Martin; you did a good thing. But don't blame yourself for anything that happened to me in Evin."

Martin said, "Okay."

"I wish I had a photo, though," Omar said. "When I sent my friend to give you the clothes, I should have told him to take a picture first."

They sat talking for almost an hour. Martin kept waiting for the meandering current of the conversation to take him to the right place, but Omar's eyelids were starting to droop. Martin felt the tightness in his chest growing; if he missed this chance he might never have another one.

He said, "Javeed's got a new friend at school, an Afghani boy. You don't mind if he invites him over to the house?"

"Of course not."

"Are you sure?" Martin pressed him. "It's just that I've heard you say some things about Afghanis—"

Omar stiffened. "My problem is with the criminals. Any friend of Javeed is welcome here."

Martin said, "So how do you know which Afghanis are criminals?"

Omar regarded him with an expression of mild irritation. "They're the ones who are stealing things and murdering people."

"So thieves and murderers are the problem, not Afghanis?"

"They're wild people," Omar insisted. "And this isn't their country. So what do you expect?"

Martin said, "Is Iran my country?"

Omar recoiled. "You're an honored guest! You didn't abuse our hospitality."

"Nor did Javeed's friend, or the boy's family."

"And *I told you*: Javeed's friend is welcome in my house, as often as he likes." Omar glared at him, wounded.

Martin said, "I'm sorry. I didn't mean to offend you."

Omar's expression softened. "It's nothing. We're both tired, and you're worried about tomorrow. You should get some sleep."

"Yeah."

Back in the guest room, Martin lay cursing himself, running through the conversation in his head, trying to imagine how he could have put things more tactfully. But he'd lost his chance; there was nothing he could say now. If he raised the subject with Omar again it would already be too tainted with a sense of grievance.

Javeed had permission to take a day off school. Martin woke him at five o'clock, an hour before they needed to leave.

"Why are you cooking breakfast?" Javeed asked sleepily.

"You don't like pancakes?" Martin spread his arms around the stove possessively. "I can eat them all if you don't want any."

"No!"

Omar joined them. He kept Javeed distracted, swiping food and messing around with condiments so Javeed didn't notice that Martin wasn't actually eating anything.

The rest of the family rose just before six. Martin still felt like an interloper around Mohsen and Nahid, but they both offered a few gruff words of encouragement. Rana shook his hand, Farshid embraced him briefly, everyone mindful of not making a big scene in front of Javeed.

Omar drove them to the hospital. Martin sat in the back beside Javeed. "I spy with my little eye something beginning with L," Javeed declared.

"In English, or in Farsi?" Martin asked.

Javeed sighed. "I said L, not *lam*."

"Lamppost?"

"No."

"Light pole."

"No."

Martin stared out into the traffic. "I give up."

"Liver." Javeed cackled at his own ingenuity.

"That's cheating," Martin said. "You can't see it."

Javeed held his hands up to his face in the shape of binoculars. "I can already see it in the jar at the hospital. My eyes are better than yours."

It took half an hour to get admitted; Javeed sat on a chair in reception and dozed. In the ward, Omar and Javeed waited outside while Martin changed into a paper gown. In the shower the night before, he had used the depilatory gel the hospital had given him; below the neck his body was completely hairless.

Someone knocked. Martin climbed beneath the sheet.

"Come in."

It was Omar, alone. Martin said, "Where's Javeed?"

"The nurse is watching him for a minute."

"Okay." Martin waited.

Omar approached the bed; he looked nervous. "I don't have time to say everything properly. I just want to tell you… I know he's your son. I know you want him to have your ideas, not mine. I won't forget that, Martin *jan*. Whenever I talk to him, you'll be looking over my shoulder."

Martin searched his face, but there was no trace of resentment. "And that won't drive you crazy?"

"Maybe a little bit," Omar conceded. "But that can't be helped. I want everything right between us."

"It is," Martin said.

Omar reached down and squeezed his arm. "Okay, you should talk to him now."

Omar brought Javeed in and sat him beside the bed, then he left the room.

Javeed yawned. "You have to get better now, Baba," he said.

"Okay, I'll try hard," Martin promised.

"Then we'll go up in the balloon together?"

"Absolutely." Martin hesitated. "Can I tell you something, though?"

Javeed nodded.

"I'm going to try as hard as I can, but if I can't get better, you mustn't be angry with me. You have to believe that I was really trying."

Javeed looked down, confused and dejected.

"*Pesaram?* Do you believe me?" Martin raised himself up and put an arm around his son. "Listen to me. I love you more than anything else; all I want to do is stay with you. But don't be angry if I can't do that."

Javeed shuddered as if he was about to cry, but then he whispered in Martin's ear, "If you can't stay, the Simorgh will look after me." It was not a reproach; it was meant to comfort him.

"Okay." Martin understood that he had caught only the faintest glimpse of the world Javeed was building in his head; Zendegi had offered no more than a crude imitation. But between the version of himself hovering around Omar like a nagging insect and whatever form he took in Javeed's private mythology, he would not be erased completely.

Martin held Javeed until the anaesthetist came in, wheeling a small steel trolley.

He said, "Do you want to stay and watch me go to sleep, *azizam?*" That was Mahnoosh's name for him, but Javeed didn't object; Martin had the right to speak for her when she could no longer speak for herself.

Javeed said, "I'll stay."

The anaesthetist inserted the line. "This lady's just going to make me sleepy for the operation," Martin explained. "It doesn't hurt at all."

Javeed nodded solemnly, staring at the drip bags and monitors, distracted for a moment by the mechanics of the process.

The anaesthetist said, "Count backward from a hundred."

Martin kept his eyes on Javeed, smiling. Nothing mattered now except drawing all the bitterness out of this moment, leaving behind something that his son could carry lightly for the rest of his life.

He said, "One hundred elephants, all from Zavolestan."

30

Nasim put on the augmentation goggles and took a seat in the boardroom. Caplan had not explained the purpose of the meeting, but she assumed he wanted to discuss the Houston bombing.

She had been turning the event over in her head for days. It was impossible not to feel unnerved by the attack; she could barely step into the building now without picturing herself and her colleagues pinned under smoking rubble. The fact that Zendegi's most vigorous opponents to date had shown no inclination toward violence was of little comfort; the prospect of a whole new player with an unknown agenda only made things worse. Rollo had honored his promise to leave Zendegi in peace once they'd agreed to his demands, and while the wish he'd professed to move beyond electronic sabotage and mount a purely political campaign might well have been insincere, if the cis-humanists were going to blow up anything it should have been Eikonometrics in Zürich, where the side-loaded slaves that would power the next Industrial Revolution were being forged. At the Superintelligence Project there had been no AI, downtrodden or otherwise, and the prospect of it ever arising there had been negligible.

Caplan appeared across the table. They greeted each other curtly, but before Nasim could mention Houston, Caplan said, "I wanted to let you know that I'm going to be out of touch for a while."

"You're taking a holiday?"

"Not exactly," he said. "I'm going to ice."

Nasim took a couple of seconds to decode that, but given the speaker it could really only mean one thing.

"You're freezing yourself?"

"Yes. Just for a short time: maybe twenty or thirty years. So unless one of us is very unlucky, this is *au revoir*, not good-bye."

Nasim felt a stab of betrayal. They were not exactly the closest of allies, but the mess they'd made, they'd made together. Now he was going to turn his back on everything and sleep through the coming firestorm in a bomb-proof vault.

"You coward," she said.

Caplan looked stunned for a moment, then amused. "I *am* still on Zendegi's board; you might want to take that into account before you offer me your uncensored, spur-of-the-moment judgments."

Nasim was not in a mood to back down. "You're happy to share the glory and the profits until the bombs start going off. If that's not cowardice, what is it?"

Caplan said, "I'm not doing this because of Houston. Apart from anything else, I don't believe that incident represents the slightest threat to my own safety. Or yours, for that matter."

Nasim was utterly confused now. "Why, then?"

"It's a medical decision. I have no choice."

Caplan made a hand gesture, and his conferencing icon did a jump cut. At first Nasim thought he'd taken the form of a gaming creature of some kind, but then the combination of baldness, wizened skin and elfin features reminded her more of a documentary she'd seen on children with progeria, the genetic condition that caused massive premature aging.

Caplan said, "Who'd have thought that human and murine telomerase could respond so differently to the very same drug?" His voice had acquired a rasp that made it sound as if half the cells in his vocal chords were being sloughed off with every word.

"A biochemist?" Nasim suggested. She would not have put it past him to fake life-threatening side-effects from one of his faddish longevity treatments just to weasel out of her charge that he was heading for the hills at the first sign of danger.

"There might have been an unexpected interaction with the SIRT2 modulators," Caplan mused. "I doubt the problem was due to isotope loading, or it should have abated as soon as I went back to a standard nuclide diet."

"You really are sick?" Nasim was loath to trust him, but she was afraid of crassly mocking a man who might actually be dying.

"Either that, or special effects technicians are assaulting me with latex in my sleep."

"I'm sorry," she said. "I had no idea."

Caplan reverted to his old icon, but that image of sparkling health now carried the air of a botched face-lift or an ill-fitting toupée. "You weren't to know. I wasn't spreading it around."

"How long have you—?"

"A couple of years," he said. "I thought it might be under control, but the last few months it's gone downhill fast. It's going to take some future medicine to fix it."

Nasim didn't know how to respond to that. Caplan genuinely expected his heirs to find a way to defrost him and patch him up.

"By the way," he said, "I'm very sorry about your friend."

"Thank you." She'd emailed him her final report on the side-loading project the day before, just after she'd learned of Martin's death.

"It wasn't all in vain," Caplan added. "I'd actually been considering side-loading a special-purpose Proxy to manage my affairs while I was on ice. But I think it's clear now that I'll be in much safer hands trusting to human executors and existing legal instruments."

"I see." Nasim bit back her anger; she had never expected him to bankroll the experiment out of sympathy for Martin's situation. Having sold it to him on pragmatic grounds, she had no right to recoil from the news that he'd got his money's worth.

"So what do you think happened in Houston?" she said. "The CHL played nice with Zendegi because we were easy to extort, but in this case there was no Cloud computing, no customers to mess with—nothing but the facility itself?"

Caplan said, "I doubt it was the CHL. I'm thinking fundamentalist Christians."

"*Christians?*"

"The Superintelligence Project stated their goals in explicitly religious language," Caplan pointed out. "'God is coming into existence. We're building Him right here.' What did they expect, trespassing on the territory of people with strongly held ideas about the meaning of the word?"

"But they've been talking like that for years," Nasim protested. "Why should anyone start taking them seriously now?"

"The HCP," Caplan replied. "Virtual Azimi. Some of the credibility of those achievements would have rubbed off on them, in a lay-person's eyes. You must have seen their me-too press release, saying they'd have God up and running within five years. For people who'd previously thought they were full of nothing but blasphemous hot air, it might have started looking too close for comfort. The Antichrist was coming to rule over the nations."

Nasim was no expert on Christianity, but it didn't quite add up for her. "I thought the whole idea of religious prophecy was that it was... *prophecy*. If it starts to look as if the Beast will be born in a computer in Houston, isn't it the role of virtuous believers to live through his reign, stay true to their faith, and reap their reward in the end? You don't drive a truck full of fertiliser into the path of pre-ordained events that need to happen before the Second Coming, however unpleasant they might be."

Caplan said, "Maybe they took their theology lessons from Schwarzenegger movies. Or maybe I'm wrong, maybe it was someone else who thought the side-loads tipped the balance and made the chance that the Superintelligence Project could succeed start to look like too great a risk. A government agency? A foreign power?" He shrugged.

"Outside the project itself," Nasim replied, "apart from Zachary Churchland, the only person I know of who ever took them seriously was you."

Caplan laughed. It sounded sincere, but then it wasn't his real voice. "Yeah, I was pretty naïve back then."

"So what changed your mind?"

"Watching them turn five billion dollars into nothing but padded salaries and empty verbiage."

That was a reasonable answer; Nasim let it rest.

"So you believe Eikonometrics will be safe in your absence?" she said.

"Safe from the bombers," Caplan replied. "Nobody's going to mistake a souped-up factory robot for the Antichrist. The cis-humanists are likely to be a nuisance, but I'm sure that can be managed."

"How, exactly?"

"Well, that's part of why I wanted to talk to you," Caplan admitted. "Before I close the lid on the freezer, I'm thinking of poaching one of your guys: Arif Bahrami. He seemed to have some good ideas when you were under attack, using side-loads as part of the defense. Now that you don't need him for that kind of thing, I wanted to ask you what you thought it would take to persuade him to join Eikonometrics."

It was a bright spring afternoon on the day of the funeral. Martin's old friend Behrouz had flown in from Damascus to speak at his graveside, and he delivered a warm, affectionate eulogy. He was a good choice, Nasim thought, because he had a little more distance than the other mourners. That made it easier not to grow maudlin.

As Nasim watched the coffin being lowered into the ground, the thought that she'd had even a fraction of this man's memories and personality at her fingertips seemed more surreal than ever. The crude approximation she'd dragged out of his skull *had* come alive, but she could no longer understand how she'd deceived herself into thinking that it would find an equilibrium within its roughly hewn boundaries. It was hard enough for any ordinary human being to come to terms with their limitations.

Back at Omar's house, she took a while to find the courage to face Javeed.

He'd never really warmed to her, but he let her kiss his cheeks; his thoughts were elsewhere.

After the funeral, Nasim spent the evening with her mother. They had finally decided to drag all her photos out of Rubens's clutches and manage them on their own hardware. As it turned out, it wasn't too difficult; within a couple of hours Nasim had everything working again.

As they flipped through the library, her mother took the opportunity to do some reorganizing. She paused at a misfiled picture of a young man in a suit coat marching on the street, holding up a portrait of Khomeini.

"That's your father in 1978," she said. "He would have been eighteen. Nine years before you were born."

Nasim knew she must have seen the picture before, but the juxtaposition of the Ayatollah and her father's youthful face was unsettling. He wasn't the only progressive who'd made the same mistake; anything had seemed better than the Shah, and the popular exiled religious leader had been widely viewed as a useful means to an end.

They sat together meandering through the family history until her mother grew tired and Nasim helped her into bed.

Upstairs, Nasim stood on the balcony watching the traffic on the highway. She had no way of knowing whether Caplan had been genuine in his claim to have finally seen through his rivals' hype, or whether he'd decided that he could only cold-sleep in peace if they suffered a major setback first, but in a sense it didn't matter. In the long run—assuming he woke, and regained control of a thriving business empire—there were much worse things he could do than bombing an empty building. Jupiter would probably outlast him unscathed, but he might easily side-load an army of a billion slaves on his way to a slow and messy accommodation with reality.

The best way to clip his wings would be to cut off the cash flow she'd stupidly helped create for him. That meant getting side-loading outlawed in as many countries as possible—while it was still so expensive and technically demanding that it would not merely find a niche in the black economy.

Whoever was behind the bombing in Houston, it was going to make life harder for the CHL. The line between hackers and terrorists would be blurred; their cause would be tarred with the same brush. If they wanted to become legitimate and take their fight into the political sphere, they were going to need all the allies they could get. People who could speak from experience about the risks of side-loading might be useful. Nasim could not put her hand on her heart and swear that side-loaded factory workers would be living in hell, but her testimony about Martin's case might help persuade people that it was better to err on the side of caution.

Maybe in Javeed's lifetime a door could be opened into *Zendegi-ye-Behtar*;

maybe his generation would be the first to live without the old kind of death. Whether or not that proved to be possible, it was a noble aspiration. But to squeeze some abridged, mutilated person through the first available aperture was not.

Rollo had said it well enough, not in a slogan from his manifesto but in his plea to her on the Ferris wheel. Nasim had not wanted to listen then, but the simple entreaty had stayed with her as all her excuses and rationalizations had melted away.

If you want to make it human, make it whole.

Afterword

This novel was completed in July 2009, a month after the widely disputed re-election of President Mahmoud Ahmadinejad. The result triggered massive street demonstrations that were met with a brutal crackdown, but even some members of the clerical establishment questioned the election's legitimacy and condemned the mistreatment of protesters. Predicting the next few years is impossible—and the particular scenario I've imagined was always destined to be overtaken by reality—but I hope that this part of the story captures something of the spirit of the times and the courage and ingenuity of the Iranian people.

Hezb-e-Haalaa is fictitious, and is not modeled on any real organization.

The fatwa by Ayatollah Khomeini permitting gender reassignment is real (see "A Fatwa for Freedom" by Robert Tait, *The Guardian*, 27 July 2005), as is the Iranian miniseries set in Nazi-occupied Europe (see "Iran's Unlikely TV Hit" by Farnaz Fassihi, *The Wall Street Journal*, 7 September 2007; in this report the title "*Madare sefr darajeh*" is translated literally as "Zero Degree Turn," but I've used a more vernacular English translation, "No Room to Turn").

My source for stories from Ferdowsi's *Shahnameh* was Dick Davis's translation (Viking Penguin, New York, 2006). Note, though, that the versions re-enacted in Zendegi are definitely *not* scrupulously faithful to the originals.

The transliterations of Farsi I've used are simply intended to give the reader some idea of the sound of the words; I haven't followed any formal system.

Supplementary material for this novel can be found at **www.gregegan.net**.